JUDGMENT CLAY

By

IAN JARVIS

Paperback ISBN 978-1-78705-423-3
ePub ISBN 978-1-78705-424-0
PDF ISBN 978-1-78705-425-7

Published by MX Publishing
335 Princess Park Manor, Royal Drive,
London, N11 3GX
www.mxpublishing.co.uk

Cover design by Brian Belanger

Chapter 1

Robin Hood lived in Nottingham.

Many people believe this and it's easy to understand why. According to Hollywood – possibly not the most reliable font of historical accuracy – Robin camped outside the town in Sherwood Forest and constantly visited Nottingham Castle to take part in archery tournaments, to courageously rescue Marian, and to generally piss off the Sheriff. Countless movies and television shows have perpetuated the geographical mistake, but the ancient legends place this famous outlaw in green tights farther north. If indeed he actually existed, Robin Hood was most definitely a native of Yorkshire, with Wakefield, Loxley, Kirklees, Barnsdale and Bawtry all featuring prominently in his folk tales.

One of the more outlandish stories tells of Robin's favourite holiday retreat. Whenever he grew weary of fighting the wicked Sheriff and that guy from over Gisbourne way, he'd treat the Merry Men and himself to invigorating breaks on the Yorkshire coast, where they'd feast upon medieval ice cream cones, hot dogs and fish and chips. However dubious – and frankly preposterous – this legend may sound, the brigand's seaside hangout now bears his name, Robin Hood's Bay, and it remains one of the most beautiful and spectacular villages in Northern England.

The modern half of this small community stands isolated above the ocean just south of Ness Point, but the older part, the area that the tourists flock to marvel at, lies hidden below. The headland cracks open here, allowing a river to cascade down to the beach, and scores of quaint cottages, art galleries and inns fill the jagged cleft. Originally the homes of fishermen, crabbers and smugglers, the picturesque jumble of sandstone buildings are clustered around a maze of tight passageways and a twisting "main" street that resembles a lethal bobsleigh run.

The Wisteria Lodge Care Home overlooked this hotchpotch of orange rooftops from its hilltop vantage point at the end of Victoria Drive. Once a striking example of thirties Art Deco, the building had

1

been renovated in the 1970s and the frontage fitted with aluminium picture windows to take in the panorama. The day lounge, with its semi-circle of high-backed chairs and Zimmer frames, faced the sweeping bay and the distant Ravenscar village. Unfortunately, a combination of dementia, narcolepsy and eye cataracts meant that most of the residents failed to appreciate the breathtaking view.

The sun had sunk below the moorland to the west, Sunday dinner had ended and Dylan Taylor had taken up his usual position with his wheelchair parked by the television. Seventy-four wasn't particularly old, but a stroke had collaborated with his years to turn the disabled man into a grumpy creature of habit. Like many such homes, the television sound was constantly set to a volume consistent with a heavy metal concert, and Taylor had to virtually shout to make himself heard.

"Well it's a lovely afternoon," he scoffed, sarcastically. "We should all grab a towel and get ourselves down to the beach for a swim."

No one responded.

Bored and bitterly craving an after-dinner cigarette, Taylor noticed his geriatric neighbour was engrossed in the Bible. "Your novel there…" He gestured to the woman with a shaky hand and grinned mischievously. "Is it any good? I think I've read something by the same author. Is that their latest one?"

Stone deaf, she ignored the poor joke.

Taylor tutted with contempt and began to brood about a cigarette. He could absolutely murder one, but Wisteria Lodge had strict rules about smoke break times and he'd have to wait another hour. The rules had little to do with health concerns and everything to do with the lack of staff. The owner wouldn't pay for sufficient carers, so there was rarely anyone free to take the smokers outside to indulge their habit.

Taylor turned to watch Becca Hughes as she hurried around with a squeaky trolley dispensing cheap biscuits and plastic beakers of lukewarm tea.

"Hey," he called out. "I hear the White Rose Party are holding a meeting near here tomorrow. Where are the newspapers? Were you

2

too idle to bring them in from your staffroom?"

Becca glanced at him and rolled her eyes. The teenager could never be bothered to remember the resident's names, but she certainly knew *this* rude and mouthy one. Dylan Taylor reminded her of the television wildlife documentaries she'd seen. With his bald head and scrawny neck, he looked as if he should be jostling and squawking with a bunch of large birds as they rummaged inside the fly-covered carcass of a zebra.

"White Rose? Yeah, I've heard something about that," she said, absent-mindedly chewing gum. She pressed a cup into the trembling fingers of an aged lady and hoped it remained vertical. Quite often they didn't. "It's tomorrow in Scarborough, I think."

"Why don't you go and bring me the newspaper, you lazy slag?"

"Whoa, that's enough," snapped Becca, glaring at him. "Now there's really no need for that, is there?"

"Hündin," muttered Taylor under his breath. It was no secret that he didn't like the girl and he certainly wasn't afraid to let her know. *Still,* he mused, *at least the bitch wasn't some ethnic immigrant. He had a special loathing for those creatures and the nursing homes were employing more and more of them. It was disgusting.*

Like many elderly folk, Taylor loudly spoke his mind and didn't care who he upset. Such behaviour is rightly viewed as borderline sociopathic, but once past a certain age, the advanced years are viewed as a reasonable excuse and the recipients seldom took offence. No matter how racist, sexist or downright abusive the comment, people rarely punched a geriatric.

Popping her gum bubble, Becca felt a cool draught and glanced around to see a bald man standing silently in the doorway to the reception hall. "Ah, are you the new guy?" she asked. "Er, it's Tonga, isn't it?"

The young man stared blankly for a moment and then slowly nodded. Just over five feet tall, broad and muscular, Tonga's smooth skin was a reddish coffee colour, suggesting a possible Middle Eastern

3

origin. Like Becca, he wore a compulsory blue plastic apron over a green nursing tunic and trousers.

"Tonga?" she grinned. "So what kind of name is that? Is it a nickname or something? Short for Tony, maybe?"

He continued to stare silently.

Becca shrugged. "Do you know you're supposed to be here at five for the night shift?" She ran an appreciative eye over his bulky biceps, then frowned to see his naked feet. "Eh? Where are your shoes?"

Tonga looked down, but didn't answer.

"I don't believe it. Your first night here as a carer and you turn up late." Becca pushed past with the rattling trolley and gave him a cheeky smirk. "Andrea the owner won't like that, so it's best if we don't let her know."

Tonga nodded.

"Everything is a big rush here," said Becca. "We don't really have time to chat right now. Can you take the other trolley, clear away everything in the dining room and load up the dishwasher?" Waving in the direction of the kitchen, she headed for the hallway lift. "I need to make a start on the bedrooms while most of them are sitting down here sleeping off their dinner." She glanced again at his feet. "And for God's sake get your shoes on. If Andrea sees you like that, you'll get one of her famous health and safety bollockings."

"Taylor," said Tonga. "Which is Dylan Taylor?"

"Oh, do you know him?" Looking again at Tonga's muscles, Becca smiled sexily before gesturing past him to the elderly man in the wheelchair. "He's over there next to the television. Listen, we'll grab a cup of tea together later and I'll explain all about how this place works."

Tonga watched her enter the lift and then walked slowly across the lounge. "Dylan Taylor?" he asked.

"That's me," said Taylor, noticing the man's reddish brown skin.

He felt a surge of hatred. *Could this new carer be part Indian, or worse still, a Muslim? He'd never seen a North American Indian, but they used to be known as "redskins". Surely Wisteria Lodge weren't*

4

employing Apaches here now? Fortunately his features looked European which suggested otherwise, but the weird name he'd overheard definitely sounded foreign.

"I'll tell you what," said the old man, "Becca might be a little tramp and a bit of a dim bitch, but she's right in what she says. Believe me, Andrea Spedding the owner of this shithole is a real nasty cow. You don't want to cross her. Maybe if she employed enough staff, you lot wouldn't be constantly rushed off your feet, eh?"

Tonga stared quietly down at him.

Taylor glanced around furtively and gave a yellow grin, reminiscent of the sickly crescent that's often seen in student flats where the bathroom carpet abuts the base of the toilet.

This was too good an opportunity to miss, he decided. *Andrea was away at some council meeting in Whitby, the no-nonsense Deputy Manager wouldn't be around for another hour and that thick tart Becca was now upstairs and out of the way. This kid had only just started and he wouldn't be conversant with the rules. Especially the ludicrous smoke break rule.*

"Listen," he said, "before you go get your shoes and start washing up, I have a little job for you. Do you smoke?"

Tonga shook his head.

"Well, it's smoke break time, son. What's your name again?"

"He has called me Tonga."

"Er, right." Taylor looked puzzled at the odd answer, then grinned again. "Well I'm Dylan and I could bloody well kill for a cigarette. How about pushing me outside and I can have a quick one, eh? Rules are usually a load of old crap, but they have *one* particular rule here that I'm all for. Because I'm a nicotine addict, it's my human right to smoke. Janice takes me out whenever I want, but she isn't here until later and I need one right now. Come on, son. We'll only be gone for five minutes or so."

Nodding, Tonga pulled at the wheelchair, but it didn't move.

"There's a brake down there." Taylor wagged an impatient finger at it. "You need to knock it off to move me." *He was a carer, for*

God's sake. How come the idiot didn't know that?

Clicking the lever with his naked toe, Tonga backed the old man's chair out of the lounge.

Taylor chuckled triumphantly. *The dickhead would probably get fired if Andrea got to know about this, but she was out. Anyway, looking at his brown skin, he was probably half black or Asian, so what did it matter? There were plenty more unemployed foreigners out there and Wisteria Lodge would soon find another to take his place.*

Tonga pushed him through the kitchen passage and into the darkening garden. A flagged patio area of plastic seating and tables ran along the rear of the building with a disabled ramp leading down to a neat lawn and shrubbery. The constant staff shortage ensured that the outdoor seats were usually empty. With a never-ending cycle of work and not enough carers, wheeling residents out here to enjoy the sunshine and fresh air ranked low on the Wisteria Lodge priority list.

"You want to be through there." Taylor waved to the latch gate that led down the side of the house. "I know it's getting dark, but we don't want Becca or anyone looking out from the bedroom windows and seeing me smoking. Janice normally takes me through..."

"No," said Tonga, trundling the chair down the ramp and onto the grass.

Flanked by high hawthorn hedges and sloping gently towards a rhododendron thicket, the lawn terminated at a white picket boundary fence with the land falling precipitously away beyond. The lights of the Robin Hood's Bay cottages twinkled below, the coastline swept around to the south and the soft indigo twilight reflected on the Ravenscar Hotel windows in the distance.

"So what kind of name is Tonga?" Taylor turned awkwardly as he took out his cigarettes and lighter. "Is it foreign or something?"

"No." The carer wheeled him out of sight of the building behind the rhododendrons and kicked on the chair brake.

"You don't talk much, do you?"

"No."

Taylor looked around approvingly. "Hey, this is a nice spot

you've chosen. The guards can't see us from the prison camp back there and, I've got to admit, the view is better than the shit alleyway down the side of the house." Lighting a cigarette with difficulty, he inhaled deeply, coughed a couple of times and spoke around it. "I've had a stroke and I can only use my right arm. Believe me, it's a real bastard, especially when…" The old man paused, his eyes narrowing curiously at a sudden thought. He'd forgotten to ask earlier. His concern and disgust at the carer's skin colour had taken priority. "I've just remembered something – didn't you ask for me by name when you spoke to Becca? It was as if you knew me, but I certainly don't know…"

Taylor caught his breath and shuddered to feel the temperature plummet. The evening air was still, but it had suddenly turned icy. He heard the harsh sound of tearing cloth behind him and twisted around to see the carer's trousers, tunic and apron lying in tatters around his feet. The old man's eyes widened and the cigarette fell from his gaping mouth.

This couldn't be happening, it was impossible.

Tonga's features had somehow changed and his naked brown body had grown slightly in height and bulk. It was as if another much larger person now stood in his place, yet *this* was no person. This was most *definitely* no person. Taylor gasped in terror at the sight, his right hand flailing about in a useless effort to keep the horror away from him.

Had he fallen asleep in the day lounge? This couldn't be real. Reason and every rational law meant this couldn't possibly be real. No, this had to be a nightmare.

His thrashing arm was grabbed tightly, twisted and effortlessly wrenched out of the shoulder socket.

"Mein Gott…" Shock nullified the pain and he watched, almost dreamily, as the torn limb was tossed onto the grass. Inches away from his bulging eyes, steaming gore pulsed in surreal red jets from the tattered shoulder. "Nein. Gott in Himmel, nein…"

No, this simply wasn't possible. It WAS a nightmare. There was no pain so this could NOT be happening.

Taylor took a breath to scream, but Tonga's huge fingers

7

clamped over his mouth and the other hand closed firmly on the back of his head. Three seconds passed, allowing him time to stare into the blank face that peered down at him, then the hands came together, crushing his skull to a gruesome scarlet pulp. A spray of brain matter splattered the rhododendrons, adding vivid colour to the dull autumnal shrubbery.

Upstairs in one of the Wisteria Lodge bedrooms, Becca hummed to herself as she thought about the sexy new carer and how she'd ask him out for a drink later tonight. Those muscular arms were quite something, she decided, and if she played her cards right, she'd hopefully feel them tightly squeezing her.

* * * *

Chapter 2

Bernard Quist had always favoured the British coast in autumn and winter. The seas were wild and spectacular at this time of the year, with enormous waves exploding over rocks and booming thunderously as they slammed into cliffs. The towns, villages and shorelines were more picturesque, and cloud-scudded blustery skies replaced the monotonous pastel blue of summer.

Although the weather had been mild for late October in Yorkshire, Quist wore his calf-length overcoat, and a cool afternoon breeze tugged at the black leather, ruffling his shaggy dark hair as he walked along the harbour. Watching the turnstones and oystercatchers flying past the fishing boats, he took a deep breath and smiled.

Yes, thought Quist. Cold ocean air and northern winds whipping at the headlands were much better than stifling heat, flies buzzing around melting ice cream, and the sickly stench of overflowing litter bins.

Tourists and holidaymakers, or rather their noticeable absence, played a major part in his outlook. Towns were quieter, the roads were less congested, parking never presented a problem, and the empty beaches were striking in their scenic bleakness. Instead of plastic bottles, sizzling red flesh and screaming kids, flocks of wading birds and lounging seals filled the sandy panoramas. Quist knew his preferences were purely personal, of course, and his feelings certainly wouldn't be shared by the hotel owners and other businesses here in the seaside town of Scarborough.

Pausing by a stack of lobster pots, he lit a cigarette, cupping his hands to shield the flame and almost singeing his large nose in the process. An attractive, lean man who appeared to be mid-forties, his aquiline nose rivalled the beaks of the yelping herring gulls that soared around him. He stood by the old lighthouse at the end of the harbour wall, drawing on the tobacco and peering over the bobbing boats at the panorama of Scarborough's South Bay.

North Yorkshire's premiere resort, Scarborough lies forty miles east of the city of York, where Quist lived and operated a small detective agency. The private investigator, or *consultant detective*, as he preferred to be known, puffed out a cloud of smoke and ran his eyes along the colourful seafront. Pubs, cafes and fast-food outlets lined the promenade, along with amusement arcades, entertainment facilities and those ubiquitous seaside shops that, for some unfathomable reason, sold nothing but cheap crap. The land rose steeply from the harbour and the detective looked upwards, past the streets and houses, to the breathtaking ruins of Scarborough Castle. A massive promontory of limestone rock thrust out into the North Sea, dividing the town into two wide bays, and the remains of the twelfth century fortress covered the summit, its stone walls running along the cliff edges and its great keep rising from the centre.

Quist glanced at a passing gull that screamed angrily at him. The birds were highly intelligent and invariably approached seafront visitors, checking to see if they were carrying anything edible. Strangely, none came anywhere near the detective and all eyed him warily as they flew by. He smoked his cigarette, meeting their flint-eyed looks with a lopsided cynical smile.

Scarborough has been a spa town since the English civil war. A stream of acidic water was discovered, which supposedly possessed medicinal qualities, and wealthy visitors travelled here for their health. Bathing machines rolled across the sand and the town became a tourist mecca with the arrival of the railway in 1845. Quist could well understand how this would be a paradise to northern workers, who spent their lives in mills, factories and coal mines, but the gentry flocked here too, filling the splendid Victorian hotels on the south cliff to his left. Built in the 1800s, two funicular railways still operated, ferrying the less athletic and the downright lazy up the headlands. Quist had a real passion for history and Scarborough was steeped in it. From here he could see the hilltop church near the castle where Anne, the youngest of the famous Bronte sisters, lay buried.

He smiled thoughtfully, remembering the time he'd discovered an artist sitting in this very spot on the harbour wall. The short man had been admiring the same view and painting the church and the ruined fortress. Recognising him immediately, Quist had walked over to inspect the half-finished watercolour on his easel.

"Excellent," Quist said, sitting with the painter and offering him a salad sandwich, part of the packed lunch prepared by his hotel that morning. "I have to say, I've always been an admirer of your work. The way you capture the light is truly uncanny."

"Why, thank you." The artist had taken the food. "And thank you for your compliment. I enjoy painting Yorkshire. It's a delightful part of the world, isn't it? Really quite splendid."

"Oh, I agree. It's exceptional."

"Good Lord! Is this just salad?" The artist had frowned curiously as he munched on the sandwich. "Where's the meat?"

"No, I'm afraid it's lettuce, tomato and cucumber. I never consume animal flesh."

"That's a little odd." The man stared at him, then took another bite and began to chuckle. "But I suppose I can relate to that. Most people view *me* as somewhat strange and eccentric." He held out a hand. "Turner."

"Very pleased to meet you, Mister Turner. Quist's the name. Bernard Quist."

That had been in the summer of 1825 and another twenty-four years would pass before Anne Bronte would be laid to rest in the churchyard upon the hill. Most people who saw Quist estimated him to be mid-forties, but he was older than he looked. *Much* older.

* * * *

The detective checked his watch; he'd arranged to meet a friend at three-thirty this Monday afternoon, and it was time to head up to the Grand Hotel. Retracing his steps along the sea wall and leaving the harbour, he walked along the promenade where pop music blasted out from the gaudy amusement arcades. Quist had a highly developed sense of smell and the fresh scent of the ocean was almost overpowered here by the powerful aromas of candy floss, waffles, hot dogs and ice cream. The predominant odour was the boiling vegetable oil used for cooking

11

battered fish, chips and sugary doughnuts – hopefully not in the same fryer.

Way up above the seafront stood the huge Victorian building he was heading for. Constructed of tawny yellow brick, the Grand Hotel dominated the Scarborough skyline, an iconic coastal landmark that almost outshone the castle. When this place was completed in 1867, it was one of the world's largest hotels and the biggest brick-built structure in Europe. Quist had never been inside before and something told him his sense of smell would be picking up a particularly bad stench there today.

The jingling of bridle bells drew his attention to the beach where six saddled donkeys stood waiting to be ridden by children. Spotting the detective, they grew restless and he quickened his pace to put some distance between them before they began to panic. Animals were always frightened around Bernard Quist. The promenade pavement was wide here, allowing for a beachfront kiosk that sold burgers and ice cream, and a white wooden cabin plastered with pentagrams and pictures of tarot cards. He hurried past and away from the jittery animals.

"Hey, you. Hey, Mister Wolf."

Quist heard the woman's voice behind him, but ignored it.

"You in the leather overcoat. Mister Wolf."

Halting abruptly, the detective turned with a puzzled frown. An elderly purple-haired woman in a black shawl gestured from the doorway of the cabin.

"Excuse me?" he said, walking over. *Mister Wolf? What on earth could she mean by that?* "Can I help you?"

"Perhaps *I* can help *you*," she said. "I'm Madame Selene."

"Madame Selene?" Quist repeated the name in his eloquent voice. Some had said the English accent belonged on a stage reciting Shakespeare. "Ah, I see you're a clairvoyant."

Looking at the exterior wall of her cabin, it was pretty much impossible *not* to see she was a clairvoyant. He ran his eyes over the painted advertising information. Apparently, Madame Selene *knew all* and *saw all*. She was descended from a psychic Romany family and well-versed in the mystic arts of tarot and palmistry. Photographs in the cabin window showed minor celebrities having their palms read by her over the past couple of decades. Most looked to be entertainers from summer seasons in the old theatre that had once stood nearby and a few were actors in Yorkshire television shows. The interior of her "parlour" was mysterious and spookily inviting, with candles, an incense burner and velvet door curtains for privacy. A lace cloth covered a table and comfortable chairs stood on either side.

"Selene like the Greek Goddess of the moon?" asked Quist.

"That's the one." She smiled, her grey eyes twinkling. "Well, to be honest, my name's Vera, Vera Lewis, and I'm not *really* a Gypsy. Er, I wonder if I could possibly hold your hand for a moment?"

Although many older ladies used adventurous hair dye colours these days, Quist knew *this* purple hair was a wig. Glancing into the cabin, he saw three bottles of pills on the table by her teacup. "You really must forgive me," he said. "I'm actually on my way to meet someone right now, so I'm afraid I don't have time for your palm readings."

"It isn't a reading. It's more of a confirmation." The elderly woman gripped his hand and caught her breath sharply. "Well, I was right. Good Lord, that's amazing."

"Amazing?"

"I'm almost seventy years old, but there are many things I've never experienced and I don't suppose I ever will now. I've never tasted caviar, for example." Vera smiled mischievously and lowered her voice. "And, as far as I know, I've never met a werewolf before."

Quist stiffened and gave a lopsided grin to mask his shock. "Er, *right*. Well, I really have to say, that's a somewhat bizarre and unexpected statement. Why on earth would you possibly imagine…"

"Oh, you've no need to worry, Bernard." She drew the black shawl tighter around her shoulders and gave his arm a friendly pat. "I won't tell anyone. It happened to you in 1790, didn't it?"

The detective stared in astonishment, his heart racing. She

knew his name and, more to the point, she obviously knew about his lycanthropy. *Did he know her from somewhere? He couldn't recall ever meeting this woman.* She said her name was Vera Lewis, but just who the hell was she?

"You don't eat meat, do you?" said Vera. "That's how you manage to control the blood lust and the beast within."

Quist swallowed uncomfortably and remained silent. His heart pounded faster still, but his blank expression didn't betray his alarm and confusion. He didn't eat any animal product whatsoever. No one, but a very select few knew these things. *No, he hadn't met her before, he was certain of that, which led him to a bizarre deduction.*

"Your illness…" He cleared his arid throat and spoke quietly. "It's a rather serious condition, isn't it, Vera?"

She let out a mirthless laugh. "About as serious as it's possible to get. How did you know that?"

"I'm very sorry, my dear lady. I realised when I saw the medication on your table back there. Morphine-based painkillers and cancer drugs."

"You read the tablet labels from there?" Vera nodded. "You have good eyesight, but I suppose that's to be expected with a werewolf."

"You're also wearing a wig and your eyebrows are painted on. The thing is, I've heard of this supernatural phenomenon before. It's rather rare, but when some individuals are close to the end, they can develop this form of psychic gift. It's stronger in some than others, but they're able to see and sense things…" He paused and gave a tight smile. "Not that I'm in any way confirming the fantastical things you believe you sense in me."

"Oh, of course not," she said, grinning. "But I've been working as a psychic on this seafront for over thirty years. What makes you think I've only just developed my gift?"

"Without wishing to appear discourteous, if you'd been able to do this for the past three decades, you'd be a very wealthy lady. Looking at this realistically, by now you'd probably be employed by the CIA or some similar clandestine group."

"Yes, incredible, isn't it?" Vera sighed. "All this time I've been *pretending* to be clairvoyant. I've been cold reading the tourists and talking drivel and now suddenly it's real. I have less than a month to live and I'm a genuine psychic at last. Talk about irony?"

"Have the doctors informed you…"

"Like I said, Bernard, I'm psychic. I know exactly how long I have."

The detective nodded sadly. "I'm sorry, but I have to enquire, why on Earth are you working here? Shouldn't you be at home with your family or…"

"I don't have any family as such. It's just me." Shrugging resignedly, Vera looked around the promenade. "I've spent so long telling lies for money, I thought I might spend my last few days here helping people for a change with genuine *free* readings. People like you." She gazed at him. "Listen, you need to know that when I held your hand I sensed approaching darkness. I must warn you that you're heading towards darkness and evil."

"You're right about that." Quist glanced up at Grand Hotel on the headland and checked his watch.

"What time is it, Mister Wolf?"

He laughed. "Isn't that what children say in one of their playground games?"

"Yes, but you have somewhere important to be and a friend you need to meet. I could feel you were going to meet him at the Grand, but that isn't it. There are dark forces gathering around you and I sense a large figure. Very soon you will encounter a large, dark, dangerous figure."

"Now you're beginning to sound like a typical seafront charlatan. What sort of dark forces?"

"I'm not sure," admitted Vera, "but I sense evil, fear and death in the very near future. If I had something substantial to go on – something to touch – I could give you more details to help you, but this is just a general feeling of impending danger and a sense of this large, dark… *figure*." She shook her head. "I sensed you were a werewolf when I saw you, but I had to hold your hand to know your name and all the details about you."

"Vera…" said Quist, uneasily. "I'm really sorry about your illness. I don't know if you're thinking it could be *cured* with a bite, but lycanthropy isn't something which…"

"No." She smiled wistfully. "Maybe if I were younger I might be considering that, but trust me, I'm a big believer in fate. I'm at peace with this and I know when it's time to go."

The detective regarded her thoughtfully. Strangely enough, he *did* trust her. He had no idea why, but his initial shock and fear at her knowing his dark secret had vanished. "Just as a matter of interest," he said, "if I *am* what you believe me to be, surely you should be warning people? Organising some sort of Hammer horror movie lynch mob with burning torches and pitchforks?"

Vera reached out and squeezed his hand. "I can sense you're a good man, Bernard. A kind man. I know you control your *other self* with yoga and by not consuming meat, and I can sense that you use your…" she hesitated, "your *gift* to help people."

Quist nodded slowly, still amazed at her psychic abilities. "I'm not confirming your suspicions in any way, but thank you for that. Listen, it's been good to meet you, Vera. Truthfully, it's been utterly astonishing, but…"

"I see someone wearing a uniform," she broke in, staring intently at him. "I see a child learning to play a musical instrument, either a young relative, or possibly the child of a friend. I see someone in a very unhealthy relationship – you know exactly who I'm referring to – and they need to see sense and end it quickly. Also, someone you know is thinking about changing their job."

"Good Lord!" he gasped. "You see all that?"

"Don't be silly." Her laughter turned into a bout of painful coughing. "That's part of my old routine. I thought I'd give you a *seaside psychic* treat before you left." She pointed to the Grand Hotel. "I know you have to go and meet your friend up there. I also know that we'll meet again." Vera vanished into her white cabin, heading for her medicine. "Goodbye for now and take care, Mister Wolf."

* * * *

Chapter 3

Wisteria had never grown upon the walls of the Wisteria Lodge care home, or anywhere near it for that matter. Then again, the majority of British houses called *Mount View* don't have mountains in the vicinity and the commonly named *Orchard Houses* are rarely built in or near orchards. The place didn't get too many visitors. Most folk left their elderly relatives here and then drove away from Robin Hood's Bay at high speed, their guilt offset by the immense feeling of relief that came from not having to look after them. This Monday afternoon, however, Wisteria Lodge was filled with visitors, although the majority were wearing police uniforms and none of them were related to the residents.

Detective Inspector Katie Bradstreet stood at the Lodge reception desk, gazing around the hallway and feeling decidedly tacky in her grey suit. Like all care homes, the central heating was set higher than the temperatures she'd encountered in illicit cannabis farms. This was the sort of warmth found in zoological reptile enclosures. Liberal amounts of air-freshener failed to mask the ever-present aromas of urine and worse. Katie knew that if visitors looked past the chic décor – and few ever did, as they already felt uncomfortable about consigning their loved ones to this – they'd see that hardly anything was spent on staffing. If twenty care workers were needed, and thirty would be preferable, some of these privately run businesses attempted to get by with twelve. It was more economical to let residents soil themselves and clean them later, than employ enough staff to escort them to the toilet when necessary.

It was sad, decided the Inspector, *but the tradition of having aged relatives live with us has long since vanished in Britain.*

Nowadays, caring for old people within a loving family environment was usually only to be found in places like Asia and Africa. No London professional, single and living in a stylish four-bedroom apartment, could possibly be expected to find room for an elderly mother. No, these care homes were a regrettable necessity, but

Katie Bradstreet did NOT want to live in one. Unfortunately, the time seemed to race past much faster as she matured. Twenty years ago, when Katie joined the North Yorkshire Police, old age was some vague future possibility, much like androids, flying cars and an honest government. Katie was now forty-one and it no longer seemed so distant.

Unable to believe what she'd just heard, the Inspector closed her eyes and ran a hand through her short fair hair. Her Sergeant, Tariq Aslam, was equally astounded.

"Seriously?" said Aslam. "You're telling us that you didn't find the body until noon?"

The teenage carer Becca Hughes leant on the reception desk and rolled her eyes. Andrea Spedding, the owner of Wisteria Lodge, stood beside her and stiffened defensively. Her golden brown perm looked like an overcooked Pot Noodle, decided Katie, and the mean face reminded her of the neighbour's vicious whippet that had once bitten her as a child.

"We're understaffed," snapped Andrea. "We naturally assumed Mister Taylor had gone to bed last night and hadn't bothered with breakfast this morning. We didn't know he was missing until lunch when we realised he wasn't..."

"Yes, that's understandable," broke in Katie, attempting to conceal her angry sarcasm. "But perhaps employing a few more staff would solve the problem of being understaffed?"

Andrea gave her a harsh smile and Katie knew that would never happen. This was a lucrative business, where old folk were converted into cash, and the fewer carers they employed, the less they had to pay out. Not that they paid out much.

It was a funny old world she lived in, thought Katie. Some people, like pointless "celebrities" in reality shows, were paid obscene amounts for doing literally nothing, yet care-home staff, who spent every day wiping excrement, changing soiled beds and cleaning up vomit, received next to nothing. How such things could be allowed in any sane society was beyond comprehension.

Tariq Aslam was ten years younger than his Inspector and felt the same disgust. "So you're the manager…" began the Sergeant.

"I'm the owner," corrected Andrea. "I'm also the manager, yes."

Aslam nodded. "And you *did* employ a new member of staff; this young man going by the name of Tonga who was supposed to begin work here yesterday evening. Surely you have a surname and an address?"

"I don't know anything about him," admitted Andrea. "We placed adverts in the local jobcentres for a carer and someone rang on Saturday morning. It was an older sounding man, maybe his father, and if he mentioned a surname at the time, I can't remember. He just called him Tonga and said he'd bring his details and paperwork when he arrived."

"Which, of course, he didn't," pointed out Katie. "If the name is even real, it's quite obviously a nickname. Tell me about him."

"I was the only one who saw him," said Becca, chewing gum. "Well, maybe one or two of the residents saw him, but that lot are half-blind and the silly sods won't remember anyway. He seemed a bit quiet, but kind of good-looking and sexy. I like quiet guys."

"Perhaps you'd *like* to give us a fuller and more helpful description?" suggested Katie.

"He was about twenty or so and a little taller than me." Becca held up a hand to gauge the height. "Just over five feet, very muscular and dark skinned."

"Dark skinned like me?" asked Aslam.

"No, he wasn't a Pakistani."

"Well, that makes two of us. I'm Indian."

Becca shrugged. "I mean, his skin was brown, but his face didn't look Asian like your lot. He looked English."

"So darkly tanned then?" Katie glanced at her Sergeant. "He could have his own sunbed, but I'll need a list of local salons and gyms with tanning facilities. If he's very muscular, as Miss Hughes here says, we'll concentrate on the gyms."

20

"It was a weird brown," said Becca. "A sort of red brown. Oh, and he had bare feet."

"Bare feet?" echoed Katie, frowning curiously. "Why on earth wasn't he wearing shoes?"

"Who knows? I warned him he couldn't go barefoot because of health and safety. He'd shaven his head and his eyebrows too. I notice stuff like that."

Aslam looked around the ceiling. "I understand you don't have any cameras here?"

"Well, no," said Andrea. "There's no point, is there?"

Katie nodded. *CCTV costs money, which would have to come out of the profits.* "Right," she said. "So we have no images of this suspect and no record or evidence of who he might be. You say Tonga asked for Dylan Taylor by name, suggesting he knew him? You left them alone in the day lounge and no one has seen your new carer since then?"

"I looked for him when I'd finished cleaning the bedrooms," said Becca. "But he'd vanished."

"Dylan Taylor had vanished too," pointed out the Inspector. "But no one bothered to look for *him* until today at noon."

"I've explained that," said Andrea, icily.

"You'll need to explain it to his family," said Katie. "I'm afraid they may react less professionally than I."

"He only has a brother," said Becca. "An old guy who visited him two or three times a month. I think he's called Stephen and he said he came from Beverley."

"Were there any other visitors?" asked Katie. "Friends and acquaintances? Did anyone call recently?"

Shaking her head, Becca popped a gum bubble. "No, his brother was the only one who came here."

"Ma'am." Zoe Planer, Katie's young Detective Constable, appeared in the reception doorway. "If you have a moment, the Scenes of Crime Officer would like to see you."

Nodding and leaving the questioning to her Sergeant, Katie

followed the girl out onto the rear patio. She took a deep breath of sea air, grateful to be away from the smell, the jungle heat, and the criminally negligent businesswoman who dared to claim she ran a *care* home.

"Jesus," she murmured, irately. "No one missed him until noon."

Zoe raised her eyebrows. "Ma'am?"

"Nothing." She shrugged her suit jacket straight. "What does Matthew have for me?"

"The suspect transported Taylor out of the home in a wheelchair," said Zoe, pointing down the garden. "He took him behind those bushes out of sight of the building. The staff say Taylor was always wanting to go outside for a cigarette and there's a half-smoked one next to the body. That's probably why they went there."

The constable led Katie across the grass and lifted the police tape that cordoned off the rhododendron shrubbery at the bottom of the lawn. The SOCO, Matthew Carson, and his assistant were still working on the crime scene, but the processing had been completed and it was safe to enter the area without forensic oversuits. Dylan Taylor still sat in his wheelchair facing the sea, although the lack of head meant the stunning view would probably be unappreciated. Taylor's neck terminated in a congealed mess of dark red gunge, most of which had oozed down into his lap.

The Inspector moved slowly around the body, gazing incredulously at the blood-soaked grass and the brain-splattered rhododendrons. She noticed the cigarette mentioned by Zoe and – rather more conspicuous – the detached right arm, then glanced over the garden fence at the older part of Robin Hood's Bay below. Cascading down the narrow river valley, the mishmash of cottage rooftops resembled a romantic illustration from a book of fairytales and provided quite a contrast to Taylor's horrific corpse.

"It's quite a mess," she said. "It doesn't look as if he was decapitated."

"No, it's a little more bizarre." The SOCO tugged down his

22

forensic hood and gave her a strained smile. "Unbelievably, the victim's head appears to have been crushed to a pulp. From the finger indentations in the flesh on these skull fragments here, it seems someone used their bare hands, one on either side, like so." Carson mimicked the clapping action.

Katie stared silently. The muffled rumble and hiss of the sluggish ocean could be heard below as it washed over rocks and sucked at shingle.

"As I'm sure you've noticed, the right arm was torn off too." The SOCO gestured to where it lay in the grass. "There are hand prints where it was gripped and, again, great strength was utilised to simply wrench it away from the shoulder joint."

"Incredible," murmured Katie, recalling Becca Hughes saying how the man named Tonga had looked muscular. She shook her head in disbelief. *But how could anyone be THIS muscular?*

"I'm sorry to tell you there are no fingerprints or traces of DNA." Carson sighed. "The wheelchair and the body have been processed and your suspect has left nothing for us."

"Well, the fingerprints I can understand," said the Inspector. "These carers wear latex gloves, but no DNA? Wait a moment – the girl back there claimed our suspect had shaved his head and he had no eyebrows. Did he purposely do that so as not to shed hairs? Is he that clever?"

"Who knows?" Carson gestured to the plastic apron and the green tunic and trousers behind the wheelchair. "What do you make of this?"

"A carer's uniform," said Katie. "The girl I've just spoken to is wearing something very similar. Are you saying the killer removed his clothes after doing this? Wait a moment – they look to be torn."

"They *are* torn," confirmed Carson. Everything had been examined and photographed, which allowed him to lift the tunic and show her. "Instead of being removed in a conventional manner, these items of clothing were literally ripped off, and this occurred *before* Taylor was killed. The blood spray and brain matter on the garments and the grass proves they were already lying here when the head was crushed. Look, there's a clean area of grass where I took this from."

"What are these traces of brown dust?" asked Katie, pointing at the tunic.

"I don't know; it appears to be some form of stone dust. The traces are mostly on the inside of the garments, as if it was on the suspect's skin, and the hand prints on the victim's arm have the same dust too. I'll be able to tell you for certain once I get my samples to the lab."

"Ma'am?" Zoe Planer cleared her throat and gestured to the tall hedgerow that ran along the side of the garden. "We believe the suspect exited the crime scene this way."

"Yes," said Carson. "Rather than going back through the house, he seems to have torn his way through the hawthorn bushes over there."

"Leaving DNA on the thorns?" said Katie, hopefully.

"Sorry, but I've checked." The SOCO shook his head. "It's pretty obvious where he pushed his way through and, from the torn clothing he left behind, he was probably naked. There are further traces of that brown residue on the twigs and leaves, but incredibly, no blood or skin."

Katie's mouth fell open. *"What?"*

The Inspector walked with Zoe to the hole in the hedge and peered through. From here, it was a short walk through a patch of grassy land to the cul-de-sac that ran down the side of Wisteria Lodge.

"He could have had a vehicle waiting there," said Katie.

"I've taken a look around, Ma'am," said Zoe. "If that's where he parked, there are no lights or overlooking windows. I called on the neighbours too, but no one saw or heard anything."

Katie nodded slowly, examining the broken twigs and seeing the dusty brown marks. "No blood from scratches," she murmured. "But traces of what appears to be brick dust? What the hell is going on here?"

* * * *

24

Chapter 4

The town centre of Scarborough covers the rocky promontory beneath the castle, with a deep valley separating this from the neighbouring headland of South Cliff. Rows of elegant Victorian hotels line the South Cliff promenade with the old spa complex and public gardens below. The Spa Bridge, a lofty walkway of ornate iron was constructed in 1827 to connect the two headlands, and Bernard Quist leant on the handrail, smoking a cigarette and peering seventy-five feet down into the bottom of the gorge.

The Grand Hotel stood on the town side to his left, with hundreds of kittiwakes soaring and clamouring noisily around the huge building. Viewing the faces of the hotel as cliffs, these dainty gulls used the countless ledges and baroque ornamentations to sleep and nest. Their shrill cries supposedly sounded like "kitty wake," but to the guests, especially in the early hours of the morning, it would sound more like an absolute bloody racket. The private detective had arranged to meet his friend Rex Grant here on the bridge at three-thirty. It was easier than meeting at the front entrance as, knowing Rex, he'd probably get the wrong door.

Quist sighed. Knowing Rex, he'd probably get the wrong *hotel*.

Drawn by the mournful cries of the birds, he turned to gaze at the building. He knew the Grand had been designed around the theme of time, with the domed towers representing the four seasons, twelve floors for the months, 52 chimneys for weeks, and 365 bedrooms for days. There were far fewer rooms now, as many had vanished when internal renovations took place and ensuite bathrooms were added. The bathing habits of modern guests extended to more than a bowl of tepid water and most seemed to prefer the concept of flushing toilets to using a stinking chamber pot under the bed.

Pulling on his cigarette, the detective thought again about his bizarre meeting with the Scarborough clairvoyant earlier. He stared at her distant white cabin on the promenade below and remembered the various mediums he'd encountered over the past three centuries, especially in the years following the first world war. Many had set up business back then, eagerly rubbing their hands and cashing in on the countless bereaved folk who had lost young relatives in the fighting. Only two of the psychics he'd ever met had been genuine and Madame Selene, or Vera Lewis, now brought that total to three.

Vera had clearly known everything about him, but highly dangerous as that could be, he didn't feel worried in any way. There was an indefinable *something* about the old woman that told him she'd keep his secret.

A loud squeal of tyres ended his thoughts and momentarily drowned out the sound of the kittiwakes. Quist winced to hear a powerful engine being over-revved and looked past the hotel to see a car hurtle around the corner – a gleaming black supercar, like a Batmobile with a severe eating disorder. The square behind the Grand provided parking for residents and operated a strict speed limit, but the driver of the McLaren MP4 had clearly missed the 10 mph signposts. Tearing in at over forty, he also luckily missed the scattering bystanders and stationary vehicles, to perform a handbrake turn and skid to a sliding halt by the fence. The detective closed his eyes and slowly shook his head as Rex Grant climbed from the car.

"Unbelievable," murmured Quist, as Rex spotted him on the bridge and cheerfully waved.

As usual, the young man was dressed from head to toe in black and wore mirrored sunglasses that cost the best part of a thousand pounds. His leather jacket and shoes were Gucci and the shirt and jeans had been knocked out by a similar designer for a similar obscene price. The Grant family owned one of Britain's largest housing construction companies and Rex wisely invested his share of the profits in the lifestyle of a spoilt footballer. Twenty-five years old, with short black hair and movie star looks, the London millionaire was often referred to as an eccentric, shallow playboy. Other people, who had got to know him better, used the word "arsehole."

There was a time when Quist would never have associated with such a crass idiot, but that was before he'd employed Watson at the detective agency, and before this new assistant coaxed him from his reclusive shell and into the twenty-first century. This was the reason he'd chosen the happy-go-lucky teenager; he'd needed someone youthful, jovial and streetwise to help him integrate more with modern society on every level. The reason he socialised with Rex Grant, however, was that, reckless, chauvinistic and dim as Rex was, Quist felt he *had* to remain friends and discreetly keep an eye on him. Unfortunately, Quist was now responsible for this young man. Not responsible for him being such a twat, but for his dark supernatural secret.

"Hi there," said Rex, strolling onto the bridge. He resembled the young Tom Cruise in *Top Gun* – if Cruise had worn nothing but black and had taken lessons in being pretentious. "So how's the private eye business going?"

"Consultant detective," corrected Quist, holding out a hand. "It's going swimmingly. How are you?"

"Terrific as usual." Rex shook hands and winked over his sunglasses. "Three girlfriends currently on the go in London, all models, and I've just returned from Saint Lucia with one of them. How about you?"

"Oh, pretty much the same, apart from the plethora of young ladies and the Caribbean sojourn."

"Plethora and sojourn?" Rex grinned. "Yeah, I love the way you speak and that refined English voice. Like I always tell people, you remind me of Chaka Khan."

Quist stared blankly, unsure of how to reply.

"You know – the suave tiger in Disney's *Jungle Book*."

The detective took a deep breath. "I see you drive a McLaren now," he said, offering his cigarettes. "When I heard you were replacing your Porsche, I assumed you'd purchase another Ferrari."

"Not a chance." Rex took one from the pack. "Ferraris are getting to feel a bit old-fashioned, aren't they?"

"Really? That must be why most people don't drive them."

"Exactly." He nodded towards the sleek black vehicle. "I

wanted something a little more state-of-the-art, and the McLaren is a real beauty. I couldn't have flown here from London any faster. I have Marilyn Monroe on the satnav and that sexy voice of hers really makes you press the accelerator."

"Monroe's voice?" Quist smiled. "She probably recorded it for the satnav company before she died."

"Well, obviously."

Rex tended to miss irony. Even if the irony was brightly wrapped and handed to him with IRONY printed on the packaging.

"Have you spoken to your Uncle Rupert yet?" asked Quist. "You mentioned you'd be residing with him on his estate whilst you're here in Yorkshire."

"No, I rang to say I'd be staying for a few nights, but I drove straight here from London." Rex flipped open his Zippo lighter and lit his cigarette. "You were a bit vague on the phone. What's this problem you want me to help with?"

"I'll explain shortly." Quist gestured to the seafront below. "I really have to tell you, I've just had the most bizarre conversation with an elderly lady down there on the promenade. She's one of those fake mediums who operate in seaside towns, but now it seems she's developed a genuine psychic gift and she's able…"

"Psychics?" laughed Rex. "I have a psychic aunt, as you probably remember, and most of the models and celebrities I date are forever paying to see those people. It's like an obsession with them. I always tell them about the time I visited a medium myself. I told her a joke and, when she was giggling at it, I punched her in the face. The thing is, I always like to strike a happy medium."

The detective sighed. "Are you finished?"

"What? You don't think that's funny?"

"This is a serious matter, Rex. The point is, this lady knew about my lycanthropy. She sensed it immediately as I walked past her cabin and, had you been there with me, I have no doubt she'd have known about you too. About how I bit you last year to save your life."

"Yeah." Rex grinned and peered over the bridge handrail. "It's been a while now, but I'm still getting used to the amazing fact that I'm a werewolf. Strange to think that I could jump off this bridge and I'd be okay. How brilliant is that?"

Quist glanced into the gorge. "You'd be quite a mess and the pain would be excruciating, but please…" He gestured to the drop. "If you want to try it, I'd be more than happy to hold your designer jacket and that £20,000 Rolex."

"No, you know what I mean. I'd survive the fall and the wounds would heal pretty much straight away. Only silver, fire and decapitation can kill us."

"Very true. Is that why you insist upon driving the way you do?"

"To be honest, I used to drive like that before you bit me." Rex laughed again. "Hey, come on. You have to admit that being a werewolf is cool and exciting." He held up his cigarette. "*And* you get to smoke as many of these as you like without them harming you."

The detective gave one of his odd lopsided smiles. "You're still in the honeymoon period, so to speak, and you're far too enthusiastic about this for my liking. Wait until you have to leave your loved ones and friends behind, change your name and move towns to prevent people from becoming suspicious."

"Yeah, whatever." Rex nodded to Madame Selene's cabin. "So is this the problem you mentioned? This psychic knowing about who you are and *what* you are?"

"No. It's difficult to explain why, but I sense I can trust this woman." Killing his cigarette stub underfoot, Quist headed for the hotel. "Come along. The problem lies this way. I need your assistance here and I'll explain inside.

Rex gazed up at the big building ahead. "So is this the latest case you're working on?"

"Not as such. It's actually something I've embarked upon as a favour for Watson, and I asked you to come because it relates to you directly."

"Me? How do you mean?"

"All in good time," said Quist. "The White Rose Party is holding a promotional meeting here at the Grand this afternoon."

"A gardening society?"

"Not quite. As you're probably aware, the white rose is the emblem of Yorkshire."

"Yes," lied Rex. He had no idea.

"*White* is definitely the appropriate word for *this* group." Quist paused on reaching the hotel doorway and lowered his voice. "White Rose is fairly new. They're a political party based in York that claims to work for the local folk of the county. They campaign for Yorkshire independence, similar to the Scottish campaign, and these meetings are being held to accrue members and to find candidates to stand for them."

"So what's the problem?" asked Rex, smoking his cigarette.

"Basically it's all a front," said Quist, smiling thinly. "In reality these people are an extremist right wing organisation and fully committed to white supremacy. A smooth character named Dominic Churchill leads them and I recently tracked down one of his party deputies. I managed to *accidentally* bump into him in a pub and we chatted at length. I heartily agreed with his right wing views and those views became more disturbing and openly racist as the alcohol flowed."

"Are we talking about braindead skinheads with swastika tattoos?" Rex frowned. "I thought groups like that were outlawed in Britain?"

"Not at all," said Quist. "This is a free country and the authorities only become involved if an organisation uses terrorism like the National Action group. There are many neo-Nazi groups filled with the kind of morons you've just described, but they're small, easy enough to identify and simple to monitor. The problem is, White Rose is far more intelligent and insidious than the usual cretins and they're gaining plenty of support. They have numerous candidates in constituencies across the county and they're exceedingly careful in what they say and how they push the boundaries of intolerance. They only hint at their true colours and their so-called policies are engineered to instil local pride and appeal to the masses. They demand more police on the Yorkshire streets, big changes to the immigration laws, an end to faith schools…"

"Well, I can see how such people would dislike Muslim schools, but aren't Catholic schools faith schools too?"

"Yes, and many of the nationalities they despise *are* Catholic. Romanians and lots of East Europeans and some black nations too. White Rose maintains a high media profile by being slightly comical and proposing eccentric ideas to catch the attention of the tabloid press and social media. They want the Yorkshire pudding adopted as Britain's national dish instead of the foreign chicken Tikka Masala, which is typical of their media tactics."

"I thought our national dish was roast beef," said Rex. "Er, or is it fish and chips?"

The detective shook his head. "Britain doesn't *have* a national dish. The press, however, have publicised the myth of Tikka Masala since it was voted the most *popular* dish a few years ago, not the *national* dish. By the way, it's a British invention and not foreign, but White Rose never mentions that inconvenient fact."

"So why are we here?" quizzed Rex. "You say it's a favour to Watson, but why is he interested in these characters?"

"A friend of his was recently assaulted by them," said Quist. "I wouldn't have involved you, but something pertinent has just arisen."

"Which is?"

"Follow me." He gave a lopsided smile. "You'll soon see."

"We'd better tread lightly." Rex gave a dry laugh as they walked in. "If these people don't like foreigners, they probably won't like werewolves."

The front doorway of the Grand certainly lived up to the hotel name – an enormous entrance of marble pillars and carvings that wouldn't have looked out of place on the mausoleum of King Midas. Although the vast lounge inside was pleasant enough, it didn't live up to the promise of the doorway. Decorative columns and arches supported a painted ceiling with chandeliers, but like so many of these old British hotels, the Victorian grandeur had faded over the decades.

Halloween was just three days away and bright orange pumpkins were strewn about the place, with bats and fake black cobwebs hanging from many of the light fittings.

A wide carpeted staircase led off the lounge with more columns, ornate banisters and statues of nymphs – the sort of staircase where brides are filmed by wedding photographers, and drunken guests from the bar hum the *Rocky* theme as they unsteadily ascend. Rex followed Quist up the steps to the first floor and into the Palm Court, one of the hotel function suites.

With its dance floor and window bays overlooking the sea, the Palm Court could be hired to accommodate christenings, weddings and other large gatherings such as this afternoon's political event. The room was full, with rows of chairs facing one of the bays where a middle-aged man stood speaking on a small stage. Five men sat behind him and, seeing Craig Battersby, the obnoxious character he'd plied with drink a few nights ago, Quist guessed this was the inner circle of White Rose deputies.

"This is Dominic Churchill," whispered the detective, heading for two empty chairs at the rear of the assembly. Sitting, he turned to Rex and sighed to find he was still wearing the sunglasses. "It would appear we've missed the start of his promotional talk, but if you've ever seen any of those old Hitler speeches at Nuremburg, you'll have some idea of how it probably went."

Journalists at the front of the crowd listened and occasionally snapped photographs of the party leader on his microphone. Churchill was attractive in a rugged way, clean-shaven, with a thick mass of silvery hair and a dark blue suit. A banner hung above him with one of the party slogans.

YORKSHIRE FOLK SPEAK COMMON SENSE. A VOTE FOR WHITE ROSE IS A VOTE FOR COMMON SENSE.

Rex leant close to Quist's ear. "I recognise him," he whispered. "He looks like a younger George Clooney and I've seen him in the media with one or two well-known faces."

"I'm sure you have," said the detective. "Churchill stands

32

beside any celebrity he can find, especially Yorkshire celebrities. His people take pictures, post them all over social media and release them to the press. All those photographs work on a subliminal level and make it appear as if the famous sportspeople, pop stars and actors are endorsing the party."

Dominic Churchill paused in his speech to flash an expensive set of dazzling teeth. "Now some have called my views racist," he said, chuckling. "But that's the loony left for you, and where's the racism in common sense? Remember, the White Rose Party only speaks common sense. No one wants to see mosque minarets towering over the beautiful Yorkshire Dales or the Yorkshire Wolds. That isn't racist, it's a simple fact. Any right-thinking person would tell you they'd be totally out of place. We all want to see ancient Norman churches and historic chapels."

One of the cleverer journalists raised a hand. "So have the Muslim community actually said they *want* to build mosques in the national parks?" he asked.

"It certainly wouldn't surprise any of us to discover that they *had*," said Churchill, deciding this was better than the actual answer which was *no*. "And that's another thing; why haven't the Yorkshire Wolds been given national park status like the Dales and the North York Moors? This is something we're campaigning for, and a vote for this party will ensure the Wolds are recognised at last. No one else seems to care about our wonderful Yorkshire heritage and that, to me, is a crime."

"This is how they invariably operate," murmured Quist. "They constantly plant seeds of hatred – visions of minarets above beauty spots – and then instantly change tactics to work on misty-eyed Yorkshire pride."

"I've told you about my Uncle Rupert and his weird right-wing views," whispered Rex. "This is the kind of crap he's always spouting."

"The Wolds aren't a priority," laughed Churchill. "That's what the other parties say. They aren't a priority and they don't have the necessary money, but how much money would it take? They have plenty of money to give to immigrants. To provide every immigrant with a free apartment and a brand new phone, but when it comes to our amazing heritage, to our stunning landscapes and our rich history, that I for one am incredibly proud of…"

"What a dickhead," whispered Rex.

"Eloquently put," said Quist, raising his eyebrows. *If Rex could see it, how come thousands of others couldn't?* "Yes, it's all thinly-veiled racism put across in an exceedingly patriotic manner. They constantly strive to paint a picture of old England. A return to the wondrous days of *Cider with Rosie* and…"

"Shush, you wankers," hissed a nearby White Rose supporter. "I'm trying to listen."

"Sorry," murmured Rex, glancing at the broken nose and the British bulldog tattooed on his large bicep. He turned back to Quist. "To be honest, I can't believe my Uncle Rupert hasn't joined this mob. You still haven't said, what's this problem that relates to me personally. What does any of this have to do with me?"

"Speaking of money," said Churchill, beaming widely and holding out a hand. "I'd like to introduce you all to one of our latest financial backers and the new candidate for the Pickering constituency."

Rex lowered his sunglasses, his eyes widening to see an obese man rise from the crowd. "Oh, you have to be joking?" he muttered, as Uncle Rupert stepped onto the small stage.

* * * *

Chapter 5

York is rightly classed as one of the most beautiful, if not *the* most beautiful city in Britain. The Yorkshire Tourist Board would never argue with this, but neither would the international hordes who pour in continuously to gasp at the wealth of historic sights – over eight million people each year. The stunning thoroughfare named the Shambles is England's most visited street, the 13th century Minster is the largest Gothic cathedral in Europe, and the enormous National Railway Museum overflows with excited visitors who marvel at the huge collection of trains on show. Over two miles of medieval defensive walls surround this small city on the River Ouse, a city quite literally crammed with Elizabethan, Georgian, Edwardian, Tudor and Victorian buildings.

Leaving the town centre, John Watson strolled across Skeldergate Bridge into Clementhorpe and headed south along the lively Bishopthorpe Road. He wore a fashionable green canvas jacket, faded blue jeans, trainers and a chirpy smile. Frank Zappa's guitar strummed loudly in his head, transmitted to tiny earphones from the vast collection of albums on his mobile. An attractive black youth of nineteen, Watson had been Bernard Quist's assistant for the best part of a year and really enjoyed the thrill and diversity of the job. Not many young people could say they worked in a private detective agency and fewer still could say they worked for a two-hundred year old werewolf. Both were pretty cool and exciting claims, but only one could actually be mentioned when bragging to friends and chatting up girls.

It was late Monday afternoon and, humming along to his music, the teenager looked around at Clementhorpe's vegan restaurants, delicatessens, bookshops, art galleries and coffee shops. The pavement cafes were filled with stylish young people drinking organic fair-trade lattes and staring at their phones. Risking a sexual harassment charge, he grinned and winked at three girls sipping cocktails at a table outside a pub and paused to read the blackboard list of guest ales.

Trendy beer drinkers went through noticeable phases,

contemplated Watson. In the past, fashion dictated that they should drink real ales with names like *Bilton's Old Pisswood* and *Frumpy Hedgehog Bitter*. Then it was cask ales, and now all the inns here sold a vast range of silly-priced European craft beers. He much preferred the strong local lager, brewed by the Sam Smiths brewery down the road in Tadcaster that retailed at a fraction of the price.

Clementhorpe was filled with modern young professionals and had a definite village vibe. It was an energetic place, but with a cosy insular feel, that seemed to set it apart from the rest of York like a little independent community. Most cities had areas like this – Highgate and Hampstead in London for example – and an official survey had compared Clementhorpe to Notting Hill, although probably not when the famous Notting Hill Carnival was in full swing.

Ebor Books stood on Bishopthorpe Road between an outlet trading in aromatherapy oils and an ethnic gallery selling aboriginal paintings – colourful artwork that was so lousy, Watson could only assume the native Australians worked blindfolded. His friend Sara Hoffman was a firefighter, but during her days off she sometimes helped out here in her grandfather's book shop. Watson hadn't seen the girl for over a week and he'd arranged to meet her here before going for a drink in town. Sara had recently changed shifts at the fire station, a colleague on her old shift was retiring, and a group of them had been on a six-day trip to Ibiza as a farewell party. Sara wasn't technically Watson's *girlfriend*, but he was working on it.

He smiled to himself. *There was only so long any girl could hold out without falling for THIS sexy charm.*

It would be Halloween this coming Thursday and the window of Ebor Books had been filled with volumes on witchcraft and ghosts, along with the usual pumpkin lanterns, cobwebs and plastic spiders. Watson had never visited the place before and wrinkled his nose at the stench of white spirit outside. Not being much of a book lover, he wondered if book shops were *supposed* to smell this way, before spotting the splatters of yellow paint on the pavement beneath the window. The corniced frame and glass had obviously just been cleaned, but traces of the bright paint could still be seen in the wooden cracks.

An antiquated bell gave a jolly jingle as he opened the door and a rich aroma of leather and musty history replaced the turpentine stink outside. Tugging out his earphones and switching off his phone, the teenager looked at the old volumes on the shelves and shook his head. He'd never seen the point of books. Why would anyone in the twenty-first century bother with this paper crap, he wondered, when there were phones, tablets and computers? Whenever Watson read anything it was usually on a screen of some sort, but he had to concede that, with printed paper, you wouldn't get hundreds of idiotic and abusive comments at the end of the text.

Adam Hoffman appeared from behind a bookcase. Sara's grandfather was sixty-two, with white hair, a trim white beard and bright grey eyes. He reminded Watson of a kindly toymaker in a kid's fantasy movie.

"Afternoon," said the old man, smiling warmly. "Are you just browsing or can I help you?"

"Hello there, mate," said Watson. "I'm guessing you're Mister Hoffman? I'm actually looking for your granddaughter."

"Ah, you must be Watson." His smile widened. "Yes, Sara told me you'd be calling and I've heard a lot about you. A private detective, I believe?"

"Well, I work for one," said the youth. "Bernard Quist's detective agency on Baker Avenue, but I seem to do most of the work, running around and taking photographs for him, so yeah, I guess that makes me a detective too."

"I'm Adam." Hoffman shook hands enthusiastically. "I know Sara was supposed to meet you here, but she's running errands for me and she'll be on her way to the house by now."

"Wow, just look at all these books." Watson gestured to the shelves and gasped in sham amazement. "Hey, I wonder, do you have that French revolution classic about a sofa in Paris and a couch in London?"

"Er…" Hoffman looked puzzled.

"A Tale of Two Settees."

"Oh, very good." The old man burst out laughing. "Yes, Sara said you were a joker. I'm closing the shop now that you've arrived and we can walk over to my place." He pointed to two cardboard boxes. "It isn't far, but you could do my back a favour by carrying those books for me."

"Someone sounds like they're in a good mood," said Watson, picking them up. "And it's probably due to more than my crap joke."

"Does it show?" Hoffman grinned, excitedly. "Yes, something incredible has happened. Something truly amazing and I can think of little else…" He hesitated and clearly decided against continuing. "Yes, come along."

Watson waited outside whilst the alarm was switched on and the shop was locked.

Hoffman checked the window to ensure it was clean. "Can you believe this?" he muttered, his smile vanishing. "Someone painted a yellow swastika on there in the middle of the night."

"Are you kidding?" gasped Watson, almost dropping the books. "Because you're Jewish? Are you telling me that kind of insane shit still happens? And here in York of all places?"

"It's the scum from White Rose," sighed Hoffman. "This all began three weeks ago when I wrote several letters to the newspapers saying that, in my opinion, the party is too right wing and it has racist views. Since then, the shop has been vandalised four times and I get death threats and abusive calls telling me to leave town."

"So what are the cops doing about it?"

"Not much." The old man laughed dryly. "Apparently, the phones they use are untraceable and the police can't prove who's responsible for the vandalism. They've advised me to install video cameras outside, but even if I did, I'm sure they'd only show unidentifiable figures in hooded coats."

"Because of a few letters." Watson shook his head. "Whatever happened to free speech? I saw Sara's black eye after she was assaulted. She told me how useless the cops were with that too."

"Yes." Hoffman nodded angrily and, leaving the shop, he crossed Bishopthorpe Road with the teenager. "Her cheekbone was almost broken and I blame myself."

"Don't be daft. The only ones to blame are the two twats who hit her."

"But I caused it by writing to the newspapers. Those thugs came to the house to intimidate *me*, but I was out and Sara answered the door. Both of them assaulted her; one grabbed her hair and punched her twice in the stomach and the other punched her in her face. '*That's from Dominic*,' one of them said. '*Tell your Jew grandad to mind his own business*.'"

"Sick," muttered Watson, following him down Madeley Street. "It's hard to believe there are animals like that out there."

Hoffman nodded. "Both men had criminal records and Sara identified them from police photographs as Harvey McMurdo and Lee Millican, but neither is a member of White Rose. There was nothing to connect them to the party and they left no physical evidence. Both men had solid alibis too, presumably provided by their cronies, so the police said Sara must have misidentified them."

"Yeah?" The teenager let out a harsh laugh. "These days I'm surprised they aren't suing her for stress and defamation of character."

"Churchill obviously employs hoodlums to do this kind of thing for him. They've painted filth on the shop and attacked my granddaughter…" Hoffman paused, smiled to himself and suddenly brightened. "Still, not for much longer. Here we are; this is my place."

Watson gave him a curious glance. *Not for much longer? What was that supposed to mean?*

Madeley Street was a cul-de-sac comprising of two rows of Victorian terraced houses with little buffer gardens. Hoffman and his granddaughter lived in the end house, where the short street terminated by an infant school.

"Sara isn't home yet." Stepping into his porch, the old man unlocked the door. "Her car isn't here. She was saving up for a Mini, but I bought her one after the assault. I said it was to cheer her up, but to be honest, it was to alleviate my own guilty feelings."

"I can understand that," said Watson. "Hey, feel free to punch me and feel guilty any time you like."

"Come on in," laughed Hoffman. "So, you're her new boyfriend, are you?"

"I'm just a friend. We…" The youth bit his tongue. *We haven't slept together yet* probably wasn't the kind of thing grandpa would want to hear. He followed him through the hallway into a large lounge and set down the boxes of books. "Sara got back last night, didn't she? Did she have a good time in Ibiza?"

"From what she's told me, yes," said Hoffman. "But then again, I don't suppose she'd tell me *too* much, what with her spending six nights on the island with a bunch of partying firemen."

Grinning at this, Watson looked around the room. With its wooden floors, decorative ceiling plasterwork and the multitude of books, it reminded him of his employer's cottage in the nearby village of Askham Richard. Many of the books appeared to be Jewish folklore and mysticism, and Watson knew Quist would love this stuff. Glass-fronted bookcases lined one wall and more volumes filled two free-standing oak units. The youth raised his eyebrows. *Didn't this old guy see enough of them at his shop?*

A television hung on the wall and he was surprised that Hoffman didn't switch it on as he walked in. Watson lived with his mother and the television in their lounge was turned on all day, from getting up to retiring to bed. It even remained on if they were out; his mum claimed it deterred burglars and it was company for their ginger cat Hucknall. Most of the teenager's friends were the same, and he'd been to funeral gatherings where the television remained on throughout, albeit with the sound muted. Watson smiled to himself. *Quist was probably weird like Hoffman and left his television switched off… if he even owned one.*

"I wonder…" said the teenager, gesturing to the books. "Do you have that old Charles Dickens classic about the twin glove puppets living in Paris and London?"

"Huh?" Hoffman pondered for a moment and erupted in a fit of giggling. "Ah, very good – A Tale of Two Sootys? No, you won't catch me out twice with those daft jokes."

Watson watched curiously as he laughed and laughed. He'd made this up himself, but it wasn't *that* funny – in fact, most people who heard it didn't even smile – but this laughter was clearly a manifestation of the pent-up excitement he'd noticed earlier.

"Come along, I'll pop the kettle on." Wiping his eyes, Hoffman walked through a pair of glass doors into a large kitchen diner. "So tell me, how do you know my granddaughter?"

"I met her in the King's Arms by the river. Some of the fire service call in there for a drink after work." Watson followed him. "How do you feel about her being a firefighter?"

"Oh, I'm very proud of her. I know her mum and dad would be too."

Watson nodded. He was aware of how Sara's parents had died when she was five years old – their car was flattened by a huge lorry on the M62. The driver was jailed for six years, which wasn't long, but hopefully long enough for him to realise that texting his girlfriend at 85 mph wasn't particularly bright.

"You brought her up, didn't you?" said Watson.

"I did, and I'm very protective of her." Hoffman grimaced slightly. "Although, seeing the state of her face last week, my *protection* leaves much to be desired. Well, that's about to change."

"Listen, about that…" said Watson. "My boss hates the White Rose Party too and I asked him to investigate them. I don't want to get your hopes up, but he's pretty good at this kind of stuff. He'll find a way in and I'm sure he'll be able to link Sara's assault to them by…"

"These people are clever," said Hoffman. "Too clever to be infiltrated by journalists or private detectives."

"Believe me, you really don't know my boss."

"I'm sure you both mean well, but he won't find any evidence. The police aren't helping either, so I intend to do something about this myself."

"You?" Watson frowned. "Like what?"

"Oh, young man..." Hoffman stroked thoughtfully at his white beard, a twinkle in his eye. "You'd be truly astounded at what's possible; at the wondrous things a person can achieve with dedication, with study and..." He peered through the kitchen door into the lounge and laughed again. "And with the right books."

Watson had no idea what this could possibly mean. "Er, okay."

The old man noticed his granddaughter's car pulling up outside. "I now have the means to avenge Sara's assault and to do something about this vile excuse for a political party."

"Dedication and the right books?" said Watson. "Are these books on karate or something?"

* * * *

Chapter 6

The time was almost five o'clock, the late October sun had set over Scarborough and the seaside resort basked in deep twilight. Flocks of starlings whirred past the Grand Hotel, their nasal screams combining with the yelping kittiwakes to create a deafening cacophony. Quist decided the racket was far preferable to the insidious garbage he'd been listening to *inside* the building. The White Rose Party was finishing their meeting in the Palm Court, but Rex and the detective had slipped out before the end.

Standing by his friend's black McLaren in the parking area, Quist lit a cigarette and offered the pack to the young man, who took one and used his own lighter. The detective noticed he was still using the shiny steel Zippo with the wolf's head engraving. He rolled his eyes. *Yes, Rex definitely looked upon the lycanthropy as being cool and exciting, which had always worried him.*

"Well…" said Rex, looking up at the hotel over his sunglasses. "I don't know about you, but after that meeting I could use a shower."

"Absolutely, and perhaps a scrub with bleach," agreed Quist. "Did you notice how Churchill kept repeating *common sense* and *White Rose*? It's a fairly standard psychological technique to have listeners associate the two. Mention something often enough and many people will actually accept it as truth. It's similar to the gutter tabloids printing: "I'm not gay, claims Michael Wilson". The simpler readers invariably assume there's no smoke without fire and believe the person mentioned *is* gay, even though the entire story is attributed to a nameless *source* and is invented."

"Who's Michael Wilson?" asked Rex.

"Well, no one, obviously. It's just a name I plucked from nowhere to illustrate my point."

"Oh, right." The young man gave a puzzled frown. "So *is* he gay?"

Quist stared for a moment. Like many young people born into vast wealth, Rex wasn't the sharpest tool in the box. "I believe so," he said. "Michael has great hair and dress sense."

"This bunch would hate him." Rex scowled at the hotel. "I wouldn't mind betting they want to make homosexuality illegal again. You say one of them punched Watson's friend?"

The detective nodded. "A young lady named Sara Hoffman. Her grandfather wrote letters to various local newspapers voicing his concerns about the organisation's closet racism. Two people were sent to rough him up and threaten him into silence. He wasn't home, so they assaulted his granddaughter instead."

"Incredible." Rex shook his head. "And my uncle actually intends to finance this bunch of morons."

"I told you how I plied that party deputy with drink last week," said Quist. "Craig Battersby is his name. He became rather inebriated, we had a good old racist chat and he revealed far more information than he should have. Apparently, Churchill employs a small group to do his dirty work, four hardened thugs whom he refers to as his *Task Force*. They have no links to White Rose and he uses them to intimidate anyone who speaks out publicly against the party. In their spare time they vandalise foreign businesses and generally create racial tension, which Churchill then has the audacity to condemn in the media and loudly blame on the lack of police. He says immigrants are a huge problem, but the problem shouldn't be settled with violence."

"He's a real beauty, isn't he?" Rex sucked angrily on his cigarette. "So you're clearly planning to do something about this?"

"Absolutely. I intend to expose White Rose as neo-Nazis and finish them. They've recently been increasing their advertising campaigns and boosting their media profile with these promotional meetings, their objective being to recruit candidates in every area before they begin campaigning in the by-elections. They're in Harrogate tonight and then Selby, Thirsk, Wakefield and Whitby later this week. All this takes large amounts of money, they've overstretched themselves and Battersby claims they desperately need Rupert Grant's cash injection. That's why I asked for your assistance; your task is to somehow persuade your uncle to see sense and to cancel his funding."

"No problem," nodded Rex. "Don't worry, I'll soon get him to change his mind."

"It may be more problematic than you envisage. From what you've told me, he isn't the most open-minded person."

"Hey, this is me you're talking to, remember? I have amazing people skills and a rather sexy silver tongue."

"Er, yes." Quist raised his eyebrows, but didn't argue. "With your Uncle Rupert out of the picture, I'll then pose as a candidate and financial backer myself, gain Churchill's trust and obtain recordings of him revealing his true self."

"Brilliant." Rex grinned. "And hopefully a nice photograph of him playing with himself as he reads *Mein Kampf*."

* * * *

Chapter 7

"So, to finish off..." said Dominic Churchill, speaking into the microphone in the Palm Court function room. "We live on an island – it's that simple. This is a beautiful, historic island and one which we're all justly proud of, but an island can only hold so many people and we already have far too many here. Our underfunded health service is on its knees, the schools can't cope, prisons are over-spilling, and immigrants are *still* being allowed to come here in their hundreds of thousands. Every day, thousands more people arrive here to systematically drain our social services and cripple our limited resources."

Churchill never bothered to check actual numbers. There was little point, when his wild, concocted figures sounded much better and far more frightening. Lee Millican, one of Churchill's planted people in the crowd, nodded wisely and began to clap. Various others joined in, although many looked uncomfortable.

"Now I'm sometimes called a racist by the loony left," said Churchill, picking up a glass and a water decanter from a nearby table. "But this isn't racism, it's simple mathematics, science and common sense. You should all know by now that the White Rose Party lives and breathes common sense. You see, I don't care if the people coming here are black or white, African, Danish, Asian or Canadian. Our tiny island is unbelievably overpopulated and we have to use common sense before it's too late." He held up the glass. "Look, this is our beautiful little country. As anyone with intelligence can clearly see, it's a certain size and it can't possibly grow any larger. We don't need a degree in physics to know it can only hold so much."

He poured the water, filling the glass and allowing it to cascade over his hand onto the carpet. Two of the crowd plants clapped louder and many more joined in this time.

"Immigration needs to be stopped," said Churchill, firmly. "Common sense dictates that it must be stopped *now*, for all our sakes. The foreign crowds on this little island of ours are growing and multiplying every day. We don't have the police resources to vet them and terrorists and other violent criminal elements are arriving in droves. Soon these crowds will grow so dense and become so vast that our children will be literally pushed into the sea. I won't allow that to happen." He smiled broadly. "That's something for us all to think about and it's all I have to say this afternoon. Thank you very much, ladies and gentlemen."

Churchill smiled again for the flashing cameras and left the small stage. Several journalists approached him for questions, but they were beaten to it by a young woman who, from her uniform and name badge, was obviously one of the hotel staff.

"Excuse me," she said. "There's a telephone call for you, Mister Churchill. The gentleman rang reception, but you can take the call on the Palm Court phone over there. Just lift the receiver and press 9."

"Why thank you, my dear." Churchill headed to the wall phone by the doors and did as instructed. "Hello?"

"Dominic?" The voice was elderly. "It's me."

"Oh, right. I assume you've been ringing my mobile?" Taking out his phone, Churchill saw several missed calls stacked up. "I've been chairing a press meeting all afternoon so my phone was switched off. It must be important for you to ring the hotel like…"

"It's Dieter…" The caller cleared his throat. "Dieter is dead."

"Really? Shit."

Lee Millican, one of Churchill's muscular underlings, heard the profanity as he walked past into the corridor. "Is everything okay?" he asked.

Churchill closed a hand over the mouthpiece. "It's fine." He waved the burly man away and spoke again into the phone. "What was it? Another stroke?"

There was a lengthy pause. "No, he was murdered. He was killed in the care home by one of the staff."

"Well, he could be quite abrasive, to say the least," snorted Churchill. "I imagine someone had finally had enough."

47

"Dominic, for God's sake."

"Oh, come on. I'm sorry about this, but you know we were never close. And why are you using his real name? He was Dylan Taylor..."

"He was my brother, Dieter," snapped the caller. "You two never got on, but he was proud of what you've accomplished and..."

"What I *will* accomplish," said Churchill. "Which will be infinitely more than the two of you ever did."

"Lee Millican," said a voice behind Churchill. "Where is Lee Millican?"

"He went that way." Churchill didn't turn, but jerked a thumb towards the hotel passage. He took a deep breath. "Listen," he sighed into the phone. "I'm really sorry about Dylan, but much as I'd like to come over and talk about this, I'm busy with another meeting in Harrogate tonight. I'll see you tomorrow."

* * * *

Lee Millican left the Palm Court and headed along the wide corridor to the male toilets by the Grand Hotel elevators. His fair hair was tightly cropped, he wore a denim jacket and walked with an arrogant, musclebound swagger. Millican had always loved violence and often approached total strangers in pubs to enquire who they were looking at. He enjoyed the terror in their eyes, the satisfied feeling of achievement as the ambulance took them away, and the admiring looks from any thick-as-pigshit girls who might be present.

The meeting had gone really well, he decided. As usual, he'd posed as an anonymous supporter, loudly applauding at all the right moments and asking a list of prearranged questions for Churchill to tackle with well-scripted answers.

Working outside the party in the Task Force, as Churchill had jokingly labelled his shadowy assistants, had plenty of benefits. These four handpicked hard men were given all the juicy jobs – slapping people around, threatening the families of journalists who spoke out against White Rose, and burning down Pakistani shops. Millican chuckled to himself. *Plus he never had to wear a stupid suit and tie.*

The toilets were empty and the brawny man stood at the line of ceramic urinals, smirking as he directed his steaming jet to swill a discarded Polo mint along the trough. The door opened and someone quietly entered, someone who walked up and stood right behind him.

Men had long ago worked out a set of unwritten macho rules in these places. At a row of urinals, where one was in use, you never, *ever* used the next one along. You never made small talk, unless it was to drunkenly proclaim this was the "best room in the house," you always stood further down the line, and you *never* stood closely behind someone as you waited.

"Hoy, twat," snarled Millican, without turning. "Have you never heard of personal space? You might have noticed there are ten places at this trough. Are you seriously telling me you're waiting for *this* one?"

"Lee Millican? Are you Lee Millican?"

"Yes, I am." He glanced around to see a bald, dark skinned man in a lengthy raincoat. "And I'm telling you to fuck off further down there right now."

The temperature fell, as if someone had opened the door of a freezer. Millican heard a noise and realised the man had removed his coat and dropped it on the floor.

What the hell was he doing? If this was some pervert hoping for some toilet fun and games, he'd definitely picked the wrong guy.

He didn't get the chance to voice his thoughts, due to a large hand fastening onto the back of his head and slamming his face into the tiles. Millican's skull exploded and a crimson mess of blood and brains splattered the room, transforming the walls and floor into something the artist Jackson Pollock would have been truly proud of.

* * * *

Chapter 8

The epitome of a traditional English inn, with gnarled beams and a charming timber and stone décor, the King's Arms in York has only been serving ale for two-hundred years. Before that, it had been a money counting house, but the ancient building has hardly changed in appearance since the days when Guy Fawkes lived a few streets away. The King's Arms is traditionally known as *the York pub that floods*. The tavern stands on the very edge of the River Ouse in the centre of town, so close that a vertical wooden measure has been fixed to the wall inside the bar which allows patrons to see the dates of past water levels. 1982 and 2000 both record depths of over six feet, presumably requiring the customers to use canoes and the staff to wear snorkels.

Illuminated by spotlights, the arches of Ouse Bridge cross the river beside the inn and a flight of old stone steps descend from the road above to the cobbled esplanade and outdoor tables. The early evening was still warm enough to drink outside and Watson sat at one of the table benches. The teenager watched the passing pleasure boats and pictured the Viking longships that were an everyday sight here before 1066. Watson's employer was constantly moaning about how he should take an interest in the history of his birthplace, and although museums were near the bottom of his "fun list", he'd grudgingly accompanied Quist to the Jorvik Viking Centre on Coppergate and picked up various titbits of information.

The symbol of Odin, a black raven on a blood-red background, the Viking flag had once flown above the bridge here. Halfdan and his brother, Ivar, took York from the Saxons and Halfdan became the first Viking king. The Roman invaders had called the city Eboracum, but the Norse warriors renamed it Jorvik and the street plan hadn't changed since their reign. Fossgate, Ousegate, Spurriergate, Gillygate – the central thoroughfares still follow the same winding routes and bear their original Viking names.

Watson looked up at Ouse Bridge, which apparently had been there since those times. The current sandstone arches were a mere two centuries old, but they supported one of the main routes into the centre from the Micklegate Bar gateway and many constructions had spanned the water on this spot since the Viking original. Resembling the Ponte Vecchio in Florence, a jumble of half-timbered buildings had covered the medieval bridge, with dwellings, shops, a small prison, and England's first ever public toilets.

That must have been fun for the boats passing underneath, contemplated Watson.

"Penny for your thoughts." Sara Hoffman arrived from the bar with two drinks and sat beside him. "What are you thinking about?"

"Huh?" Jolted from his daydreaming, Watson turned to her. "Public toilets."

"Oh, nice,"

"No, the boss took me to the Viking museum last week and…" He laughed and picked up his lager glass. "It doesn't matter. Thanks for the drink and cheers."

Sara clinked her wine glass against his lager. She was an attractive girl, petite and trim, with short black hair and, at the moment, the dusky remains of a black eye.

"Like I said," she smiled. "The drink makes up for me not bringing you a gift from Ibiza. I was going to get you a pair of maracas."

"I already have a pair, thanks." Watson grinned. "Although I call them by a different name. I'm guessing you had other things on your mind." He gestured to her facial bruising. "It's pretty much faded, which is a shame because I find pandas kind of sexy."

"I'm over the attack now." Sara fingered the discoloration. "It's one thing to be assaulted in the street, but when someone calls on you and it happens on your doorstep, it's frightening. The thought that people like that know where you live…"

"I can imagine," agreed the youth.

"Gramps blamed himself and grew really upset and depressed over it."

"He was telling me about that earlier. He bought you the car because he felt so guilty."

51

"That's right, but I don't think it worked. The only thing that snapped him out of his depression was a book someone gave him."

"Well, it must have been a good one." Watson laughed. "What was that one my mum used to rave about? I think it was a cookery book. Oh, yeah – *Fifty Shades of Gravy.*"

"It was some old leather book on the occult," said Sara, "and I mean *really* old. He has this new German friend called Daniel Geller who's wealthy and apparently has the right kind of connections. They can find any antiquarian book you want. Geller brought it to the house a few days before I left for Spain and they were both over the moon. Gramps never stopped reading it and it certainly cheered him up."

Watson sipped his lager. "Your grandad is a great old guy and yes, he seemed quite happy and excited today."

Sara nodded. "He's been like a different person since I got back. It's like he's secretly won the lottery or something."

"Anyway, enough of all that," said Watson. "How did your friend's retirement party go? Six days in Ibiza? Wow, whatever happened to a York pub crawl, or a night out at the seaside?"

"Ibiza was brilliant. Nothing but swimming, joking, dancing, drinking and lounging around, and it was good to go out with some of the old crew. My new watch are great, but I have some real friends on the old watch."

A guffaw of laughter came from further along the quay where Sara's work colleagues were sitting around an outdoor table. She glanced over and one of them waved and blew a kiss at her.

"Don't you want to join them?" asked Watson.

"I see enough of their ugly faces at the fire station," said Sara. "My leave is over and I'm back at work in the morning. Besides, they'd only take the piss out of us – you especially."

"Me? Why?"

The girl smiled. "No reason and certainly nothing personal. It's just what firefighters do. I suppose it's like the cops and the armed forces. A lot of normal folk find it difficult to understand and handle." She pointed to her crew. "That's Jabba over there, so called because he was once overweight. Next to him is Deidre, who wore specs before getting laser treatment and someone noticed he had a look of Deidre Barlow from *Coronation Street*. The ginger-haired guy is Prince, named after Prince Harry. Then there's Dobbin, who's hung like a seaside donkey. I wasn't present, but he once famously used it to swat a fly in the station kitchen."

Watson nodded. "It's probably because I work in a detective agency and my boss is always talking about deduction, but I'm deducing that nicknames are quite popular in the fire service?"

"You could say that. Everyone at York fire station has one. The good-looking Indian guy there is Josh Patel, or Rogan Josh, as his mates call him."

Being black, Watson knew there was nothing racist in this kind of humour amongst groups of close friends. The only people who found such things offensive were slightly dim white people who overheard the banter, the sort of uptight folk who believed tabloid headlines and didn't have any real grasp of what racism actually *was*.

"So what's your nickname?" he asked. "I'd go for something like Winona. You're really attractive and have a look of the actress Winona Rider. Er, back when she was twenty, that is. Not now that she's a great granny or whatever."

"Sorry to disappoint you, but it's Waggy. I was caught listening to Wagner on the running machine in the fire station gym and that was my name for a while. It was soon shortened."

"You like classical music? Wow! You should meet my boss, Cyrano."

"My parents enjoyed it and I have their CD collection," said Sara. "Playing their music makes me feel close to them." She glanced back at the firefighters. "I haven't been on this shift long, but they're a really nice bunch."

"So what's it like working in the fire service?" asked Watson. "The public think you sit around waiting for fires, playing snooker and volleyball all day."

The girl shook her head. "It may have been like that decades ago, but now we never stop. We spend all day on fire prevention, safety inspections and putting up smoke alarms in houses. Plus we train all the time to deal with the new hazards that are constantly appearing."

"And all for a few quid more than the minimum wage," pointed out Watson. "New hazards? A fire is a fire, isn't it?"

"All fires are different," said Sara, "and now there are all kinds of weird chemical fires. But I'm also talking about new types of building cladding and cheaper construction that collapses on you in heat. Plus, all the modern motor vehicles have built-in dangers. We have scrap cars delivered to the station that we train with, but they've always been old cars that didn't have the risks that we need to be aware of. New cars are safe when you're driving them, but after a crash they can become death traps. There are magnesium components that you can't extinguish, explosive charges built into seat belts and countless air bags that burst out from everywhere."

"*Explosive* doesn't sound too nice, but you're saying air bags are dangerous?"

"They have a habit of going off when you're working inside the crashed vehicle, holding the head of a driver with a fractured neck. Or when you're using a hydraulic tool in there that can slice off an arm. Fortunately, we're getting modern cars to train with now. Believe it or not, we've just taken delivery of three that are less than a year old. A superb Range Rover, a BMW and an Audi. Cutting them to pieces will be educational, but tear-jerking."

"Nearly new cars? Bloody hell. Where did they come from?"

"God knows, but they're real beauties."

"Shame," sighed the teenager. "I've always fancied an Audi, but I doubt I'll get one working for Cyrano."

"I have to ask," said Sara. "Why do you call your boss Cyrano?"

"He has a big nose." Watson smiled. "Kind of like Cyrano de Bergerac."

"So private detectives have nicknames like firefighters? What's yours?"

"Well…" Watson's smile widened and he gave her a wink. "I don't talk about it, but I'm sometimes known as *the Black Love Machine*."

* * * *

Chapter 9

A rugged landscape of purple heather and Jurassic rock outcrops, the North York Moors lie twenty-five miles to the north of York, bordered by the North Sea, the Cleveland Hills and the chalk folds of the Yorkshire Wolds. Sedgefield Grange stood in a wooded vale on the southern edge of this desolate terrain between the village of Levisham and the market town of Pickering. Rex Grant paced up and down in the grange library, fuming over the heated argument he'd just had with his uncle.

Rupert's views on race and class were fairly eccentric, to say the least, thought Rex, *but why was he wasting his time and, perhaps more to the point, his money on these White Rose people? It was difficult to imagine anyone more right wing than Rupert, but surely he'd never condone the vandalising of ethnic shops? The very idea of beating up girls, like Watson's Jewish friend, would outrage him, so how could he be so stupid as to get involved with this group?*

The young man paused by the library French doors to stare angrily over the stepped terracing behind the grange. Standing in an area of parkland on the outskirts of Sedgefield village, this small mansion dated back to the 1500s, but various features had been added over the years, including Rupert's two swimming pools, his clay pigeon shooting range, outdoor hot-tub and the huge motorised satellite dish. The construction company *Grant Homes* had paid for it all. Rupert and his brother Lionel were joint owners, although Rex's father Lionel ran the firm and Rupert was more of a silent partner now, the majority of his cash coming from shrewd stock investments and a little insider trading that he never cared to speak about.

Watching the peacocks strutting around the gardens, Rex noticed how the hundreds of pheasants he'd seen on his last visit had vanished. The shooting season begins on the first of September and, by the fourth, the last of the terrified birds had been driven over a battery of expensive shotguns and blasted from the sky like a live game of *Space Invaders*. Rupert was fanatical about blood sports, his passion having begun in public school, where he'd excelled in thrashing fags, roasting new boys and waterboarding sissies.

Rex glanced over his shoulder as his uncle returned from the kitchen. The argument had left him feeling peckish and he'd had his chef rustle up a light snack – six fried bacon and peanut butter sandwiches steaming on a tray. *Yes*, thought Rex, *he loved blood sports, but from the size of him, clearly not any other form of sport.*

The fifty-eight year old man was enormous, reminiscent of an overweight version of the old actor Fatty Arbuckle. *If he were ever to lay on a beach*, decided his nephew, *well-meaning wildlife lovers would probably gather around in an attempt to return him to the water.*

"I honestly can't believe you," said Rex. He watched Rupert flop onto one of the library couches and begin devouring his meal. "You're not an idiot. You must be able to see through this White Rose organisation."

"You're still going on about this?" snapped Rupert, through a mouthful of sandwich. "I thought we'd finished with it."

"Did you know that your new pal Churchill had his men beat up a girl?" demanded Rex.

"It was a couple of weeks ago." Rupert nodded. "Dominic told me about this. Some young woman wrongly accused him of assault, but the police investigated and found it was nonsense. She was probably a tabloid journalist making it up to create a story."

"*What?*" gasped Rex. "She was a friend of someone I know."

"This isn't some group of thugs," laughed Rupert. "It's a British political party."

"That's the image they're trying to project, but surely you can see past that? At the very least you must be able to see they're racist?"

"You say that likes it's a bad thing."

Rex wondered if this was an attempt at humour, but saw that it wasn't. Many regarded Rupert as eccentric because of his right wing, reactionary opinions. He loathed the lower classes and immigrants and Rex wondered if he ever fantasised about combining this pet hate with his love of blood sports. *He'd probably like nothing better than to chase unemployed "scroungers" across the moors with a pack of hounds.*

"Dominic is right in what he says," said Rupert, chomping on a sandwich. "Britain is an island and it can only support so many. They come over here and clog up our National Health Service…"

"Why should that bother you?" snorted Rex. "When did *you* ever use the NHS?"

"Half of them can't even speak our language."

"That shouldn't be a problem; you don't talk to the ones who *can* speak English. Not unless they're millionaires like yourself." Rex shook his head. "We're no longer living in the Victorian days. Dad employs dozens of foreign workers on his building projects…"

"Really?" Rupert grimaced. "Good Lord, I'll have a word with him over that."

"There's something you should maybe consider," said Rex. "You know dad hates racism and he's never agreed with your views. He holds the majority of shares in the family business and I don't know what he'll do when he finds out you're intending to give money to the White Rose Party."

"Mmh, that's a point." Rupert narrowed his eyes thoughtfully, wondering if this would affect him financially. He shook his head. "Well, I'll cross that bridge if and when I come to it."

"Honestly, you have some peculiar ideas." Sighing with exasperation, Rex sat on the couch. "Didn't you famously say that the unemployed should be used on the land? Not as farm labour, but ploughed in as fertiliser?"

"And so they should. Idle layabouts."

A petite young woman walked into the library, her raven hair flowing over the shoulders of a tight red mini dress. Rex swallowed uncomfortably as she smiled sexily at him. Marika Grant was half the age of her husband and, fortunately, around a sixth of his weight. She never wore make-up, save for black pencil lines around her large brown eyes which gave her the look of a coal miner who hadn't washed properly – a stunningly attractive coal miner.

Rupert had already been contemplating the idea of a Thai bride when he met the young girl on a Romanian hunting holiday. She was working as the receptionist in his Bucharest hotel and they'd married after a whirlwind courtship. Marika was easily wooed by his English charm, but also by the pictures of his country mansion and the bank statements she'd seen on his phone. Rex often called at Sedgefield for short breaks with Rupert and Marika, and couldn't help feeling secretly attracted to his "aunt".

"Hello, Rex," she purred, in her husky accent, her breathing becoming shallower.

The unspoken attraction was definitely mutual. Thanks to his Hollywood looks and glib charisma, women had always been drawn to Rex. The McLaren supercar and the carefree way he threw his father's money around helped too. Since the werewolf bite, however, this sexual magnetism had been augmented. Quist had explained how females subliminally sensed his supernatural darker self and it excited and aroused them without them knowing why. Marika was no exception – whenever she saw him and subconsciously picked up his pheromones, her dark brown pupils dilated, her pulse accelerated and on a couple of occasions she'd almost swooned.

Sensing the tension, Marika gave a puzzled frown. "What's wrong?" she asked. "Are you two arguing?"

"You could say that." Rex rolled his eyes. "Did you know that Rupert is joining the White Rose Party as their Pickering candidate and he's agreed to finance their campaign?"

"Are you joking?" Sweeping back the mane of black hair, she turned disbelievingly to her husband. "White Rose? That horrible bunch of racists I keep seeing in the news?"

"I've tried to reason with him," sighed Rex. "But it's like pulling teeth. Maybe *you* can talk some sense into him."

"I certainly will," snapped Marika, her hands on her hips. "Listen to me. You can forget about financing these people right now. In fact I don't want you going near them anymore."

"Calm down, dear." Finishing his plate of sandwiches, Rupert smiled sympathetically. "We're talking politics and it's all above your head. Girls don't understand anything about politics or science."

"Really?" Marika laughed. "Listening to the speeches on the internet, I know one thing – if White Rose had their way, they'd deport me back to Romania."

"Don't you worry your pretty little head about that." Her husband gave a condescending laugh. "No one will be deporting you anywhere because I won't let them. Now all the *other* East European immigrants, however..."

"Rupert..." she broke in, angrily. "You know that game you like to play with the carpet beater? Lord Henry and his naughty servant girl?"

"Now, now..." Rupert coloured up and shot Rex an uncomfortable grin. "Er, I don't think we need to mention such things in front of my nephew."

"There won't be any more *such things* if you don't rethink this." Marika stooped close to his ear and lowered her voice. "You can certainly forget about that latest idea of yours. Me running around the gardens in a crotchless fox outfit while you hunt me naked with..."

Rex's eyes widened as he listened to her private mumbling, his hearing augmented by the lycanthropy. Some country landowners, it seemed, got up to far more interesting things than shooting pheasants, contracting gout and avoiding taxes.

"I've reconsidered," said Rupert, abruptly. He cleared his throat and smiled uneasily at Rex. "You were right, and after careful deliberation I've decided to cancel my White Rose membership and the financial contributions. Somebody bring me a phone."

* * * *

Chapter 10

Many years ago, the government fire authorities applied a mathematical algorithm to the map of North Yorkshire and decided that England's largest county didn't need much in the way of fire protection.

Only four of the fire stations there are whole-time, in that they're constantly manned by professional firefighters and are operational twenty-four hours a day, every day of the year. The handful of others, intermittently positioned around this vast rural area, are only staffed during office hours, or run by people with other jobs who sometimes work there part-time. This is due to the county having little in the way of built-up areas and industry, and also because it's more economical for the British government. Firmly crossed fingers and nervous optimism are a hell of a lot cheaper than adequate fire cover.

York is one of the whole-time stations. Sandwiched between an indoor car park and a small block of apartments, the modern building with its three-bay garage stands just outside the city centre on a quiet thoroughfare named Kent Street. It was six-thirty, the night shift had begun and the seven firefighters would man the place until they were relieved by the day shift at eight in the morning.

"Bon voyage," muttered Moggy, watching the fire engine speed away along the street.

Many fire service nicknames were clever and imaginative. Others were less so, and Moggy had come by his after accidentally running over a cat some twenty-four years ago.

The engine had just been dispatched to a house fire in the suburb of Clifton, but Moggy and his colleague, Zorro, remained on the station. The two men were crewing the hydraulic platform tonight, the appliance with the cage and huge extendable booms on top which wasn't needed for small domestic properties. Little children used to have wonderful playtime adventures with toy versions of these machines in the days before mobile phones.

Moggy stepped out onto the forecourt as the automatic garage door slid down and closed behind him. It was impossible to say how long the crew would be. If this was a burning building with people trapped or fatalities, the engine could be away all night. If it turned out to be a false alarm or an easy job, they might be back in twenty minutes or even less. No two jobs were ever the same.

The firefighter smirked. *However long it took, he'd definitely have time for a cigarette.*

Fire service personnel weren't allowed to smoke at work, but no one would find out. His partner Zorro was busy cooking spaghetti in the kitchen and he wasn't going to say anything. Facing the rear of the Barbican theatre, the York station was illuminated by floodlights at night and Moggy strolled around the corner from Kent Street and down the side of the appliance garage. His "unofficial smoking area" had been carefully chosen – a position near the station car park gate that wasn't overlooked by windows or covered by cameras. The shadowy blind spot was beside a metal container bank where the passing public could deposit old clothes and shoes for charitable organisations.

"No smoking," he mumbled, leaning against the bank to light his cigarette. "Yeah, well screw that."

Slender, with a lean face and a thin pencil moustache that belonged on the upper lip of a wartime spiv, Moggy was fifty-two. He'd be retiring in less than twelve months and he couldn't wait for the day to arrive. He'd grown sick of the job over the last few years and he suffered from a serious condition which the brigade doctor had diagnosed as "terminal cynicism." When Moggy joined the service twenty-nine years ago, lots of firefighters smoked and, in his opinion, the working environment was much friendlier. The shifts were filled with black humour, camaraderie, endless practical jokes, good-natured harassment, light-hearted sexism, and plenty of jovial prejudice.

Drawing on his cigarette, he pulled a sour expression. That had all changed and not for the better. Nowadays everything was squeaky clean and politically correct and the old ways were sadly missed. Gone were the merry days of handcuffing effeminate sounding firefighters to the station pole to hose them down, and locking new recruits in the kitchen chest freezer for up to thirty minutes. Moggy tutted with disdain. It wasn't bullying – it was robust, good-natured high jinks that, admittedly, would sometimes end in tears, stress problems and the occasional bout of medicated depression. Besides, it was common knowledge that bullying made a man of you.

The good old days needed to be brought back, he mused. *This White Rose Party seemed like a decent bunch and they spoke common sense; he'd certainly be voting for them. Hopefully they'd get in power because, given the chance, they'd soon reintroduce fun and genial bigotry into the workplace. The lads might, once again, be able to have a good laugh and whistle at large-breasted women who walked past the station.*

Moggy inspected the cigarette and shook his head in disgust. Incredibly, he could now be fired for smoking this. Brigade policies that covered every tiny aspect of the job, and the officers who slavishly obeyed them, had outlawed most of the fire service humour and had ensured that smoking firefighters were a rarity. Smoking was originally banned inside the stations, then the ban was extended to cover every inch of fire service property. Finally, they just banned smoking anywhere whilst on duty and the serious threat of instant dismissal ensured that very few people risked breaking the rule. Smokers like Moggy had to suffer fifteen hours without a cigarette and, weirdest of all, new recruits had to sign a bizarre prenuptial-style agreement to say they didn't smoke and nor would they begin at a later date.

Surely that sort of shit couldn't be legal?

Moggy gave a contemptuous laugh and looked around. The view from his "unofficial smoking area" wasn't up to much. Kent Street was a quiet thoroughfare and the station car park gates behind him faced the rear wall of the theatre. Stars twinkled in the sky above and he gazed up at them, drawing again on his cigarette.

Back in the good old days, not only were stations filled with a fog of tobacco smoke, but on night shifts the lads sat down to enormous curries, or fish and chip suppers. Now the young kids spent all their time in the station gym and carefully weighed their portions of brown rice, quinoa and tofu. He'd watched them separating egg whites before throwing away the yolks, and searching the internet on their phones to discover which obscure vegetables had the slower carb release.

Yes, he thought, *those bloody mobile phones. Constantly staring at them in silence had taken over from watching television together and yelling at sport. What the hell had happened to the fire service and why didn't...*

"Excuse me," said someone to his left, halting his dour thoughts.

Turning, he saw a large man approaching across the tarmac from the empty Kent Street. *Large? This man was huge, like a heavyweight boxer.*

Moggy swiftly hid the cigarette in a semi-closed fist with the dexterity of a conjurer palming the ace of diamonds. This could easily be an off-duty officer excitedly hoping to score promotion points by getting him sacked for smoking. "Er, yeah?" he said, warily. "Can I help you, mate?"

"Yes, you could help me by lying on the ground."

The firefighter felt something hit his shirt and looked down to see two small barbs attached to wires.

"What the fuck do you think…" His teeth clenched as the Taser pumped a burst of crackling electricity into his skinny torso. "Shittttt…."

Moggy dropped to his knees and another large figure quickly approached to swing a fist and smack him hard on the chin.

"Hah, the good old Jerry jawbreaker," chuckled the man with the stun gun.

"Don't use my name." Jerry flexed his knuckles and dragged the comatose firefighter behind the charity clothing bank. "Mind you, he won't hear anything, will he? He's out cold."

Jerry's accomplice pocketed the Taser. "Wait here and keep watch," he said. "We need to work fast before the fire engine gets back." He glanced again at Moggy and grinned. "Doesn't he know smoking is bad for you?"

* * * *

Chapter 11

Bernard Quist lived four miles to the west of York in an isolated house on the outskirts of Askham Richard village. With its walled garden at the rear, the wisteria-draped gable and rose-covered porch, Briar Cottage was the sort of place Beatrix Potter might reside, or even one of her furry characters. Pretty houses like this were often referred to as "chocolate box" cottages, but instead of strawberry creams and lemon fondants, the interior of Quist's home was filled with bookcases, paintings, antiques and old bric-a-brac.

Sipping a black coffee in the lounge, the detective answered his vibrating mobile. "Ah, good evening, Rex."

"Mission accomplished," announced Rex Grant, smugly. "You'll be pleased to hear that Uncle Rupert cancelled his White Rose funding and he's no longer standing as a candidate for those idiots."

"That's splendid news." Quist checked his watch. "You managed to persuade him in such a short time too. I never envisaged your uncle would be so easy to talk around."

"Well, what did I tell you? If ever you need something doing, I'm your guy." Rex couldn't see any point in mentioning that he'd played no part in Rupert's U-turn. "Speaking of which, what's our next step? How are we going to get inside the White Rose Party?"

"We?" echoed Quist. "No, I'm afraid you won't be needed for that."

"*What*? No, I'm really looking forward to this. It'll be another exciting adventure together, with us going up against an evil bunch of neo-Nazis."

Quist sighed "This *adventure*, as you term it, won't be anything at all like our past escapades. I intend to discreetly infiltrate this organisation and that can only be accomplished alone. This requires subterfuge and these people would quickly see through your attempts to blend in with…"

"Are you crazy?" gasped Rex. "I'll blend like scotch and soda. Me and subterfuge go together like a Catholic priest and a choirboy.

I'm perfect for dangerous undercover stuff like this."

"I'm sorry, but I disagree," said Quist. "Getting your uncle to back out was excellent work – I don't know how I'd have managed that myself – but I really don't see how you can assist further."

"Oh, so that's it?" snorted Rex, angrily.

"Rex, you mustn't take this personally…"

"You used me and now you're done with me?"

"Good Lord," chuckled Quist. "You remind me of a wronged lover. You make it sound as if I've had my wicked way and then discarded you."

"Yeah, like *that* would happen," snapped Rex. "Believe me, I'd be the one dumping *you* after we'd screwed." Realising what he'd said, he thumbed off his phone. "Shit!"

* * * *

Quist enjoyed running in the woodland behind his cottage two or three times a week, but whilst many people ran there during the day, he preferred exercising at night, and on four legs instead of the more conventional two. Unfortunately, a local wildlife problem was currently preventing this. A group of badgers had built themselves a large sett, this year's youngsters were particularly active and the Yorkshire Wildlife Trust was filming them at play. Solar-powered cameras had been hidden in the trees and stealthy naturalists were often prowling Quist's favourite jogging spot with zoom lenses. The last thing he needed was to show up in lupine form on video footage. His supernatural wolf scent could also scare the badgers away, which was something he didn't want to happen.

It wasn't always easy being a werewolf, especially a considerate, ecologically minded one.

The detective drove along a dark country lane and parked in a small gravel lay-by, where a dirt track branched off to enter a dense area of woodland. The half-moon was obscured by cloud and he climbed out, peering into the trees and across the meadows to ensure there was no one around. He was near the village of Moor Monkton and he'd exercised in this area many times before. A good alternative to his local patch, it was only a short drive north from his home.

Quist finished his careful check of the surrounding landscape before kicking off his trainers and slipping out of his track suit. The naked man removed his watch and signet ring and looked at the engraved initials RQ on the latter. Richard Quist had been attacked by the werewolf in 1790 and had never grown a day older since his recovery. Changing names and moving around every few decades was an unfortunate necessity to prevent suspicious questions, but he'd always used a similar name to his original – Bernard Quinn, Richard Quayle, Robert Quist. He popped the ring in his shoe for safekeeping, locked his clothes in the blue Ford and hid the car keys beneath a stone.

Unlike the legends and full moon myths, Quist and his kind were able to shapeshift any time between sunset and sunrise. Squatting by the door, he grimaced and grunted as his bones crackled and lengthened and the swift transformation began. The six-second metamorphosis hurt like hell, but he was used to the pain and also the familiar temperature drop as the supernatural change leached ethereal energy from the atmosphere. His face extended into a broad lupine muzzle, human teeth falling and turning to dust as large white razor fangs replaced them. Thick fur sprouted to cover an increasing body mass and his grey eyes changed to a shade of deep amber. Taller and far bulkier than the naked detective, the huge black wolf arose from the squat to stand upright on its rear legs.

Quist looked around again, twitching his pointed ears and sniffing the night air. His senses were greatly augmented in this form and he could easily detect unwelcome observers. A passing barn owl spotted the monstrous furry figure, screeched in terror and whipped away into the darkness. Quist was unable to see in pitch-blackness, but just like the owl, his glowing lupine eyes collected the available moonbeams and starlight to enhance his night vision. Wagging his tail, the wolf flexed its muscles, dropped onto all fours and darted into the trees.

Despite its size, the powerful creature sped almost silently through the woodland, easily spotting twigs and other debris and the large paws effortlessly avoiding them. Watson had often commented on his employer's appearance in this lupine form, claiming he looked nothing at all like a *normal* wolf and he certainly had a point. The wolves the teenager had seen on television documentaries resembled scruffy husky dogs and Watson had witnessed much scarier animals strolling around his council estate. Quist was far larger and sleeker, with a head that resembled a furry alligator. *This* black wolf was the stuff of nightmares and belonged in a *Little Red Riding Hood* illustration, a book illustration by an artist who detested children and really delighted in terrifying them.

A fox barked somewhere to Quist's distant left and he stopped abruptly, his heightened senses picking up a low human cough and the scents of cigarette smoke and body odour. The poacher had the sense not to smoke, but the tobacco smell still lingered on his clothing and breath. The man was setting a snare thirty feet away and the wolf watched him for a several seconds before bounding over a log to continue its run in the opposite direction.

Melding with the night-time forest was always sensually liberating. It felt good to connect fully with nature and to breathe in the myriad of exhilarating smells – the damp soil, the moist mosses and plants and the lingering scents of nocturnal creatures. It cleared the mind and helped Quist to focus on his current investigation into the White Rose Party.

He smiled grimly, his fangs glinting in the dim moonlight. He'd witnessed unbelievable racism over the centuries – the Nazis, the horrors of slavery, and even the British Raj – and he'd always detested it. White Rose were merely playing at it by comparison, but people like this made his skin crawl and they needed to be stopped. These things grew and metastasised, and there was no place for race hate in the twenty-first century.

Racism began as an instinctive means of protection in humans - an inbred fear and distrust of anyone who looked different. *Different* people, who weren't part of the small prehistoric society, would probably pose a threat, and outsiders with different coloured skin were chased away or killed. Unfortunately, despite there no longer being any reason for the instinct, it's still present and can be seen in thicker children. They instantly fixate on the tiniest difference in other kids, like a black face, a stammer or a facial birth mark, and make life hell for them. Way before reaching adulthood, intelligence and social understanding join forces to eradicate the instinct in most folk, but it still remains in the deranged, the very stupid and those who enjoy violence. Thugs with a liking for brutality use differences as an acceptable excuse for their crimes. *He's gay, he supports a different football team, he's a foreigner who's taking our jobs* – all are seen by these people as perfectly good reasons to kick someone to death.

The wolf arrived on the edge of the woodland and paused to scan the field ahead.

This business with White Rose shouldn't take long. He'd swiftly infiltrate the party, gain Churchill's trust and find definite evidence of his white supremacist beliefs and racist violence, specifically the recent attack on Sara Hoffman.

What could possibly go wrong? thought Quist.

* * * *

Chapter 12

Katie Bradstreet stood in the first floor gent's toilet at Scarborough's Grand hotel. It wasn't often she spent time in male lavatories and, whenever she did, it was usually to inspect a grisly corpse like this. The Detective Inspector raised her eyebrows. Thinking about it, she'd seen stab victims and drug overdoses, but she'd never seen a corpse *this* grisly.

The body lie face-down by the urinal trough and, from the bloody brain splatter on the tiles above, it looked as if the wall had been pelted with overripe tomatoes.

"Lee Millican," murmured Katie. She wore a white forensic suit and moved from one plastic stepping stone to the next, careful not to touch the floor which was still being processed. "Good God, what kind of strength does it take to slam a man's face into a wall and completely destroy the skull?"

"I don't know," said Matthew Carson, the Scenes of Crime Officer. "Probably the same sort of strength you'd need to tear off a limb and crush a head between two hands."

"Are you saying Millican here and Dylan Taylor could be the work of the same person?"

"I'm not saying anything; that's your job." The SOCO attempted to smile at her, difficult when wearing a forensic mask. "I'd only just finished off at Wisteria Lodge when I got the call to come here, and there *are* similarities. You see the blood splatters and sprays across the floor here? Do you see the clean area where…"

"The shape of a coat?" The Inspector nodded. "It looks as if a garment was lying on the floor before the blood sprays occurred. A lengthy coat."

"Exactly," said Carson.

"So whoever did this removed their coat and dropped it on the floor prior to killing Millican. Just like our friend at the nursing home removed his clothes before he killed Taylor."

"But unlike Wisteria Lodge, where the torn clothing was left behind, this coat was picked up and taken with him." Carson gestured to the tiles. "There's a similar brown stone dust on the floor too, very like the nursing home crime scene."

"The same?"

"I can't say until I get to the lab, but looking at it, I'd say it's highly likely."

Tariq Aslam appeared behind Katie and she turned to him. "Did anyone see a man in a long coat?" she asked. "Coming in here or leaving?"

"No one remembers seeing anything," said Aslam. "Uniform think the killer arrived and left through the service door along the corridor out there. It leads down to the staff parking area."

"CCTV?" asked Katie, hopefully.

"Afraid not."

The Inspector pulled a sour face. Even back in the old days, the general public witnessed very little, but now that most people spent the entire time staring at their phones, a dragon in a fluorescent jacket could walk through the hotel and no one would notice.

"Are we absolutely certain this *is* Lee Millican?" Katie pointed to the body. "I doubt his own mother would recognise this mess."

"It's definitely Millican," confirmed Aslam. "Constable Planer fingerprinted him and he's in our system. He has previous convictions for assault and affray."

"Okay." Katie nodded. It was so simple these days to take prints electronically and mail them to the police computer for an instant match. "So what do we know about him?"

"Very little so far." The Sergeant shrugged. "As you're aware, White Rose was holding a meeting here this afternoon, but according to the party, Millican is nothing to do with them. He isn't a hotel guest, so it's fairly likely he was attending the meeting as a spectator. Uniform have the hotel guest list for you. They also collected all the memory cards from the press cameras that were present and copied the images from them onto our computer."

"Very good," said Katie. "Let's take a look at who was at this meeting. We might see Lee Millican, or better still, someone in a long coat. Even *better*, a bald, dark-skinned care worker named Tonga in a long coat."

The Inspector followed Aslam down the ornate staircase to the main hotel office where Zoe Planer, her Detective Constable, was working on her police laptop.

"I have all the photographs from the Palm Court here, Ma'am." Zoe clicked on a file and went through the shots as Katie pulled down her forensic hood and peeled off her gloves. "The journalists weren't interested in the spectators and, as you can imagine, most of the pictures are Dominic Churchill speaking. A few of them show the assembly, however, and here's one with the left section of the..."

"Hold it." Katie clutched Zoe's arm. "Zoom in on that one, would you?"

The Constable did as instructed and Katie frowned. "I thought so," she murmured. "Now there are two rather interesting spectators."

"Oh, a blast from the past," said Aslam, squinting at the figures seated at the rear of the crowd. "That's York's consultant detective."

"Yes," smiled Katie. "Our old friends Bernard Quist and Rex Grant. Now why would *they* be there, and just before a murder too?"

* * * *

Chapter 13

Adam Hoffman walked through his hallway to answer the front door, his face lighting up to see the man standing in the porch. "Daniel." He embraced his visitor and squeezed tightly. "I was just thinking about you. To be truthful, I've thought about little else over the past few days. You and our... shall we say our *project*? I still can't believe we did it. We actually did it, Daniel."

"We certainly did." Daniel Geller's English was perfect, although his German accent was noticeable. "*You* did it, Adam."

Geller was in his late fifties, fit and extremely well-groomed, with manicured hands, a full head of iron-grey hair and a thick moustache that unfortunately gave him a look of Joseph Stalin. From the dark blue Italian suit, handmade shoes and gold Breitling wristwatch, this was a man who obviously never shopped at Primark.

"Come in, please. Come in." Hoffman excitedly ushered him into the passage and lowered his voice to a whisper. "Just be careful what you say here. My granddaughter has just arrived home from the pub and she's up in her room getting changed."

"Ah, she's back from Spain?" Geller glanced up the staircase and nodded. "Did she have a good trip?"

"Yes, but I'm sure you don't want to hear about Ibiza." He stifled a slightly manic giggle and led the way into the rear kitchen. "I've been finding it almost impossible to keep my feelings in check. We can talk in here, and oh, we have so much to discuss. As I say, we'll need to keep our voices down, but I feel like shouting about this from the rooftops."

"Probably not a wise idea," said Geller. "I'm sorry to call on you at this late hour."

"Don't worry about it. It's so good to see you."

A pair of glazed French doors opened onto the garden and Geller looked out, smiling at the large hole that had recently been dug in the shrubbery. Hoffman took a bottle of scotch from a cupboard, offered a glass to Geller with a shaking hand and quickly poured two drinks.

"To our *project*," said Hoffman, gleefully clinking the glasses together. "To reason and light triumphing over racism, and to the downfall of the White Rose Party."

"Yes." Geller sat at the oak dining table. "I think it's safe to say their days are numbered."

"Absolutely." Hoffman sat beside him. "I had another swastika painted on my shop window last night. I spent two hours today cleaning it off."

"Rest assured…" Geller sipped his drink. "That will soon all be over."

"That's the plan." Hoffman let out an excited laugh and clamped a hand to his mouth. "Daniel, I still can't believe it worked. I mean, I always knew it was possible; I told you about the one I saw as a child in London. I just never thought I'd be able to do it."

"Really? I certainly had faith in you, Adam. You're a rabbi."

"Well, I was never ordained, but…"

"Irrelevant, as it turned out." Geller shrugged. "You had the wisdom and knowledge for this. You're fully conversant with the Torah, the Kabbala and Hebrew mysticism."

"We refer to it as mysticism and the occult," said Hoffman, stroking his white beard. "But it's actually a science – a very old science that most people have forgotten about and can no longer comprehend. It was the author, Arthur C Clarke, who said that any sufficiently advanced technology is indistinguishable from magic. I imagine even the jungle tribesmen of Borneo sit around texting these days, but imagine if you'd showed them a mobile phone with a webcam conversation fifty years ago. Imagine showing an X-ray with the insides of a human body to physicians three-hundred years ago. You'd be burned at the stake."

"True," agreed Geller. "Well, whatever your mysticism is, it certainly works."

"But it wasn't possible without the book and I wouldn't have dared to attempt it were it not for you. You were the one who persuaded me."

"I disagree," said Geller. "I'd say those people from White Rose persuaded you by attacking your granddaughter. I merely pointed you in the right direction afterwards."

"I suppose it was fate." Hoffman nodded. "You contacting me when you did three weeks ago."

"It *was* fate," agreed Geller. "These people have eluded me for thirty years and I only discovered their new names and details when the forger was caught in Munich last month. That was fate."

"True."

"It was all fate, Adam." Geller began to list the examples on his fingers. "I tracked them to Yorkshire and informed the police, but they were useless. I saw your letters in the papers at the same time and rang you, and then came that disgusting assault on Sara. I located the book for you without any problems and Sara went away for six days which gave us the opportunity to work on this incredible undertaking. All of that, happening so fast and coming perfectly together in that way, it *has* to be fate." He lifted his glass. "To fate."

"Yes, to fate," said Hoffman, raising his own drink. "This is so amazing. I can hardly believe it's real."

"Oh, it's real."

"Speaking of the book…" Hoffman gulped his whisky. "Now that I've had the time to read and translate it properly, I'm certain I've solved the energy consumption issue."

"I wouldn't worry yourself." Geller smiled. "I really don't think it will matter."

"Daniel…" Hoffman grinned nervously. "Of course it matters, and ultimately it will be highly dangerous. We rushed into this while Sara was away and I didn't have the chance to study the book fully. I know now that I made minor mistakes with the prototype and the energy consumption problem won't repair itself. We need to create something more stable before we can begin."

"No, the one we already have is ideal."

"But we can't begin the project until we correct the ethereal energy…"

Geller shook his head. "As a matter of fact, we've already begun."

"I'm sorry?"

"This morning I lit two yahrzeit candles for my parents," said Geller.

"Is it the anniversary of their passing?"

"No, but I felt it was appropriate." He regarded Hoffman. "Haven't you seen the local news?"

Hoffman looked puzzled.

"About the death in Robin Hood's Bay yesterday."

"Yes, I saw something about a murder, but there were no details on the news report. The police haven't released…" His eyes widened. "Wait a minute. Are you saying the dead man was this Dylan Taylor you told me about? You said he lived in a nursing home there."

"Yes, Dieter Schneider, or Dylan Taylor as he called himself."

"No." Hoffman almost dropped his whisky glass. "No, Daniel, surely you don't mean…"

"Don't worry," said Geller. "Everything went smoothly."

"No, no, no," whispered Hoffman. "What the hell have you gone and done? What were you thinking?"

"I did what needed to be done." Geller shrugged and sipped his drink. "The police didn't believe me or, more likely, they couldn't be bothered to dig too deeply, so I resolved the matter myself."

"But this isn't what we planned," stammered Hoffman, his complexion draining. "I would never have agreed to it. No, this is so wrong. You didn't need to kill him."

"Of course I did." Geller frowned. "Yesterday was Judgment Day for Schneider and today Lee Millican went the same way. As I said, we've begun."

"Millican too?" Hoffman slowly shook his head, horrified. He felt physically sick. "Oh, God, no. Why would you do that? No, this isn't what we talked about at all. We never once said *anything* about murder."

"No, we didn't," confirmed Geller. "But that was always *my* intention. I knew you wouldn't be too happy and that's why I began this without you."

"I don't want this," hissed Hoffman. "I don't want any part in killing them."

"Dieter Schneider and Lee Millican." Geller clinked his drink against Hoffman's glass. "One for me and one for you, as it were. I'd say it's a little too late to back out now."

"Oh, hi there," said Sara. The girl walked into the kitchen wearing a white towel robe and smiled to see their visitor. Her grandfather's back was to her and his white face went unnoticed. "Nice to see you again, Mister Geller."

"Please…" said Geller, "you must call me Daniel. How are you? Adam tells me you were attacked by two thugs from that White Rose group?"

"Yeah, but that's ancient history and I'm over it." She ran an affectionate hand over Hoffman's shoulder and squeezed. "Hey, I have to tell you, Gramps was really excited by that book you brought him. It cheered him up no end."

"Yes." Geller grinned at her grandfather's shocked expression. "We were *both* excited. What a marvellous find that turned out to be."

Sara grabbed a carton of apple juice from the fridge. "I'm watching a programme before turning in," she said, heading for the lounge television. "Let me know if I have the volume too loud."

Hoffman turned to watch the kitchen door close. "Listen…" he croaked, clearing his dry throat. "We really have to talk about this."

Geller nodded. "We *are* talking, Adam."

"I mean alone." He glanced uneasily at the door again, knowing that Sara could come back in at any moment. "I mean talk *properly*. We were supposed to break up their organisation and damage them."

"Well, we're certainly doing that."

"No, *you're* doing that," hissed Hoffman, his voice a harsh whisper. "This was *never* the plan and it has to stop right now."

Geller shook his head. "But Adam, we've only just begun."

"*We*? This is all *your* doing."

"I disagree. I could hardly have managed this without you, now could I?"

Hoffman closed his eyes, realising he was right. *No, he could never have accomplished this himself.*

Geller may have killed these two men, but Hoffman had provided the rather unique murder weapon and he was ultimately responsible.

"Oh, God, Daniel," he groaned. "What have you done?"

* * * *

Chapter 14

Standing high and proud upon their Roman foundations, the white limestone walls of York date back to the thirteenth century and encircle the ancient city centre. Square crenellations for the medieval archers top these battlements and several barbican gateways punctuate their two-mile elliptical course like miniature fairytale castles. The grassy embankments below are dotted with mature trees and covered with wild flowers and bright yellow daffodils in the springtime. The overall effect is romantically picturesque and a magnet for the tourist cameras, making it difficult to associate the fortifications with their turbulent history of invasion, harsh fighting and bloodshed.

Bernard Quist's private investigation agency stood just outside these ramparts on the junction of Fishergate and Baker Avenue, the bustle of traffic here presenting a raucous contrast to the leafy residential streets on the other side of the walls. The detective's small office was situated on the upper floor of the two-storey corner building, with Bramley's Deluxe Kitchen Showroom below and Ted Duggan's debt collection company next door. People who'd been tempted into buying things they couldn't afford, such as a deluxe kitchen, were soon tempted by Duggan's brawny collectors into paying back their loans. Quist's agency comprised of two magnolia-painted rooms – a small reception and the main inner office containing a desk, three chairs, two shelves of books and a filing cabinet.

The "consultant detective" had arrived earlier than his assistant this Tuesday morning, which was often the case. He drove into York from the nearby village of Askham Richard and Watson travelled by bus from the Grimpen council estate in the suburb of Acomb. Quist sat on top of his desk in a cross-legged lotus position reading the *Yorkshire Post* and drinking a black coffee. He glanced up as the door sounded and Watson strolled in with a plastic carrier bag.

"Morning yoga as usual, I see?" Wearing his customary outfit of zip-up canvas jacket and jeans, the youth flopped down in a chair by his employer, removed his music earphones and laughed. "Those special meditation exercises to keep the wolf at bay, so to speak. So what happened at the meeting yesterday, Guv? Is Rex okay?"

"Our investigation into White Rose?" murmured Quist, looking through the newspaper. "Rupert Grant has withdrawn his financial backing, as we hoped, and Rex is Rex, of course. He doesn't change."

"Well, he'll *never* change." Watson smirked. "You made sure of that."

"How droll." Quist gave a tight smile. He still experienced pangs of guilt over biting the young man. "If there had been any other way to save his life…"

"Yeah, your *remedy* certainly did the trick. Who needs penicillin and shit when there's a werewolf around to chomp on your arm?"

"Have you seen this?" The detective held up the front page of his paper. "The Scarborough hotel where yesterday's meeting was held. Apparently there was a suspicious death after Rex and I left. The police have yet to release the details." He sipped his drink and turned the page. "And this may interest you − your friend Sara works at the York fire station, doesn't she? An unnamed firefighter was assaulted outside the building last night. Apparently someone used a Taser on them."

"Weird." Watson took a tinfoil carton and plastic fork from his bag, an exotic, sickly aroma filling the office as he peeled off the container lid. "Those things are banned in Britain. Who goes around zapping people with an illegal stun gun? Anyway, it wasn't Sara. She doesn't start back at work until this morning."

"So what do you have there?" asked Quist, peering suspiciously.

"Special chow mein, or *brunch*, as us posher folk call it." Watson held out the carton. "Do you want some? I know you can't eat meat, but I can fish out the lumps of pork and stuff."

"I'll graciously decline your offer." Quist frowned at the contents swimming in brown oil and almost retched. Watson consumed huge amounts of junk food, but nothing seemed to alter his wiry frame. "I have to say, it doesn't appear very *special*. As a matter of fact, it looks as if someone has wormed their dog. It's a little early for Chinese food isn't it?"

The teenager shrugged. "In China they eat Chinese food all day long."

"It's rather difficult to argue with that logic."

"I've noticed how the supermarkets do all kinds of stuff for you vegans these days. Apparently you can't tell the difference. Rashers of vegan bacon, vegan steaks that look just like real beef, vegan burgers…"

"Yes, and I'll never understand why," said Quist, glancing down disapprovingly as Watson sat back and rested his feet on the desk. "Vegans have clearly made the decision not to consume flesh, presumably because they abhor the concept of slaughter, yet many of them still desire food that has been purposely engineered to resemble and taste like pieces of dead animal." He shook his head. "Anyway, speaking of your firefighter friend, how is she now?"

"Well, she's over the beating," said Watson, through a mouthful of chow mein. "Mind you, I guess six nights of partying in Ibiza will cure most things. I met her grandad yesterday and the White Rose nutters are still harassing him. Since he contacted the papers, they've been phoning him with death threats and painting big yellow swastikas on his shop window."

"Unbelievable." Quist sighed bitterly. "Presumably the police are unable to prove anything?"

"Yeah, just like the attack on Sara. He blamed himself for that and he was really depressed, but he seems to be okay now." Watson shoved another forkful of food into his mouth and laughed. "It takes all sorts, I suppose. Sara says he cheered up when his friend gave him a book."

"Really?" The detective used a tissue to patiently wipe bits of sprayed chow mein from the desk beside him. "What book?"

"Dunno." Watson shrugged. "Probably one of those self-help things you see. *How Not to be Depressed*, or some such crap."

Quist gazed at him. "I've never asked before, but have *you* ever been subjected to racism?"

"Me?" The youth looked puzzled. "Why would I?"

"Oh…" It wasn't often that Quist was thrown. "Well, er, I thought, er…"

"Only kidding," grinned Watson. "Because I'm black, innit? No, to be honest, it's never been much of a problem for me. I think racism is more for older folk like you, Guv. Well, there's no one as old as *you*, of course, but you know what I mean. There were loads of black and Asian kids at my school, but I reckon younger people are used to different coloured skin and they're more tolerant these days. Most of the white kids I knew were into black rap music."

"I'm pleased to hear it," said Quist. "Although what you describe probably doesn't apply to the leafy suburbs of the home counties and schools like Eton. Oh, get that would you?" He gestured to the door with his coffee mug. "It could be a client and it would be imprudent to keep them waiting."

"What the hell are you talking about?" Watson munched his meal. "No one knocked."

He rolled his eyes as a sharp knock sounded on the door of the outer office, recalling how Quist's senses were heightened by his lycanthropy. Tutting and leaving his food on the desk, the youth walked out through the reception room.

"Two sets of footsteps," called out Quist. "One is a female and lighter. I heard them turn left at the top of the stairs, so they were clearly heading here."

"Why, grandma…" mumbled Watson, sarcastically. "What big ears you have."

"I heard that," shouted Quist.

The teenager opened the door, cleared his throat and stood more upright, as many people did on finding two police officers on their doorstep. Katie Bradstreet and Tariq Aslam wore suits, not uniforms, but he recognised them immediately.

"Inspector Bradstreet," said Katie, showing her wallet I.D. "North Yorkshire Police. This is Sergeant Aslam. Then again, we probably don't need to introduce ourselves, do we? I'm sure there's nothing wrong with your memory."

"No, I certainly remember *you*, luv." Watson grinned nervously and stepped aside. "Come in."

"Good to see your voice problem has cleared up," said Katie. "As I recall, you weren't able to speak the last time we met." She walked through into the main office and raised her eyebrows in surprise to see Quist's yoga position on the desk. "Mister Quist, we meet again. It feels like only yesterday that I interviewed you over that nasty business with the dermatology lab."

"Ah, Inspector Bradstreet." Untangling his legs and jumping down, Quist took her hand and kissed it. "This is most unexpected. Shall I have Watson pop the kettle on for a coffee?"

"Oh, how chivalrous," drawled Katie, derisively. Retrieving her hand, she ran it uneasily through her short fair hair. "No need to bother with drinks. We were just passing and I decided to call on you with a few questions."

"Intriguing." Quist sat in the chair behind his desk. "Please, fire away."

He smiled at her involuntary hair grooming, her flushed skin and the way her pupils had dilated. Despite her sarcastic comment, she'd gulped when he kissed her hand too. Like many women, the Inspector was attracted to him, but it was the supernatural wolf she subconsciously sensed.

Aslam walked to the window and looked out at the city walls over the busy thoroughfare of Fishergate. Katie sat in the chair opposite Quist and crossed her legs.

"I was never happy with our previous dealings on that dermatology investigation," she said, eyeing his large nose and automatically fingering her hair again. "The case was closed, but as far as I was concerned there were many irritating loose ends that were never satisfactorily tied up. Lots of nagging questions left unanswered, if you know what I mean?"

Quist shrugged. "I'm afraid I don't."

83

"There's something about you, Mister Quist. A certain something that I can't put my finger on, and when you pop up on my radar, I become very interested."

"I've popped up?" He gave one of his lopsided smiles. "How fascinating."

"The White Rose Party," said Aslam, joining his superior at the desk. "You attended one of their meetings yesterday, didn't you?"

"In Scarborough." Quist nodded. "That's correct."

"Are you a member of this organisation?" asked Katie.

Watson paused in eating his Chinese food and let out a short laugh. "You may have noticed he employs a black assistant. What do *you* think, luv?"

"Good point," said Aslam. "So why were you there?"

"Why on earth do you need to know that?" asked Quist.

"You don't have to answer," said Katie. "I'm simply curious."

Quist thought for a moment and decided there was no need for subterfuge. "Firstly, as you're probably aware, White Rose are not particularly nice people. I recently discovered my friend's uncle was about to finance their campaign and I suggested he try to talk some sense into him..."

"A friend?" said Katie. "Would this be Rex Grant from London?"

"Correct. Someone obviously saw us there?"

"Don't worry," said Aslam. "You aren't under surveillance or anything. We have the pair of you on press photographs taken during the meeting."

"It's because of me," said Watson, chomping his meal. "He's looking into these nutters as a favour. A girl I know was assaulted by them."

"Really?" Aslam turned to him. "Assaulted because she's black?"

Watson laughed again. "Good guess, mate, but no. She's Jewish, actually."

"An anti-Semitic assault by members of the White Rose

Party?" The Sergeant glanced at his superior. "Did your friend report this?"

"Yeah," snorted Watson. "You questioned the guys who did it, but they denied everything. You said their alibis were good and there was no evidence. It all came down to her word against their word." He glared angrily. "The thing is, you obviously know the White Rose Party are racists; that's why you asked if she was black. Why the hell haven't the police done something about them?"

"Listen," said Katie, "I don't like these people one bit and you can be damn sure my Asian Sergeant here doesn't. The thing is, they have good legal advisors and they never overstep the line. Believe me, if they do, or hopefully *when* they do, I'll be the first one to come down hard on them." She narrowed her eyes. "This attack you mentioned... I wonder, would your friend be Sara Hoffman?"

"So you're aware of it." Watson nodded. "Yes, Sara."

"Your girlfriend?" quizzed Aslam.

"Well..." The teenager grinned. "Let's say I'm working on that."

"I see," said Katie. "Are you aware of the murder?"

"Murder?" echoed Quist. "What murder would that be?"

The Inspector watched the two men closely. "Someone was killed in the Grand Hotel after the meeting you and Rex Grant attended. The victim was Lee Millican, one of the men Miss Hoffman accused of assaulting her."

"That's right," said Watson. "Millican was one of the scumbags. I'll put a reminder in my phone to send flowers and a sympathy card."

"How did he die," asked Quist. "Do you know who was responsible?"

"He died in a manner that we like to term *confidential*," said Aslam. "As to suspects, you and Grant were there. Maybe you could help us with that?"

"Hey, how about that?" drawled Watson, caustically. "When Millican punched Sara, the cops couldn't find any link between him and

White Rose. Now he's been killed at one of their meetings."

"There's still no link," pointed out Katie. "Lots of people were present at the meeting, such as Mister Quist here."

"Please, Inspector…" said Quist. "Call me Bernard."

Katie coloured up slightly and felt angry with herself. *Why on earth did she always feel sexually aroused by him?* "We need evidence for an arrest," she said. "There wasn't anything to implicate Millican in your friend's assault. Just as a matter of interest, do you have any connection with a gentleman named Dylan Taylor of Robin Hood's Bay?"

Quist shook his head. "I know from the news that he was killed in a nursing home there. Why do you ask?"

"Like I said…" Katie smiled tartly. "To establish whether or not you're connected to him. And to gauge your reaction of course."

"How did I do?" Quist smiled. "Am I to assume there's a link between the care home murder and this Lee Millican's death?"

"You're free to assume whatever you like." Katie smiled too, but with a hint of sarcasm. "If there was, we'd be hardly be likely to tell you, would we… *Bernard*?"

Not to worry, thought Quist. *We know a certain young man who WILL tell us.*

* * * *

Chapter 15

Once an upmarket residential area of doctors and legal professionals, Holgate lies to the west of York's city centre and the National Railway Museum. Sara Hoffman sat in one of the two fire engines parked on Holgate Road, part of the main A59 running north from York to Knaresborough. Set back from the pavement behind railings and small gardens, elegant houses with bay windows and corniced doorways lined the road here, and Birlstone House had recently been rented by the White Rose Party to serve as their headquarters. The size of these terraced dwellings – most had three spacious storeys with lofts and basements – meant that the majority had been converted into several apartments, or small hotels with imaginative names like *the Cedars* and *the Windermere*.

"Why does every town have a B&B called *the Windermere*?" muttered Sara to herself.

She sat by the window in the rear cab of the fire engine, wearing her full firefighting outfit and a breathing set on her back, the compressed air tank giving her the look of an overdressed scuba diver. An anonymous caller claimed a bomb had been planted in the White Rose building, a specialist team were searching, and the fire service were stationed outside as a precautionary measure. Tapping her fingers on the window ledge, Sara stared irately at the house. She felt she had a right to be annoyed; this was her first day back at work and she'd been sent here to help protect the head office of the racist scum who assaulted her.

The fire engines had been waiting for over sixty minutes now and most of the firefighters were staring at their phones.

"Oh, come on," sighed Sara. "How long does it take to find a non-existent bomb?"

Sporting an identical air cylinder, Sara's breathing apparatus partner Josh Patel – or Rogan, as his friends called him – sat beside the opposite window across the rear cab from her.

"They had three bomb hoaxes here last week," he said. "It's

probably some left-wing nutter who thinks he's harming the White Rose Party."

"True," agreed Sara. "In reality he's just tying up the fire engines and cop cars and depriving people who genuinely need the emergency services."

"My arse is numb," groaned Patel, opening his door. "Come on, Waggy, let's stretch our legs for a bit."

Nodding, Sara gripped the hand rail and clambered down the three high steps. The cabs on these huge machines were almost four feet above the ground, a problem that would definitely need addressing when the inevitable happened and the politically-correct authorities insisted upon disabled people being allowed to join the service. Adjusting the weighty tank on her back, she walked along the pavement and met Patel at the rear of the engine by the water pump.

"Have you heard anything about Moggy?" asked Sara, watching the passing traffic. "I can't believe some twat zapped him with a taser right outside the station."

"Yeah, weird." Patel nodded. "I doubt we'll see him again."

"Jesus!" The girl's mouth fell open. "I'm sorry, Rogan, but no one told me how serious it was. I didn't realise the attack was so bad that..."

"Don't be daft," laughed Patel. "There's nothing wrong with him, but knowing Moggy, he'll be off sick with stress and a bad neck from his fall for the rest of the year. He's off work with flu three or four times every year and the simplest trip has him walking with crutches for a month. He'll play on this right up until his retirement."

A toot of a horn drew Sara's attention to a passing car where three grinning youths blew kisses at her through the open windows. She smiled at them, then gazed curiously at the next car to cruise slowly by. The driver and his passenger both gazed at her with obvious interest and she got the definite feeling these large men knew her.

"Er, listen, Waggy," said Patel. He glanced back at the cab to ensure they were out of earshot. "I couldn't say anything in front of the others in there, but I really need to talk to someone. I think I might have done something stupid."

"Really?" Sara smirked. "Well, there's a surprise."

Josh Patel was thirty and quite attractive, with his black hair, dusky skin and flashing white smile. With several lovers on the go, he often had *girl problems* and always confided in Sara, asking her advice and appreciating the female point of view. His latest girlfriend was Kacey, or "the Squealer", as he romantically referred to her. From what he'd told Sara, their sexual frolics in his car were the stuff of blue movies, but there were drawbacks. He hated the idea of any mess in his treasured BMW and always covered the upholstery with towels before the fun began. The other drawback was his wife and the ever-present risk of her finding out.

"I'm assuming you want to talk about Kacey?" said Sara. "Are you still seeing her?"

"Er, yeah." Patel looked uneasy. "Funnily enough, this kind of relates to her in a roundabout way. The thing is, Waggy, the other night…"

"Gentlemen," called out Dominic Churchill. Wearing a grey suit and tie, he walked down the garden path from Birlstone House to the two fire engines. "Our bomb threat has been officially declared a hoax and as a small token of appreciation for the fire service standing by here, I have something for our courageous boys."

"Gentlemen and *ladies*," pointed out Sara, turning. She saw he carried a tray of non-alcoholic cocktails with tiny umbrellas. "Some of the courageous boys have breasts."

Two of Churchill's deputies were filming their silver-haired boss on phones and Sara guessed this would be posted straight onto social media and sent to the television stations. The videos would show how he gallantly supported the emergency services and how much the fire service loved White Rose.

"My mistake." Churchill's smile widened as Patel turned too. "Ah, it's so good to see diversity at last. For so long the fire service was made up exclusively of white males and I was one of the leading campaigners for change. Now we have our ethnic friends from all races and cultures, and young ladies too. Rather attractive young ladies."

"Yeah, that almost sounded convincing," scoffed Sara. "You just love ethnic people, don't you? And if you genuinely think I'm attractive, you obviously aren't aware that I'm Jewish."

"Are you really?" He turned to the phone cameras. "Pessimists said I was wasting my time campaigning for diversity in the fire brigades, but they were wrong and my efforts paid off."

Sara laughed. "You honestly don't know who I am, do you?" she asked, folding her arms.

"Jewish and sassy?" Churchill smiled sweetly. "Are you Joan Rivers?"

His two deputies laughed sycophantically at the joke, although neither had heard of the late comedian, or knew what *sassy* meant.

"Please forgive my witticism," said Churchill, "but I fail to see what…"

"I'm Sara Hoffman and you sent someone to attack me," said Sara. "You wanted to hurt my grandfather, but I was there alone and…"

"What a ludicrous idea." Churchill brushed past Sara and Patel with his laden tray and walked to the fire engine cab. "I can see from your face that someone hit you, but this has nothing to do with me." He turned to inspect her cheek and winced. "It's been over a week and the bruise is still there. Ooh, that punch must have been painful, but I can't imagine why you'd wrongly hold me responsible."

Sara followed him along the pavement. "Well, the guy who did it said "this is from Dominic" which kind of gave it away."

Churchill laughed quietly. "Young lady, whatever these two men might have said, I can assure you that I…"

"How do you know it was *two* men, and how do you know it happened over a week ago?"

Sara noticed Churchill's cronies had stopped filming the moment she'd begun to challenge him; this definitely wasn't the sort of conversation they wanted on YouTube and the local afternoon news. The door into the fire engine rear cab was wide open as she'd left it. Smirking and gauging her movements carefully, the girl grabbed the hand grip, lifted her right leg onto the top step, then brought up her left knee, "accidentally" catching it beneath Churchill's tray of drinks and upending it. Eight full cocktail glasses poured down his suit.

"Oh, I'm so sorry," she gasped. "This air tank on my back makes it difficult to balance when I climb the steps. Are you alright?"

"How *dare…*" Churchill glared at her, cold fury blazing in his eyes, before somehow managing to force a smile back onto his face. "Don't worry about it," he hissed. "These things happen and it's fine."

"Sir?" One of his men approached. "You're needed inside."

"I'm on my way," snapped Churchill. Soaked and dripping, he glanced at the grinning crew in the fire engine, his rigid smile welded in position. "You're all doing a wonderful job and the White Rose Party is proud of you. Stay safe out there."

"Hey, thanks," said Sara. "Yeah, we'll try."

"The drinks are on *you*, mate," shouted Stan, one of the wittier firefighters.

Laughter erupted in the fire engine and Churchill stormed back up the path in icy silence. Entering the front reception room, he flung the empty drinks tray at the wall, destroying a picture of Prince William and the Duchess of Cambridge.

"Er, are you okay?" asked one of the deputies, tagging on behind and glad that he was no longer filming.

"*Okay?*" shouted Churchill. "I was going to wear this suit at the Wakefield meeting tonight and now look at the state of it. That fucking Jew bitch." He tore off the jacket. "This is Italian and just fucking look at it."

Another deputy appeared from an office. He saw the man's furious expression and wished he'd delegated someone else to deliver the news. "Sir, there was a phone call just now."

"From who?" snarled Churchill.

"Rupert Grant." The man visibly cringed. "The millionaire guy who was going to stand as our Pickering candidate and finance us."

"Yes, I know who he is. What did he want?"

"It seems he's reconsidered." The deputy gulped. "He's

decided to withdraw his offer."

* * * *

Chapter 16

Nine-hundred years old, and allegedly the most photographed street in Europe, the narrow thoroughfare known as the Shambles winds through the centre of York and resembles a quaint illustration from a book of medieval folk tales. Elizabethan buildings loom on either side, jutting out in lateral steps, so that their ancient timber-framed walls overhang the cobblestones. Many liken it to Diagon Alley in the Harry Potter stories, but one thing is for certain – this is definitely no place for anyone of a claustrophobic disposition. Shambles is the archaic term for slaughterhouse meat market, and the raised pavements once formed a channel between the butcher's shops, down which visceral rivers of blood and offal gushed towards the River Ouse. The tourists wouldn't have taken so many pictures back then, not unless they were particularly *weird* tourists.

Watson had always found the Shambles a little creepy after dark. When the dim yellow light from the mullioned widows illuminated the place, goblins, cackling hags and possibly the occasional werewolf wouldn't look out of place lurking here.

Speaking of which…

He glanced at Quist. It was daylight, but his employer's long leather overcoat still reminded the youth of a vampire's cloak as it flapped around his lean frame. Watson strolled along the cobbles beside the detective with his hands in the pockets of his canvas jacket.

"I rang the White Rose headquarters earlier," said Quist. "I've made an appointment to see Dominic Churchill tomorrow afternoon."

"To pose as a financial backer like Rupert Grant?"

"Yes, but I'll need to exercise caution. One financier pulling out and another instantly appearing could arouse suspicions. I've told them I'm interested in being their candidate for the York West constituency. Once I have their attention and I've subtly established my support for white supremacy, I'll mention the large amounts of money I'd like to invest in their courageous campaign to save Britain from the dark-skinned likes of you."

"Cheers, Guv," laughed Watson. "So why are we bothering about these two murders?"

"The police visit stirred my curiosity," admitted Quist. "We have an entire day before I meet Churchill and these deaths could be of interest. We're hoping to establish a definite link between White Rose and your friend's two attackers and one of them has just been killed at a campaign meeting. I want to see what information the police have on this."

"Why do you suppose the cops asked about the other killing on Sunday? This old guy in Robin Hood's Bay?"

"I can't imagine," said Quist. "But the Inspector wouldn't have mentioned the murder if there wasn't a connection of some sort. We'll soon know what the link is courtesy of your friend Gareth."

* * * *

Gareth Lestrade, or Gazza, as Watson called him, lived in a converted granary, a redbrick Victorian building on Saint Andrewgate at the end of the Shambles. The windows of his upper floor apartment looked onto the nearby York Minster and the lounge was filled with framed cinema posters, models of starships and rare science fiction memorabilia in glass cases.

Lestrade's freelance work in computer troubleshooting for companies paid well, but he supplemented his income with the occasional handout from Watson's employer. He'd learned not to question why the private investigator needed the bizarre information he requested and they'd arrived at a rather simple understanding – occasionally, Lestrade would illegally hack into heavily encrypted sites, and Quist and Watson paid up and kept their mouths shut.

"Welcome back to the cyber-cave," said Lestrade. Slender and bespectacled, with lank fair hair, the young man sat at a large monitor screen surrounded by networked computer banks. "Last week you had me hack into the White Rose database. Are we going back there?"

"That was a waste of time," snorted Watson, pulling up two chairs. "We wanted to find evidence of their racist views and hopefully links to radical groups."

"And I couldn't help," admitted Lestrade. "Everything was clean."

"No, there was nothing incriminatory in their files," said Quist, examining a Star Trek phaser that lay on the table. "Today I need you to access the North Yorkshire Police computer."

"Deja-vu." Lestrade laughed and began tapping at his keyboard, his fingers a blur. "We've been here before, haven't we?"

"We have indeed," said Quist, sitting beside him. "Do you never worry about being caught?"

"That isn't going to happen," said Lestrade. "As Watty will tell you, I use untraceable pathways through the dark net, constantly rotating the ISP identification and bouncing from one mirror site to another on a non-programmed cyber loop. If any genius ever managed to track my encrypted ISP, which they won't, they'll find I'm operating from a bakery in Paraguay."

"I understood *bakery in Paraguay*." Quist stroked thoughtfully at his large nose. "As for the rest, you could just as easily have been speaking to me in a Namibian clicking language."

Lestrade winked at him. "The thing is, no one will be looking because they've no idea they're being hacked. As I told you before, I have a secret back door into the police system and I'm invisible. I circumvent all the access logs and I leave no trace." He clicked a final key. "And there we are – I'm in. Okay, so what do you need to see?"

"Truly amazing," muttered Quist. "Can you find me the police report on yesterday's murder at the Grand Hotel in Scarborough? The victim's name is Lee Millican."

The young man worked through several menus. "There you go," he said. "As always, press that key there when you want to scroll down."

"Thank you." The detective sat forward to read, his eyes widening. "Good Lord, the man's head was completely crushed."

"Friggin' Nora," whispered Watson. "It says someone slammed his face into a wall and reduced his entire skull to pulp."

Quist nodded slowly. "That requires colossal strength."

"Hey, you think, Guv?" Watson let out a short laugh and continued reading. "It happened in the gent's toilets. They believe the killer removed his coat before the assault and dropped it on the floor."

The detective pointed to an onscreen photograph. "Yes, there's the perfect outline of a coat in the blood spray, as if he removed it just prior to killing Millican." He quickly read through the report. "They found no DNA or fingerprints, but there were traces of coarse brown dust on the corpse and the bathroom floor which is currently being analysed. Gareth, could you see if Lee Millican has a criminal record? Let's see if he has any connection to White Rose."

Exiting the murder report, Lestrade typed and sat back as arrest records appeared onscreen.

"Yeah, he has form," said Watson. "Three short spells in prison. Well, there's a surprise."

"Indeed, murmured Quist. "Dangerous driving, driving under the influence of alcohol, affray and several counts of violent assault, intimidation and grievous bodily harm."

Watson nodded solemnly. "He'll be sadly missed."

"Inspector Bradstreet was correct," said Quist. "There's nothing here to link Lee Millican to Churchill or White Rose, but from my conversation with the party deputy Craig Battersby, we know they employ a separate group to do their dirty work. As Millican assaulted Sara, we can safely deduce he was part of it."

"The Task Force, as Churchill calls it?"

"Exactly. We need to find the connection to the other death she mentioned." The detective turned to Lestrade. "Could you bring up the murder report on Dylan Taylor who was killed on Sunday at the Wisteria Lodge care home?"

The young man obligingly typed again.

"Ah, there we are," said Quist. "Taylor's head was completely crushed too and, like Millican, there was no murder weapon. The pathologist claims immense strength was utilised to squeeze the skull between two hands."

"Is that even possible?" gasped Watson. "It says they also

96

found identical stone dust too."

"Yes, just like the Grand Hotel bathroom, there was no DNA evidence at the scene, but multiple dust traces were deposited on the clothes and on both bodies, suggesting the killer had it on his hands."

"His feet too," said Watson. "Again, like the bathroom floor, there were dusty footprints on the grass around Taylor's corpse."

Quist scrolled down and gestured to the report. "Mmh, that's intriguing. The killer's torn clothes were discovered by Taylor's body, suggesting he literally ripped them off before crushing the man's head." The detective frowned. "With Millican, the killer removed his coat and dropped it on the floor before he murdered him. Then, seeing as it wasn't left at the scene, he presumably put it back on and left?"

Watson nodded. "So why would he take it off?"

"I've got to say it," muttered Lestrade. "You two weirdos are into some really fucked-up shit."

"Ooh, the cops have a suspect," said Watson, pointing to the onscreen description. "He's called Tonga and he posed as a carer at the nursing home. What kind of name is Tonga?"

"I would surmise it's a nickname and almost certainly a false one," said Quist. "Yes, this male individual is probably in his early twenties. He's quite muscular and around five feet, three, with reddish brown skin, a shaven head and no eyebrows. Oh, and bare feet." He glanced at his assistant, perplexed. "The man wore nothing on his feet."

Watson shook his head. "You're telling me this killer went to murder someone *barefoot*?"

"That would seem to be the case, and this brief description from one of the teenage carers would appear to be all the police have to go on. They have no video footage from either crime scene. It says the suspect asked for Dylan Taylor by name, suggesting this wasn't some random killing."

"So do you reckon it was the same murderer?" asked Watson. "Did baldy Tonga kill both of them?"

"The police aren't jumping to conclusions," said Quist, reading, "but they suspect as much and I'd tend to agree with them. But why would someone kill an old disabled man in a care home and a thug who works freelance for Churchill? I wonder why he targeted these two people."

"Yeah, well I'm wondering about the bastard's strength." Watson took a deep breath. "Where does this Tonga guy buy his steroids?"

"Does Dylan Taylor have a police record?" Quist gave Lestrade a lopsided smile. "If you'd be so kind?"

Lestrade busied himself at the keyboard and found the relevant information.

"Ah, this is interesting." The detective worked through the report. "He and his brother Stephen Taylor were both arrested several times over the years and paid many court fines. They were members of the *British National Party*, the *Send Them Back Party*, and later *Britain First*. It says they participated in violent disturbances on right wing street protests in Doncaster, Leeds and Wakefield. Well, I believe we can safely deduce their political leanings."

"All that was over five years ago," said Watson, reading the file. "Dylan Taylor was never involved with White Rose."

"Not according to this," agreed Quist. "It's very odd, but the arrest records only go back thirty years."

"Why is it odd?"

"Elementary." The detective shrugged. "Taylor was seventy-four, so his aggressive participation with radical groups apparently began when he was forty-four. I can assure you this kind of violent person would be far more involved and active with the right wing movements in their younger days."

"Maybe he *was*, but he just didn't get arrested back then."

"Perhaps." Quist gestured to the screen text. "Dylan Taylor lived in Doncaster for twenty-eight years and then moved into Wisteria Lodge following a stroke. His brother Stephen was his only visitor at the care home. He called there twice a month and there's an address for him on the outskirts of Beverley."

Watson nodded. "The police say Stephen Taylor was

uncooperative and openly hostile during questioning."

"Reading of his arrests, that sounds right." The detective sat back in his chair and pulled out several banknotes to pay for Lestrade's help. "Thank you, Gareth. There's more here than the usual fee for your rather excellent services. I'd like you to keep an eye on the police website and check these investigation case files on a regular basis for updates. I'm particularly interested in any new evidence that may emerge, or if they find anything on this Tonga suspect."

"Cheers." Lestrade pocketed the money. "No problem."

Deep in thought, Quist tapped his ring finger for a while on Lestrade's desk. "Taylor was disabled and living in the nursing home when White Rose were formed, yet from his past dealings with right wing organisations, I feel certain he'll have been connected to them in some way, just like Millican was."

"But how?" asked Watson.

"Exactly – how? Perhaps in a clandestine capacity, like Millican in the Task Force, or simply through correspondence. Whatever it was, this may be the reason both men were killed. Stephen Taylor will probably be able to help us."

"Or probably not," said Watson. "He didn't say anything to the cops."

"We're not *the cops*." Quist smiled. "I'm sure he'll be more amenable with us."

* * * *

Chapter 17

Stephen Taylor lived outside the market town of Beverley in a redbrick house off Hull Bridge Road. Isolated and set back from the main A1035 behind a large garden and driveway, the detached dwelling backed onto open meadows which extended to the River Hull. Taylor answered the front doorbell to find Dominic Churchill on his open porch holding up a bottle.

"I decided upon a brandy," said Churchill, walking in. "It's the one you like."

The elderly man nodded. Shaven heads really suit some people – certain actors and other celebrities are famous for the look – but it didn't do Taylor any favours. Coupled with his sallow complexion and the dark shadows beneath his eyes, it left the sixty-nine year old resembling an extra from a science fiction movie, the sort of character who staggers around radioactive wastelands following an apocalypse.

"Asbach brandy?" he asked, closing the door behind his visitor.

"Yes. We can drink a toast to Dylan."

"Thanks," said Taylor in German. He led Churchill into the lounge, a minimalist room with a green three-piece suite, a television and a small bureau. Save for one large painting in pride of place above the tiled fireplace, there were no pictures or ornaments. "I'd prefer you to call him Dieter when you're here. You know that."

"What I *know* is that you're Stephen Taylor," snapped Churchill. "He was Dylan Taylor. Stop speaking your native tongue and maintain your identity at *all* times. It isn't difficult, yet neither of you could ever seem to understand that simple rule." He gestured irately to the painting. "I mean to say, how many times have I spoken to you about *that*, for God's sake?"

"It's *my* house." The old man smiled proudly at the oil portrait of Adolf Hitler. "I can hang whatever I like on the walls."

"But it'll be seen by any visitors you might have. It's all about guarding your anonymity and projecting the correct image. Admirable as the great man was, we can no longer express our love for him to outsiders." Sighing, Churchill unbuttoned his suit jacket and sat in one of the armchairs. "But tonight we should be talking about Dylan. Look, I'm sorry for your loss and I can imagine how you're feeling."

Taylor shrugged. "My brother was seventy-four, he'd had a stroke and he used to chain-smoke." He brought two glasses to the coffee table. "I knew he wasn't going to last forever, but I never expected this. The idea of him being murdered in his nursing home is beyond belief."

"Do the police have any idea who's responsible?"

"Not really," said Taylor. "Apparently their suspect is some young man who claimed to be a new carer at Wisteria Lodge. He used the nickname Tonga, but that will be false and they don't know who he is. I didn't speak with them for long. You know I don't get on with the police."

"Would it have been so difficult?" Churchill opened the brandy bottle. "Couldn't you have reined in your hostility for once and found out as much information as possible?" He poured the drinks. "Who could it have been? Was it some maniac hoping for an easy target in a nursing home?"

"It wasn't random," growled Taylor. "This bastard went there specifically to kill my brother. They said he asked for him by name."

"Is that so," said Churchill, thoughtfully. "I'll speak to my contact in the police and see what they know. Tell me, have you heard anything more from that Daniel Geller character?"

"I've been thinking the same thing," admitted Taylor. "No, not since he sent me the letter saying he knew the identities of Dylan and me. He contacted the police at the same time, but your insider brought the letter to you."

"That was three weeks ago," said Churchill, handing him a brandy. "He hasn't contacted the authorities since, but don't worry. I'll have the Task Force pay this Geller a visit to find out who he is and exactly what he knows."

"He identified us and Dylan was killed a couple of weeks later. Do you honestly think that's a coincidence?"

"I couldn't say, but if he's involved in any with Dylan's murder, believe me, I'll find out." Churchill grimaced. "I should have investigated this man sooner, but I've been busy with these constant meetings."

"I thought you had a meeting tonight?"

"I have, in Wakefield, but I came to see you first." He raised his glass. "To Dylan."

"To Dieter." Taylor lifted his drink and gulped the brandy.

Churchill ignored the indiscretion; under the circumstances, it was understandable. "This promotional tour of Yorkshire is going well," he said. "The press are always there and I play to their cameras. They see me as colourful and outspoken and that sells their newspapers."

"That's good to hear." Taylor nodded. "I just wish I could have been a part of White Rose. I wish I could have helped in your rise to power."

"You're too set in the old ways." Churchill pointed again to the Hitler picture and shook his head. "Not only are those methods outdated, but they actually work *against* the cause these days. Intelligence and subtlety are needed to begin a race war in the twenty-first century, not muscle and chanting skinheads."

"Oh, but what great days they were." Taylor's eyes misted. "Burning down shops and homes belonging to the blacks and the Jews."

"Subtlety," repeated Churchill, firmly. "I use subliminal messaging all the time. When you and Dylan moved here and changed your names, you picked Taylor, the English version of Schneider. When I changed *my* name, why do you suppose I chose Churchill? It appeals to the British people on a subconscious level. They can't help thinking of their great leader Winston Churchill who fought for them against the foreign menace."

"The foreign menace being Germans like me."

"It doesn't matter anymore." Churchill sipped his drink. "Today the white British look upon white Germans as their brothers and the word *foreigner* has taken on a very different and frightening

102

meaning. The mongrel races are the foreigners now and the public are growing to fear them."

"With your help," said Taylor, grinning.

"To be honest, my job is becoming easier," laughed Churchill. "A few crackpot terrorists have made the stupid masses suspicious of all Muslims. Drugs and gang violence are now associated with the blacks and people are becoming afraid of illegal immigrants. I harness all that apprehension, distrust and fear and I gently fan the flames, but it has to be done in the correct *legal* manner."

"I'll drink to that." Taylor raised his glass again.

"We need to fight the mongrel races, but as I keep telling you, the white supremacist organisations that operate openly don't work anymore. Groups like your old mob in Germany and the movements you joined here in Britain are despised. They're small and easily stamped out."

"We had plenty of devoted followers in Munich," said Taylor.

"No you didn't," laughed Churchill. "Not by White Rose standards. Your members were violent thugs and already converted to the cause. Everyone else was against them, including the German media and the police. That was because they were *openly* against the mongrel races. I believe in taking normal people and slowly converting them to the correct viewpoint. I started White Rose with an agenda that no one can argue against – I'm fighting for the Yorkshire people. You need to gain their support and then introduce your ideas and win them over gradually. They tell their friends and you legitimately expand into a true political force to be reckoned with."

"I suppose you're right." Taylor shrugged. "As you say, Dylan and I joined many of the British right wing groups, but it felt like we weren't really accomplishing anything. Then we became too old for it all and Dylan had his stroke."

"Too old for what?" asked Churchill. "Burning shops and beating blacks to a pulp? You can't do that if you're looking for support from the masses. When I need such things carried out, I use a Task Force of four professional individuals who have no connection to me or my party."

Taylor smiled. "Like the old Jew you told me about who wrote to the papers?"

"Adam Hoffman." Taylor grinned. "My Task Force called on him, but he wasn't home. They roughed up his granddaughter instead and they're currently targeting his business with graffiti and damage to drive him out. You see I'm not averse to the traditional methods, but these *outrages* have nothing to do with White Rose and I loudly condemn such appalling behaviour in the media."

"But I'm betting you'd like to be more hands on with such things?"

Churchill's smile suggested he was correct. "Speaking of that little Jew bitch, I met her today and she made me look foolish in public. She'll soon wish she hadn't."

"So what about the man who identified me?"

"Geller? Yes, like I say, I'll send the Task Force to speak with him. They're going to be busy this week. We had a wealthy financial backer who has just pulled out. He's about to discover you don't do that to White Rose." Churchill finished his brandy. "I need to go now. I can't be late for the Wakefield meeting."

"Are these promotional meetings working?" asked Taylor. "Are you getting plenty of members?"

"Absolutely, and I have an appointment with another potential candidate tomorrow afternoon." Churchill stood up to leave. "His name is Quist."

* * * *

Chapter 18

Feeling utterly wretched, Adam Hoffman walked slowly along Madeley Street deep in thought.

What on earth had he done?

What he'd *done* was astounding and truly beyond belief. It should have been impossible, naturally, and had he not seen one with his own eyes many years before, he'd never have even attempted it. He groaned, shaking his head miserably.

But he had attempted it, and he'd succeeded.

"Stupid, so stupid," he muttered to himself. "Oh, you old fool, why did you hand the control over to Geller?"

He couldn't have foreseen how Geller would completely disregard the plan and instead use it to kill. He couldn't have known and yet he still felt responsible.

Well, of COURSE he was responsible; this was all his doing. Without his unique knowledge and involvement, these people would still be alive. These murders, and any future killings, were down to him.

"Stupid," repeated Hoffman, quietly. "You believed every word he said."

One evening, after Sara's assault, he'd invited Geller to the house for a drink. This had quickly escalated into several drinks and a lengthy conversation had ensued about White Rose and the various hypothetical ways in which the organisation could be stopped. His mistake was telling Geller about the events he'd witnessed in his childhood and explaining half-jokingly how it could theoretically be replicated.

Geller had believed his astonishing story, he'd instantly seen the possibilities and had insisted he try. Hoffman had the knowledge and training, but this was nothing without the correct book of Hebrew mysticism and only three copies were known to exist. The cost had been no problem to Geller. He contacted his sources and, in just three days, the rare volume had been located, purchased from a Los Angeles collector and flown to England.

Hoffman laughed harshly. He'd honestly believed they were doing something decent and righteous – it would have been a huge blow against racism – but he hadn't reckoned with the secret hatred that festered inside his new acquaintance.

Geller had contacted him three weeks ago after seeing his newspaper letters and had realised his unique potential from the drunken conversation that night. He'd persuaded him to go through with the bizarre project and had then deviously taken control. Hoffman could easily understand the man's anger and hatred, but he still couldn't believe he'd go to these terrible lengths.

Geller had been hoping to find the Schneider brothers for thirty years, ever since they disappeared from Munich using false identities. He finally located them when the German forger who produced their fake documents was arrested and, using the information his police contact had uncovered, Geller had tracked the Schneiders to their homes in Yorkshire. The police hadn't helped him so he'd rented an apartment in York and had obviously been planning his own brand of justice.

Hoffman had no idea what Geller's original intentions could have been, but it no longer mattered. He'd unwittingly provided this man with the horrendous means to kill whoever he pleased. A guided missile that could be used over and over again. The problem was *this* missile had a major flaw which rendered it highly unstable and Geller didn't care.

Hoffman arrived at his house at the end of the terrace and unlocked the front door, frowning curiously to feel the draught. *Something was wrong here.* The inrush of air told him that another door or window was open somewhere in the house, but Sara was at work.

"Hello?" He stepped into the passage and looked up the stairs. "Sara, are you there?"

His granddaughter was supposedly at the fire station, but perhaps she'd returned for some reason. Had she forgotten her sandwiches or something?

He entered the lounge and froze, realising the draught was nothing to do with Sara, not unless she'd called home and thrown some violent fit. The place resembled a teenager's bedroom. Drawers, cupboards and bookcase doors were wide open, and papers and books were scattered across the carpet. Walking warily into the kitchen, he found the French doors open and the remains of the lock on the floor.

Was this the work of the White Rose thugs again, or was it Geller's doing? Was he trying to retrieve the book so that he could... The book!

Hoffman raced to the cupboard in the lounge and saw the door was ajar. The safe inside was securely bolted to the wall behind and he swiftly punched in the electronic combination to open it. The large book was still there, inserted diagonally with its bulk filling the space. Sighing with open relief, he lifted it out and ran his fingers over the title carved intricately into the five-hundred-year old leather: *The Key of Honorius*.

Replacing the volume and locking the safe, Hoffman looked around at the devastation and shook his head. *Thank God Sara hadn't been here when this happened.*

* * * *

Sara Hoffman sat at a computer in one of the York fire station offices, entering the details of the garage fire she'd just attended into the county database.

"Ah, I've found you alone at last," said a familiar voice. "Waggy, I really need to talk to you."

"Really?" She turned to see Josh Patel in the doorway. "Bloody hell, Rogan. You and your constant girl problems. Is this about Kacey again, or…"

"Er, no, it's something else." He sat at the desk beside her, but his smile appeared forced and apprehension clouded his attractive features. "I tried to broach this earlier at the bomb hoax, but…"

"But that arsehole Churchill arrived with his tray of drinks. I wonder if his suit is dry yet."

"Yeah, I can't believe you *accidentally* did that." Patel laughed quietly. "Er, listen, Waggy, you know last night when Moggy was attacked?"

"When he was knocked out with a stun gun?" Sara nodded. "What about it?"

"The police believe it was just someone messing around. A couple of youths who somehow managed to get hold of a Taser."

"That's right. They were passing by, saw Moggy outside, and decided to zap him for a laugh."

"I don't think that was the case," said Patel, glancing furtively over his shoulder. "Apparently the night watch got called out to a fire a couple of minutes before. It turned out to be a false alarm."

"Nothing new there," snorted Sara.

Digital communication systems had dramatically slashed the number of false calls. When phone booths stood on every corner, the fire service had scores every week – usually idiots sending an engine, along with unwanted food deliveries and undertakers, to their ex-partners house after being dumped. False calls were still made, however. Some arseholes rang from public phones and some were too thick to realise their personal phones could now be instantly traced.

"A false call," said Patel, uneasily. "But what if it wasn't a *normal* false call?"

"Right…" frowned Sara. "Meaning what exactly?"

"Suppose someone wanted to get everyone off the station and leave it empty? The false address they gave was miles away to ensure they were out for at least a good twenty minutes. The hydraulic platform isn't sent to normal house fires, but the caller wouldn't have known that. They didn't know the platform would still be on station with the two-man crew. When they found someone was still here, they tasered him."

"What the hell would make you think this?" Sara shook her head, puzzled. "Yes, Moggy was knocked out, but no one broke in or took anything."

"No one broke into the *station*," corrected Patel, "But the padlock on the scrap car compound was sliced off, wasn't it?"

"Yeah, but *again,* nothing was taken," pointed out Sara. "Besides, I wouldn't attach too much importance to that broken lock. Finding it the morning after Moggy's attack is most likely a coincidence and it could have been cut off days ago. There's a good chance some of our lot went out to train with the cars, couldn't find the compound key and cut the lock off with the bolt croppers. They probably found the key later, realised they hadn't looked hard enough and blamed the damage on a non-existent would-be robber."

"Er, yeah." He nodded slowly, but didn't appear convinced. "Yeah, maybe."

Sara frowned. *What could be worrying him so much about Moggy's attack and why was he fantasising about imaginary intruders?*

Patel swallowed uncomfortably and opened his mouth to speak again.

"Intentionally damaging fire service property?" said Dave Soames from the office doorway. "Firefighters destroying a padlock and not reporting it to me? We can't go around making those kind of accusations."

Sara turned to see the nervous-looking station manager who had obviously overheard the latter part of their conversation. Soames constantly walked on eggshells around female and ethnic firefighters, terrified that he'd accidentally say the wrong thing and his superiors would find out. He'd learned the brigade policies parrot-fashion and those policies quite rightly stated that *racism was not to be tolerated under any circumstances*. Unfortunately, they didn't explain to him what racism actually *was* and he'd once famously attempted to fire a man for saying he was popping out to the Chinese takeaway.

"A takeaway is a takeaway," Soames had hilariously declared in his report, "and to prefix it with *Chinese* is racist."

A classic case of being promoted beyond his abilities by a clique of close friends at headquarters, Soames pounced upon anything that *might* be racist, hoping to officially discipline someone and score gold promotional points.

"I'm joking, Dave," laughed Sara. "But, let's face it, if this was the work of thieves, they must have been professionals to come equipped with stun guns and bolt croppers. I can't see why such people would cut the lock off our compound and not take anything."

"They were probably looking to steal a car," said Soames. "But they didn't know the petrol, oil and other fluids are removed before they're sent here."

"True," nodded Sara. "And they might have thought we leave the ignition keys in them."

The Station Manager stared at her, pondering whether this was humour or sarcasm. Soames was the only person who didn't call her *Waggy*, as it might be deemed sexist or anti-Semitic and he couldn't take the chance.

A robotic slave to the brigade policies and petrified of anything that could affect his promotion chances, he never took *any* risk. He wasn't even comfortable calling the girl Sara and wondered if he should address her as Firefighter Hoffman. The problem was, that could be construed as unsociable, which again could lead to accusations of anti-Semitism. Playing it as safe as possible, Soames took the tablets for his stress ulcer and didn't call her anything at all.

It was worse still with the Indian. The station manager was aware that Josh Patel went by the nickname of Rogan Josh, but he wasn't sure what to do about it. Patel even happily referred to himself as Rogan on social media and informal paperwork. Much as Soames dearly wanted to hand out official reprimands to everyone who uttered these words, he couldn't – it might make him appear stupid again, like the Chinese takeaway fiasco. The best option was to pretend he hadn't heard the name, but one thing was for certain, he wouldn't ever be calling this man Rogan.

"I sent control the report for Holgate Road," said Patel, gesturing to the computer. "I added the bomb hoax to our database too. Do you want me to mail the other three shifts, letting them know there might be further false alarms at the White Rose address?"

"Good idea," said Soames, his anxious mind whirring with frantic thoughts. *Don't slip up and refer to Firefighter Patel as Rogan. Whatever you do, do NOT call him Rogan.* "Yes, do that please, Firefighter Darkie."

* * * *

110

Chapter 19

Like York, some thirty miles to the west, the market town of Beverley had been encircled by medieval walls for several centuries, but the only section that still remains is the 15th century gateway of North Bar. Fortunately, the Minster has fared better than the defensive ramparts and, again like York, this majestic cathedral soars high above the Georgian streets to dominate the charming little town. Quist and Watson had motored to Beverley along the A1079, through Pocklington and Market Weighton, and the illuminated Minster rose from the dusky rural landscape in front of them. Eight-hundred years old, Quist knew this gothic masterpiece was filled with priceless carvings and sumptuous stained glass.

"Exquisite," murmured the detective, smiling wistfully at the distant building. Stars had begun to show in the darkening sky above the floodlit towers. "Most of the little market towns here in Yorkshire are quite lovely, aren't they?"

"Lovely?" Watson sat in the passenger seat eating a bag of crisps and chuckled through a mouthful. "Yeah, if you say so, Guv."

"You have the artistic soul and passion of a halibut," snorted Quist. "The old architecture, the quaint town squares, the narrow cobbled streets – don't you find any of that attractive? What about Malton? Didn't you say you liked Malton?"

"Well…" The youth shrugged. "I like the rock music nights they have in the Black Bull there."

"But not the amazing history?"

"Not everyone is into that crap like you." Watson turned to him. "Hey, speaking of history, I'm sure you'll know this – why did they award Malton a medal in the last war?"

"I wasn't aware of that." Quist frowned curiously. "No, I can't imagine what you've heard, but I'm sure it can't be right."

"Are you joking? Malton's famous for it." The teenager looked aghast. "You seem to know everything, yet you don't know about *this*? Yeah, apparently they awarded the town a George Cross for holding out against the Germans."

"Ah, right." The detective sighed. "I believe you may be confusing Malton with the island of Malta." Suddenly realising he'd been played, he glanced at his assistant and saw the smirk. He could usually read people, but with Watson it was often tricky.

Quist took a minor road across the Westwood, the vast area of trees and open grassland on the outskirts of Beverley. Ancient legislation still allowed commoners to graze cattle here for free in the summer months, although the fact that they'd need to keep the cows in their gardens for the remainder of the year meant that very few took advantage. An evening ground mist covered much of the wide terrain and Watson spotted a group of roe deer in the low haze. More twinkling stars had appeared above the approaching town and the detective switched on his headlights.

"When Rex rang last night he offered to assist with the White Rose investigation," said Quist. "He wants to stay on longer at his uncle's place and *go undercover for me*, as he puts it."

"Well, to be fair, I probably have the wrong complexion for that," pointed out Watson.

The detective laughed. "The problem is, as usual, he's far too eager and overly excited by the prospect of infiltrating this organisation. Knowing Rex, he would almost certainly get in way above his head and…"

"Fuck it up?" offered the youth, helpfully.

"Eloquently put," said Quist. "Yes, I turned down his offer and he wasn't exactly pleased."

Driving through the compact town centre, they followed Hull Bridge Road to leave Beverley on the eastern side and head out into open countryside. The land was flat here, with drainage dykes between the fields. Watson looked over the autumn stubble to his left and saw the low haze of mist still clinging to the ground, just as it had spread across the Westwood.

"I can't see why this Stephen Taylor guy would talk to us," said Watson. Having finished his crisps, he'd moved on to chomping a chocolate bar. "But if he does, what are you going to ask him?"

"We'll play it by ear, as they colloquially say," said Quist. "But I want to know if he or his late brother were involved in any way with White Rose and if they're connected to Lee Millican."

"He didn't say much to the cops." Watson shrugged. "Like I said earlier, I doubt he'll speak to a private eye either."

"Consultant detective," Quist reminded him.

"Oh, yeah, that makes all the difference."

"Taylor may be aware of someone they'd class as an enemy, and he may know who this Tonga character is, the man suspected of killing his brother. We may not be the only people who dislike this right wing party."

The youth grinned. "If the killer smashed Millican's head to pieces in Scarborough because he dislikes the party, I'd say he dislikes them a good bit *more* than us."

Much to his assistant's disapproval, Quist lit a cigarette. "Speaking of Scarborough, I ought to mention the psychic I met there." He drew thoughtfully on the tobacco. "It was an unexpected encounter and really quite bizarre. The woman instantly sensed my lycanthropy and she was able to read me perfectly. She knew my name and everything about…"

"You mean she was for real?" Watson opened the window and wafted his hand. "I thought that lot just spouted crap: *I'm seeing someone in a uniform? I have a man here with a letter M in his name*?"

"No, this lady was most definitely genuine. She calls herself Madame Selene."

"Oh, the woman in the white hut on the seafront?" Watson nodded. "Yeah, she was there when I was a little kid. She's been there forever. I have to say, you don't seem very worried, Guv. Aren't you scared she might tell people about you? About what you are?"

"Strangely enough, no. I got the distinct feeling I could trust her. Plus, she doesn't have very long to live."

"Why? What are you planning to do to her?"

"Don't be facetious. The lady is very ill."

"My mum goes to see psychics with a bunch of her girlfriends." The teenager grinned. "The shit they tell her doesn't exactly make your jaw drop. The last one blew her away by saying she knew someone with a dog, and someone she knew was apparently thinking about going on holiday to Tenerife." His face lit up. "Hey, have you been watching *Psychic Celebrity Big Brother*?"

"I'm afraid not," admitted Quist. "Is this another one of those awful television shows you waste your time with?"

"It's brilliant," enthused Watson. "Just like the original *Big Brother* show except all the housemates are dead. Admittedly, there isn't much to see, as the rooms appear empty if you're not psychic, but a panel of mediums give a constant commentary explaining what's happening. The housemates in the latest series are Benny Hill, Gandhi, Lee Harvey Oswald, Princess Diana…"

"It sounds wonderful," broke in Quist, unsure whether Watson was joking. Knowing the low-cost garbage they broadcast these days, it was probably genuine. "I must remember to miss it."

The teenager laughed. "Hey, speaking of psychics and spooky shit, I've just realised this address we're heading for must be close to Barmston Drain. It's a really long dyke outside Beverley, isn't it?"

"Yes, it was constructed in the 18th century to drain the flat countryside out this way and it stretches from Hull to Driffield. I checked the map before setting off and I noticed the drain runs across the meadows behind Taylor's house."

"Well, you must have heard the stories?" said Watson. "Lots of people have seen a werewolf prowling around there. It was in all the newspapers. Famous people were talking about it on Twitter and they…"

"Actually I have a confession to make." Quist gave one of his lopsided smiles. "You're aware that I exercise by running at night, usually in the woodland near my cottage? It was before I employed you, when I'd just begun working as a consultant detective, and I drove out this way to interview a potential client over a divorce investigation."

"Seriously?" Watson turned to him. "I think I can guess what's coming."

"I'm afraid so." The detective nodded. "It had been a long day of sitting in the office and driving around and, as it was dark, I decided to park the car and take a run through the fields along Barmston Drain. It was an isolated spot and seemed ideal, but unfortunately someone saw me."

"Wow! It isn't like you to get spotted, what with those keen ears and a sense of smell like a shithouse rat."

"It was pitch-black and misty." Quist shook his head irately. "Who on earth walks their dog on a foggy night in the middle of nowhere? The thing is, I was only seen fleetingly that one time, but various other sightings were then reported, some delusional and some clearly fabricated, giving rise to the urban myth of the Barmston Drain Werewolf."

"Well, there you go, Guv," snorted Watson. "This proves what I always say – no good ever comes from exercise."

The detective glanced at the empty crisp packets and sweet wrappers in the passenger well. Watson was one of those fortunate people who remained lean and reasonably fit despite eating junk and making no effort whatsoever. The most exercise his assistant ever took was twiddling his thumbs on a mobile phone keypad.

"I have mates who spend a fortune on gyms," said Watson, shaking his head. "They drive there, go on the running machine, and then drive home." He let out a dry laugh. "Anyway, that's another supernatural mystery solved. I don't suppose you've ever been swimming in Loch Ness?"

* * * *

Chapter 20

The sun had sunk below the Beverley rooftops and darkness had descended upon the open countryside around Stephen Taylor's isolated house to the east of the town. The old man sat in the lounge drinking his recent gift of Asbach brandy and watching *the Wild Geese* on television. He'd seen the 1978 film many times, but never tired of watching the horrible black soldiers being killed by the brave white mercenaries. He also loved how one of the main cast, Hardy Kruger, was a German like himself. He smiled affectionately and raised his glass to the onscreen actor and then to the portrait of Hitler above the fireplace.

Hearing a loud knock at the front door and muting the sound on his remote, he eased himself up from his chair and checked through the lounge window before answering.

"Who the hell is this?" he muttered.

He didn't recognise the young man who stood motionless under his front porch. Stocky and shaven-headed like himself, his visitor wore a lengthy raincoat and presumably must have arrived here on foot; there was no vehicle on the dark drive.

But why would some stranger would walk here? Maybe his car had broken down, or perhaps it was a salesman? Taylor frowned. A salesman on foot didn't seem likely.

He walked into the hallway, switched on the external porch light and ensured the sturdy restrictor bar was in place on the door. He'd kicked open enough house doors in his time, when attacking black and Jewish homes, to know something about domestic protection. Instead of the usual chain that any toddler could probably snap, he'd fitted a steel security bar similar to those used in hotel rooms.

"Who is it?" he asked, turning the key.

"Stephen Taylor?"

"Yes, that's me. Who are you?"

The old man opened the door to the extent of the restrictor and squinted through the four-inch gap, his eyes widening in amazement to

116

see that his caller was now naked with the raincoat lying at his feet. He caught his breath, the amazement turning instantly to fright as the temperature plummeted and the man's reddish-brown body began to grow in height and bulk out, almost as if it were being inflated like some ghastly Halloween balloon.

Horrified, Taylor slammed the entrance shut, then staggered back as it crashed open, the deadlock and restrictor flying past his head. He couldn't recall what he'd paid for the security bar, but realised he might just as well have used steamed spaghetti.

What was this thing? More to the point, what the fuck did it want from him?

Five inches taller and much wider now, the dark figure lumbered inside and reached out for him. Taylor backed away across the hall, whimpering in terror and avoiding the grasping hand. The features had somehow changed, the eyes had shrunk, almost vanishing in the flattened face, and the wide mouth was an open black slit.

What were these red markings on its torso? What WAS it?

The old man was fit enough for his sixty-nine years, but the fear-induced adrenalin boost certainly helped as he scampered down the passage from the entrance hall to the rear kitchen. He looked back to see the dreadful creature walking steadily after him.

Walking? Why wasn't it running?

Tugging back bolts with trembling fingers, Taylor threw open the kitchen door and ran out into the darkness, his heart pounding and his breath shallow and rapid. The Leylandii hedges on either side of his rear garden were dense and impenetrable – he couldn't escape through them – but he could easily scale the waist-high fence at the bottom of the lawn. The huge figure strode after him as he hurried across the grass, his mind spinning in panic.

Whatever it was, it didn't seem able to move any faster than this weird walking pace. Once he negotiated the fence, he could definitely get away from it.

"Shit!," he hissed, wincing in pain.

It was dark and he'd forgotten the barbed wire fixed along the top of the woodwork, but who cared if he injured his hands? Right now, bleeding fingers were the least of his worries.

"Fuck you," snarled Taylor in German, awkwardly clambering over as the ponderous creature caught up with him. "I'm out of here."

With the garden fence now between them, he backed away in triumph, then stopped abruptly and looked down to see his right shirt sleeve snagged on the wire. Moaning, he jerked frantically to free himself as large fingers clamped on his wrist.

"Oh, no, no…"

The thing had been closer than he'd realised. Taylor was yanked effortlessly back over the fence and held up in two hands, his dangling feet kicking in mid-air, as the creature appeared to inspect him. Lowering him to the ground, it pulled the struggling man against its brick-hard torso, almost as if they were preparing to smooch.

"What are you doing?" screamed Taylor. It wrapped its left arm tightly around his waist and placed its right hand firmly on his ribcage. "No, don't. Don't…"

The hand pushed at his chest, bending the old man backwards over the rigid arm. Taylor heard a loud crack and briefly wondered if someone had fired a gun. His final thought was the realisation that the noise had been much nearer. It was the sound of his own spine snapping.

* * * *

Turning his car off Hull Bridge Road, Quist pulled into Stephen Taylor's driveway. "Hello," he murmured, seeing the front door was wide open. "What's going on here?"

"Could he be on his way out?" asked Watson. Climbing from the passenger seat, he walked to the porch and spotted the raincoat on the ground. "Er, Guv, this doesn't look good."

"It looks positively bad," said Quist, noticing brown dusty marks on the porch step and darting inside. "Stay behind me."

"No need to worry about that," muttered the youth.

The pair ran through the house, quickly checking the empty downstairs rooms, and into the kitchen where the rear door also stood open.

"What the hell…" Watson pointed to the bottom of the garden. There was enough light to make out a young bald man climbing over the fence. "That guy… he's stark bollock naked."

"Well spotted." The detective nodded. "Although that hasn't escaped my attention."

Hearing their voices, the nude figure glanced back at them and ran into the darkness across the meadow. They raced down the lawn and Watson recoiled at the sight of the deformed corpse on the grass.

"This is almost certainly Stephen Taylor," said Quist, grimacing. "Good Lord, he killed him by breaking his back. The old man's body has been folded backwards, completely in two like a pocket knife."

"You don't say." Watson let out a nervous laugh. "I told you he wouldn't talk to us."

"A very bad joke," said Quist, watching the killer sprinting across the misty field.

"Bloody hell," gasped the teenager. "He's fast, isn't he?"

"Too fast for me to catch like this," admitted Quist. With no time to undress, he shrugged off his leather overcoat and quickly removed his watch and signet ring. "Fortunately it's dark and this place is fairly secluded."

"Oh, here we go," muttered Watson, wincing to hear the tearing clothing, crackling bones and grunts of pain as the detective shapeshifted. His breath became visible on the icy air and he peered down at the black wolf through the cloud. "That guy has a shaven head and he looked pretty muscular. Do you suppose it was Tonga, the fake carer from Wisteria Lodge?"

"Without a doubt," growled Quist, rising from the transformation. "It's time I had a chat with him. This shouldn't take long."

The werewolf sprang over the fence and raced after the killer on all fours, bounding ghost-like through the low mist. A group of ground-roosting partridges sensed the approaching creature, spotted the glowing amber eyes and exploded upwards in raucous panic.

Hearing the alarmed birds and looking back, the naked man saw he was being pursued and turned right to crash through a hawthorn hedge into a cattle field. The wolf cringed inwardly at the thought of negotiating *any* kind of prickly vegetation whilst nude, then realised he was heading for the Barmston Drain, the twenty-mile dyke created to drain this flat landscape. The fleeing killer leapt the misty waterway and continued to the River Hull, which for the most part ran alongside the dyke on its meandering journey to the Humber. Scattering terrified cows, Quist bounded across the dyke and saw that his quarry had come to a halt on the riverbank ahead.

He glanced back at the drain and smiled suspiciously. The water he'd just crossed was over fifteen feet wide. Any human, even an Olympic athlete on steroids, would have trouble clearing *that* distance. He'd wondered about the remarkable strength used in the recent murders and now there was this.

"Don't run any further," shouted the wolf, approaching. "I can easily catch you and I believe we should talk."

The naked man stood motionless facing the river, his hands hanging by his sides. With the darkness and the mist, he probably didn't realise he'd been chased by a wolf, but if Quist's suspicions were correct, it wouldn't matter. Quist raised himself on his hind legs and moved warily towards the silent figure, sniffing the night air.

This was intriguing. There was no scent, and the man wasn't breathing heavily following his burst of exertion, the still shoulders and back were proof of that.

"I know you killed Stephen Taylor back there," said the wolf. "But I don't know why. There's something about you that leads me to deduce…"

Leaning forward, the figure toppled face-first into the water with a huge splash.

"Damn," snarled Quist, rushing to the banking, but arriving too late.

He hadn't expected this and he'd no intention of following him. From the steady flow, the River Hull looked to be deep at this point and the black ripples slowly vanished as Quist waited. He carefully watched the surface and the grassy banks left and right for any sign of the man re-emerging. It was a lonely spot with open fields on either side, and he'd be easily spotted when he appeared. Seconds turned into minutes and the wolf frowned, realising that he wasn't coming back up.

The half-moon broke through the clouds and, noticing dark dusty marks where the man had stood, he lowered his muzzle and sniffed. There was no human scent here – no scent whatsoever apart from the faint aroma of damp clay.

"Interesting," growled the wolf, smiling shrewdly and rising onto two legs.

A distant gasp of shock jolted him and he turned to see a frightened couple walking a dog some two-hundred feet away along the riverbank. He'd been too preoccupied to pick up their footsteps and smell and, cursing under his breath, the wolf dropped back onto all fours and sprinted away across the field.

"Now do you believe me?" stammered the girl to her boyfriend. "You wouldn't have it, but I told you those stories about the Barmston Drain werewolf were probably true."

Her terrified spaniel demonstrated its agreement by unintentionally defecating on her foot.

* * * *

Chapter 21

The huge black wolf crossed the meadow and paused in the darkness, dropping low in the long grass and gazing around with luminous amber eyes to check that no one was watching. Quist had been stupidly careless with the dog walkers, but his attention and senses had been concentrated on the river and then on the dusty marks in the banking vegetation. Fortunately such occurrences were rare and no one would believe the two young witnesses.

Everyone knew that werewolves didn't exist, and they were only to be found in mythology and horror films. Doubtless their exciting story would add to the Barmston Drain legend, but as time passed, they wouldn't even believe it themselves. Both would assume their fleeting glimpse of a supernatural creature was a combination of a large stray dog and their eyes playing tricks in the darkness.

Returning to Stephen Taylor's garden, Quist leapt the fence and paused to properly examine the corpse before running up the lawn to the house.

"Did you catch him?" asked Watson, closing the kitchen door behind the wolf.

"I didn't," growled Quist, standing upright.

The youth grinned uneasily. "After seeing what he did to Taylor, maybe that's just as well."

"I'm uncertain as to what it was, but it definitely wasn't a *him*," said the wolf, thoughtfully tapping his talons on the kitchen work surface. "It was something supernatural."

"You're kidding?" Watson raised his eyebrows. "You mean we're involved with the supernatural again? Are you sure, Guv?"

Quist nodded. "Whatever it is, it's faster, more agile and much stronger than a human. Plus it has no human scent. It dived into the river to escape me and didn't surface, which suggests that it doesn't actually breathe air."

"Er, right." There was a time when this would have astounded the teenager, but not these days. Not when it came from a talking wolf on two legs. "Maybe *it* drowned?"

"I very much doubt it. From what I saw of this creature, it was almost certainly the suspect mentioned in the police report. Bald and dark-skinned. Around five feet, three with muscular…"

"Guv, I think the fact that he nearly snapped a bloke in half confirms it was the police suspect."

"Good point," agreed the wolf.

Watson watched as Quist transformed back into his human shape. The fur and fangs fell out and turned to dust on the kitchen floor as the wolf's elongated muzzle retracted and the lupine features returned to those of a middle-aged man. The youth politely turned his back on the naked detective and passed him his leather overcoat.

"It's handy that you have a long coat that hangs down to your calves," said Watson. "You wouldn't look too good naked in a short bomber jacket. By the way, I collected up your torn clothes after you burst out of them; I hope they weren't Armani or some other designer. I'm guessing you wouldn't want them lying around when the police find the body and search this place."

"Very wise," said Quist, slipping on his signet ring and wristwatch. "Well done."

"Oh, and this too." Watson handed him the raincoat from the front porch. "Looks like our friend took it off before he came in. As there are no clothes lying around, he must have been nude underneath."

"Excellent deduction," said Quist, examining the coat. "I wonder why? Mmh, this is brand new and there are smudges of brown dust all over the internal lining. How interesting."

"So this is another case involving supernatural creatures?" Watson shook his head. "You seem to attract weird shit like this."

The detective smiled grimly. "If the supernatural is involved here, it's essential that we learn as much as possible about Stephen Taylor and why he was killed. Come along, let's take a look around this place." He produced a pair of thin leather gloves from his overcoat pocket and pulled them on. "Search only with your eyes and don't touch anything."

They walked into the lounge and Watson saw the painting above the fireplace.

"Friggin' Nora," he gasped. "Is that a portrait of Adolf Hitler?"

"Good heavens." Quist's eyes widened. "Either that or a particularly dire depiction of Charlie Chaplin." He walked to a bookcase filled with volumes covering military history and Aryan themes. "Taylor clearly had an interest in Nazi Germany. Something of an unhealthy interest, I would deduce, going by his choice of wall decoration."

Apart from the books and the Hitler picture, Stephen Taylor had very little in the way of possessions. There were no other wall decorations and no ornaments or keepsakes. Quist guessed, like most hardcore racists, the old man would have had little in the way of imagination and taste. The few items of furniture contained nothing of any significance, but a desk stood in one of the upstairs bedrooms and Quist found that one of the drawers was locked. Gripping the base, he yanked it forward and snapped the mechanism.

"What's this?" he murmured, taking out a roll of cloth. It contained a dagger in a black scabbard. A silver eagle clutched a swastika on the ebony hilt and, sliding out the blade, he read the German Gothic motto etched into the metal. *My honour is loyalty.*"

"I assume that's a Nazi knife?" said Watson. "The swastika is a bit of a giveaway."

"Yes, a dress dagger," said Quist. "They were presented to SS officers during World War II. Certain types of weird people are fascinated by this kind of thing and that fascination has little to do with history. They sell for thousands of pounds." He narrowed his eyes. "AW?"

"What's that?"

"This one has AW etched into the hilt beneath the swastika. It could be the initials of the officer, but it's very unusual for them to deface their dagger." Quist rewrapped it in the cloth and slipped it into his pocket. "I'm keeping this. It could prove very useful tomorrow when I meet with Churchill. Hello, who could this be?"

"It's an old school photo," said Watson, looking at the picture as Quist lifted it from the drawer. The detective turned it and his assistant read the reverse. "Kurt, aged eight."

"Strange," said Quist, "but this boy looks familiar."

"Not to me." Watson shrugged. "The name Kurt doesn't ring any bells either. What else do we have in there?"

Quist took out two letters in stamped envelopes, one addressed to Stephen Taylor and the other to the York police headquarters on Fulford Road.

"This is anonymous and quite threatening," he said, reading the first. "The author is telling Taylor he knows who he is and that he's informed the police. Apparently his days are numbered."

"Maybe Tonga sent it?"

He unfolded the police letter. "Interesting. This is in the same handwriting and it's from a Daniel Geller. It says that Stephen Taylor is really named Stefan Schneider. His brother Dylan Taylor is Dieter Schneider, they're both German and they were part of a neo-Nazi organisation in Munich. They were suspected of murder there, they changed their identities thirty years ago and relocated to England, here in Yorkshire."

"Geller?" Watson frowned. "I've heard of him."

"Really? If this is correct and these brothers *did* change their name, Taylor would make sense. Schneider is the German word for tailor."

"Do you speak German?"

"I speak several different languages; I've had plenty of time to learn." Quist read through the letters again. "If these brothers moved to Yorkshire thirty years ago, that would explain why they didn't show up being arrested at right wing protests until then. Intriguing – if this information was sent to the police, how come they didn't act upon it and why does Taylor have the letter here in his desk?"

"Daniel Geller?" Watson narrowed his eyes. "I remember now; Sara mentioned him. He gave her grandad the book last week, the one that cheered him up. I remember the surname because it's the same as

125

that old magician on television who used to bend spoons and shit."

"Geller is a friend of Adam Hoffman? Is that so?" Quist replaced the letters and photograph. "Well, save for the contents of this drawer, there's nothing in the house to tell us about Taylor and his background."

"Apart from that lovely portrait of the knobhead Hitler."

"Apart from *that*," admitted Quist. "No, he doesn't appear to keep anything in the way of personal mementos, past correspondence, records and official paperwork."

"So what are you going to do about all this?" Watson followed the detective back downstairs. "Ring the cops?"

Quist shook his head. "I can hardly do that without involving us, can I? I noticed an empty bottle on the front step, so Taylor has milk delivered. If we leave the door open just as we found it, this crime scene should be discovered tomorrow morning. If not, I'll make an anonymous call to the police and..." He spotted the dusty prints of naked feet on the hall carpet and pointed. "Ah, look at this."

"Yeah." Watson inspected them. "So why does supernatural Tonga arrive barefoot and strip naked before he kills his victims?"

"Good question. Why indeed?"

"It looks like he stepped in something. Is it earth from the front garden?"

"No, it isn't." Picking up a small piece of reddish stone, Quist examined it and sniffed at it. "I'm no geologist, but I can tell you this is clay. Dry brown clay, just like the smudges of clay on the inside of the killer's raincoat. Just like the clay dust I discovered in the grass where our friend jumped into the river."

"So is this the same brown dust the cops have been finding at the murders?"

The detective nodded. "I'm sure their laboratory analysis will confirm that." He put the fragment in his pocket and headed out to the car. "Now why would clay be discovered at every crime scene?"

* * * *

Chapter 22

Rupert Grant had two swimming pools at Sedgefield Grange, the large outdoor one for summer use and a smaller indoor pool housed in an elongated single-storey extension on the western side of the manor. He never used either himself, viewing all forms of physical exercise in much the same way that a vampire views garlic. A Rolling Stones album played from concealed speakers and his nephew Rex swam up and down, close to completing a half mile and still fuming about his telephone conversation with Quist.

Seeing as *he'd served his purpose and the detective had no further use for him*, this was his last night in Yorkshire and he'd be heading back to London tomorrow.

"Twat," muttered Rex, turning and beginning another fast length. "What a big-nosed, inconsiderate, stupid twat."

The heated pool was twenty-five feet long by ten feet wide and Rupert had loosely designed the building interior around a Roman theme. Colourful tile murals covered the walls and a line of large marble busts stood along one edge of the pool, the heads crowned with laurel leaves and their open mouths spouting water. Each bust was a British politician that Rupert greatly admired, including Enoch Powell, the Duke of Wellington, Nigel Farage, Boris Johnson and David Cameron.

Rupert's all-time favourite political leader had been reserved for the principal decoration on the end wall, a huge mosaic depicting Margaret Thatcher in the guise of Britannia, complete with shining helmet, union jack shield and trident. The face was incredibly lifelike, the cold eyes following the observer everywhere, but Rex found her naked body, full breasts and furry genitalia slightly unnerving. Although Rupert didn't believe women should be allowed to take part in politics, he made an exception for this late Prime Minister.

Completing his mile, Rex climbed out of the pool and angrily towelled himself. He usually took such opportunities to smile at his toned body and rigid abdominal muscles, but tonight he just wasn't in the mood.

"Yeah, thanks for everything, Rex," he mumbled to himself, mimicking Quist's eloquent voice. "You did what I asked, so now you can piss off."

As far as Quist was concerned, Rex's job here in Yorkshire was done, yet he'd be the perfect choice for going undercover and infiltrating Churchill's mob. He had the mirror shades, he was super-smart and he could easily spout racist crap to blend in; all he had to do was use Rupert's bigoted arguments. Rex slipped on his sunglasses, switched off the music on the wall control panel and shook his head.

Watson was clearly no use for such an assignment, so why would Quist turn down his offer? God alone knew why, but he suspected the detective viewed him as being a little dim, brash and shallow.

Quist also felt guilty and responsible for transforming Rex with a bite and still didn't quite trust him in lupine form. He insisted upon monitoring the young man every full moon when the urges were stronger, but now that Rex was sticking to the vegan diet and yoga meditation exercises, he had the werewolf side in check. On the last full moon, he'd driven his McLaren sports car at 130mph along the M25 in werewolf form, howling to the heavens through the open window.

If that didn't prove he was in complete control, he couldn't imagine what would.

Tugging off his wet shorts, Rex pulled on a white towelling robe before walking down the passage that connected the pool building to the house. He headed for the evening lounge, poured himself a red wine and sat on one of the leather couches.

"Hello," said Marika, following him into the room. "I see you've been swimming."

"Yes, in the pool." Rex realised what a stupid answer this was, then smiled as his *aunt* sat beside him. "How are you?"

"Oh, I'm fine," said the girl in her husky Transylvanian accent. Stroking back the long black hair, she eased up her mini dress and crossed her legs. "But I'm also somewhat puzzled. I've been trying for quite a while now and I still can't put my finger on it. Something feels very different about you, Rex. You know I'm a little psychic."

"Hey, not *that* little," grinned Rex, looking her up and down over his sunglasses. "You must be around five feet tall."

"It's strange, but whenever I've seen you over this past year, I've sensed something." Moving closer and pouting, she ran her eyes over the hairy chest exposed beneath his robe. "Something more exciting and intense, but also much darker."

"Well, darkness and excitement *are* my middle names," he purred.

Now that he was flirting with a sexy girl, the sullen thoughts of Quist had vanished. He could feel her body warmth and his lupine senses picked up the stimulating traces of more personal scents concealed by her musky perfume. He cringed, suddenly remembering that the sexy girl in question was his uncle's wife.

"I've told you before about those psychic dreams I have from time to time," said Marika. "They're like visions, or premonitions. They usually come to pass, but not always. Do you remember that bizarre dream I had last Christmas where you were killed by a werewolf?"

He nodded. Her premonitions were more accurate than she suspected, but he couldn't tell her. Quist had explained how a werewolf bite effectively ended the recipient's life and they were reborn as a supernatural creature.

"I still dream about you," said Marika, running the tip of her tongue over her lips. "I have lots of them when you're staying with us. When you're close the dreams are more vivid, but now they're different." She smiled coyly. "Now they're kind of like blue movies."

"Well…" He cleared his throat. "That's understandable."

"It must be this dark energy you give off; I sense it constantly." Reaching to remove his sunglasses, she stroked his temple and slowly ran a finger down his face and neck to the black hair on his chest. "I can feel it right now. Maybe if you allowed me to realign your chakras..."

Rupert waddled into the evening lounge and lowered his bulk into an armchair. Marika coughed uneasily, tossed the sunglasses into Rex's lap and moved away on the couch. Her husband hadn't noticed their closeness, but this wasn't particularly surprising. He never noticed how much time his wife spent helping the young gardener's assistant, or the two lads who cleaned the swimming pools. Despite all the visits to Juan's Spanish class in Pickering, he'd yet to realise that she couldn't speak a word of the language.

"Lord Mortimer just rang me," snorted Rupert. "He has saboteurs disrupting his fox hunt. I've offered to lend him some of my mantraps and a box of those special shotgun cartridges I had filled with rock salt. There's nothing more exhilarating than seeing a spotty art student leaping into the air when they get their rump ripped apart by salt."

"Is that legal?" asked Rex, astonished.

"Of course," said Rupert. "It's perfectly legal when all the local judges, magistrates and senior police officers hunt and shoot with you."

"Excuse me, Sir." Barrymore the butler appeared at the lounge door. "There are two gentlemen to see you. Harvey McMurdo and Peter Ryder."

"Show them in," said Rupert. He turned to Marika. "Never heard of them. Are they friends of yours, my dear? Two of those young men from the fitness club that call here to go out walking in the woods with you?"

Shaking her head, Marika noticed Rex's curious glance and gave him an innocent smile.

The huge men who strolled in and loomed over Rupert were obviously into something a touch more hardcore than fitness clubs. Their broken noses and the muscles bulking out their black windcheater jackets pointed more to steroids and sweaty backstreet gymnasiums, the sort of places frequented by unregistered boxers, bouncers and those strange individuals who really enjoy hurting people. The men had tightly-cropped hair, but no style would have enhanced their piggy-eyed features. Both were proud to look like bulldogs. *British* bulldogs.

Rex instantly stiffened. He didn't need Marika's psychic senses to feel the threatening air of raw aggression emanating from McMurdo and Ryder.

"Good evening," said Rupert, oblivious to the tense

atmosphere. Not being keen on strenuous exercise, he didn't rise from his chair, but held out a hand. "Can I help you?"

"I'm sure you can," growled McMurdo, ignoring the offered hand. "I've seen you at the White Rose meetings and I thought you were committed to the cause."

"White Rose?" snapped Marika, sitting upright. "Are you involved with those disgusting people?"

Ryder ignored her. "I understand you cancelled your membership, Mister Grant?" he said, with a rather unappealing grin. "More to the point, you cancelled your promised financial contribution."

"Are you Dominic Churchill's men?" asked Rex, climbing to his feet and tightening the cord around his robe. "What do you want?"

"No, we don't work for Mister Churchill," said McMurdo, looking him up and down. "And no, we're not part of White Rose."

"Think of us as two concerned citizens hoping to set things right," said Ryder. "As to what we *want*, we want Mister Grant here to reconsider his hasty decision."

"Yeah, I've heard about you," said Rex. "Churchill employs a Task Force, as he calls it, to carry out his grubby business. A group of big guys like you that can't be connected to his party."

"Grubby business?" McMurdo's smile grew taut. "That isn't very nice, is it? In fact, it's rather insulting and I don't like it." He turned back to Rupert. "You promised that money and then went back on your word without any…"

"There isn't any money," said Marika, her brown eyes flaring angrily. "You won't be seeing Rupert again either. I don't know what you think this visit will achieve, but it's time for you to leave."

"Ooh, nice accent there," said Ryder. "East European, are you, luv? Believe me, it's *you* who'll be fucking leaving when White Rose is in power."

"Right, that's enough," barked Rupert. "Get out of my house."

"Yeah, your house…" McMurdo looked around the lounge. "This is an old place with lots of timber. It must be very flammable."

131

"It's also *very* insured," said Rupert. "Any damage can easily be repaired while I lay on a beach in the Maldives."

"Is your wife's pretty face insured too?" snarled Ryder. "I hope so, because I know from experience that acid can do lots of damage."

"There are plenty more fish in the sea." Rupert shrugged. "Lots of other Romanian beauties."

"Yeah?" McMurdo laughed dryly. "I'm glad you can joke about it."

Rupert looked bemused. "*Joke?*"

"We've told you," said Ryder. "You need to see sense and change your mind about the cash contribution, or...."

"And the lady told *you*." Rex snatched McMurdo's arm. "It's time to leave."

"Hey, you grabbed me," said McMurdo, with an evil grin. "Big mistake, sonny. That's classed as a physical assault, just like this..."

Rex easily dodged the punch and, dropping low, he slammed a fist into the man's stomach. Winded, McMurdo bent double and Ryder flew at Rex to be met with a hard backhanded slap across the face. Rex knew he had to hold back with his blows. If he forgot himself and used his lupine strength, he might accidentally kill these two. McMurdo yelped and fell on his back as Rex cracked him across his jaw, dislodging three teeth.

"Splendid work," enthused Rupert. "I didn't know you had it in you, my boy."

Watching with wide eyes, Marika gripped the couch and trembled with uncontrollable sexual excitement. She gasped to see Rex effortlessly lift Ryder above his head and use the thug's flailing body to beat his partner on the carpet, the sound of each loud smack and crunch stimulating her. The violent sounds combined with the potent testosterone in the air and that dangerous, dark *something* that emanated from Rex to send intense tingles coursing through her lower torso.

The two visitors lay groaning on the lounge floor and Rex grabbed their jacket collars in both hands.

"Okay, time to go," he growled, dragging them to the door.

"You're both finished."

Rex heard a low involuntary moan from Marika and glanced at her. The girl gripped the couch tighter and visibly shuddered. Her shallow breath, flushed complexion and light perspiration told him these thugs weren't the only ones who had *finished*.

"Marvellous," said Rupert, clapping. "Good show, Rex."

Rex pushed open the door and began hauling them across the hall.

"Wait," shouted Rupert, heaving his vast body from the armchair. "Marika and I want to watch you throw them down the front steps." He turned to his panting wife. "Are you coming?"

Marika cleared her throat. "Yes," she gasped, quietly. "Three times."

* * * *

Chapter 23

What could that thing have been?

It was Wednesday afternoon and Quist had thought about little else since leaving the late Stephen Taylor's house the previous evening. Driving along Holgate Road in York, he contemplated the bizarre events in Beverley as he headed for his appointment at the White Rose headquarters.

Inspector Bradstreet's visit had aroused his curiosity in the murders, but the police had no idea they were dealing with a supernatural creature. If any officers managed to get near their "suspect", they'd be in serious danger, although they would have seen the state of the victims and this pretty much went without saying. Quist knew he had no choice but to track down this killer himself.

Tonga, as the police referred to him, wasn't human, but what exactly WAS that creature he'd chased after across the fields?

The detective realised that he might actually need Rex Grant's offer of assistance, not to infiltrate the right wing party, but to stop this supernatural killer. Although Watson was fairly unfazed by such strange things these days, he wouldn't be much use if they bumped into that powerful creature again, especially if on the next encounter it *didn't* run away.

He drew thoughtfully on his cigarette. There was little doubt that the Tonga creature was responsible for all three deaths, but why would it murder these specific people – Lee Millican and the Taylor brothers – and *why on earth* do it naked? Millican worked for Churchill in his Task Force and, if Daniel Geller's letters were to be believed, the Taylors were actually named Schneider and both were neo-Nazis from Munich.

And then there was the clay. Why were those traces of brown clay found near every victim?

Quist brought his car to a halt by the kerb and gazed up at Birlstone House beyond the neat garden of gravel and tiny shrubs. Compared to supernatural murders, exposing a bunch of racists seemed trivial, but it still needed to be done. His phone suddenly vibrated and he saw it was Rex.

"Hello there," said the detective. "I was going to ring you, but you beat me to it."

"Really?" snapped Rex. "Seeing as I'm no use to you, it was presumably to say cheerio before I leave for London. This is just a quick call to let you know that Churchill sent two of his Task Force to Sedgefield last night. They tried threatening Rupert into giving them the cash he'd promised, but it didn't work. I gave them both a bit of a spanking."

"I see," said Quist, puffing on his cigarette. "No, I wasn't intending to say goodbye. The situation has altered somewhat and, if you'd still like to help with…"

"Absolutely," broke in Rex, excitedly. "Definitely. Of course I'll help."

Quist smiled. "That sounds to me like a *yes*."

"Yes, it's a yes. I'm glad to hear you've seen sense. After those bastards threatened Marika last night, I'm more determined than ever to help with this. These racist scumbags need closing down and I'm your ideal undercover guy. I can't wait."

"I'm afraid you'll *have* to wait a little," said Quist, glancing at Birlstone House. "I'm a little busy right now, but I'll ring you later today and explain everything."

The detective pocketed his phone. Whatever the creature might be, it was unbelievably strong and two werewolves would have a better chance against it than one… even if one of them happened to be something of an imbecile. Right now, however, he had to put all thoughts of the paranormal aside and focus his mind on this meeting with Dominic Churchill. The first step was to gain entry into the inner circle and win his trust. He had two items in his coat that would hopefully help with that.

He remembered the nugget of brown clay found at Taylor's house that he also carried in his pocket. *Clay? Those traces of clay residue at the crime scenes must be relevant in some way, but how?*

135

"Forget it," he muttered to himself. Climbing from the car, he crushed his cigarette underfoot and straightened his leather overcoat with a brisk shake. "Concentrate on this."

Walking up the front path to the White Rose headquarters, Quist ran his eyes over the four-storey building and realised that human nature changed very little with the passing of time. When this terrace was built in the early 1800s, these large houses had been home to the professional classes and wealthy businessmen, none of whom would have welcomed the idea of black people in Britain unless they were kept out of sight and toiling as servants. Two-hundred years had passed by, men had walked on the moon and the current occupants of Birlstone House still felt the same way about dark skin.

The front door stood open and he entered a hallway with a reception desk and waiting area of chairs. Most of the building's original features had been preserved, with wooden wainscoting, ornate coving around the high ceilings and glass fanlights above the panelled office doors. Coffee tables were covered in copies of *Yorkshire Life* and other local magazines, and patriotic pictures of the Royal family hung on the walls beside Yorkshire sports stars and actors. Two men in smart suits approached.

"Bernard Quist," said the detective, smiling warmly. "Good afternoon. I have an appointment with Mister Churchill."

Nodding, one of the assistants gestured for him to lift his arms.

"Seriously?" He politely raised them. "I take it there's a justification for such stringent security?"

"Better to be safe than sorry," said the man, patting him down. "We get a lot of hate mail from left-wing nutters and you must have heard about the recent bomb threats? Like all politicians, Dominic has enemies."

"Yes, I fully understand." Quist managed to contain his laughter at the "politician" description. "Good Lord, did you just run a hand over my shirt checking for microphones?"

"You could be a journalist wearing a wire to secretly record your meeting."

"Really? What on earth do you think Mister Churchill might say?"

"Recordings can be altered to portray Dominic in a bad light."

The detective nodded. The plan was to involve Churchill in a racist conversation and tape his views, but Quist hadn't worn the secreted recording equipment today. Once trust had been established, they wouldn't bother to search him again.

The assistant found a bulging envelope in his overcoat. "What's this?"

"A little something for the White Rose Party." Taking back the envelope, Quist opened it to show a thick wad of twenty-pound notes and returned it to his pocket. He didn't want his second *gift* to be discovered. "It's a financial contribution that I'm sure Mister Churchill will appreciate. Now I've had enough of this nonsense. You've seen my donation and you've established that I have no machine guns or microphones, so I wonder if you'd be so good as to take me to him?"

Nodding curtly, the man led him along a passage and into a smart modern office with filing cabinets and glass cases of books on Yorkshire. More pictures of the Royal family hung on the wall and the leader of White Rose sat writing behind a desk.

"Bernard Quist, Sir," announced the assistant, closing the door as he left.

Sighing, Churchill climbed to his feet and walked over him; he didn't appear to be in the best of moods. Quist estimated the man to be mid-forties, six feet tall, and his toned body indicated regular training sessions in a fitness spa. His hair had obviously turned grey at an early age and the thick silver locks complimented his tanned movie star features.

"Good afternoon," said Quist, enthusiastically. "It's so good to finally meet you. I've seen you speak many times at the meetings and your words never fail to stimulate me."

"That's good to hear." Churchill shook hands and managed a tight-lipped smile. Quist noted the manicured fingernails and the expensive Omega watch. "You should have introduced yourself earlier.

Which meetings did you attend?"

"Scarborough was the last one. I have to say, your plans to end all immigration are radical, but clearly the only feasible way forward. These people are flooding in and will soon be taking over. No one in their right mind wants a Muslim Britain with Sharia law courts."

"Absolutely." Churchill shrugged. "But the mainstream parties don't agree, or they'd have already adopted my policies." He sat at the desk and gestured for his visitor to sit opposite. "You'll have to forgive me, but I'm not exactly myself today. I've had some bad news."

"Oh, I'm sorry to hear that."

"Yes." Churchill smiled sourly again, but didn't elaborate. "So what can I do for you, Mister Quist?"

"Call me Bernard, please, and it's more of what I can do for *you*." The detective sat back and crossed his legs. "The appearance and subsequent rise of White Rose is the best thing to happen in this country for decades. I really admire you and what you stand for."

"Well, thank you, Bernard. It's always good to be appreciated."

Quist lowered his voice slightly. "I've come to admire you even more since I spent an evening recently with one of your colleagues. It was a gentleman named Craig Battersby and I liked him immensely. Craig is my kind of man and, from what he was telling me, I now know you're *definitely* my kind of political party."

Churchill narrowed his eyes. "I'm not so sure I follow."

The detective gave an enigmatic smile. "In my younger days I was a member of the National Front. Later I was involved with the British National Party, the English Defence League…"

"You must know those aren't the sort of people we would ever associate with?"

"Indeed I do." Quist laughed quietly. "You're far too astute to be connected in any way with those openly racist morons, but before your party appeared, my options were somewhat limited."

"Are you comparing White Rose to them?"

"Of course not. I can see what you've achieved here and you're something *very* different indeed. Something powerful that hasn't been attempted before and a thousand times more effective than those volatile groups who claim to stand for a purer Britain. You see, my discussion with Craig was rather lengthy and *very* informative. I know we think alike and I want to stand as a candidate here in York. White Rose is the only organisation who will make a difference in Britain and it's the only party for me."

"That's good to hear," said Churchill, reaching across the desk to shake his hand again. "I'm starting to like you, Bernard."

Quist relaxed slightly. He'd been hoping he hadn't gone too far with his gushing praise for these racist idiots.

"I also know you're seeking financial backers," he said. "I'm aware of your recent setback with that fool at Sedgefield, Rupert Grant. I know the man socially through hunting and shooting and I honestly believed he and I shared the same views."

"Grant?" Churchill frowned. "If you know him, perhaps you could enlighten me as to why he pulled out?"

"God only knows." Quist shook his head. "Grant told me he'd changed his mind when I spoke to him yesterday, but he wouldn't say why." He brought out his envelope of cash. "The point is, *I* won't let you down. Here's eight-thousand pounds as an initial expression of goodwill and, once I have your banking details, I can transfer a far more substantial amount to assist the party."

"Well, this is excellent." Churchill held up the envelope and grinned. "I honestly can't thank you enough, Bernard. Yes, we really *do* need candidates like you. Intelligent and cultured Yorkshire folk with the *correct* revolutionary views."

"As I said, our politics are the same and I have another offering that I believe will demonstrate that. Something that will prove just *how* alike we are." Quist produced a roll of cloth from his coat and opened it to show the Nazi dagger he'd found at Stephen Taylor's house. "It's beautiful, isn't it? The ultimate symbol of racial purity and perfection. I've treasured this for many years and now I'd like you to have it. It's a gift you can either keep or sell to fund the party."

Churchill's eyes widened. "Breathtaking," he murmured,

reverently lifting the black knife. "Yes, these weapons really are quite exquisite, aren't they, Bernard? This would be worth a small fortune to the right collector."

"Absolutely," agreed Quist. "But its symbolic value is worth so much more and I feel you may wish to keep it. As I say, I believe we think alike."

"I believe we do." Caressing the SS dagger, Churchill slid out the blade and froze, his smile instantly fading. "Yes," he said. "I will *definitely* be keeping *this*."

His right hand reached beneath the desk and Quist heard an almost silent click. Human ears wouldn't have picked up the sound of the hidden alarm button being pressed.

* * * *

Chapter 24

Quist sat in Churchill's office smiling warmly at the leader of the White Rose Party across the desk. Something was wrong, but the detective's calm expression didn't betray his confused thoughts.

Why had he pressed the concealed alarm? What was going on here and why had the man's attitude suddenly changed?

"Interesting," said Churchill, examining the SS dagger. Standing and moving to a wall safe behind the desk, he shielded the keypad from Quist with his body and entered the combination. "You've had this knife for years, you say?"

The detective glanced at the glass cabinet of books on the opposite wall. "Yes, a much-loved piece of Nordic Aryan memorabilia that I've always…"

"We both know that's bullshit." Churchill placed the knife in the safe along with the cash, slammed it shut and twisted to glare furiously at his visitor. "It's time to stop lying. Who are you and how did you get that knife?"

Quist's mind raced. *Churchill knew the dagger wasn't his. Did he recognise it as belonging to Stefan Schneider, but if so, how? Were the two connected in some way?*

One thing was certain, using it to gain his trust had been a colossal mistake. His thoughts had been on the creature in Beverley all morning and he hadn't given this meeting enough consideration.

"Mister Churchill," he said, "I don't know what I've done to cause offence, but I assure you, my intentions are…"

"The dagger," snapped Churchill. "You should have inspected it more closely before using it as bait. The tiny letters AW are etched into the hilt below the swastika."

Yes, thought Quist. *I saw them, but I stupidly dismissed them.*

Alerted by the concealed desk buzzer, two large men opened the door and strode in. Their denim jackets, grossly enlarged muscles and streetfighter faces told Quist they were probably part of Churchill's Task Force. He noticed the bruises and realised this could be the pair mentioned by Rex earlier. Still smarting and raw from the beating at Sedgefield, Harvey McMurdo and Pete Ryder took up intimidating positions on either side of the seated visitor. If the Easter Islanders manufactured bookends, they'd doubtless look like this.

"Is there a problem, Sir?" asked McMurdo, his voice a threatening growl.

"Yes," said Churchill. "A *huge* problem for our big-nosed friend here if he doesn't tell me how he came by a certain knife." He walked to the detective and loomed over him. "You see, I know who owned it and it certainly isn't you. What do you know about these murders?"

"That's a bizarre question," said Quist. "What murders?"

"Dylan Taylor in Robin Hood's Bay, and I've just heard that his brother Stephen Taylor was found dead by the postman this morning. An acquaintance of mine named Lee Millican was also killed in Scarborough on Monday."

"Well, obviously I know nothing about any of this and I honestly can't imagine why you'd ask." Quist looked puzzled. "Stephen Taylor hasn't been in the media."

"No, I have a contact in the police."

I'll bet you do, thought Quist. *One or two police officers have occasionally been known to hold racist views. This was probably the same officer who gave Daniel Geller's letter to Stephen Taylor.*

Churchill stared at him for several seconds before returning to his seat behind the desk. "Are you Daniel Geller?" he asked. "Or are you connected to him?"

"No, I'm Bernard Quist, as I told you." The detective raised an eyebrow. *It was as if he'd read his thoughts.* "Who's Geller?"

"He recently threatened Stephen Taylor and now Taylor has been murdered."

Quist glanced up at the scowling thugs. This was turning decidedly nasty. It was safe to say his attempt at infiltrating White Rose could have gone better and his performance as a benevolent racist wouldn't be winning any acting awards. His mind had been on the previous night, he'd been sloppy, and the most prudent course of action now was to get out of here.

"Look, I can see I've upset you," he said, rising from the chair. "I apologise and I'll simply leave before…" Ryder's hand gripped his shoulder like a bench vice and slammed him back down.

"You're going nowhere," said Churchill, icily. "Tell me about the dagger with AW on it."

"AW?" Quist shrugged. "I don't know. Was it once owned by Andy Warhol?"

Churchill nodded to McMurdo who landed a hard punch on the side of his head.

"I see." The detective clutched his ringing ear. "Not Warhol, then."

"Okay," said Churchill, gesturing to the menacing creatures behind Quist. "Harvey, it's time for you and Pete to have a chat with him downstairs. Find out exactly who he is and why he came here. I want to know how he got the dagger and if he knows this Geller character. I don't care how much damage you do."

"There really is no need for this," sighed Quist. "I'm who I say I am, I don't know Geller and I know nothing about the murders you mentioned."

Churchill ignored him. "You claim you like the party," he said, smiling cruelly. "Well, let's see how *these* White Rose politics appeal to you."

Snatching the detective's coat collar, Ryder hauled the man from his seat and marched him out of the office.

"Don't try running or doing anything stupid," warned McMurdo, following. "If you do, I'll snap your arm."

"He called you Harvey," said Quist, staggering slightly as Ryder pushed him roughly along the corridor. "Would you be Harvey McMurdo?"

The big man nodded suspiciously. "You've heard of me?"

"You were identified by Sara Hoffman as one of the men who assaulted her. That must be stimulating work – hurting young women for money."

Ryder laughed. "We'll hurt *anyone* for money." He opened a door beneath the staircase and flicked a switch, lighting a flight of cellar steps. "You're about to get a demonstration."

"White spirit," said Quist. "Soap and water won't do it."

Ryder grabbed his collar again. "What the fuck are you talking about?"

"Your fingernails. When you reached for the light just then, I noticed traces of yellow gloss paint beneath them. Is that from painting swastikas on shop windows?"

"No one can prove that," snarled Ryder, manhandling him down the stairs.

"I'll take that as a yes," nodded Quist.

Extending beneath the entire building, the basement comprised of several large chambers connected by redbrick arches. Used as extra storage space by the offices upstairs, cupboards, filing cabinets, and boxes of party leaflets filled the subterranean rooms. The detective arrived at the bottom of the steps and was thrust against the wall.

"You've got some talking to do," said McMurdo. He cracked his knuckles before forming outsized fists reminiscent of frozen turkeys. "I hope those clothes aren't expensive. They're going to get messy and blood has a habit of staining."

"Oh, dear." Quist glanced down at the smart shirt and trousers beneath his leather overcoat. Yesterday he'd torn a perfectly good outfit to pieces during a shapeshift and he didn't relish the thought of ruining another. "If it's all the same," he said, "I'd much prefer to keep them clean, so before this goes any further…"

McMurdo and Ryder stood side by side and, shooting out both hands with lupine speed, the detective grabbed their heads and slammed them together hard. He winced to hear the crack echo around the underground chamber, praying that he hadn't misjudged the force and fractured their skulls. The stunned men collapsed into a tangled heap on the concrete floor and he shrugged his coat straight.

"No need to get up," he said. "I'll see myself out."

Quist darted through the cellar complex and discovered an external door with the key on a hook beside it. An intruder alarm was fitted and, quickly following the wire to where it vanished through a brickwork conduit, he jerked it free, snapped it, and fed it back out of sight. No one would realise the alarm was now neutralised and if he needed to return here covertly, this basement entrance would be the ideal way. Unlocking the door and finding a flight of steps, Quist ran up them into the rear yard and left via the alley behind the building.

Harvey McMurdo shook himself and climbed unsteadily to his knees. "Shit," he grunted. "How the hell did he do that?"

McMurdo was a professional enforcer who hurt people for a living. Sometimes, if the money was right, he did more than hurt them. He and Ryder were supposed to be experts at this and now, for the second time in twenty-four hours, they'd been beaten in a fight. To be truthful, neither episode had been an actual "fight".

First, that twat in the sunglasses at Sedgefield had wiped the floor with them using, what could only have been, a weird martial art like Bartitsu. Now some middle-aged prick with a posh voice had made them look stupid by knocking their heads together like little kids and escaping.

McMurdo rubbed his spinning head. "How did he *do* that?" he growled.

* * * *

Chapter 25

The Duck and Diogenes stood on The Green, the large triangle of parkland and trees in the York suburb of Acomb. One of Watson's favourite pubs, it was walking distance from his mum's house on the Grimpen housing estate and within staggering distance at the end of the evening. The quirkily named inn had great beers, live music twice weekly, comedy nights, and decent bar meals at reasonable prices.

Watson sat with Sara in the busy lounge where illuminated plastic pumpkins, giant spiders and other Halloween decorations hung from the ceiling. He'd decided that it might be a bright idea to take the young firefighter out for lunch. *He was a friend, not a boyfriend, but treating someone to lunch was definite boyfriend and girlfriend shit.* A cheap plate of chicken and chips could hopefully nudge her romantic feelings in the right direction – basically, in the direction of a bedroom.

The gruesome visit to Stephen Taylor's house had occupied his thoughts all morning. There was a time when such things would have terrified the teenager, but since uncovering Quist's dark secret and participating in his bizarre investigations, he was almost used to it these days – *almost.* Used to it or not, he couldn't get the shocking murder out of his head.

Probably just as well, he contemplated, with a wry smile. *If he WERE able to dismiss such horrors – dead people, with their spines snapped by nude killers – it would point towards a fairly weird psychological makeup.*

Watson thought back to his brief sighting at the garden fence. *Was the police suspect Tonga a paranormal creature?* Apart from Tonga's curious and rather antisocial pastime of murdering folk whilst stark naked, he'd appeared normal last night. Quist, however, had insisted he wasn't human and the boss was usually right about such things. As if crushing skulls with his hands didn't make this killer scary enough, he was some sort of supernatural monster, a very strong and lethal supernatural monster that Cyrano had crazily decided they should go looking for.

"Are you okay?" asked Sara, seeing his perturbed frown.

"Yeah, I was just thinking," said Watson, shaking himself and taking a drink from his lager. "Hey, I thought schoolteachers had it cushy with all their holidays and days off, but firefighting is obviously the way to go. You only started back at work yesterday and you already have *another* day off."

"It's one of my spare days," explained Sara. "They let me book it in at short notice so I could be with Gramps after the break-in and help tidy up the mess. It turns out I've wasted it though, because he says he'd rather do it himself."

"Wasted?" Watson grinned. "How can it be wasted if you're out with a good-looking guy like me?"

"Yeah, well when you put it that way." Smiling, Sara looked around the crowded lounge and sipped her white wine. "Anyway, how much time off do you private investigators get? Here we are – another day and another pub."

"We're low on work at the moment, which is one of the reasons Cyrano agreed to investigate White Rose for you." Watson raised his glass and winked. "Things are progressing too. He's already managed to get one of the party deputies pissed and he found out about their Task Force, a bunch of scumbag thugs who Churchill pays to do all the nasty stuff like hurting people."

"McMurdo and Millican, those two bastards who were sent to my house are obviously part of this group?"

"That's right. The next step is to get himself inside their organisation and find proof for the cops that this Task Force work for White Rose. Cyrano also had our friend Rex persuade Rupert Grant to cancel his party funding." He glanced at his watch. "He's at their headquarters right now posing as some racist nutter with plenty of cash."

"Isn't that dangerous?"

"Absolutely. Knowing Cyrano, it's going to be dangerous for *them*." Watson thought again about the murders, Schneider's corpse and the naked fleeing figure. If it *was* supernatural, as Quist believed, then things would doubtless be getting very dangerous indeed. "Listen, it's great you're here…" He clinked his glass against Sara's. "But after the burglary yesterday, are you sure you don't want to be at home with your grandad?"

"No, it's okay." She shook her head. "He's fine and a guy replaced the broken lock in the kitchen this morning. The police said the break-in appeared professional; it looked a mess, but they didn't do any real damage."

"They didn't use the lounge carpet as a toilet?" The youth raised his eyebrows. "They certainly don't sound like York burglars."

"No, thank God." Sara laughed. "The weird thing is, nothing was taken. Drawers were open and bits of money, items of jewellery, and things like cameras were left there in them. The police are certain the robbers just searched the place looking for something specific."

"If that's right, what do you suppose it could be?" Watson grabbed two menus from the next table and passed one to the girl. "Something to eat would probably help us think. Here you go – lunch is on me."

"Hey, that's really nice." Sara smiled sweetly and looked through the list of meals. "Speaking of the police, the detectives questioned Gramps and I about Lee Millican's murder. I guess we're suspects."

"*Suspects*?" The teenager's mouth fell open. "Keep this to yourself and don't ask me how I've seen the forensic report, but Millican's head was crushed flat against a wall using brute force."

"His head was *crushed*?"

"Yeah, and you're telling me they questioned you and your *grandad* about it?"

"Well, I suppose we could have paid someone to do it." Sara shrugged. "Millican assaulted me so they're bound to have us somewhere on their suspect list."

"Was Millican the twat who nearly broke your cheekbone?"

"No, that was the other one, Harvey McMurdo." Sara grimaced. "Millican punched me twice in the stomach."

"He certainly won't be punching any more girls." Watson nodded grimly. "Not without his head. Hey, what can you tell me about your granddad's mate, Daniel Geller?"

"Not much. Why do you ask?"

"Oh, I don't know..." He decided against mentioning the Beverley murder and Geller's letters in Taylor's drawer. "It could be important."

"I can't see how," said Sara. "He's German and pretty wealthy, but apart from that, I don't know anything about him. Being Jewish, he hates White Rose too and saw the letters Gramps wrote to the papers. He contacted him a couple of weeks ago." She closed the menu. "This is a nice idea, but to be honest, I'm not too hungry."

"That's no problem; neither am I." Watson finished his lager. "Listen, are you sure your granddad is okay?"

"Yeah, Gramps is a resilient old guy. Why?"

"Well, the thing is, Mum's away for two days at her sister's place in Sheffield." He gave the girl one of his special erotic smiles, something similar to a constipated fox. "Apart from Hucknall, our ginger cat, I have the house to myself. If you don't want lunch and you don't have to get straight home to your grandad, I was wondering if you fancied coming back to the house for a coffee or something?"

Sara smiled. "Or *something*?"

"Don't get the wrong idea, but I have more questions about Geller and White Rose and…" Watson caught his breath as Sara leant over and kissed him.

"Why not," she said, knocking back her drink. "Yeah, come on. Let's go."

Watson didn't argue and, taking her offered hand, he followed Sara out into the rear car park. They arrived at the girl's car parked by the shrubbery hedge and she gestured to the road. A dark saloon drove slowly past the pub with two men inside, both glaring their way.

"Shit, will you look at that?" she hissed, angrily.

"We're being watched," said Watson, as the car rolled to a halt. "Do you know them?"

"One of them." Sara nodded. "I recognise him from yesterday at the White Rose headquarters. He was filming Churchill when he brought out those drinks I told you about."

"When you *accidentally* knocked them all over him?" Watson laughed. "So now they're trying to intimidate you?"

"Well, I *did* ruin his suit. They'll love me even more now they've seen me with a black guy. Okay, let's give them something to *really* watch." Dragging the teenager to her and running her fingers through his curly hair, she kissed him again long and hard, searching for his tonsils with her tongue. Sara broke away breathless as the disgusted spectators drove off. "Yeah, thinking about it, I'd really like to go to your house for a bit of no strings attached *something*."

"A wise decision," mumbled Watson, his head in a whirl.

He turned towards her car, then fell backwards into the shrubbery as a man's fist landed hard on his chin. Hearing a vehicle screech to a stop and struggling to his knees, he saw Sara being bundled into the rear of a van by two large figures in tan leather jackets and ski masks. The one who had punched him turned before closing the door.

"Don't ring the cops," snarled the man. "If anyone rings them, no one will see her again. Tell her grandfather we want it back."

The van sped out of the pub car park and Watson climbed to his feet, massaging his aching jaw.

"*Brilliant*," he muttered dryly, realising how close he'd been to getting Sara into bed. "Well, talk about perfect timing. Isn't that just fuckin' brilliant?"

* * * *

Chapter 26

Quist parked outside Adam Hoffman's house on Madeley Street and Watson leapt from the car. His jaw still ached from the punch, but fear and concern for Sara overshadowed the niggling pain. He hammered on the door and Sara's grandfather appeared instantly.

"There you are," he said, almost dragging the two men through the hall. "Thank God."

"We came as quickly as we could," said Quist, looking around the lounge.

"How are you bearing up?" asked Watson. "Are you alright?"

Hoffman laughed manically. "No, I'm not in the slightest bit *alright*. You said on the phone that you were there with her. Did they hurt her in any way?"

"No, they shoved her into a van and drove off." The teenager stroked his jaw again. "They hurt *me* though, as I defended her."

"You must be Bernard Quist," said Hoffman, pumping the detective's arm in a frantic shake and completely missing the mention of heroism. "Sara told me her friend worked with a private investigator and this could almost be fate. I could really use your services right now." He held up his phone in a trembling hand. "Just after Watson rang me with the awful news I received a text message sent from Sara's mobile. It says: *Don't contact the police. Go in your safe, or wherever she's keeping it, and return it now. Give it back intact and she comes home safe.*"

Watson turned to Quist. "Just like the guy who somehow got the better of me when I was protecting Sara. He said to tell her grandfather to return it."

"I see," said Quist. "So the obvious question is *what*? Return what?

"I don't know." Hoffman shook his head. "It doesn't make any sense. I have no idea what they could mean."

Quist ran his eyes over the titles of the leather volumes in the bookcases, before gesturing to the photographs on the lounge mantelpiece. "I presume this is Sara?" he said. "The girl in uniform? Is it a recent photograph?"

"Two years old," said Hoffman. "When she finished her fire service training."

"A delightful young lady. And from the resemblance, these must be her parents?"

"My son and his wife. They both passed away some years ago." Taking the photo, Hoffman stared at his granddaughter. "Oh, God, this is all my fault."

"Why would you say that?" asked Quist.

"I sent those letters to the newspapers which started this vendetta with White Rose. First they attacked her and now this."

"I don't believe so," said Quist. "Kidnapping is an extremely serious offence. This abduction can't possibly be retaliation for a few letters which ultimately proved to be inconsequential, or even the spilt drinks Watson told me about. The text message you received would also suggest someone other than White Rose is responsible."

"Like who?" demanded Hoffman.

"Someone searched your house yesterday and Watson informs me that cash and valuables were ignored and nothing was taken. These intruders seemed to be searching for something specific – perhaps for whatever this text message alludes to."

Hoffman opened his mouth to speak, but thought better of it. He cringed inwardly, his insides knotting themselves. He'd already made up his mind that Geller had been the one who broke in here searching for his book, but he couldn't possibly mention this to them. *This kidnapping certainly wasn't Geller's work. No, Churchill must have somehow found out what he and Geller had done and this was his revenge. His stupidity had put Sara in danger.*

Quist's phone buzzed in his overcoat and he answered it. "I see," he said. "Well, thank you anyway."

"Was that Gazza ringing you back?" asked Watson.

"Yes, but I'm afraid he couldn't help." He turned to Hoffman. "I contacted a friend of ours on the way here and asked him to run a computer check on the van that was used to abduct Sara. Despite Watson here being an invaluable assistant and a credit to the detective agency, he somehow neglected to take down the registration."

"Cheers, Guv." The youth scowled. "I was kind of busy protecting Sara and getting punched."

"Fortunately, our friend found traffic camera footage of it speeding away after leaving the Duck and Diogenes pub." He held up his phone to show a still image. "*Unfortunately*, as you can see, sunlight on the windscreen prevents us from identifying the occupants and, when he attempted to trace the number plates, he discovered they were false."

"Oh, no,' whispered Hoffman.

Quist stroked thoughtfully at his nose. "No, this doesn't add up at all, does it? Churchill is a loathsome creature and yesterday Sara embarrassed him with that tray of drinks. I could understand him sending his thugs to hurt her again, but I fail to see what abducting her would accomplish. And then there's this enigmatic text…"

"Maybe they abducted her to hurt her," said Watson. "We saw Churchill's men watching Sara from a car and shortly afterwards the van arrived and grabbed her."

Hoffman whimpered and closed his eyes.

"So why do that?" asked Quist. "Why let you, a witness, see them watching her right before they snatched her, and in a completely different vehicle?" He took Hoffman's phone and read the text. "And what about this message? What on earth could they mean by *return it*? It says *wherever she's keeping it*, which specifically points to Sara having something, and not you. Has she acquired anything recently that someone might want her to return?"

"No," muttered Hoffman. "I bought her a car, but she doesn't have anything that might be valuable…" He rubbed tears from his eyes with a shaky hand. "Or maybe she *does*. Oh, I'm sorry, but I honestly don't know."

The detective nodded to one of the lounge cabinets. "Whoever took Sara is clearly aware that you possess a safe as they mention it in the message. As we've established, your recent break-in suggests that whatever the intruders were searching for, they didn't find it. Could it be something in there? You purchased the safe very recently, didn't you?"

Hoffman frowned. "How could you know…"

"Elementary." Quist smiled. "The cupboard door is slightly open and I spotted the safe when I looked around your room just now. It appears to be quite new. The instruction label is still fixed to the door, and there are traces of plaster and brick dust on either side where you drilled the masonry to secure it to the wall."

"He notices shit like that," explained Watson. "Could Sara have put something in the safe like the text says?"

"I bought it the other day when she was away," said Hoffman. "I haven't had chance to tell her the code yet. No, there's only a book in there."

"No money or valuables? Just *one* book?" Quist raised an eyebrow. "Intriguing. Watson tells me you recently acquired a book which excited you greatly. Would this be the book in question?"

"Er, yes."

"I see. Tell me, did you purchase the safe just to protect this book?"

Hoffman nodded.

"I have to say, that really arouses my curiosity. What is it?"

"An obscure medieval work." Hoffman shook his head. "Believe me, we're wasting time with this. They're not talking about the book in that text." He knew that Geller wouldn't send cryptic text messages; he'd ring and demand the book by name. "This isn't helping to find Sara."

"Speaking of books…" Quist gestured to the cases. "I see you have a great many on religion, folklore and Jewish mysticism."

"An interest of mine," sighed Hoffman. "I was once going to be a rabbi. That idea was shelved when Sara's parents died and I became her guardian…"

"This *obscure medieval work*," said Quist. "Sara told Watson that a gentleman named Daniel Geller gave it to you."

"What?" The man's colour drained. "Er, yes, he did."

"I see." Quist studied his expression. "Even before your granddaughter was abducted, I intended to call on you to ask about this man. I need to know how Geller is connected to Stephen Taylor."

"Taylor? I don't understand why you'd ask about…"

"It would appear Geller knew him, or knew *of* him. We came across a letter, sent by Geller to Taylor, in which he accuses him of being a German named Stefan Schneider."

"By the way," said Watson. "Did you know Stephen Taylor was killed last night?"

"Oh, my God!" Hoffman's mouth fell open. "I was aware that Dylan Taylor had been killed in Robin Hood's Bay, but his brother is dead too?"

"Murdered in a most unusual way," said Quist. "His body was folded in two and his spine was snapped. You can imagine the power that must have been employed, just like the immense strength that was used to kill his brother in that nursing home. The individual who did it is quite a remarkable character. Would you or Geller know anything about him?"

Hoffman shook his head nervously, then slumped in a chair and took a deep breath. "Geller told me about the Taylors," he said, rubbing his eyes. "Just as he claimed in this letter you found, Dylan Taylor was Dieter Schneider and his brother Stephen was Stefan Schneider. Decades ago they were the leaders of a neo-Nazi organisation in Germany called Aryan Truth. They were being investigated for various hate crimes and also as the chief suspects in two murders. They left the country under their new names and Geller found them here in Yorkshire."

Quist nodded slowly. "Why was your friend looking for them?"

"Personal reasons, and he *isn't* my friend." Hoffman grimaced. "I've only known him a couple of weeks. He's been hoping to find them for thirty years and he has a contact in the Munich police. The person who forged the Schneider's passports and provided them with their new backgrounds was caught last month and Geller's insider found the three

155

Schneider identities on the forger's computer list. He passed them on to him."

"Couldn't Interpol use the new information to track them down?" asked Watson.

"It seems no one cared anymore," said Hoffman. "Aryan Truth collapsed after the Schneiders vanished. There was never any proof that they committed crimes, so the files on them were eventually destroyed. Germany was glad to see the back of them and, with the budget cutbacks, the Munich police and Interpol didn't bother searching for them. They were missing for three decades and their only offense would be travelling abroad under false documents."

"Just a moment." Quist narrowed his eyes. "Did you just say *three* identities?"

"Yes, Stefan Schneider brought his twelve-year-old son to England. His new identity was John Taylor, but Geller wasn't able to find him. He used the forger's information to track the Schneider brothers here and he contacted the Yorkshire police, but they were snowed under with *real work*, as they termed it, and they weren't interested in two old men in their seventies. Their computer checks showed the Taylor's documents and backgrounds were in order and there wasn't any evidence to back up Geller's wild claims. Then Geller saw the letters I'd written to the local papers about White Rose. He knew we had similar views about this racist party so he contacted me."

"Oh, of course." Quist closed his eyes and laughed quietly. "How could I be so stupid?"

Watson frowned. "What are you talking about, Guv?"

"Kurt." The detective turned to Hoffman. "Was Stefan's son Kurt Schneider?"

"Yes, that was his original name," said Hoffman. "How could you know that?"

"You mean the kid's picture we saw?" gasped Watson.

"Yes, we came across his school photograph yesterday and now I know why the child looked vaguely familiar. He grew up to be Dominic Churchill."

156

"What?" Watson laughed. "Are you serious?"

"Are you sure?" stammered Hoffman.

"I can't believe I didn't spot the likeness immediately," Quist nodded slowly. "Yes, he had black hair as a child, but it turned silver with age. As he grew older, John Taylor obviously found his own forger in Britain and changed his identity yet again."

"I know it's easy enough to buy fake documents such as identity cards to get into pubs underage," said Watson, astounded. "But is it really so easy to become a whole new person? To have a new past invented that would even fool the cops?"

"Absolutely," said Quist. "If you have enough money and know someone with the correct skill set, an entirely new background can be created both on paper and by hacking internet archives to alter the right records. A wealthy and powerful individual can have a more acceptable history created for the Russian mail order bride he's acquired. You've seen how your friend Gareth operates."

"True," said Watson.

"And, of course, the police won't have looked too closely at the Schneider computer records. I dare say they wouldn't stand up to an in-depth investigation by a technical expert." The detective smiled dourly. "Well, this Kurt Schneider revelation would certainly explain one or two things. I met Churchill earlier today and he told me he'd just received bad news – that must have been the news of his father Stefan's death. More to the point, it explains how he recognised the… er, *gift* I gave him and why his demeanour instantly changed from grateful to homicidal."

"You gave him the SS dagger?" asked Watson.

"I did. The tiny letters etched into the hilt were AW, and Aryan Truth in German would be Arische Wahrheit."

Watson grinned. "If this is true, the newspapers are going to love it."

"It's true alright," said Quist. "But we can't contact the media or the police without proof and I'm sure Churchill has done an excellent job of concealing his parentage and his dark past."

"By now the cops will have that picture of him as a kid," pointed out Watson. "Will they recognise him?"

"I didn't at the time," admitted Quist. "But I'm sure they could be gently nudged into examining it more closely, along with his manufactured background."

"This is all very interesting, Guv," pointed out Watson. "But none of it is helping Sara."

"Very true. The clock is ticking and we need to find her." Quist glanced again at the cabinet that concealed the safe. "*Return it now*. Are you certain they're not referring to this book that Geller gave you?"

"I'm certain," said Hoffman. "I genuinely don't know what they want."

"Very well," said the detective. "If you have no objections, I'd like to search Sara's bedroom for anything out of the ordinary and then there's a further avenue we need to explore – York fire station. Please try not to worry, Mister Hoffman. We'll find who took her."

"Her room is this way." Hoffman led them to the stairs and glanced through the window at the sky over York. "The afternoon is turning to twilight," he whispered.

"Meaning?" asked Quist, climbing the steps.

"I was talking to myself," said Hoffman. "The sun is setting."

* * * *

Chapter 27

A huge redbrick building, taking up the corner of Clifford Street and Cumberland Street, the York Dungeon had been the York Institute back in the early nineteenth century, teaching art, science and literature. Now it taught horror, along with the city's gruesome history and the darker side of humanity. The Dungeon was home to a multitude of gory displays and working examples of torture equipment, the linking corridors cleverly dressed to resemble dark medieval streets where concealed speakers broadcast recordings of screams, groans and evil whisperings.

Savannah momentarily glanced up from her phone, really hoping they *were* recordings.

Feeling the young girl shudder, Harvey McMurdo smirked and ran a comforting hand over her taut bottom, squeezing one of the cheeks for added reassurance. He much preferred thrashing female posteriors with a leather belt to petting them – and *seriously* thrashing a backside if the woman stepped out of line or answered back – but that kind of fun would have to wait until later tonight. His cruel smile widened, instantly changing to a pained grimace as the facial movement reactivated the ache in his bruised cheekbone.

McMurdo shook his head angrily. *Two beatings in two days and both courtesy of arseholes who didn't look as if they could fight a five-year-old, let alone a professional enforcer like himself.* Massaging his face, he dismissed the glum thoughts, knowing that a look around the York Dungeon followed by some hard sadistic sex would cheer him up.

There were several of these "chamber of horrors" attractions in cities like London and Edinburgh, and this one depicted the local and indigenous atrocities. The current room represented an ancient York street, with cobblestones underfoot, half-timbered Tudor houses looming above and a town gallows complete with a mouldering corpse. An exhibit on their left showed the mutilation of York gunpowder plotter Guy Fawkes, medieval racks held the broken bodies of other torture victims and large metal pots contained the boiled remains of religious zealots.

McMurdo had been right – this was the ideal fun place to impress his new girlfriend.

Resembling a superficial "glamour" model, Savannah wore ludicrously expensive jeans and a tight designer top to expose her spray-tanned midriff and accentuate her silicone breasts. Her perfume counter co-workers couldn't understand why she was sleeping with McMurdo, a thirty-year old thug who resembled a shaven Rottweiler in a leather jacket. Savannah wasn't the brightest of girls, however, and dating a violent "bad boy" was pretty cool in her shallow and somewhat limited imagination.

The couple moved into a further chamber where the struggling highwayman Dick Turpin was being strung up for his crimes and disfigured plague victims writhed in agony surrounded by rats. It was late in the afternoon and the York Dungeon would soon be closing. McMurdo and his girlfriend were two of the last few visitors and the emptiness of the place made it far more creepy.

"I don't like this," said Savannah, clutching her phone tighter for comfort. The screen illuminated her frightened pout in the darkness. "It's really scary."

Savannah never put the phone down, taping a clear plastic bag over her hand when showering and even staring at it in bed. Fortunately, McMurdo wasn't dating her for conversation and her addiction wasn't a problem. He'd found the best sexual position with her was doggy style; when he was on top in the missionary position, it was difficult for her to see the screen over his shoulder. Hopefully she'd never become pregnant as it would be virtually impossible to change nappies using one hand.

"Hey, look at this," said McMurdo, excitedly. He led her into a side chamber. "Oh, yes, these are the boys. This is brilliant."

"What the hell is it?" she asked, horrified.

A dimly lit waxwork filled the centre of the dark room and Savannah glanced timidly over her phone at the lifelike torture scene.

A half-naked man had been lashed face-down over a boulder and a trio of Norse warriors worked on his exposed vertebrae, tearing into his flesh with knives and a crude bone saw.

"The Blood Eagle," said McMurdo, proudly, almost as if he'd devised it himself. He read aloud from the illuminated information plaque. "Often described in the Norse sagas, this was the most feared and gruesome method of Viking execution. The prisoner's back was sliced open and the ribs cut away from the spine before being wrenched apart to resemble the blood-drenched wings of a soaring eagle. Caution was exercised to prevent the victim expiring too quickly. Wow! Can you imagine that?"

"Horrible," mumbled the girl. "That would really hurt."

"That's the idea," laughed McMurdo, continuing to read. "Salt was tossed into the exposed organs for maximum pain. Finally, both lungs were pulled out of the torso and spread over the broken ribs, a combination of trauma and suffocation concluding the agony and ending the victim's life. Yeah, right. I'm no doctor, but I can't see many folk surviving after that."

McMurdo didn't need the information panel. He knew all about the blood eagle and felt the authorities should be using it today, on terrorists, sex offenders and any immigrants who broke the law.

"This depicts the death of Aella," he said. "Aella was the King of Northumbria and the Vikings executed him after the Battle of York. The big guys supervising are Halfdan and his brother Ivar. Aella had killed their father Ragnar in a previous battle and this was their revenge." McMurdo smiled proudly. "Like I said, these were the boys – Vikings were the true Nordic Aryans and their blood was unpolluted by the mongrel races."

"I can't believe this happened," said Savannah, pouting. She permanently pouted, like a whistling cod, ever since paying a salon to inject something unpronounceable into her lips. "Surely the police would have made it illegal."

McMurdo stared at her, wondering if this was a joke. He saw that it wasn't. "Oh, it definitely happened," he said. "I'm into Viking

161

history and the famous Gotland picture stones from Sweden show a man being killed in exactly this way."

A Viking in full battle attire, cloak and helmet strode through the dark room and gave Savannah a fierce snarl, one of the many budding actors employed by the Dungeon to instruct and entertain the tourists. His bushy golden beard flowed over the upper half of a leather breastplate and his large axe looked formidable.

"Talk about perfect timing," said McMurdo. "I'm sure this guy will know all about it."

"Can I help you?" The burly warrior smiled warmly. "Hello there, young lady. I'm Erik Bloodaxe."

"Oh, my God!" Savannah's eyes lit up as she photographed him with her phone and sent it to Facebook. "Are you a real Viking?"

"I work here part-time," he laughed. "I'm the last Viking King of York, but that's only on Wednesdays. On other days I'm Guy Fawkes, or the highwayman Dick Turpin. My real name is Vince."

"Er, okay." Savannah looked confused. "So are you a real Viking or not?"

"No, I'm not." Winking, Vince passed her the axe. "It doesn't weigh much, does it? It appears genuine, but it's made of rubber. Don't go telling anyone, but I'm wearing a false beard and a wig too. The beard's made from real hair so it's a lot better than the ones Father Christmas uses in the shopping centres at..."

"But Father Christmas *is* real," said Savannah.

"The Blood Eagle," snapped McMurdo. *Thank God this girl was amazing in bed, because she could be fucking embarrassing to take out.* "It was a genuine method of execution back then, wasn't it? She finds the idea of this unbelievable."

"To be honest, no one is certain." Vince glanced around and saw that a stocky figure in a raincoat had entered the dark chamber and was standing right behind them. "Some experts accept the old stories as fact and some don't, but if such executions ever *did* take place, it was over a thousand years ago. All this frightening stuff you see here in the dungeon, these horrible things don't happen anymore."

"Harvey McMurdo?" said the man to their rear. "Which is Harvey McMurdo?"

"I'm McMurdo." He turned and squinted in the darkness to see the newcomer removing his coat. "Why? Who are you and what do you want?" He made out the features, or lack of them, on the muscular naked figure.

Naked? What the hell was this? The man was growing larger and the eyes... What was going on with the eyes?

An arm shot out, sweeping the Viking aside and slamming him into Savannah. Instinct joined with youthful reflexes and she gripped the phone tightly, protecting it with her body as a mother would protect a baby. The pair hit the wall hard and slid down into a stunned heap.

"What the..." gasped McMurdo, staring in horror at the glowing eyes. "What the fuck *are* you..."

The bulky figure grabbed his head, a hand on either side, then turned to gaze at the waxwork behind. Three seconds of deliberation passed before the struggling McMurdo was twisted around and shoved face-down on the fibreglass rock. Fingers, as hard as steel, tore through his jacket and crunched deeply into his back, grasping his ribs and wrenching them away from the spine. The last thing to go through his head were Vince the Viking's words.

These horrible things don't happen anymore.

* * * *

Chapter 28

Sara Hoffman slowly raised her head. Her mouth felt unnaturally dry and she was bemused to find she'd been sleeping upright on a leather office chair. Attempting to lift a hand and discovering she couldn't, she looked down dreamily and saw why – her arms were secured to the seat, her wrists fastened to the armrests with nylon cable ties. The enormity of what had happened hit home like a bucket of ice water and, jerking herself into full consciousness, Sara twisted frantically, pulling at the restraints and looking around with wild eyes.

She was alone, but where? How long had she been here?

From the appearance of the brick walls, the naked light bulb hanging above her and the smell of damp, this was probably a cellar. Churchill must have had her brought here and tied to this seat. *Was the man completely out of his mind?*

She remembered being dragged into the van in the pub car park and someone shoving a needle in her arm, but there was nothing after that. She'd been drugged and brought here, but why? *Why on earth would Churchill do this?*

The girl froze, her heart beating faster, as the door opened and three men walked in. One was short and stocky with spikey blonde hair. He looked to be late twenties and wore a smart grey suit with both hands stuffed in the pockets. His arrogant, strutting manner told Sara he was in charge of the two muscular characters behind him. From their size and the identical tan leather jackets, she guessed these were the masked men who had abducted her in the van. Their faces seemed vaguely familiar, but she couldn't place them.

"Who the fuck are you?" she snapped. Her anger concealed the fact that she was very scared, but she had no intention of showing it to Churchill's thugs. "And where am I? Is Churchill completely insane?"

The blonde-haired man looked puzzled. "Churchill? Who the hell is Churchill?" He turned to his large companions who both shrugged. "I'm Jake," he said. "Pleased to meet you, sweetheart. I won't shake hands as you look to be a little tied up at the moment."

This was hardly cutting edge comedy, but his gorillas chuckled sycophantically.

"This is kidnap," said Sara, trembling. "I can't believe White Rose would be so crazy as to..."

"White Rose? Churchill?" Jake shook his head. "What are you babbling about? You must have guessed why you're here."

"Huh?" Sara frowned. "You're saying you don't work for White Rose?"

"Stop pissing around. You know what we want."

"What is this? I have no idea what you're talking about."

"Oh, yes, you do."

Sara thought it was only girls who played this stupid game with their boyfriends. "I was injected with something," she stammered. "When these two dragged me into their van, someone stuck something in my arm."

Jake nodded. "Something to knock you out. We couldn't have you screaming and shouting all the way here."

"Where exactly is *here*?"

"It doesn't matter where we are." Jake sighed. "Look, we know it's you, sweetheart. When we discovered it had gone, a friend of ours hacked into your fire station computer and checked out all the people who work there. Their social media and credit card accounts were checked and guess what? You stuck out like a sore dick. You're the only one throwing money around."

"Throwing money..." Sara's head began to spin. "What are you talking about? What *is* this?"

"You really want me to spell it out?" laughed Jake. "You've just been to Ibiza, haven't you? Three days ago you bought a brand new car..."

"*What*?" shouted Sara. "The trip was a leaving party for someone at work and my grandfather bought me the car. Why in God's name am I tied up here answering questions?"

"You *aren't* answering them, are you?" Jake's smile became

165

darker. "But you will. I had Ben and Jerry here break into your house yesterday, but they didn't find anything."

One of the giants nodded. "Then again, we saw you had a safe. It's bolted to the brick wall and we weren't equipped to deal with it."

"Seriously?" said Sara. "You're telling me I was kidnapped by two guys called Ben and Jerry?"

"If you're a good girl, they'll make you an ice cream," said Jake. "I had them bring you here and text your grandfather from your phone telling him to return our property. If it's in the safe, he'll exchange it for you."

"There's nothing in the safe except a book." Sara felt more confused than ever and her heart hammered. "Is that it? Did that old book belong to you and you want it back?"

"Don't be stupid," said Jake. "Apart from the letters section in porn mags, I'm not much of a reader."

The door flew open and a man stormed in. Stocky, spikey blonde-haired and expensively dressed, he looked to be early thirties and was almost certainly Jake's older brother. A bald man in spectacles followed him.

"Tony…" Jake held up a hand. "Let me explain."

"I wanted her under surveillance," growled Tony. "Not brought here. Roylott tells me you sent these two to search her house."

"You were in London so I took charge," said Jake. "The lads have been watching her and it's been a waste of time. There's no sign of it in her house, but she has a safe and they couldn't open it. Believe me, my way will speed things up."

"Maybe it's time I gave you more authority." Calming down, Tony stared at the terrified girl. "Because you might be right for once. Roylott's pharmaceuticals could solve this problem." He turned to the middle-aged man behind him. "Go get your bag of tricks."

Roylott left and Sara squirmed, the cable ties cutting into her wrists. *Pharmaceuticals? What did he mean by that?* It was obvious these two were brothers and this older one was clearly in charge, but in charge of what? Tony was harder looking and more frightening than

Jake, but what the hell did they want from her and just what did they intend to do? She'd recently watched a box set of the *Hostel* horror films at work with the lads and gory torture scenes from the DVDs unhelpfully whizzed through her head.

"Ben and Jerry have been in York," said Tony. "I've had them watching you, but Jake is right. It hasn't helped us so…"

"So you kidnapped me," whimpered Sara, suddenly remembering where she'd seen them before. They'd driven past her outside the White Rose headquarters during the bomb hoax. The two men had appeared interested in her and now she knew why. "Listen, just let me go. I don't know who you are or where this is. If you blindfold me and drop me off somewhere…"

"You're going nowhere," laughed Tony. "Not until we have our property. You must have some idea of the money involved and you can see we're not fucking around, so just tell me where it is and you'll be released as soon as we get it back."

"I have no idea what you're talking about." The girl shook her head. "What do you want?"

Roylott returned with an attaché case. He placed it on the floor beside the chair, opened it, and Sara's eyes widened in horror to see the countless bottles of drugs and hypodermic needles.

"To be honest, you sound convincing," said Tony. "Maybe it *wasn't* you, but now we'll see. If you're lying, you'll soon tell us where you've hidden it."

"Hidden *what*?" croaked Sara. "Who *are* you people?"

"Some would torture you," said Jake. "But we're not that primitive. We have Roylott, our very own doctor."

Sara stared at the bald man squatting beside her chair. He sorted through his bottles of drugs and checked the syringes.

"An animal doctor," corrected Tony. "Roylott used to be a vet, but he was struck off, so we have him working for us instead. When his customers had their pets put to sleep, they'd pay to leave the bodies at his surgery for cremation afterwards. Naughty Roylott here used to sell the dead animals for vivisection. It helped to pay the gambling debts he owed us."

"Then he got greedy," added Jake. "The cops discovered he was lying to the owners, telling them that healthy animals were sick. He pretended to put them down and sold the live animals for experiments."

Roylott held up a syringe. "This is the sedative I administered in the van." He gave Sara a reassuring smile. "Don't worry, it's perfectly harmless."

She stared at the hypodermic, shaking uncontrollably and openly petrified.

"He has more than tranquilisers in his medical case," said Tony. "All kinds of weird truth drugs that will make you talk and…"

"Keep away from me with that shit," yelled Sara. "Stay away."

The terror finally took control. Screaming, thrashing and violently throwing her head from side to side, she lashed out at the vet with her foot, then screamed shriller as he jabbed the needle into her arm. Sara stared momentarily at the syringe, then slumped forward in the chair, motionless and silent.

"What the fu…" Tony gaped. "Roylott, what the fuck did you just do?"

"Er, yes, sorry." The vet grinned uneasily and showed him the empty syringe. "I'm really sorry. I was holding the tranquiliser and my instincts just kicked in. It's standard practise when a patient begins to panic, you see? You always sedate them and then…"

"Patient?" shouted Tony. "You're talking about a frightened Labrador. Is she okay?"

"Tell me you didn't kill her," said Jake.

Roylott quickly checked the girl with shaky hands. "No, it's okay," he spluttered. "Her pulse is slow, but steady. Breathing is slow, but regular." He ran a hand over Sara's short black hair and lifted an eyelid. "Her coat is shiny, her eyes are clear and her nose is cool. Yes, she's fine. I didn't put her down."

"You'd better *not* put her down, you stupid bastard." Tony seethed with anger. "I need you to give her one of those truth drugs. How long will she be out?"

"It's difficult to say." The vet shrugged. "You really need to weigh the patient first. I once sedated a spaniel without knowing its weight and it was out for hours. She's smaller than a Great Dane, but larger than…"

"You stay with her in the cellar," snapped Tony, storming out. "Let me know the moment she wakes. Do you understand?"

Roylott nodded nervously.

Jake followed his brother. "You call us when she's awake," he growled. "You do *not* take her for walkies."

* * * *

Chapter 29

The search of Sara's bedroom had proved fruitless, as had the swift examination of the rest of the house. There was nothing in Hoffman's home, obvious or secreted, that could have been the reason for the girl's abduction. The safe had remained locked, but Quist accepted the old man's assurance that the enigmatic book stored inside had nothing to do with his granddaughter's kidnapping. If it had been in any way relevant, he knew that Hoffman would have told them.

The detective drove over Skeldergate Bridge and turned onto Tower Street, glancing to his left at Clifford's Tower. The majority of York's historic buildings are illuminated after dark and a battery of floodlights gave the huge limestone fortress a golden glow. Circular and imposing, the tower stood over one-hundred feet high upon its conical defensive mound, one of the few surviving features of William the Conqueror's York Castle. Thinking about Hoffman, Quist grimaced sadly. Strikingly beautiful as it was, he found it impossible to forget the tower's terrible history. One of the worst anti-Semitic massacres of the middle ages took place in this building when York's entire Jewish community, some 150 people, were wiped out here in 1190.

"Sara's grandad," said Watson, ending his grim thoughts. "What makes you think he's hiding something?"

"Trust me, he *is*," said Quist. "One only had to read his body language. Didn't you see him when I asked about the book that Geller gave him? His mouth dried, changing his voice slightly, and he was very uneasy speaking about it. You must have noticed how he avoided mentioning the title?"

"Whatever." Watson grinned. "I have one or two books under my bed that I wouldn't want to talk about."

"Hoffman also knows more about these murders than he's disclosing. He's clearly very frightened of something."

"Maybe he was just frightened and upset about Sara. Who could blame him?"

"No, it's far more than that," said Quist. "Although one thing is certain – his reticence to speak has nothing to do with his granddaughter's abduction, or he'd have opened up to us. Just like that book in his safe. He claims it's unrelated to Sara's kidnapping and I believe him."

"Talking of fear," said Watson, "I keep thinking about that murder last night. You say the killer we saw was a supernatural creature of some sort? You know all about this kind of stuff, Guv. What do you reckon it was?"

"I don't know yet, but I *do* know the clay dust is relevant. The police discovered it at the Wisteria Lodge murder scene and the Grand Hotel. There's plenty of boulder clay in the cliffs of Robin Hood's Bay. They famously find fossils in it…"

"But it'll be in short supply in the Grand Hotel," said Watson. "Maybe the killer works with the stuff? Like one of those guys who makes vases and shit on a potter's wheel."

"Maybe," agreed Quist. "And when he goes out murdering people he doesn't bother to change out of his potter's smock or wash his hands."

The teenager pulled a sarcastic face. "Could it be another werewolf like you, but one who's into pottery?"

"Somewhat doubtful, but whatever it was, I spoke to Rex earlier. I've asked him to assist us."

"Lovely," drawled Watson. "Well, what could possibly go wrong with that dickhead on board?"

Quist gave one of his odd lopsided smiles and turned the car onto Kent Street. "Right now, however, Sara Hoffman's predicament takes precedence over supernatural creatures."

Watson peered down the side of the building as they drove slowly past the fire station frontage. "So you really don't believe Sara's kidnap has anything to do with White Rose?"

"No, I don't," said the detective. "Do you recall me reading to you from the Yorkshire Post yesterday morning? About the incident here at the station on Monday evening?"

"Yeah, one of the guys went outside and got knocked

unconscious by a taser."

"Correct. No one entered the building, but they later found that the padlock had been cut from the compound where the old scrap cars are stored for training exercises."

"What did they steal?"

"Nothing whatsoever."

Watson frowned. "So what does that have to do with…"

"Think about it." Quist pulled up and executed a three-point turn. "Someone phoned in a false alarm to clear the station of personnel – I checked. Two men arrived minutes later equipped with a Taser and bolt croppers to remove padlocks. These intruders were clearly looking for something specific in the vehicle compound, but perhaps they didn't find it. I'm wondering if this *something* could be the mysterious item mentioned in Adam Hoffman's text message."

"Something that someone believes Sara now has?" The teenager sighed. "That's a shit-load of *somethings* and *someones* and it's all a bit vague, isn't it?"

"Extremely vague," agreed Quist, driving steadily back to the fire station. "But hopefully not for much longer."

"If you're right and they were looking for something in the compound, why would they think Sara has whatever it is they're after?"

"I don't know. Perhaps she *does* have it." Glancing at the station security gate that led into the rear training yard, Quist shook his head. "This is no good," he murmured. "We're far too exposed on this brightly-lit street and there are cameras. I wonder what we'll find behind the station."

The detective turned out of Kent Street and left onto Fawcett Street, before turning left again into the quiet cul-de-sac of Escrick Street. A two-storey terrace of self-catering apartments ran along the left of the thoroughfare obscuring the station from view.

"Ah, what's this?" Quist spotted an archway through the building that led into a rear parking area. He slowed down to glance through and saw that this yard backed onto the fire station grounds. "Yes, this is ideal," he said.

172

Turning the car, he pulled up by the pavement near the dark arch and looked around. A school playground wall stood opposite and, for the moment, the street was empty of people and traffic.

"So what's the plan, Guv?" asked Watson. He realised Quist was quickly undressing. "Oh, right. *That's* the plan."

The youth had always felt the sharp temperature drop on the occasions he'd witnessed his employer's bizarre transformation – according to Quist, the supernatural change sucked ethereal energy from the surrounding atmosphere – but in an enclosed space like this, it felt as if he'd entered a deep freeze. His breath instantly clouded, his teeth began to chatter and he trembled uncontrollably. This was mostly due to the intense cold, but also due to the enormous black wolf appearing behind the steering wheel.

"Surely you're no longer alarmed by this?" asked Quist, his extending muzzle of razor fangs grinning reassuringly. "A big brave boy like you?"

"Not at all." The teenager gulped to see the glowing amber eyes. "I watch plenty of horror films and this shit is nothing compared to the CGI they have in them these days."

"Here we go." The shapeshift complete, Quist glanced up and down the empty cul-de-sac, switched off the car courtesy light and opened the door. "Stay here. I shouldn't be too long."

Leaving the car and creeping quietly through the archway on two legs, the werewolf crossed the small parking area watching out for CCTV. He leapt the wall into the fire station grounds and squat low in the shadows, sniffing the air and checking again for cameras and observers, before darting on all-fours to the high mesh fence that surrounded the training compound. Scrap vehicles were stored here before being pushed out into the centre of the yard to be worked upon with cutting tools. A brand new lock secured the gate, but rather than break it, Quist jumped over.

"Ah," murmured the wolf, gazing at the three cars parked inside. "How interesting."

Scrap was definitely the wrong description. A smart Range

173

Rover stood beside an Audi and a BMW, and from the registration plates, all were less than a year old.

Perhaps he'd been wrong in theorising that Sara Hoffman's abduction was connected to this break-in. Whoever cut the lock off the compound could have been hoping to steal one of these.

But no, of course that wasn't the case. Any respectable car thief, if indeed there was such a thing, would know this was impossible without the keys. The fire station yard was protected by an electronic security gate on Kent Street too. The intruders would have climbed this to reach the compound, but it prevented the cars from leaving.

The wolf circled the three cars in the darkness, its eyes glowing. *So why did they come here? What could they possibly have been searching for that would necessitate assaulting a firefighter with a Taser and, far worse, kidnapping someone?*

Frowning curiously, he eased open the door of the Range Rover, certain that the courtesy light wouldn't flash on. The batteries in all these vehicles would definitely have been removed for health and safety reasons. *Again, any car thief worth his salt would know that too.*

He quickly looked through the vehicle, sniffing and checking the empty glove compartment, beneath the seats and the boot space. Something in one of these cars had brought those intruders here, but they'd either taken it on Monday night or, more likely, discovered it was missing, hence the "give it back" text message. He didn't expect to find anything, but there could be some clue that would help.

He moved on to carefully examine the Audi, then turned finally to the BMW, his lupine senses picking up the scent of the owner's Cuban cigars as the door opened. The aroma still lingered and wasn't yet masked by the smell of upmarket leather and dashboard polish. Quist's furry brow furrowed suspiciously. There was something else here too, another vague scent on the very fringe of his senses.

The wolf moved around quickly, sniffing every surface, before realising the faint smell was emanating from the rear kerbside door. He snuffled at the panel and noticed the twin indentations. Two sharp objects had been jammed into it, damaging the material, and he peered closely. The material in question was a different shade of silver grey; *almost* the same as the other panels, but not identical.

"Hello," he murmured.

Sliding in his talons, he carefully prised it from the door. Two retaining clips were already snapped off, telling him this panel had been removed and replaced before. The scent was stronger inside the cavity and he felt around, his furry fingers searching behind the airbag assembly and the electrical motors for the window and locks. Whatever had caused the smell was gone, as he knew it would be.

The wolf smiled grimly. *This was beginning to make sense.*

He'd smelled this before and it was a scent that some people seemed to find exceedingly moreish. It was heroin.

* * * *

Chapter 30

Watson followed Quist to Granary Court on Saint Andrewgate and rang Lestrade's doorbell. "So what was it?" asked the youth. "Why won't you tell me what you found?"

"I didn't find anything," said the detective. "Nothing at all, but I now have a very good idea of what happened to Sara."

"And as I'm worried out of my friggin' mind, I'm sure you'd like to share this idea?"

"Just allow me to confirm a few things first." Quist gave Lestrade a lopsided smile as he opened the apartment door. "Ah, good evening, Gareth. I need you to check something on the internet."

"Oh, there's a surprise." Lestrade ushered them into the apartment. "I thought you'd called to see my Spider-man comic collection. I was just about to ring you – you asked me to keep an eye on the police website for updates in this murder investigation. There was another killing a short while ago at the York Dungeon; the cops are there right now. It was some guy called Harvey McMurdo and the SOCO analysis found traces of brown dust…"

"McMurdo?" said Watson. "That's the other scumbag from the Task Force who assaulted Sara."

"Indeed," said Quist. "A vile character. I met him today at the White Rose headquarters in his role as Churchill's paid enforcer."

"When you screwed up your undercover shit?"

"When I screwed up my undercover shit," confirmed Quist, deadpan. "So Sara's attackers are now both dead. That's interesting, isn't it?"

"They say someone with great strength Blood Eagled him." Lestrade shrugged. "Whatever the hell that might mean."

"*Blood Eagle* doesn't sound like fun," said Watson.

"No, it isn't fun." Quist's shocked expression suggested it was about as far from *fun* as you could possibly get. "It was an ancient and rather gruesome method of Viking execution."

"Oh, and that coarse brown dust at the crime scenes," said

Lestrade. "The forensic lab completed the analysis yesterday and it was dry clay."

"You could have told them that, Guv," said Watson. "You sniffed it and knew straight away."

"They're required to follow the correct procedures," pointed out Quist. "I very much doubt that sniffing it would constitute evidence in a British court."

Lestrade gave him a peculiar look.

"You're always fast, Gareth," said Quist, walking to the computer, "but we need you to excel yourself tonight. The life of a young lady could literally be at stake." He handed Lestrade a slip of paper with a registration number. "This BMW is currently being used by the fire service and I need to know everything about it. All about its *previous life*, so to speak."

"Leave it to me," said Lestrade, sitting at his keyboard and flexing his fingers. "If someone's in trouble, there's no charge for this one.

Quist paced slowly up and down as he waited.

"Sara mentioned this BMW," said Watson. "She says they train with cars all the time, cutting them up and releasing trapped people, but the old bangers they're sent have none of the new hazards. They complain that they don't get anything modern to work on…"

"And the authorities have finally listened?" said Quist, smiling. "They've now begun to provide them with more up-to-date cars, but from where? That's the question, and I'm fairly certain I know the answer. Perhaps you're aware of the *proceeds of crime* initiative? When the police prosecute felons they confiscate any goods, including vehicles, that were paid for by their criminal activities. They usually sell them, but recently they've begun giving some to various fire brigades for training purposes."

"Here we go," said Lestrade, typing. "Yes, the BMW *is* a proceeds of crime car. Until very recently it was owned by Trevor Brisson, a Leeds underworld figure."

"I thought as much," said the detective, stooping to look over his shoulder. "Do you have an address for him?"

"Yeah, and I'm sure you'll find him home if you call on him." Lestrade grinned. "He's in Armley Prison. The police swooped three months ago, arrested him for the sale and trafficking of drugs, and confiscated various expensive assets including the car. It says here that his son Tony Brisson now runs the family firm, along with his brother Jake. They own the Touchy-Feely Club on Chadwick Street in Leeds. It says Tony lives above there in an apartment."

"Chadwick Street?" said Quist. "Where's that?"

Lestrade brought up another window and found the club's gaudy website. "Ah, it's in the renovated dockland area near the Royal Armouries. They describe it as *upmarket lap dancing.*"

"Upmarket?" Watson raised his eyebrows. "Oh, right. The naked birds must wipe their bums properly before wriggling about on your knee."

"Why wasn't the club closed down when Trevor Brisson was imprisoned?" asked Quist.

"They couldn't touch it," said Lestrade. "According to this, it didn't belong to the father. It's in the eldest son's name."

"I see." The detective nodded. "Now could you possibly hack into the North Yorkshire Fire Service database?"

"Let's see." Lestrade shrugged. "If I can hack the police, I shouldn't imagine *their* site will be too hard."

Quist walked to the window as he waited, staring out at the floodlit Minster and tapping his fingers on the sill.

Watson joined him. "So come on," he whispered. "What *didn't* you find in the car?"

"Narcotics," murmured Quist. "A substantial quantity of heroin had been secreted in one of the door panels. It was recently removed, but I detected the scent."

"Ah." Watson nodded. "Yeah, I can see why the owners might send a text saying *return it.*"

"Here we go," said Lestrade, bringing up the website onscreen. "What do you need?"

"Personnel files for York," said Quist, returning to the computer and sitting beside him. "A list of everyone who currently works at the Kent Street station."

Watson stood behind, leaning over the two men and watching as his friend worked through the menus. He pointed to a photograph as the files appeared. "Hey, there's Sara."

"The bird you told me about?" Lestrade gave an approving whistle. "Nice going, Watty, but I'd say you're punching above your weight there."

"Excellent," said Quist. "Thanks to government cutbacks very few people work there; that will save time. Could you possibly cross check these names with the DVLA database to see if any of the firefighters at York own a BMW?"

Watson whispered into Quist's ear as Lestrade typed. "So you think these guys at the lap dancing club have Sara?"

"Underworld figures who deal in drugs?" The detective turned to him. "Considering the scent I picked up in the car, I'd say it was highly likely, wouldn't you?"

Ten minutes passed by and Lestrade gestured to the screen. "Yes, one of them has a BMW," he said. "Josh Patel. Oh, and here's a coincidence for you – it's the same model and year as the proceeds of crime car they're cutting up."

"I deduced as much," said Quist. He read Patel's personnel file and noted the address before jumping to his feet. "Come, Watson. We need to go."

* * * *

Quist drove along the side of York racecourse and turned off Tadcaster Road into Pulleyn Drive, entering a small estate of leafy streets, hedgerows and modern redbrick houses. He pulled up outside a semi-detached property and saw the car on the drive.

"Yeah, there it is," said Watson, climbing out and nodding to the sapphire blue BMW.

The detective glanced through the rear window, but already knew what he'd see. The kerbside door panel was almost the same

179

shade as the others, but not quite. Smiling tightly, he nodded and pressed the house doorbell.

An external light clicked on and Patel appeared in T shirt and jeans. "Hi, can I help you?" he asked, noticing Watson. "Hey, aren't you Waggy's friend? The private detective guy? I saw you with her at the King's Arms on Monday night."

"That's right," said the youth. "This is my boss and yes, he thinks you'll definitely be able to help."

"Good evening," said Quist. "I'll make this as brief as possible. You currently have a BMW in your fire station compound."

"Er, yeah." Stiffening slightly, Patel swallowed, but remained calm. "We're using it for training. What about it?"

"I discovered two sharp indentations in one of the door panels," said Quist. "But of course, it isn't the original panel. When the vehicle was delivered to your station and you saw that the interior trim was virtually identical to your own, you exchanged it. You swapped it for the damaged one in your own BMW."

"No, you're wrong." Patel glanced nervously over his shoulder. "Listen, I don't know what you think you…"

"Are you alone?" asked the detective.

"No, my wife is in. She's watching television and…"

"You had to exchange the panels," continued Quist. "I deduced those indentations were caused by stiletto heels." He gestured to the BMW on the drive. "Heels worn by a young lady who jammed them hard into the material during the throes of passionate…"

"Yes, yes, yes." Patel looked around again, panic in his eyes. "Keep your voice down, for God's sake."

"Your wife doesn't know?" asked Watson.

"Hey, ten out of fucking ten," whispered Patel, his voice a hiss. "Yeah, I can see why *you're* a detective."

"I really don't think you're in any position to be sarcastic," said Quist. "You found something behind the panel and I want it."

"Er…" Patel glanced at the garage. "I don't know what you mean."

"I mean you can give me the drugs right now and we'll never mention this again, or we can chat about swapping door panels with your wife. *Now*, Mister Patel. Someone is in grave danger because of your actions and we really don't have the time for this nonsense."

Gulping, the firefighter darted out to the garage, rolled up the door and vanished inside to a cupboard of tools. He rummaged around in the rear and returned with a tightly-wrapped package of white powder. "Listen," he stammered. "I'm no drug dealer or smackhead, okay? I found this hidden away in the door when I swapped the panels and I wasn't thinking straight. I just took it."

"Good Lord!" Quist weighed the package in his hand. "There must be two kilos here. I can't begin to imagine the street value."

"What on earth were you going to do with it?" asked Watson, amazed.

"I didn't think that far ahead." Patel grinned, nervously. "So that's it? No one needs to know about me screwing Kacey in the car?"

"That's it." Quist glanced over the man's shoulder and raised his voice. "So, if you aren't interested in God's wonderful teachings, we'll leave you be. Hopefully you'll see the light and change your mind. When you do, you'll find us in the Kingdom Hall of the Jehovah's Witnesses."

"What the fuck are you talking…" Patel looked aghast as they turned to leave, then felt the hair rise on the back of his neck. He realised his wife had come to the door and was standing three feet behind him, trembling with anger. "Yes, yes, thank you," he croaked. "Praise be to Jesus."

* * * *

Chapter 31

Springing to his feet at the sound of the doorbell, Hoffman raced to answer it hoping to find Sara. He groaned wretchedly to see Daniel Geller in his front porch. "Now isn't a good time," he muttered. "I'm not in the mood for this."

Ignoring him, Geller brushed past and held open the door. "I'm not alone," he said.

Hoffman's mouth fell open as a stocky figure in a lengthy raincoat walked in behind him. Bald and just over five feet in height, the young man looked to be in his early twenties and his reddish-brown skin suggested a Middle Eastern origin. Hoffman grimaced, knowing he'd originated much closer to home.

"Why have you brought him here?" hissed Hoffman, watching as the two visitors walked into the lounge. "What's going on?"

"Sit down, Tonga," said Geller, gesturing to an armchair.

The young man slowly lowered himself onto it and stared at the wall.

"*Tonga?*" Hoffman shook his head, astounded. "Good God, you've actually *named* it?"

"After a dog I once owned as a child." Geller nodded. "Tonga was the most faithful pet you could ever imagine and he'd do anything for me. Rather fitting, don't you think? He'll get a little clay dust on your upholstery, I'm afraid, but a vacuum cleaner will soon fix that." Smiling, he ran a hand over Tonga's smooth head and held up a brown palm. "He doesn't have pores, as you know, but he appears to exude the dust in much the same way we perspire. He often leaves small pieces of clay behind too."

"That isn't supposed to happen?" Hoffman touched the young man's cheek with a trembling hand and examined the dust on his fingers. "I haven't studied the science behind this fully, but it has to be connected to the energy flaw."

"Then the obvious remedy is to provide him with *more* energy." Geller patted Tonga's shoulder. "My partner in this crusade needs to be kept fully charged."

"*I* was your partner when we planned this project. I'm talking about the original plan, of course, not this killing."

"Plans change," said Geller. "You don't have the stomach for doing what's necessary, so I decided it would be best to leave you out of it. All you need do is remain silent and allow Tonga and I get on with it." Geller gestured to the seated figure. "I'm constantly learning about how he functions. Right now I probably know far more than you, but then again, Tonga lives with me, doesn't he?"

Hoffman nodded miserably. When they began the project, Geller had insisted upon keeping it at his apartment. It couldn't possibly remain here where Sara might see it, he'd said, but it was obvious now that his motive had been much darker.

"Tonga has rudimentary reasoning skills like an ape," said Geller. "A definite sense for self-preservation too and both are constantly improving. Last night he was pursued by someone and avoided them by hiding underwater. He actually walked along the bottom of a river towards where I waited in the car. He sensed where I was and he came to me."

"Incredible," whispered Hoffman.

"I haven't provided him with footwear. I allow him to walk barefoot because he'd only lose his shoes when he removed them to change. As I mentioned, fragments break off his feet when he walks in his larger form, but they grow back when he's like this." Geller regarded Hoffman curiously. "You appear upset, Adam. What's wrong?"

"Are you serious?" snapped Hoffman. "*Everything* is wrong. I understand you've killed Stefan Schneider."

"My *partner* and I called there last night." Geller nodded. "And then we killed Harvey McMurdo today."

"*What*?"

"Tonga is rather proficient at tracking down his targets. I give him the name and any relevant details and send him into wherever they are. He locates these people, usually by politely asking for them by name, then slips off his coat, changes and delivers justice."

"It isn't justice," muttered Hoffman. "It's murder."

"As I said, you don't have the stomach. We've just been to the York Dungeon; I followed Harvey McMurdo and his girlfriend there and Tonga broke in through the rear fire exit. Some of the Dungeon exhibits are quite lifelike, especially their current tableau depicting a Viking Blood Eagle." Geller regarded Hoffman closely. "Schneider and McMurdo are dead, but you're clearly more concerned with something else. I'll ask again, what's wrong?"

"Sara is in trouble," stammered Hoffman. "As if I didn't have enough to worry about with you killing people, someone has abducted my granddaughter and warned me not to inform the police. At first I thought it was the White Rose people, but Quist doesn't believe..."

"Who's Quist?"

"A private investigator that..." Hoffman's phone rang, startling him, and he fished it from his pocket with a shaky hand. "Mister Quist?" he gasped. "Have you found her? Please tell me you've found her."

"Well, speak of the devil," whispered Geller, grinning. "Put it on speaker."

Hoffman pressed the button.

"The Brisson family in Leeds," said Quist. "Have you or Sara ever had any connection with these people? Trevor Brisson, or his sons Tony and Jake?"

"I've never heard of them," said Hoffman. "Is that who took her? Do you know where she is?"

"Very probably. The Brissons are an underworld family who own a Leeds nightclub and I'm certain now that this abduction is drug-related. I realise it's an odd question, but have you or Sara ever visited the Touchy-Feely lap dancing club on Chadwick Street?"

"Of course not," said Hoffman. "Do you think she's there?"

"I intend to find out," said Quist. "The police wouldn't be able to obtain a warrant without proof and, if they start asking questions, the Brissons may panic and do something stupid. Churchill may not be the only one with informants in the police force. Don't worry, I'll check this out myself and as soon as Sara is safe, we'll report the Brissons to the authorities. Speaking of Churchill, we'll also destroy the White Rose Party by proving to them that he's Stefan Schneider's son."

"Thank you so much." Hoffman glanced warily at Geller. "Please ring me the moment you find out anything. Anything at all."

"I see," murmured Geller, watching as he pocketed the phone. "Were you going to tell me?"

"Daniel, this information has only just come to light. Of course I was going to…"

"Dominic Churchill is Kurt Schneider, Stefan Schneider's son?"

Hoffman nodded. "It would appear he changed his identity again at some point many years ago, but you don't have to kill him, Daniel. Yes, his people hurt Sara, but…"

"I'm not doing this because of Sara," snapped Geller. "I'm doing it because of his father. What the Schneiders did to my parents will be paid for in full."

"Revenge?"

"Surely *you* must have thought about revenge? I'm talking about that wagon driver who killed *your* son, Sara's father? Don't tell me you haven't thought about making him pay? Just imagine the warm satisfaction of sending Tonga to visit him."

"Daniel, please think about this." Hoffman looked at Tonga and swallowed. "The Schneider brothers are dead and so are the men who attacked Sara. The idea of taking their lives disgusts me, but they're dead now and we have to leave it there. I could learn to live with the secret and I'd never mention our involvement. There's no need to carry on with this."

Geller shook his head. "There's *every* need to continue this crusade, but not tonight. I believe your private detective friend said the address was the Touchy-Feely Club on Chadwick Street? Well, this is ideal, isn't it? Tonga needs life energy and these drug dealers can provide it."

"No," snapped Hoffman, his eyes wide. "Whatever you're

planning…"

"They've taken your granddaughter, Adam. I'll drive Tonga to Leeds and free her." Geller smiled thinly. "I'll be honest with you, Churchill being Stefan's son is just a bonus. As the leader of White Rose, I was going to kill him anyway, along with his deputies. When they're gone, there are plenty of other white supremacist groups and people who deserve a nocturnal visit from Tonga. Have you heard of the multi-millionaire Rupert Grant?"

Hoffman shook his head.

"I attended White Rose meetings to identify the ringleaders and saw him there. He was about to finance them, so I rang him this morning posing as a party member to arrange a meeting with Tonga. Luckily for Mister Grant, he's changed his mind and resigned from White Rose. For some reason, he now hates them. Fickle or not, his change of heart saved his life."

"Listen to yourself," gasped Hoffman. "You don't have the right to decide who lives and who dies. You can't set yourself up as judge, jury and executioner."

"I can and I have. Judgment Day has come for the Schneider family and White Rose." He glanced at Tonga and grinned. "Actually, let's call it *Judgment Clay*."

"You're enjoying this." Hoffman stared at the motionless figure in the chair. "I should never have allowed you to insert the scroll."

"But you *did*," said Geller. "Which fortunately means I'm the one in total control."

"We rushed into this." Hoffman rubbed his eyes wearily. "I explained how this constant requirement for ethereal life energy is a design flaw. It isn't supposed to be like that. Now that I've read more about this and translated the book correctly, I can render Tonga dormant and end this. I believe I've found the correct incantation to change him back."

"Well, we certainly wouldn't want to do that, would we?" Geller laughed quietly. "I think it would be much better if I looked after the book."

186

"No, it's secure in the safe. Anyway, you can't read it and you don't know how to use it."

"I don't want to use it," said Geller. "The point is, I don't want *you* to use it."

"But this is insane." Hoffman shook his head in desperation. "You can't keep it like this, constantly needing energy and having to kill."

"Why not? There's plenty of *fuel* out there. Like I said, when I've finished with White Rose there are many other organisations just like them. I'll take the book, Adam."

"No," said Hoffman, emphatically. "The book stays here."

"Very well." Geller turned to the silent figure in the chair. "Stand and follow me."

Tonga raised himself and walked to the door.

"Whatever you say, Adam." Geller stared at Hoffman for a moment before leaving. "If that's how it has to be."

* * * *

Chapter 32

Leeds has been the commercial heart of West Yorkshire for almost two centuries. Once nothing more than a farming settlement on the River Aire, the industrial revolution of the eighteen-hundreds brought numerous textile mills, the production of their fabrics transforming this unremarkable little market town into an affluent sprawling metropolis.

Just outside the city centre on the southern bank of the Aire is the old riverfront quarter and its docks. Annual winner for many decades of the *Yorkshire Shithole Award*, the area underwent a complete metamorphosis in the 1980s and swiftly became an upmarket district of chic restaurants, designer apartments, modern office buildings and deluxe hotels. The riverfront cake was well and truly iced when the prestigious Royal Armouries were moved from the Tower of London to a cutting-edge exhibition hall here. The enormous collection of weapons and armour had been crammed into underground storage rooms, like the treasures in Tutankhamun's tomb, but now for the first time, the British public was actually able to see them.

Quist drove by the Armouries along Chadwick Street and past the Touchy-Feely Club on the corner of Ash Street. The dockland thoroughfares were fairly quiet, but a line of cars were parked along the kerb and he found an empty space a hundred feet away from the two-storey building. From the look of the redbrick exterior, the nightclub had probably been a small factory in its previous incarnation.

Watson looked nervously over his shoulder. "So Leeds gangsters run that place and the chances are Sara is inside?"

"Chances?" Quist weighed the package of heroin in his hand. "This two kilos of narcotics says it's a certainty."

"I hope you're right. So what's the plan, Guv?"

"It's rather straightforward." The detective gazed at the club in his wing mirror. "I'm going in there to speak with the Brisson brothers. You'll remain in the car and I'll ring if I require you to bring the package. I very much doubt that will happen."

"What do you mean?" Watson gave him a puzzled glance. "I thought we were going to swap the heroin for Sara?"

"Actually, no. I'm going to retrieve your friend from these people without returning their drugs."

"Er, right." The teenager grinned uneasily. "I'm not too sure how drug dealers operate, but I don't think they'll see that as a good deal."

"I imagine not." Quist lit a cigarette and climbed from the car. "But believe me, I've no intention of allowing these criminals to distribute two kilos of lethal narcotics on the streets of Yorkshire. Besides, I've thought of a far more constructive use for it."

"Take care, Guv," said Watson. "Bring her back safe."

"That's the idea." Quist pulled on his leather overcoat and gave his assistant a reassuring smile. "Try not to worry."

The detective strolled along the pavement, watching as two nondescript cars drove by and covertly eyeing the nightclub and its security cameras. Pausing to draw on his cigarette, he quickly calculated the size of this corner building before walking down Ash Street to check the narrow alleyway with its row of dumpsters at the rear. The half-moon and starlight provided very little illumination here and, unlike the frontage on Chadwick Street, there was no CCTV. Quist noted the number of windows and rear doors, which ones were fitted with security mesh, and how they were positioned in relation to the metal fire escape. If he needed to get out quickly with the girl, he now had some idea of how to accomplish this.

Returning to Chadwick Street, he smiled grimly. Because when dealing with drug dealers who kidnapped young women, it was fairly certain that he *would* need to get out quickly.

Three steps led up to the front door, where the words *Touchy* and *Feely* flashed alternately on a red neon sign above the lintel. The bass rhythm of a pop song thumped in the dark corridor behind two large characters in tuxedos, gentlemen who clearly spent a great deal of time in gymnasiums and who didn't look particularly opposed to violence.

"Good evening," said Quist, disposing of his cigarette. "Agreeable weather for the end of October, don't you think?"

"Evening, Sir." One of the bouncers waved him in, exposing a set of broken teeth in a slightly intimidating smile. "Enjoy yourself."

"Yeah," grinned his partner. "I know what this place is called, but don't go touching or feeling anything you haven't paid for. That's a bit of advice well worth remembering."

Quist handed the admission fee to a Thai girl behind a desk and walked down the passage. The throbbing musical beat grew louder, almost masking the sound of sexual grunting in the toilets, as he arrived at the dimly lit club interior. He paused in the shadows by the swing door, looking around the main room for any sign of the management and wrinkling his large nose at the scent of masculine perspiration.

Groups of smirking businessmen and single males of varying ages mingled with scantily dressed cocktail waitresses. Some customers drank at the bar, flirting with the staff, but the majority stared at a waist-high stage where two bored-looking Albanians in thongs gyrated around chrome poles to the old Kylie Minogue song: *Can't Get You Out of my Head*. Quist peered curiously, his enhanced lupine gaze running over their young bodies. Their naked breasts were solid hemispheres that appeared to have been inflated with a tyre pump. Something bizarre had been injected into their lips too, leaving their mouths resembling the swollen red posteriors seen on baboons.

The detective shook his head. He'd never understood why any sane and healthy person would pay a surgeon to carve open their torso and stuff bags of silicon inside, but however blatantly false and ridiculous the result might be, these customers clearly found it attractive.

A hard-faced young blonde in satin underwear spotted the new arrival and darted across from the bar. She looked Quist up and down for signs of wealth and, more to the point, signs of an eagerness to give it away – perhaps a wristwatch costing over £1000, clothes with expensive labels stitched into them, or the right kind of overpriced footwear. This punter wore a leather overcoat; it wasn't the first time she'd seen lengthy raincoats in this *adult* club.

"Hi there, I'm Tori." She gave Quist a smile that would have made an alien autopsy photograph appear genuine. "Ooh, I took one look at you and I just knew that you'd like a sexy private dance."

"Actually no," he said, noticing that she too had a fondness for cosmetic surgery. "I'm afraid your perceptive skills have failed you, Tori. What I'd *really* like is to meet the Brisson brothers. Are they here this evening?"

"Yeah, but they're usually busy." Tori shrugged. "They probably won't see you without an appointment."

"I have something far more pertinent than an appointment: a large package of heroin that belongs to them. Be a good girl, Tori, and let them know, would you?"

The girl's false smile became even more rigid, as if her teeth were glued together, and she hurried across the club as Quist headed to the bar.

"A whisky, please," said Quist, eventually catching the eye of a young woman. "A large single malt."

"That's on the house," announced a voice behind him.

The detective turned to find two stocky men in expensive suits. From their sharp features and identical spikey blonde hair, they were clearly brothers. The huge men looming behind them could also have been related; not to each other, but to a troop of gorillas. Much larger than the bouncers on the front door, the minders moved to take up intimidating positions to the rear of Quist.

"Don't let Ben and Jerry scare you," said Tony Brisson. "They're big lads, but they're really sweet, unless I tell them not to be."

"Oh?" Quist glanced over his shoulder. "You're called Ben and Jerry?"

"Yeah," snarled one. "You got a problem with that?"

"Not at all." The detective took his whisky from the barmaid and sipped it. "Thank you for the drink. That's most kind of you."

"I'm Tony," said the older of the brothers. "This is Jake, and we own this place, as you probably know. We also own something else which Tori tells me you have?"

Quist nodded. "If this *something else* is around two kilos of pure heroin, then yes, that would be correct."

"Ah, Christmas has come early." Jake grinned at his brother. "So where is it?"

"Well, obviously I didn't bring it in," said Quist. "Your package is perfectly safe with an associate of mine nearby. I believe you have something here that *doesn't* belong to you – a young lady named Sara. I'd like to see her and then we can discuss the return of your property."

"Yeah, *our* property," said Tony. "Dad was taking that package to Manchester in the BMW. It was stashed in the door when the cops arrested him and took the car. We couldn't get it back from the police vehicle compound, but luckily for us they sent it to York as a proceeds of crime car."

"*Our* property," repeated Jake. "But your friend found it first, didn't she? The stupid bitch should have left it where it was. She must have guessed the value and known the owners would come looking for it."

"Sara didn't take it," said Quist. "I'm afraid you kidnapped the wrong person, which is probably why she won't have been able to answer your questions as to its whereabouts."

"Is that so?" Tony smirked. "Well, I'm sorry that she had to go through this unpleasantness for nothing, but not to worry. We now know its whereabouts – *you* have it." He gestured to the minders. "Search him."

Quist glanced at the nearby clientele as Ben and Jerry went through his pockets and roughly patted him down.

"The punters won't help you," said Jake. "This isn't the first time they've seen our boys search a troublesome customer. Besides, they're more interested in tits and ass than you."

"Give it here." Tony held out a hand and took the offered phone and wallet. Opening the latter, he raised an eyebrow. "Bernard Quist? Oh, you're a private investigator?"

"Consultant detective," he said. "I'm helping Sara Hoffman's grandfather with this matter. Hopefully we can have a smooth exchange. The young lady for your narcotics."

"Yeah, hopefully." Tony laughed. "Okay, lads, bring him downstairs."

Quist was marched through a door off the main club area, through the rear of the establishment and down a staircase into the cellars. Jake led the way along a passage to a large room filled with beer barrels where a middle-aged man sat playing games on his phone. Bald and bespectacled, he jumped to his feet as the brothers approached.

"What's going on?" he asked, nervously. "Who's this?"

"He's here to take our guest home." Tony glared at him. "Is she awake yet?"

"Er, not quite…"

"So that's a *no*, is it? For fuck's sake, Roylott. How much did you give her?"

"I'm sorry." The vet cringed. "I usually weigh my patients and work out the dosage, but it was an accident and..."

Quist glanced around as they angrily spoke, noticing the stone steps at the end of the room which led up to a door. From the robust appearance, the metal lining and security bolts, it was almost certainly an external exit. Working out his position in the building from his earlier reconnaissance, it would open into the alleyway he'd seen at the rear of the club. *This could be the perfect way to get out of here.*

"Unbelievable," snarled Tony, shaking his head angrily. He took out a set of keys and unlocked a storeroom. "Here we go."

The underground chamber was twelve feet square, a single bulb lit the brick walls and the concrete floor sloped gently to a drainage grate in the centre. Quist was more interested in the young woman slumped on a chair by the wall.

"What's wrong with her?" he asked, suspiciously.

"She's been sedated by our *expert* medical practitioner here," said Jake, with more than a hint of sarcasm. "Check her. You'll see she's fine."

The detective walked forward, noting the nylon cable ties securing the girl's wrists and ankles before raising her limp head. He recognised her from the picture on Adam Hoffman's mantelpiece and turned to see that Ben and Jerry were now holding small automatic pistols. This rescue might not be as easy as he thought. Bullets wouldn't harm him, but they wouldn't do Sara any favours if these two began firing.

"What did you administer?" asked Quist, checking her carotid pulse and lifting an eyelid.

"Er, it's a form of Acepromazine," said Roylott. "It won't harm her."

"A veterinary tranquiliser?" The detective shook his head. "People like you amaze me."

"Yeah, right." Tony held up Quist's phone. "Here's how this will work – you'll tell me the code to unlock this and you'll tell me the number of the friend who's holding my property. I'll ring them and put the phone on speaker. You'll reassure them that you've seen the girl and you'll tell them to bring my package here right now. They'll ask for Tori upstairs and give it to her. She'll bring it down to me. Could that be any simpler?"

"And you'll let Sara go and no one will be hurt?" asked Quist, smiling.

"That's right," said Jake.

"You have our word, but any problems and Ben here will shoot you in the leg." Tony wiggled the phone. "The code and the number, now."

Nodding slowly, the detective ran a hand through his hair. If he could get Ben and Jerry to put away their guns and attack him, he could overpower them, stun the Brisson brothers and carry Sara out. "Ah, your word," said Quist. "Yes, well that's the problem, isn't it? Drug dealers aren't the most trustworthy of individuals and I'm not so sure you'll let us go."

"He has a point," said Jake, grinning.

"Shut up," snarled Tony.

"I mean, I can identify you and I've seen what you've done here," continued Quist. "That heroin must have a colossal street value and you have a serious kidnapping charge sitting right here in this chair. I just don't know if I can trust you."

"You don't have much choice," said Tony. "Now give me the pass code to this phone."

"I'll have to give this some thought."

"Not a problem," said Jake. "Our friends here will help you think." He turned to Ben and Jerry, but didn't get chance to issue any orders as a loud thumping sounded on the outer door at the top of the steps. "What's this?" he snapped. "Who did you bring here?"

"Nothing to do with me," said Quist, shrugging. "Perhaps it's the Jehovah's Witnesses."

"Well, let's find out, shall we?" Tony slammed the door and locked it, leaving the detective in the storeroom with Sara.

The pulsing music still sounded from the club upstairs, but Quist's lupine hearing picked up the muffled footsteps on stone as the five men moved across the cellar to check on whoever was knocking. He looked around the small room for a way out, but the sturdy door was the only exit and, forcing his fingers into the jamb, he realised he didn't have the strength to pry it open. Not in human form.

"Damn," he whispered.

Sara was unconscious and wouldn't see anything if he shapeshifted, but the Brisson brothers would be returning at any moment. Taking the opportunity to snap the girl's bonds and lay her limp body on the concrete floor, he glanced up at the dangling light bulb, an idea quickly forming.

"What the hell…" Quist froze as male screams and gunshots sounded. *What could be happening out there? He had to do this fast and pray that it worked.*

Removing the bulb and plunging the room into darkness, the detective soaked two fingers with saliva and stuck them into the live socket, grunting as his hand sizzled and intense pain crackled through his arm. The shock flung him backwards into the wall, but the tell-tale bang outside told him the fuse for the lighting circuit had just blown. The entire cellar should now be pitch black, but it had done nothing to stop the mayhem; loud crunching and terrified squeals of agony still sounded.

Dizzy from the electrical surge, Quist shrugged off the overcoat, kicked off his shoes and removed his signet ring before dropping onto all fours and transforming. "I don't believe this," he growled, his furry frame bursting from his shirt and trousers. "Two outfits ruined in two days."

Standing upright, the werewolf jammed talons deep into the door crack, wrenched it inwards and peered out into the darkness with glowing eyes. The exit to the rear alleyway stood wide open, allowing dim moonlight to filter in. A stocky figure darted up the steps and through it. Quist briefly wondered if it was Tony or Jake and then saw this wasn't so. The illumination was negligible, but enough for his enhanced night vision to pick out the brothers, the minders and the other man who had drugged Sara. All five were dead, their broken bodies and torn limbs scattered in an expanding puddle of glistening black.

"Ah," said the wolf, spotting the discarded raincoat beside the corpses. This told him all he needed to know.

Dropping onto all fours and bounding into the cellar, the wolf sprang across the pool of blood and raced up the steps. The alleyway was empty, but this didn't come as a surprise; Quist had seen this character run before and he wasn't exactly slow.

He paused, sniffing the night air and eyeing the row of dumpsters that lined the narrow passage. *Then again, could he be hiding inside or behind one of these?*

His pointed ears twitched as a car engine burst into life on Ash Street and he ran towards the sound of the vehicle accelerating away. Fortunately, he didn't need to catch up with it. All he required was a glimpse of the registration number for Gareth Lestrade.

The wolf arrived at the road in time to see a grey Ford saloon turn at the junction with Chadwick Street, but the angle concealed the plate. Cursing quietly, Quist remained in the shadows of the alley, knowing he couldn't pursue it. He'd be filmed by the club security cameras and the bouncers on the front entrance would see him. Plus, it would mean leaving Sara unattended and getting her away from this place was the priority. The loud thumping music in the club would have prevented anyone upstairs hearing the gunshots and screams, but an employee could go looking for the Brissons at any moment. He had to get back there quickly.

Returning to the grisly carnage, the wolf stooped over Tony's corpse to sniff and examine the horrific wounds, before retrieving his wallet and phone from the jacket pocket. He found another mobile and, switching it on, saw the screen picture of firefighters in Ibiza. This clearly belonged to Sara and, from the look of him, Brisson would have no further use for it. Stepping backwards to view the entire scene, Quist's paw crunched on something and, glancing down, he saw it was a piece of dry clay.

Smiling knowingly, he headed into the storeroom to quickly shapeshift back into human form and pull on his overcoat and shoes.

"The same killer," he mumbled to himself, stuffing his torn clothing into the coat pockets. "First the Schneiders and Churchill's thugs and now *these* people?" He scooped up the unconscious girl and carried her to the cellar door. "There only appears to be *one* connection."

* * * *

Chapter 33

Carrying Sara into her room, Quist laid the insensible girl on the bed, carefully positioning her on her right side. He stepped away and watched as Adam Hoffman covered her with a duvet and kissed her forehead.

"Is she okay?" whispered Watson.

"As well as can be expected," said the detective. "Her heart rate and breathing are both normal and she hasn't been harmed as such. I've placed her in the recognised medical recovery position. If she vomited whilst lying on her back, she could easily inhale the regurgitated matter into her windpipe and asphyxiate."

"You silver-tongued old devil." The youth grinned. "You have a way with the romantic talk, don't you?"

"All we can do now is leave her to sleep off the tranquiliser." Quist turned to Hoffman and handed him Sara's phone. "Are you sure you don't want me to take her to the hospital?"

"No." Hoffman shook his head. "They'd only keep her under observation until she wakes and I can do that here myself. I've been terrified these past few hours and, now that I have Sara back, I don't want to let her out of my sight."

Quist and Watson followed him downstairs to the lounge where the old man embraced the detective and squeezed tightly.

"I honestly don't know how to thank you," he said, weeping. He stepped back, frowning slightly to see the man's naked legs beneath his overcoat. "You found Sara for me and saved her. You got her away from those criminals…"

"Those criminals who abducted your granddaughter are dead," said Quist. "Five of them were murdered, Adam, and you could thank me by telling us the truth now."

"Five dead?" Hoffman's eyes widened. "What happened?"

"I didn't see who did it; not clearly, at any rate. From the horrific way they died, however, it was the same powerful individual who dispatched the Schneider brothers and Lee Millican."

"He left a raincoat behind too," said Watson. "With this guy, that's a kind of calling card. Like a crappy version of Zorro scratching his big Z on the wall."

"Did you know that Harvey McMurdo was also murdered earlier tonight?" asked Quist.

"McMurdo? Yes, I heard that…" stammered Hoffman. "I don't know where. Er, the radio, I think…"

"What was it, Adam?" sighed Quist. "What killed them?"

"How should I know who it was?"

"Not *who*. I asked what *it* was." The detective held up a small piece of clay. "I found this by the bodies in Leeds. The killer dropped it." He produced another. "Here's an identical piece that we discovered at Stefan Schneider's house."

Gulping, Hoffman shook his head, his face white.

"I'm asking you because of the obvious connection," said Quist. "There were similar traces of clay on Dieter Schneider's body in Robin Hood's Bay. Clay dust was found on Lee Millican and Harvey McMurdo too. Why do you suppose clay is found at every murder scene, Adam?"

"I don't know."

Quist took a deep breath. "Whoever, or rather *whatever* was responsible for the Schneider brothers also killed the two men who attacked your granddaughter. Now that same individual has murdered a group of drug dealers. The first killings were all linked to White Rose, but not tonight's massacre in Leeds. No, the only real connection between all of these deaths is Sara."

Hoffman stared at the carpet.

"Yeah," said Watson. "The thing is, you were the only person who knew we were going to Leeds."

"You clearly know something," said Quist. "To be truthful, I'd say you know a hell of a lot. I have no idea what it is you're hiding, or why you're so frightened, but you really need to tell us."

"I can't…" he mumbled. "I can't help you."

"I see." Quist nodded, irately. "You obviously realise that you can't contact the police and tell them about Sara's abduction or my rescue. No one is aware that the Brissons were holding her in Leeds and I can't be involved with these murders. I can't possibly explain what happened in that basement without mentioning what I know about the killer, the supernatural creature known as Tonga."

Hoffman noticeably shuddered at the name and, for a moment, the detective thought he was about to faint.

"Do you or Daniel Geller know this creature named Tonga?" asked Quist.

"I've told you I can't help you," croaked Hoffman, trembling.

"Then perhaps this Mister Geller can help us," said the detective. "Do you have his address?"

"I don't want to talk anymore." Hoffman shook his head emphatically. "I can't thank you enough and I'm in your debt, but right now I need you to leave so I can sit with Sara and watch her. I have to make sure she's alright after that tranquiliser drug."

"Of course," said Quist. "That's perfectly understandable and we'll leave you to attend her." He turned to go. "But, Adam, this isn't finished. You know far more than you're telling us and our conversation concerning these matters is *far* from finished."

* * * *

Chapter 34

Quist drove steadily along Beckfield Lane in the York suburb of Acomb. Deep in thought, his fingers tapped rhythmically on the steering wheel. "Tell me," he said, breaking the silence, "what did you deduce from Adam Hoffman's demeanour and attitude back there?"

"It's hard to say." Watson shrugged. "I mean, he was out of his mind with worry over Sara being grabbed by those nutters in Leeds…"

"But now he has her safely back home."

"Yeah, but he's still really upset…"

"He wasn't upset just then; he was frightened by my questions. Hoffman is clearly terrified of something and he's concealing a huge amount. He knows a great deal about these murders and I feel certain he also knows who or what is responsible. He almost passed out when I mentioned the name of the police suspect, *Tonga*. The fact that he's stubbornly withholding the information from us can only mean one of two things. Firstly, he could be protecting someone…"

"Well, he definitely isn't protecting this Geller guy," said Watson. "He claims he isn't a friend and, from the way he talks about him, he doesn't like the bloke one bit. I'm also certain that Sara isn't involved in this stuff. I've been speaking to her and she knows absolutely nothing about what's going on, so he isn't protecting her either."

"I agree," said Quist. "Which leaves the second option – Adam Hoffman is directly involved in this horrific business."

"Hey, careful what you say about him, Guv." The teenager grinned. "You could be talking about my future father-in-law. Er, better make that my *grandad-in-law*."

Quist shot him a cynical look. "He's far more likely to be the future gentleman who says: *When are you going to take the hints and stop pestering my granddaughter?*"

Watson laughed. "Yeah, yeah, whatever."

"We have one further task tonight." The detective checked his watch and turned the car into the notorious Grimpen housing estate.

"Unfortunately, it will be after midnight and I have things to prepare. I'll drop you at home to eat and get a few hours rest and I'll pick you up again at half past one."

"No problem, Guv. Where are we heading?"

"Birlstone House," said Quist, smiling tightly. "The Holgate headquarters of our favourite political party."

The detective drove along Grimpen's main thoroughfare, weaving around the abandoned supermarket shopping trolleys and broken bottles. Sensing what was in the car, the small packs of half-feral dogs growled in fear and scattered as it approached. Quist looked around the streets and shook his head gloomily, dismayed that such places could still exist in one of the world's wealthiest countries with such a high proportion of billionaires.

Graffiti-plastered steel shutters covered some of the windows beneath the ubiquitous satellite dishes, and many overgrown gardens sported knackered fridges, cookers and old piss-stained mattresses. Quist could only assume the residents viewed these as fashionable horticultural alternatives to shrubs and flower borders. Broken trampolines were also much in evidence, presumably left in the gardens for the barking attack dogs to shelter beneath during bad weather. He noticed how many people had already fixed up their Christmas decorations on the rooftops and house frontages. He then realised this wasn't the case; they'd been there for years as no one could be bothered to take them down.

The detective smiled dourly. Successive Tory governments and their smug "couldn't give a shit" attitude to unemployment and the harsh difficulties surrounding the lower end of the social strata ensured that the Grimpen estate was definitely no Mayfair.

Quist turned into one of the better crescents and pulled up outside Watson's home. The house was remarkably smart for this particular area and, peering over the low wall, he saw the small figurines dotted about the neat garden.

"I see your mother is still in the garden gnome business," he said, raising his eyebrows.

"Yeah." The teenager grimaced. He'd always found them embarrassing. "She sells them through her mail order websites, but as you know, she uses our garden as extra advertising."

"Yes, they're a little different from the customary little chaps who sit on toadstools with fishing rods."

"You could say that," agreed Watson, cringing. "The thing is, I have to live here."

Quist wasn't wrong. Klansman gnomes in robes and pointed hoods gathered around a cross on the grass. Some gnomes sat with rolled-up sleeves injecting smack into their arms, suicidal gnomes in nooses dangled from a horizontal branch with toppled stools beneath their feet, and black-garbed SAS gnomes in balaclavas abseiled from the gutter. An escaped prisoner gnome with an arrowed tunic and spade emerged from a pile of earth and, next to it, a gnome was enjoying unnatural sex with a slutty-looking squirrel.

"Amazing," muttered Quist, taking out his phone and lighting a cigarette. "But returning to more pertinent matters, this man Geller intrigues me and I really want to speak with him. Let's see if we can obtain he address."

Dropping the window to let out the smoke, Watson watched as he rang Lestrade.

"Good evening, Gareth," said Quist. "I'd like to thank you for the information earlier; you'll be pleased to know that the young lady I mentioned is now safe because of your help. Now I wonder if you could find me the Yorkshire address for a German gentleman named Daniel Geller. He entered the country a few weeks ago and he'll either be staying in a hotel or renting a property here. I won't need the information until the morning so there's no rush. Needless to say, you'll receive the usual remuneration for your outstanding work."

"How about Rex?" asked Watson. "Didn't you say you were getting him to help us?"

"I did indeed." Sighing, Quist keyed in a new number and drew on his cigarette. "Ah, Rex. Sorry I was unable to speak earlier, but I was quite busy. Doubtless you'll be surprised to learn that someone has targeted the White Rose Party and they're using a supernatural weapon to murder individuals who..."

Watson grinned as his employer winced and held the phone away from his ear. He heard the yelp of excitement and the enthusiastic chattering.

"Yes," sighed Quist. "Supernatural murders. It would appear Watson and I are going to need your assistance with this, so why don't you pop over to the office first thing tomorrow and we'll do our best to track down the perpetrator? Er, quite, it does sound *totally fucking awesome*, doesn't it? Goodnight and I'll see you in the morning."

"Whoo, he sounds eager," laughed Watson.

"Mmh, that's something of an understatement," murmured Quist, thumbing off the phone. "Unfortunately, I'm afraid we'll need him."

"By the way..." Watson climbed out of the car and frowned. "You say we're going to the White Rose headquarters later tonight?"

"That's correct."

"Er, won't it be closed?"

"As we'll be visiting at two in the morning, that's pretty much a certainty." Quist gave one of his lopsided smiles. "I ought to mention that I'm not exactly proud of what we'll be doing."

* * * *

Chapter 35

The A1036 into York changes names several times along its route to Micklegate Bar – Tadcaster Road, the Mount, Blossom Street – and just past the racecourse it becomes Mount Vale. Set back from the main road traffic on a grassy rise, several huge residences stand in spacious private grounds with mature trees. Many have been converted into upmarket apartments and Geller had rented one on the ground floor of Pelham House, an elegant Georgian building of white-painted walls and enormous sash windows.

Churchill's Task Force of four musclebound thugs had been reduced to two, and the remaining pair sat in a car on the dark gravel parking area behind the house. Pete Ryder and Brad Kipling had yet to hear about Harvey McMurdo's death in the York Dungeon. Both men shared their late colleague's passion for Norse history and violence, along with his views concerning "pure" Aryan blood. Had they known he'd died in a Blood Eagle execution, they were stupid enough to assume this was how McMurdo would have wanted to go.

"Here he is," murmured Kipling, as a grey saloon turned into the drive. Churchill's informant in the police had checked the York rental records and this was Daniel Geller's car. "Time for some fun."

Headlights washed over their vehicle as Geller drove past and parked by the rear entrance.

"Two fuckin' hours we've been here," seethed Ryder. "It's about time."

They watched the man jump from the driver's seat and open the rear door to allow a stocky figure in a raincoat to slowly clamber out.

"The Jew's supposed to live here alone," said Kipling. "He has company."

"Unlucky for them," grinned Ryder.

They waited until Geller had unlocked the communal door to Pelham House and ushered in the younger man before quietly approaching.

"Daniel Geller?" growled Ryder, preventing the door from

closing with a brawny arm. He pushed his way through into a smart entrance hall with two apartment doors leading off and a staircase to the flats above.

"Hello there," said Kipling, following him in. "We've been waiting out there for you."

"Have you really?" Geller looked the two large men up and down. "You should have let me know you were calling. Tonga and I have just returned from Leeds."

Ryder bristled with anger, fighting his inner turmoil. *The Jew had a foreign accent and he hated foreigners, especially Jewish and black foreigners.* The problem was, this was a German accent and he admired the Nazis. It was a quandary.

"You're a hard man to find," said Ryder, watching as Geller unlocked the apartment door and waved his young bald friend inside. "Fortunately we have people in the right places who can find the information we need. You flew here from Germany three weeks ago and you rented this place fully furnished."

"That's right." He gestured for them both to enter. "Please, come in."

Ryder shot his Task Force colleague a puzzled look. *Hadn't this old fool picked up on the menacing atmosphere? How stupid could he be?*

He swaggered in behind Kipling and glared at the younger man in the raincoat. His skin was dark, but he didn't look Asian. *Maybe he was Egyptian or something? It didn't matter – his brown complexion had earned him a fucking good kicking.* Ryder had been overpowered earlier by that big-nosed guy in the Birlstone House cellar. The previous evening he'd taken a hard beating at Sedgefield Grange. Both episodes had left him fuming with hatred and ready to seriously damage someone. Anyone.

"Sit down," said Geller to Tonga.

The man silently obeyed, lowering himself onto a chair.

Ryder frowned to see his bare legs and feet. *Jesus, was this young guy completely naked beneath the coat? Was Geller some Jewish pervert who picked up rent boys? If so, this would feel like the best birthday ever.* He always carried a knife and knew exactly what to do with those sort of freaks.

The apartment was spacious and chic, with high ceilings, a marble tiled floor and several Indian rugs laid out between the items of furniture.

"You made a big mistake," snarled Kipling, walking close to Geller, almost nose to nose. "You sent a letter to the police claiming that the Taylor brothers are called Schneider and they're from Germany."

"That's right." Geller nodded. "Dieter and Stefan Schneider. They moved here from Munich using false documents many years ago."

"How did you come by that information?"

"Oh, it's a long story," said Geller.

"And we want to hear it," said Ryder. "You also sent a threatening letter to Stefan Schneider at his home address and now he's dead. You're going to tell us everything you know about that."

Geller laughed. "You talk to *me* about threatening people? From what I understand, you do that for a living."

"We do more than threaten," chuckled Kipling. "A lot more."

"I'm sure you do." Geller turned to the seated figure. "Gentlemen, I'd like you to meet Tonga, my partner in a little crusade I'm currently waging. Tonga, stand up and take off your coat." He turned to Ryder and shrugged. "I bought him four raincoats because I knew they'd get messy and he'd probably lose them. One was soaked in blood and brains, he lost one in Beverley and another in Leeds earlier. This is the last one, for now at any rate. As you can imagine, I'd prefer to keep it clean."

"What the fuck are you talking about?" Ryder watched the young man stand and unbutton his coat as instructed. "What's he doing?"

"Shit!" gasped Kipling. The raincoat fell to the floor and he gaped in amazement at the naked man. "What's going on here?"

"I don't understand," stammered Ryder, more terrified than

amazed. Tonga had no hair on his head and body, but *far* weirder than this, no sexual organs – just smooth brown skin where they ought to be. "How's that possible?"

The absence of genitalia didn't concern Kipling, a man of limited intelligence and imagination. He'd always felt uncomfortable around naked men and he'd long since discovered that the best way to deal with discomfort was to punch someone very hard. He slammed a fist into Tonga's face, then stepped back, aware that something was very wrong. The man hadn't flinched, and another two seconds passed before the pain from the broken fingers reached his brain.

"Fuck," he hissed, nursing the fractured hand. "That was like hitting a wall."

"This is fortunate," said Geller. "Tonga needs to consume life energy and here we are – a home delivery. Oh, wait, we don't want to ruin this." Stooping to the rug that lay between them, he grabbed the edge and pulled it away to reveal the marble tiles. "Tonga, kill them both, now."

It didn't last long. Geller watched gleefully, grinning to hear the snapping limbs and choking grunts of agony. He walked forward to view the two broken corpses and nodded with satisfaction.

"Well done, Tonga," he said. "But you'll need to clean up this mess before we head out on our next visit. You're certainly getting your fair share of energy tonight."

* * * *

Chapter 36

Quist and Watson walked east across the old Holgate railway bridge, the detective checking his watch as they approached the row of large Victorian houses ahead. It was two o'clock on Thursday morning. The dark, empty thoroughfares of York lay silent and, standing in the centre of the terrace, Birlstone House, the White Rose headquarters would be unoccupied until nine.

Quist's mind raced with questions, mostly relating to Adam Hoffman. From his behaviour, Hoffman knew far more about the murders than he was telling, but what was he hiding and why? The two men who assaulted his granddaughter were both dead, but did he have anything to do with this? Did he know the killer and, more to the point did he know that it wasn't human? He was definitely frightened by something, but what?

The detective shook himself, dismissing such thoughts for now. The last time he'd visited this place, his meeting with Churchill had been ruined by his preoccupation with the supernatural creature at Beverley. He wasn't about to repeat that mistake.

"So why did we leave the car a quarter of a mile back?" asked Watson, quietly. "What's the idea of walking the last bit of the journey here?"

"Public surveillance cameras," murmured Quist. "We have a truly staggering number in this country, not to mention all the road traffic cameras. The police use them to identify vehicles with their *Automated Number Plate Recognition* and I don't want my registration recorded in this neighbourhood tonight. What we're about to do here is highly unethical, not to mention downright criminal, and we can't be connected in any way with the outcome."

"What exactly *are* we about to do?" Watson glanced up as a tawny owl spotted his employer from a nearby tree and let out a melancholy hoot of fear. "You've been kind of tight-lipped about this little venture. I assume we're going to break into the headquarters?"

"Your assumption is correct." Quist looked back over his

shoulder along the empty road. "Believe me, I wouldn't have brought you along, but the chances are I'm going to need you once we're inside."

"For what?"

"You'll soon see."

"Unbelievable," muttered the teenager, turning off the road down Cambridge Street. "Yeah, you really believe in keeping your assistant fully informed with what's going on."

Quist saw a fox trot out from a garden ahead, then tear away in terror on sensing his lupine presence. The detective smiled and carefully checked the buildings and lampposts for cameras. Being seen by the nocturnal wildlife was one thing, but just like his vehicle registration, he'd no desire for their faces to be recorded on video. Buttoning his black leather overcoat and turning up the collar, he walked quietly along the dark alleyway that provided private access to the rear of the lengthy terrace. Watson tagged along behind, warily scrutinising the surrounding windows for insomniac observers.

Most of these large houses had been converted into hotels and each had a small rear car park for the guests. The White Rose headquarters was no exception and three party vehicles stood on the square of tarmac behind the building. The two men moved stealthily past them and descended the stone steps to the cellar door. It was pitch-black and, slipping on his leather gloves, Quist felt around for the handle.

"Today's the last day of October," whispered Watson, smiling uneasily at a sudden realisation. "It's Halloween tonight. If it wasn't for the fact that I'm standing in the dark with a werewolf, this might be scary."

Quist turned the handle and, as quietly as possible, shouldered the door inwards.

"Bloody hell, Guv," hissed Watson, hearing the metal tenon snap inside the lock. "Surely this place is alarmed?"

"Of course it is, but I disconnected the wires to this entrance yesterday." The detective stepped inside, listening intently and sniffing the air for any signs of humans. "I noticed there were no ceiling motion sensors in the corridors and offices upstairs. Alarms are fitted to the windows and external doors, but once inside, we can move about freely."

"Even *you* can't see a thing in here," said Watson. "How the hell are we supposed to..."

Quist clicked on a small pen torch. "The wonders of modern science."

Pulling the door closed, they walked cautiously through the complex of basement rooms and ascended the steps to the offices above. Street lighting from the windows filtered in here, allowing Quist to switch off the torch and see along the passage with his enhanced night vision. Watson followed close behind as he found Churchill's private office and tried the door.

"Just as I suspected," he whispered. "It's locked and it has to remain that way. We can't allow anyone to know that intruders have been inside, which is why I brought *you*."

"Really?" The teenager watched curiously as his employer hurried to the reception area. "I'm not exactly famous for my lock picking skills."

"No, you're not." The detective returned with a chair and nodded to the rectangular glass fanlight above the door. "But you're smaller than me and wiry enough to squeeze through *there*."

Watson's eyes widened. "Seriously?"

"Seriously." Standing on the chair and taking out a pocket knife, Quist carefully slid the blade inside the frame, flicked the catch and swung the small window outwards. He jumped down and handed Watson his leather gloves. "Put those on before you touch anything."

"Er, right." Grinning nervously and pulling on the gloves, Watson saw that the detective had interlocked his fingers. "Never a dull moment in *this* job."

"Come on," said Quist, wiggling his hands. "Up you go."

The youth took a deep breath, placed his right trainer in the makeshift stirrup and was boosted up to the opening. Squirming his upper body through the gap, he struggled awkwardly to ease his hips and buttocks past the wooden frame and landed with a thump on the office carpet.

"Are you alright?" quizzed the detective, standing on the chair and peering through the fanlight.

"I'm fine." Watson climbed to his feet. "Okay, Guv, what am I supposed to do in here?"

Quist passed him the torch and pointed. "You'll find a wall safe behind the desk there. Churchill stood in front of it yesterday to shield the keypad as he entered the digits, but it was mirrored in that cabinet door on the opposite wall. Most people would have been unable to read the numbers, especially as they were reversed in the glass reflection, but most people don't have my keen lupine sight."

"Why, Grandma, what big eyes you have." Laughing quietly, Watson clicked on the torch and sneaked across the dark room. "Okay, let's have it."

"Two, seven, three, five," whispered Quist. "Then press the letter B."

The teenager held the torch in his teeth, entered the electronic code and swung open the safe door.

"You'll find an envelope of money," said Quist. "My £8000 donation to White Rose. I can't think of any reason to leave *that* in there."

Taking the cash, Watson returned to the office door and handed it to Quist through the fanlight.

"Thank you." Quist pocketed the envelope, pulled a bulky carrier bag from his coat and passed it down to his assistant. "Now if you'd be good enough to leave the contents of this in its place. Naturally I'll be needing the carrier back; it has my fingerprints on it."

"Christ on a bike!" stammered Watson, shining the torch inside. Quist had repackaged the heroin from the fire service BMW into several smaller bags. "Wow, you've been a busy boy since you dropped me off earlier. I can't believe you're actually going to plant this shit on Churchill."

212

"Believe it," said Quist. "If this man had any saving graces whatsoever, I'd have decided against this blatantly illegal undertaking, but this is someone who happily endorses intimidation and hate crime."

"Absolutely," agreed Watson. "A twat who pays a team of hardened nutters to assault women and attack Jewish shopkeepers." He headed back to the safe. "Yeah, let's do this."

"The clerical staff won't be opening Birlstone House until around nine," said Quist. "I've checked the White Rose timetable and Churchill has a meeting at ten in Thirsk today, followed by Whitby in the afternoon. Hopefully he and his entourage will be heading straight there without visiting the office; more to the point, without opening this safe. Place the majority of the bags inside and leave two or three in the desk drawer there."

Shoving the drugs into the back of the safe, Watson closed it and turned to the desk, stashing the final three bags beneath papers in the top drawer."

"Are those car keys in the drawer?" asked Quist, peering down from the fanlight.

"Yeah." The youth held them up. "A set of Ford keys."

"Let me see them." Holding out a hand, the detective nodded thoughtfully as Watson passed them up to him. "One of the party vehicles we passed in the parking area was a Ford and, from the registration tag attached to this ring, these are the keys. Right, remove one of those packages from the desk and come on back."

Watson did as instructed and, ensuring everything in the office was as he'd found it, he jumped up to grab Quist's outstretched hands. The teenager scrambled back through the open aperture and waited as Quist closed the fanlight behind him and returned the chair to the reception room.

"Very good," said the detective, patting Watson's back. "Time to go."

The pair swiftly retraced their steps back down to the basement and out into the rear yard. Sure enough, the keys opened the Ford saloon and Quist left the drugs in full view on the passenger seat.

"There," he muttered, dropping the keys down a drainage grating in the tarmac. "Now all that's needed is for me to make an anonymous call to Inspector Bradstreet at first light and this undertaking should hopefully prove to be far more productive than my initial idea of flushing the narcotics down the toilet."

"You can say that again" agreed Watson.

They left the yard and walked back along the dark alley.

"This clandestine visit will hopefully hammer several nails into the White Rose coffin," said Quist. "It's now time to turn our attention to something far more important."

The teenager swallowed nervously. "Tonga?"

"Exactly. It's time to find that creature and stop it before it kills again."

* * * *

Chapter 37

Sara awoke with a raging thirst and checked the digital clock by her bed. It was three o'clock in the morning and, still fully clothed, she sat up in the darkness, rubbing her eyes and attempting to swallow. Her desiccated mouth felt like the bottom of a birdcage; this was a phrase she'd heard many times, but *this* birdcage tasted as if it had also been used as an ashtray. Water wasn't going to quench this drug-induced thirst. She needed something ice cold and crisp and there was a carton of apple juice downstairs in the fridge.

Standing up and feeling the floor tilt, she wobbled and gripped her bedside cabinet, still slightly disorientated by the veterinary sedative.

Jesus, just how much tranquiliser did that lunatic Roylott give her?

Sara shook her head to clear the dizziness, bristling with fury and outrage at the thought of being tied up and injected. She still couldn't believe it. She'd been abducted by those scumbags in broad daylight, tied to a chair in a cellar and stuck with a needle.

"Bastards," she muttered.

The girl had awoken earlier to find her grandfather sitting beside her bed. He'd given her a condensed account of the afternoon's events – the Brisson brothers in Leeds, the heroin hidden in the fire service car, and Bernard Quist's rescue. The heroin must have been worth a fortune and she could understand their urgency to get it back, but what would have happened to her when they realised they had the wrong person? It was hard to imagine the Brissons apologising with a bunch of flowers and driving her home. No, if it hadn't been for this Quist guy, she might never have been seen again.

Sara headed downstairs and found her grandfather reading a book in the lounge.

"You're fully dressed," she said. "Haven't you been to bed?"

"Of course I haven't." He jumped to his feet and held her tightly. "How could I possibly sleep after what happened? Besides, after we'd spoken and you went back to sleep, I've been coming up every five minutes to check on you. Thank the Lord you're back safe. How are you feeling?"

"Hey, don't worry. I'm okay." She walked to the kitchen. "Well, apart from a thick head and a mouth that feels like someone shovelled hot sand into it. If it puts your mind at ease, I felt worse after partying all night in Ibiza."

"Believe me, that doesn't help," said Hoffman, smiling nervously. He followed the girl to the fridge and watched as she drank half the apple juice in three thirsty gulps. "My God, Sara, I was so worried about you."

"Not as worried as *I* was." Sara kissed his cheek. "But it's over now and I can't wait to meet Watson's boss tomorrow. I want the full story of how this Bernard Quist found me and how he got me out of that shitty place. He probably saved my life."

Hoffman nodded uneasily, not relishing the thought of his next meeting with Quist. It was obvious this private detective knew he was lying and he'd want to know why, but he couldn't possibly tell him about his project with Geller and what they'd done together. He couldn't tell *anyone* that he was responsible for all these deaths.

"Heroin?" she gasped, swigging more juice. "Can you believe those lunatics actually believed I'd taken their hidden stash because I was suddenly buying cars and jetting off to Ibiza? They were going to give me some weird truth drug. When it didn't work and they realised they had the wrong person, I suppose they'd have gone through the fire station staff until they found the right one." She gave a puzzled frown. "So where are the police? I thought they'd be here waiting for me to wake up. Surely they'll be wanting my statement?"

"Er, I haven't rung them yet," said Hoffman. He couldn't contact the authorities, but he'd wait until the morning before trying to explain why. "I didn't want the police here bothering you with questions when you were drugged and…"

"You haven't told them?" said Sara, astounded. "Well, I'm fine now and those bastards in Leeds need locking up as soon as possible."

Hoffman nodded. The *bastards* in question had been torn apart, but how could he explain that to her? "I was devastated when I heard you'd been taken," he said, attempting to change the subject. "I still can't believe you were kidnapped. Oh, my God, you must have been so scared."

Scared was putting it mildly, but Sara decided it was best not to worry him. "Hey, I've been inside burning warehouses with gas cylinders exploding. I've been to fires on the Grimpen estate with yobs throwing bottles at me." She grinned reassuringly. "It takes more than a bunch of scumbag drug dealers like that to frighten me."

"Well, you're okay now and that's all that matters," said Hoffman, wrapping his arms around her. "You're completely safe now."

They both stiffened to hear the sound of the front door bursting open and Hoffman reconsidered his reassuring words. The pair looked through the open kitchen door and saw Tonga in his raincoat standing silently at the far end of the lounge.

"Who on earth…" gasped Sara.

"Adam Hoffman?" said Tonga. "Sara Hoffman?"

"Yes." Sara stared anxiously at the brown-skinned stranger. *Did he work for the Brisson brothers?* "What the hell do you think you're doing smashing your way into our…"

Tonga's coat fell to the floor revealing the muscular naked body beneath. Sara's jaw dropped at his complete lack of genitalia, then dropped further still as the intruder impossibly changed, swiftly growing in mass and height before her wide eyes. The muscle tone disappeared as the dark body seemed to inflate and become just solid bulk, the neck swelling so the head almost appeared to be part of the torso.

"What…" croaked Sara, feeling a draught of icy air. "No, this can't be…"

Tonga's face flattened and the nose vanished, leaving an open slit of a mouth and tiny piggy eyes which smouldered with a dull red light. The same gleaming light emphasised several mystical symbols on

217

the wide torso. The bizarre red markings resembled fiery cracks on the skin, a skin that now appeared to be reddish brown stone. Almost six feet tall now, the creature strode to the cabinet containing the safe.

"No." Sara stepped backwards shaking her head. "This can't happen. This is imposs…"

"Move." Snatching his granddaughter's arm, Hoffman dragged her across the kitchen. "We need to get out of here right now."

Sara didn't need any persuasion and quickly unlocked the French doors with shaking hands. Hoffman pushed the girl through as a metallic clang came from the lounge. The safe had been wrenched open.

"Come on," gasped Hoffman, running into the garden. A security light sensed their movement and clicked on. "It can't move any faster than a walking pace."

"How can you possibly know that?" yelled Sara, petrified. "What the hell is it?"

Her grandfather didn't answer. He turned as they reached the garden gate to see the huge figure lumbering out of the kitchen after them, the book from the safe tucked under its left arm. Throwing open the gate, he ran with Sara up the dark alleyway by the side of the house and out onto Madeley Street. A grey Ford car stood a short way along the cul-de-sac and Hoffman saw who sat inside.

"You bastard," he snapped, glaring at Geller and hammering on the window. "You sent it in there for us? You thought we'd be in bed. How dare you try to…"

"Gramps," whimpered Sara, tugging frantically at his arm.

Hoffman glanced over his shoulder to see the bulky shape of the creature following along the pavement, its eyes smouldering red in the darkness.

"Oh, God," he groaned.

They left the car and raced up the silent street as Geller quickly opened the rear door, gesturing for Tonga to climb in. The terrified pair arrived at the deserted Bishopthorpe Road and Hoffman pulled his granddaughter out of sight into an art gallery doorway as Geller's car

218

turned out of Madeley Street and drove away.

The old man closed his eyes, shaking with fury. He hadn't been able to tell Quist what he'd done, or the truth about the murders. He hadn't been able to tell anyone. Until this moment the guilt and fear had forced him into complicit silence, but now Sara was in danger. Tonga had come for the book, but he'd also asked for them both by name. That maniac Geller had sent it in there, not just to get rid of him, but his granddaughter too. This had gone on long enough and the time for silence was most definitely over.

Sara's frightened panting slowed enough to enable her to speak. "What was it, Gramps?" she stammered, her words tripping over one another in a babble. "What the hell was it? It changed. It's impossible, but I saw it change. I saw it, Gramps. Did you see its eyes and those glowing tattoos?"

"I saw them," said Hoffman, quietly. "Those were the Kabbalistic symbols of Kada estra. The ancient Hebrew runes of life."

The girl stared at him with wide eyes. "How do you know that?"

"I know because I carved them on its body." Hoffman held her tightly. "Because I created that terrible thing down in our cellar."

* * * *

219

Chapter 38

Watson sat in rear of Quist's parked car chomping on a double cheeseburger and fries and slurping a chocolate shake. Needing to make a phone call, the detective had parked outside the York McDonald's on Blake Street, giving his assistant the chance to rush inside and alleviate his hunger pangs. The teenager was ravenous. It was now almost noon and, save for a pack of cheese sandwiches, three bags of crisps and two chocolate bars, he hadn't eaten *anything* since his breakfast at eight.

Rex Grant turned in the passenger seat, inhaling the scent of hot meat and peering enviously at the burger over his designer sunglasses. He knew he could never eat animal products again, not if he was to keep the ferocious lupine urges in check, but maybe the shake would be okay. Sniffing again, Rex picked up the faint cocoa aroma and wondered whether McDonald's used actual milk chocolate in their milkshakes. Or even actual *milk*. Deciding not to chance it, he tugged up the collar on his black leather jacket and winked at a passing girl, thrilled that he was once again involved in one of Quist's investigations.

Rex grinned eagerly. A fantastic investigation too, from what he'd been told, with a supernatural monster going around Yorkshire killing people. Not too fantastic for the murder victims perhaps, but exciting fun for anyone tracking this thing down.

Quist finished his telephone conversation with Gareth Lestrade and started the engine.

"So are we cooking on charcoal or what?" asked Watson, noisily sucking out the last dregs of milkshake. The sound was reminiscent of a pig being violently throttled. "Did Gazza get you Geller's address?"

"He tracked him down this morning," said the detective, pulling away into the traffic. "Lestrade found the immigration data from when Geller entered the country at Leeds airport and cross referenced that with rental records. Geller hired a car at the airport, interestingly a grey Ford car like the one I saw at the nightclub yesterday, and he's renting an apartment in one of those large houses on Mount Vale near the racecourse."

"Okay," said Rex. "And you're pretty sure this guy is involved in these murders and the supernatural monster stuff?"

"Absolutely." Quist nodded. "He's definitely involved in some way."

"Great." Rex cracked his knuckles. "Let's go get him."

"We're going to speak to him, not rough him up," said Quist, glancing incredulously at Rex and wishing he'd curb his excitement. "If Adam Hoffman won't answer my questions, then perhaps this man will. Geller approached Hoffman right before the murders began. Apparently they were friendly to begin with, but there was a falling out of some sort and now Hoffman dislikes him."

"And there's some old book," said Watson. "The Guv wants to know what it is."

"That's right," said Quist. "Geller gave Hoffman a book which I'm certain has something to do with this. Hoffman described it as *an obscure medieval work*, but he was somewhat unforthcoming with the title. I want to see what Geller has to say about this."

"Hey, I wish I'd been with you last night," said Rex, enthusiastically. "I can't believe you broke into the White Rose headquarters and planted those drugs."

"Yeah," laughed Watson. "That was a pretty cool idea, Guv. Mind you, you couldn't have done it without your underpaid assistant, the human ferret who can squeeze through tiny holes."

"*Cool* isn't the descriptive term I would choose," admitted Quist, with an awkward smile. "I derived little pleasure and satisfaction from such a criminal undertaking, but these people are truly repellent and this might be a speedy, if rather unethical, way to end their political campaign. I rang Inspector Bradstreet anonymously this morning and disguised my voice to inform her of Churchill's drug dealing side-line. It was a very early call; I couldn't risk White Rose finding the narcotics first and disposing of them."

"No, *cool* is definitely the right word," said Watson, recalling Sara's bruised face. "Screw them."

221

Quist drove through the city centre and turned off Mount Vale into the wide driveway of Pelham House. Parking on the gravel behind the white-painted Georgian building, he climbed out of the car and walked to the communal door with its panel of four call buzzers.

"Geller has one the ground-floor apartments," he said, pressing the button. "Number Two."

"What if he won't talk to us?" asked Watson. "Or, if the past couple of day are anything to go by, what if he's dead?"

The detective shot him a cynical look, then realising the man wasn't answering, he pressed the other three buttons. Like Geller, two were obviously out, but the light beside apartment four lit up.

"Hello?" A woman's tinny voice came from the speaker. "Who is it?"

"Maintenance," said Quist, stooping to the microphone "Good morning, my dear. I'm here to fix the faulty hall light reported by Mister Geller in apartment two."

A buzzer sounded and the door unlocked electronically allowing the three men into the hallway.

"Great security," mumbled Rex.

The detective knocked on Geller's apartment door and waited for over a minute before giving his companions a guilty look, turning the knob and quietly shouldering it inwards.

"What do you think you're doing?" hissed Watson. "How the hell will you explain *this* if he comes home?"

"It was like that when we arrived," said Quist, pulling on his leather gloves and walking into the lounge. "Keep your voices low and touch nothing."

"So if he's out, what are we doing here?" asked Rex, excitedly. "Searching for clues?"

"Something like that." Quist gestured to the brown clay dust on one of the armchairs. "I didn't know what we'd find here, but *this* tells me we haven't wasted our time."

"Yeah," whispered Watson, looking around nervously. "It definitely looks as if our bald friend Tonga has been here. Like I said outside, Geller is probably dead."

"The room smells strongly of bleach," murmured Quist. Moving into the centre of the lounge and jerking back the huge rug, he dropped onto all fours to sniff the marble-tiled floor. "Ah, this whole area has been cleaned very recently. *Really* cleaned."

"He's obviously into hygiene," said Rex.

A passage led off the lounge and, walking along it, Quist paused at the open bathroom door. "Not *too* hygienic," he said, raising his eyebrows. "I'd say this bath could certainly use a good clean."

"Fuck!" whispered Watson, looking in.

"Fuck!" echoed Rex, slowly sliding off his sunglasses.

Two large men lay in the blood-splattered tub. Both were fully clothed, which told Watson they weren't enjoying a hot soak – this and the fact that one of the heads and a leg were detached from their broken bodies. The horrified teenager glanced at the two closed passage doors beyond the bathroom and wondered whether or not the killer could still be in the apartment. From here back to the entrance looked to be around ten paces, but if Tonga suddenly appeared, he'd cover that distance in four.

"I recognise one of these gentlemen," said the detective, stepping forward to carefully search their pockets. "I met him at the White Rose headquarters yesterday. He's a member of Churchill's Task Force and, from the size of him, I presume his companion here is too. Mmh, their identification has been removed."

"And one of their heads," pointed out Rex, gagging.

"What are they doing here?" Watson swallowed hard as his burger and milkshake threatened to unexpectedly reappear. "And where's Geller's body?"

Leaving the bathroom, Quist opened a bedroom door and saw the clay dust staining the bed quilt. He lifted it and found it was clean below. "Our friend Tonga has been lying here," he said. "Not *in* the bed, but on top of it. Have you noticed the clay dust footprints everywhere? It appears to me that Tonga has been living in this apartment, although *living* is definitely the wrong term."

"Like some sort of supernatural killer's boarding house?" Watson threw open the door to the last room and jumped back warily. Clearly the master bedroom, with a king-size bed and tasteful furniture, it was empty. "No more dead bodies? So Geller is still alive? You think he's been looking after Tonga here?"

"That's one way of phrasing it," nodded the detective, following him in. "Tonga left the Leeds nightclub in a grey Ford saloon last night, doubtless the car that was rented by Geller. Well, I said this man would have the answers we need and I believe that has certainly been established." He gestured to a large leather-bound book on the dresser. "Oh, hello…"

"What is it?" asked the youth.

"*The Key of Honorius.*" Quist read the title carved into the ancient cover. "I've heard of this magical grimoire. It's a very old and rather rare work of Hebrew mysticism."

"Yeah, sounds like a real page-turner," drawled Rex.

"It looks like a friggin' doorstep," said Watson, still decidedly queasy after his bathroom shock. "Personally, I'd have gone for the paperback version."

Opening the volume and looking through the yellowed handwritten parchments, the detective came across a slip of paper bookmarking a particular section. The text was indecipherable, but he was able to identify some of the words, the Kabbalistic symbols and magical illustrations.

"Good Lord, of course." Quist grimaced and snapped the pages shut. "I knew that clay was relevant. I really must be slipping in my old age; I should have worked this out earlier."

"Anything you'd like to share?" quizzed Watson.

"I believe I'll allow Adam Hoffman to explain." Shaking his head with exasperation and taking the weighty book under his arm, Quist looked around and picked up a small nugget of clay. "Come along. We need to speak to him without delay."

"What about the cops?" asked Watson. "Are we going to report the bathing beauties in the tub?"

"After we illegally broke in here?" said Quist, walking across the lounge. "No, we can't get involved in their murder investigation and they certainly wouldn't believe anything I told them." He paused at the apartment door, pondered for a moment and then ran back along the corridor to the bathroom. "Wait there a moment."

"What's he up to now?" asked Rex.

"Your guess is as good as mine." Watson shrugged. "He probably needs the toilet. After seeing those two lads in the bath, I've been thinking about a visit myself."

Quist returned holding a hair comb.

"Well, I have to say…" The teenager gave Rex a deadpan look. "I never expected *that*."

The detective's phone rang and he answered. "Ah, Mister Hoffman…" He stiffened slightly. "Good Lord, really? Are you and your granddaughter alright? Are you both safe now?"

"What's happened?" demanded Watson. "Is Sara okay?"

Quist held up a hand, gesturing for his assistant to remain quiet. "Yes, you're right, Mister Hoffman." He smiled tightly. "I'd say we definitely *do* need to talk."

* * * *

Chapter 39

Quist parked outside Hoffman's house on Madeley Street and walked into the hallway with Watson and Rex. Announcing their arrival by the traditional method of knocking was awkward, as the broken front door lay in the buffer garden, its locks and one of the hinges completely smashed. The detective noticed the smudged clay handprint where someone, or more precisely *something*, had slammed it open from the outside.

"Afternoon," said Watson, nodding politely to the two joiners who were repairing the damaged frame. "How's it going?"

Hoffman met them in the lounge and nervously ushered the three men through to the rear kitchen.

"How are you?" asked Quist, noticing the damaged safe as they passed. "You were frightened, but rather vague when you called me. You say you were attacked here in your home last night?"

"Yes, but I wanted to speak face to face." Hoffman closed the lounge and kitchen doors to prevent the workmen from overhearing anything. "I couldn't say anything on the phone. You'd think I was insane."

"I wouldn't be so sure about that," said Quist.

Sara sat at the table, nursing a coffee in both hands and eyeing them uneasily. The girl was clearly frightened.

"Are you okay?" Watson ran to her. "You *look* okay, but then again you always look pretty sensational. The last time I saw you, you were unconscious after going for a drive with your new friends."

"Yeah," she laughed, dryly. "That was scary, but believe it or not, things got a lot more scary after you brought me home."

"Good afternoon," said Quist, smiling warmly. "We've met, and I have to say, although it was a rather stimulating encounter, I'm afraid you won't remember."

"You're the one." Sara climbed to her feet and hugged him. "You're Watson's boss, Bernard Quist. Gramps told me about how you rescued me from those Leeds gangsters. I don't know what to say."

He patted her back. "You don't have to say anything, young lady."

"Yes, I do." Sara kissed his cheek and felt her stomach flutter, unaware of how the wolf pheromones worked on a subliminal level. "When we have the time, I have so much I want to ask about how you got me out of there, but I honestly don't know how to thank you."

"I'm sure that kiss will suffice," said the detective, sitting at the kitchen dining table with the others. "You both know my assistant Watson, of course, but this is a friend of ours, Rex Grant from London. Rex, this is Adam Hoffman and his granddaughter, Sara."

"Well, hello there." Rex peered over his shades and smiled sexily as Sara sat opposite him. "So you're Watson's girlfriend?"

"Well…" She ran a curious eye over the jet-black clothing and wondered why he was wearing sunglasses indoors. "I'm his friend."

"Oh, I see." Rex flashed his white teeth and gave her a wink. "Good to know."

Sara smiled back, slightly confused; despite the tension and fear, she was feeling faintly aroused. It was hardly surprising, being in a closed room with the pheromones of two werewolves.

Watson shook his head. Even with everything that was going on, Rex was hitting on her. It was nothing new; he'd once propositioned a girl at a funeral. This in itself would have been tactless enough, but she'd been the widow.

"Mister Hoffman," said Quist. "I believe you have something important to tell us. Please don't worry – you can speak openly in front of Rex. He's assisting us with this bizarre situation."

Hoffman cleared his throat. "Firstly, I want to thank you again for everything you did for Sara last night and for coming when I rang just now." He hid his face in both hands and Sara squeezed his arm reassuringly. "I'm sorry, but I haven't had any sleep and I'm a little tearful. I should have told you everything yesterday, but I didn't know how and I was so scared. You see, I achieved something truly amazing, something wonderful, but Geller corrupted it and now people are dying. I really don't know where to begin."

227

"Something amazing and wonderful?" repeated Watson. "What did you do?"

"The easiest way is to just say it." The old man swallowed nervously. "It sounds crazy, but I created a... I know you won't be able to accept this, but I created..."

"A golem," said Quist. "Basically, a supernatural automaton fashioned from clay and animated by Hebrew mysticism. In Jewish folklore they were used as servants to perform strenuous tasks."

Hoffman's eyes widened. "You *knew*?"

The detective shook his head. "I knew that the individual responsible for these recent murders was some form of powerful supernatural being. I didn't know you were behind its creation, however, nor what it actually *was* until the realisation dawned earlier in Daniel Geller's apartment. Geller has been keeping it there with him and driving it to various locations to kill people. I glimpsed his car as he aided its escape from the Leeds club last night. I understand he's named it Tonga?"

"After his pet dog," confirmed Hoffman.

"Right," murmured Watson. "Yeah, that's nice."

"I should have deduced this sooner," said Quist. "I knew about your interests in Jewish mysticism and your training to become a rabbi, but the principal clue was the clay. In my defence, it's been so long since I read about these creatures in the annals of mythology."

"Hardly mythology," said Hoffman, quietly. He gestured through the glass kitchen doors to a sunken area in the rear shrubbery where recent digging had obviously taken place. "Yes, a golem. A band of clay runs under the garden, so the basic materials were taken from there and sculpted in the cellar. I created a makeshift occult temple down there to perform the necessary rituals."

Watson and Rex glanced at one another and Rex broke the silence.

"Gollum?" he said, frowning in puzzlement. "You mean like in *Lord of the Rings*?"

"Golem, not Gollum," said Quist, patiently. "A golem."

Hoffman nodded. "It was easier explaining this to Sara because she saw it, but…"

"It was terrifying," muttered Sara, nodding timidly. "It came for us last night and I watched it change from a young guy into a monster. It almost killed us both. I couldn't understand why Gramps didn't ring the police once I was safely back home, but now I know."

"The authorities couldn't be informed about your abduction," said Quist. "It would have been rather difficult for me to explain how I found you and what happened in that cellar."

"Plus there was no one to arrest," pointed out Rex, helpfully. "Apparently, they were all torn to bits."

"I'm so sorry you had to encounter the golem." Hoffman wrapped an arm around Sara's trembling shoulders. "I never thought Geller would be mad enough to send it to kill us." He turned to Watson and Rex. "But I don't blame you for not believing this. I knew you'd think I was crazy."

"Not at all," said Quist. "You're mistaking a lack of astonishment for disbelief."

"Speak for yourself, Guv," said Watson. "Yeah, I've seen a lot of weird shit recently, but this sounds impossible. A clay robot made by friggin' magic?"

"Believe it," mumbled Sara. "It's true alright."

"I've always known it was possible," sighed Hoffman. "What the layman refers to as *magic* is simply a science that few people realise exists, a very ancient and esoteric science known only to a very few. The truth is, I saw one of these creatures as a child in London. A rabbi friend of my father had a huge interest in Jewish folklore and the occult sciences. He made several secret attempts to create a golem and on the final occasion he actually succeeded. It couldn't walk very far and didn't last long, less than two days, but my father took me to see the creature before it crumbled to dust. I was eight years old and it was the most amazing thing I'd ever seen – an actual being, moving and seemingly alive, yet constructed from clay."

"Wow," whispered Watson. At eight years old he'd seen *Star*

Wars on television and thought *that* was amazing. Sara's grandad had beat this hands down.

"From that moment onwards," said Hoffman, "I was spurred into reading books, devouring them, learning the sciences and studying such things myself."

"Incredible," muttered Rex.

"The mistake I made was telling Daniel Geller." Hoffman rubbed his tired eyes and laughed bitterly. "Once he knew such creatures were a reality, he instantly saw the potential. He'd read about golems – their mythical strength and obedience – and he knew that I was a rabbi. He knew I was well versed in mysticism and the kabala and he persuaded me to try."

"He also supplied you with the necessary Hebrew grimoire," said Quist, *"The Key of Honorius."*

"Yes, it was rare and very expensive. How do you know the title?"

"I found the book at Geller's flat and I have it in the car." Quist gestured to the lounge. "I see the door has been wrenched from the safe where you kept it. I can only presume the creature did that last night?"

Hoffman nodded. "Geller has been using the golem to murder certain people, which he knows I'm totally against. I can't get him to stop. He sent it in here last night to recover the book and also to..." He winced and shook his head.

"To get rid of us," said Sara, angrily.

Quist nodded his understanding. "He needed you to create the golem, but I presume he now has no further use for you. You're opposed to these murders, but you couldn't speak to the authorities, or us, because of your involvement. You're very much a loose cannon, however, and he knew you might ring the police anonymously. He didn't know how much you'd told your granddaughter, so he obviously decided to get rid of her too."

"I never thought he'd do that," stammered Hoffman. "You're right, of course. I couldn't say anything because I was frightened I'd be implicated in the murders, but that doesn't matter anymore. The police

230

have to know about Geller and the golem, but I don't know how I'll convince them."

"The police can't help," said Quist. "I believe I'll have a much better chance of stopping this thing."

"You?" Sara frowned. "How?"

"I'm working on it." The detective smiled tautly. "I've seen this creature twice. Once at Beverley when it killed Stefan Schneider and very briefly as it fled from that Leeds cellar. Tell me about it."

Hoffman nodded. "As I said, it's basically an animated clay servant. The golem has no bodily hair or genitalia, but when clothed and in human form, it can pass for a young man. It can only transform into the true golem form between sunset and sunrise. When it does, it grows slightly and bulks out into hardened stone. The features change, the eyes turn red and the Kabbalistic symbols of life appear on its torso and glow."

"Glowing tattoos?" Rex whistled. "Now those would *really* catch on. Can this thing be killed?"

"Not as such – it's pretty much indestructible."

"Marvellous," sighed Watson.

"In golem form its strength is greatly augmented, but it's much slower. It can't run in that shape and only moves at a walking pace." A tear rolled down Hoffman's face. "But that hasn't prevented it from killing. It wasn't supposed to kill anyone; that was never the plan."

"What *was* the plan?" demanded Watson, incredulous. "Why the hell did you want to make a clay monster?"

"It was never supposed to *be* a monster." Hoffman let out a mirthless laugh. "It was just after those White Rose bastards attacked Sara. I wasn't myself and I'd have done anything to get back at them."

"Oh, Gramps." Sara kissed his cheek. "I wish you hadn't."

"Believe me, I wish that too." Hoffman held her hand. "Geller and I talked at length about golems one drunken evening. He knew I was telling the truth about my childhood encounter and he suggested creating one. The police weren't going to do anything about the Schneider brothers or the men who attacked you, and we were just two old men. We had no means of exposing these people or damaging White Rose ourselves."

"That was the intention?" asked Quist. "You'd use the golem to damage White Rose?"

Hoffman nodded. "I admit I wanted it to hurt the thugs who vandalised my shop and assaulted Sara, but I'd never dream of killing them. Churchill had his paid thugs and the idea was that, with a golem, we'd have a thug of our own that could wreck their headquarters and vehicles. The creature would have approached the White Rose personnel individually at night and terrified them into leaving the organisation. Night after night, we'd frighten off their followers, cost them money and bankrupt the party. The creature would also terrify the Taylors into confessing who they really were. Geller agreed with all this, but he was just using me. Right from the start he had other plans."

"Why would you want to frighten tailors?" asked Rex, bemused.

"Taylors, not *tailors*," said Quist, testily. "Two brothers living in Yorkshire under assumed names. Their real name was Schneider and they came here from Munich where they ran Aryan Truth, a white supremacist group."

"I didn't tell you everything," said Hoffman. "Geller's parents had a business in Munich and, because they were Jewish, the Schneiders wrecked the place one day. His mother was stabbed and his father chased them into the street where he was beaten to death. The brothers were arrested, but released on a lack of evidence. There were other pending allegations against them and things were becoming hot in Germany so, as you know, they changed identities and moved to England. Geller claimed he wanted to punish the Schneiders by bringing them to justice, but that was a lie. He hated them, as you can imagine, and his plan was always to kill them."

"Both brothers are now dead," said Watson.

"Yes, but he has no intention of stopping and Churchill will be next on his list." Hoffman paused for a moment. "The problem is, this golem has a major flaw. When Sara went away on her Ibiza trip it

232

seemed like fate had lent a hand. I had the house to myself, the book had just arrived, and Geller and I had the perfect chance to attempt the experiment. Unfortunately, with it being such a small time window, I didn't read the *Key of Honorius* fully and my translation could have been better. The temple wasn't prepared correctly and I rushed the rituals. I made minor mistakes and the creature is defective."

"A defective golem?" Watson frowned, realising how stupid this sounded. "What do you mean?"

"In layman's terms, it constantly requires boosts of ethereal life energy to remain intact and animate."

"That's layman's terms?" said Rex. "Okay."

"He means it needs to kill," said Quist, quietly. "On this magical level, a human death will release the life energy it requires. But you have the occult knowledge and you know the rituals. If it can't be killed, can you stop it using the *Key of Honorius*?"

"Yes, and I wanted to destroy our faulty prototype and create another, but Geller wouldn't hear of it. This creature is constantly on the brink of decay, shedding dust and small fragments of clay. Eventually it would become dormant, break down fully and crumble to dry powdered clay, but Geller intends to keep feeding it with energy. As he says, once he's finished with White Rose, there are many other white supremacists in Britain. He looks upon it as a crusade."

"I see," murmured Quist.

"There's a further problem." Hoffman cringed. "During the Kabbala ritual of life, mystical incantations and symbols are written on a tiny scroll, about two inches in length, which is tightly rolled up and placed in the golem's mouth. I trusted Geller and stupidly allowed him to insert the scroll, which gave him total control. It only listens to him."

"Ah." Watson nodded. "Probably not the brightest move."

"Geller insisted," explained Hoffman. "I couldn't have the golem here because of Sara. Geller lives alone so it made sense that he should keep it hidden in his apartment, but he needed to be able to order it around."

"There must be some way to stop it," said Sara.

"There is," said Hoffman. "I've been reading the *Key of Honorius* ever since the creation. I now know the correct incantation to release it from Geller's control. Then all we would need to do is retrieve the scroll from its mouth and it should transform back into clay. Geller is aware that I can do this and that's why he took the book last night."

"And also why he attempted to er, *dissolve your partnership*," said Quist. "Well, the book is now safely in my possession. Could I read out this incantation?"

"I'm afraid not." Hoffman shook his head. "You don't know the correct pronunciation and inflection. I need to read it, so I have to be there when you find the golem and hopefully the ritual will work."

"Not a chance," said Sara. "I don't want you going anywhere near that thing."

"Bloody good advice," said Watson. "I don't want to go anywhere near it either."

"I don't like it," admitted Hoffman. "But this is my responsibility. It's all my fault and I *have* to do this."

"If we can find this Geller guy, we'll find Gollum," said Rex. "He isn't at home right now, so any idea where he might be heading?"

"He's going after Churchill," said Hoffman. "He intended to kill him before, but now he's aware that Churchill is Stefan Schneider's son Kurt, I know he'll be his main target."

"You told him?" said Quist, amazed.

"Actually *you* told him," said Hoffman. "He was here when you rang last night and he overheard. The White Rose Party had a meeting this morning in Thirsk and then they're heading to Whitby. If I'm right, he'll choose the later venue in the Whitby Pavilion to attack Churchill as he needs it to be after sunset."

"Whitby? Tonight?" Watson cringed. "It's Halloween."

Rex grinned. "Surely you're not scared?"

"Have you visited the place on Halloween?" Watson pulled a sarcastic face. "The entire town is full of Goths, vampires and ghosts."

"Interesting," said Quist, thoughtfully. "That could work in our favour."

The teenager glanced at him. *Cyrano was right. If he needed to change into the big bad wolf, he probably wouldn't stand out quite so much amongst all the vampire and werewolf costumes. Probably.*

"I really don't like this," said Sara, her mouth dry. She cleared her throat, still confused as to why she felt sexually aroused. "But when are we setting off?"

"We?" Quist smiled. "No, young lady, I'm afraid you won't be accompanying us."

"Typical sexism," she snorted. "You think I won't be able to handle such things? I've already been chased by this thing and…"

"Actually this has nothing to do with chauvinism," said Quist. "Five people won't fit into my small car."

Watson ran a nervous hand through his hair. He considered offering to stay with Sara, but knew she'd then take his seat to be with her grandfather and he didn't want her in danger. Hunting for a lethal clay monster on Halloween was pretty much the last thing he wanted to do, but he couldn't back out and show Sara how frightened he was.

"Sara could sit on my lap," suggested Rex, winking at the girl. "It's a good thing we aren't using *my* car. I drive a McLaren MP4 supercar and there are only *two* seats in those beauties."

Sara stared for a moment, the weird arousal triggered by the lupine pheromones actually causing her to consider this. "Just bring my grandad back safely," she snapped, irately.

"No problem." Rex grinned. "As a treat, I'll take you for a spin when this is over."

"Well, I'm not exactly over the moon about doing this," said Watson, checking his watch. "But if we set off now, we'll get to Whitby before sunset."

"We have a brief call to make on the way," said Quist, rising from his chair. "You're probably correct about Geller heading for the Whitby Pavilion, but I believe there's another way to locate him."

* * * *

Chapter 40

Geography played a major role in protecting Whitby from the brash changes that transformed many British coastal towns into raucous holiday centres of neon arcades, funfairs and candyfloss. Sandwiched between the ocean and England's largest expanse of moorland, the North York Moors, the little fishing port remained relatively isolated and, for the most part, the developers passed it by. As holidaymakers eventually deserted their native shores for cheaper Mediterranean lager, hotter sunshine and larger melanomas, many of the garish resorts faded and died, but Whitby's unspoilt beauty and evocative charm of yesteryear enabled it to grow into a major attraction.

Opened by the Victorians in the eighteen-seventies, the Whitby Pavilion houses a theatre, function rooms, cafes and bars. Similar buildings can be found in most coastal tourist towns, where top-of-the-bill variety acts played the summer seasons in decades long past. A large redbrick construction, the Pavilion stands on the edge of the sea below the West Cliff. The main theatre had been booked for tonight's White Rose meeting and the party entourage had just arrived from another productive engagement in the market town of Thirsk.

Churchill was preparing his speech notes at a table by the stage. One of the main points at this meeting was his proposal to have a statue of Bram Stoker, the author of *Dracula*, erected in the town. He smiled to himself. *Surely anyone with common sense and local pride would prefer to see a monument to this great British writer instead of Muslim minarets.*

"Mister Churchill? I wonder if we could have a word?"

He turned to find a smartly dressed couple approaching, an attractive middle-aged woman and a younger Asian man.

"Good afternoon," he said, looking the Indian up and down and suppressing a sneer. "Are you here for the meeting?"

"I'm afraid not." The woman held up a warrant card. "Detective Inspector Katie Bradstreet and DS Tariq Aslam. North Yorkshire Police. You'll be interested to know that someone rang me this morning with information about you selling heroin to finance your White Rose campaign."

"Heroin?" laughed Churchill. "That has to be the most hilarious thing I've heard all week. *Someone*, you say?"

"An anonymous caller from a public phone," said Katie.

"Well, that certainly sounds like a trustworthy source. Are you telling me we still have public call boxes? I thought they'd all been smashed up by the immigrants." He glanced pointedly at Aslam. "There was a time when an old lady could safely use a telephone box in this fine country without…"

"We have public phones in cafes and similar places," broke in Katie. "The caller disguised his voice, but said he'd phoned me personally because he trusted me. Apparently there could be someone in the police who is sympathetic towards your party and they could be passing information to you. The caller didn't want them alerting."

"A ridiculous notion." Churchill grinned. "So you're here to ask me if this nonsense is true. You're actually going to ask me whether or not I'm selling heroin?"

"No, I sent uniform to your Birlstone House headquarters on Holgate Road earlier and shortly afterwards Sergeant Aslam and myself conducted a search of the premises when you were in Thirsk."

"My lawyer will be interested to hear that. You need a warrant to…"

"Yes, and I obtained one," said Katie. "Uniform saw a packet of white powder in one of your vehicles in the rear car park. It was sitting in plain sight on the seat and I was alerted. I had no problem obtaining the warrant from a magistrate friend who hates drugs."

"White powder?" snapped Churchill. "What kind of garbage is this?"

"Further narcotics were found in your private office," said Aslam. "Small packets of heroin were discovered in your desk…"

"Obviously planted," laughed Churchill. "This is utterly ludicrous. My office is always locked and you can't search it without me being present."

"This isn't your private dwelling," pointed out Aslam. "It's a rented building used by an organisation and one of your deputies had a key."

Churchill glared at the Asian, biting his tongue.

"Three White Rose deputies were present," said Katie. "They were all quite amenable too and gave us full permission. They smugly assured us we were wasting our time."

"Exactly. They'd know this is total bullshit."

"I had one of them open your office safe and we found more heroin. Quite a lot more, with a huge street value. The anonymous caller said that's where the bulk of the narcotics were stored and it turned out to be true."

"Planted," repeated Churchill.

"Really?" said Aslam. "Planted by whom? How many people have access to your locked office and know the safe combination?"

"I don't know." Churchill smouldered angrily, wondering who could be responsible. It didn't matter. He could threaten or pay someone into taking the blame for this and then figure it out later. "I know nothing about these drugs and you can't prove that I do."

"We found something else in the safe," said Aslam. "A Nazi SS dagger."

Churchill swallowed hard. "Planted," he growled, but with far less conviction.

"If you say so," said Aslam. "But it's currently in an evidence bag and we'll be checking it for your fingerprints. If it turns out that you keep items of SS memorabilia in your safe, it won't look too good for your career as an upstanding politician."

"Now listen, you jumped up little darkie," hissed Churchill. "You don't ever speak to me like..."

"Excuse me." Katie turned to the Pavilion manager who stood listening nearby. "Did you hear that?"

"Er, yes. I did," admitted the man.

"Thank you. I'll take a brief statement before we leave." She turned back to Churchill. "On top of everything else, that makes a total of three witnesses to an incident of verbal race hate. It seems to me as if my Sergeant could be right; this isn't looking too good for you politically."

"Just how stupid *are* you?" Churchill leant forward, trembling with rage. "Can't you see that I'm fighting to help the police, you silly bitch? I want more armed officers out there with better wages to fight against the Muslim terrorists and the black street gangs who…"

"Aren't you curious as to why we took the SS dagger as evidence?" asked Aslam. "I mean, it's a pretty repulsive thing to keep, but it isn't illegal."

"That's right," said Katie, producing two photographs from her suit jacket. "So here's why. My anonymous caller suggested I take a closer look at a picture we found at a recent crime scene. According to the writing on the reverse, it's a young boy named Kurt."

Churchill stared silently at the school photograph she held up, his teeth clenched and heart thumping. He had no idea his father had kept this. When he'd watched him beating up the Jews and blacks all those years ago in Munich, he'd never taken him for a romantic.

"It's many years old," said Katie, handing him the second picture. "I had my lab friends digitally age this child using our police computer programme and the older version looks exactly like *you*."

"The resemblance is striking," agreed Aslam. "The anonymous caller claimed you're the son of a German neo-Nazi named Stefan Schneider, who was posing as Stephen Taylor under false documentation. He ran a group in Munich called Aryan Truth, or Arische Wahrheit, and the letter AW are etched into the SS dagger found in your safe. Obviously we'll need to prove such allegations with DNA. We have Taylor's on file and we're obtaining a warrant for a sample of yours. We'll be fingerprinting the dagger and investigating the Schneider allegations as we wait for it."

"This was just a courtesy call to let you know what's happening," said Katie, turning to leave. "We'll see you again for that DNA sample very soon."

"Enjoy your meeting," said Aslam, smiling at the seething man and following his superior.

Churchill watched furiously as they spoke to the pavilion manager on their way out. *The smart-mouthed little darkie was right. The planted drugs could be worked around, but incredible as it seemed, that dagger with his prints and the school photograph would finish him.* This was beyond belief. After all the hard work and careful planning, White Rose would be ruined because of this.

He felt his phone vibrate and answered it.

"Good afternoon, Mister Churchill," said the caller. "I work for Mister Rupert Grant."

"Who are you?" snarled Churchill. "His fucking lawyer?"

"Simply an employee. As you're aware, Mister Grant intended to finance White Rose, but changed his mind. He has now reconsidered that rash decision and hopes you're still open to his generous offer."

"Is that so?" Churchill raised a curious eyebrow. "Well, you can tell him that cash would be preferred." *According to the Task Force, they'd failed at Sedgefield, but apparently this wasn't so. The fat bastard had obviously had time to think and had become worried by their threatening visit.*

"Cash is exactly what Mister Grant assumed and he's provided me with a substantial amount to give to you. I have the funds here in a holdall."

Very shortly there would be no party to fund, but "holdall" sounded like plenty of cash and it would certainly help with his relocation and a fresh start.

"Really?" growled Churchill. "Where are you?"

"I understand you're currently hosting a White Rose meeting in Whitby? I'll meet you at St. Mary's, the church at the top of the 199 steps."

"*What*? That's a weird place to meet, isn't it?"

"Mister Grant wants our meeting to be discrete," said Geller, smiling. "I'll see you there at sunset."

* * * *

Chapter 41

Quist parked outside a café on the Scarborough seafront and jumped from the car. The sun was low and yelping gulls wheeled in the afternoon sky above Madame Selene's white-painted cabin on the promenade.

"I won't be long," he said. "You three had better wait here."

"Is he serious?" gasped Hoffman. He paused in reading *the Key of Honorius* to watch from the passenger seat as the detective negotiated the traffic to reach the shed. "He's actually going to ask a seaside psychic where Geller might be?"

"That's the plan." Watson shrugged. "Apparently Madame Selene is the real thing. The boss met her the other day and apparently she knew everything about him."

"You mean like how gullible he was?" Hoffman nodded, amazed. "I can't believe he's doing this."

"Really?" The teenager let out a short laugh. "I can't believe we're driving around searching for a friggin' monster that's capable of crushing people's heads."

"Hey, I once visited a psychic medium myself," said Rex, grinning. "I told her a joke and, when she was laughing, I punched her in the face. The thing is, I always like to strike a happy medium."

Watson and Hoffman stared blankly at him.

"You honestly don't think that's funny?" Rex shook his head. "Why doesn't anyone find that funny?"

Madame Selene appeared at her open cabin door. "Well, hello again," she said. "I was just about to close."

Quist was surprised at how much the woman had visibly deteriorated in the few days since he'd first met her and he smiled sympathetically. "You weren't expecting me?" he said. "Well, I have to say, Vera, that isn't exactly reassuring."

"It doesn't work like that, but I can sense that you need my help." She coughed into her handkerchief. "So what can I do for you, Mister Wolf?"

241

"Er, you could begin by not referring to me as *that*." Laughing uneasily and stepping inside, Quist reached into his pocket and produced the small piece of clay he'd picked up in Geller's apartment. "The name is Bernard and yes, I could definitely use your assistance today. You were correct when you told me I was heading towards darkness and death. You mentioned a dangerous dark figure too. I have something here for you to touch. I'd like you to try your psychometry skills and tell me if you feel anything."

Vera took the brown nugget, instantly dropped it and staggered slightly.

"Careful how you go there." The detective caught her arm and guided her to a chair. "Let's sit down."

"Do you know what that *is*?" she gasped, trembling. "That piece of clay, it came from... It came from a creature known as a golem."

"I'm afraid that's right." He brought out Geller's comb. "I also have this which I took from someone's bathroom earlier. It contains one or two hairs from the owner and I was hoping that, if you touched it..."

"Daniel Geller," she said, taking it and running her fingers slowly over the teeth. "This man is very dangerous, Bernard. Oh, yes, this Geller is consumed with so much darkness and hatred. He's killed people and he intends to kill again."

"That sounds about right. Can you tell me where he..."

"Whitby," said Vera, nodding. "Right now he's just along the coast from us in Whitby, outside a church on a cliff." She pointed to the clay. "I really don't want to touch it, but would you pass me that clay again?"

Quist retrieved the nugget from the carpet and handed it to her.

Vera winced. "This is so dark and cold," she whispered. "The golem is lethal. This man Geller has turned it into a deadly weapon and its icy darkness is even present here in this tiny piece. The creature is there with him at St. Mary's churchyard, but you'll need to hurry. The blackness is closing in swiftly and horrific death and terror are waiting there."

"Thank you," said Quist, smiling awkwardly. "I'm only guessing, but during your time working here, was that the most gloomy reading you've ever given?"

* * * *

Heading across the desolate North York Moors to the Yorkshire coast, travellers don't really see Whitby until the last moment. The River Esk cuts through the headland here, carving out a valley flanked by cliffs, and the town nestles around an ancient harbour in the deep cleft. The old fishing port clings to the eastern side of the water – a picturesque jumble of cobbled streets, red-tiled rooftops and twisting alleyways – and the Victorian crescents and stately hotels of the New Town fill the opposite horizon.

Watson sat beside Rex in the rear of Quist's car, peering at the sky as they drove along the West Cliff Esplanade. Fingers of crimson mottled the gunmetal clouds and a deep red blush tinted the darkening heavens. The colours reflected upon the expanse of ocean beyond the harbour's two stone piers, but night was swiftly overtaking the dramatic sunset. A little *too* swiftly for Watson's liking.

"Er, Guv," he said, nervously clearing his throat. "Being a brilliant detective, you might have already noticed, but the sun has gone down. I wasn't too keen on bumping into Tonga *before*, but now it's getting dark he's able to change into his golem form. You know – his nasty head-crushing, spine breaking form."

"Ah, right." Rex grinned at him over his sunglasses. "I wondered what that weird noise was, but it's just the sound of Watson's spine melting."

"Yeah, it's okay for you," whispered the teenager. "You have a *hairy* advantage over me in dangerous situations."

"We should have come straight here," pointed out Hoffman. He sat in the passenger seat with the *Key of Honorius* open on his lap. "If we'd driven to the Whitby Pavilion instead of calling at Scarborough, we'd have found Churchill at his meeting."

"Probably," said Quist. "But not Daniel Geller and he's our primary concern. We can't know for certain whether he'll approach

Churchill at the party meeting, but we know exactly where he and the golem are right now."

"Because your seaside psychic told you?" said Hoffman, incredulously.

"What?" laughed Rex. "Are you telling me you don't believe in psychics? A guy who made a killer monster using a pile of clay and a magic book?"

Hoffman smiled tensely. "Point taken," he mumbled.

Quist pulled up by the kerb and gestured to the huge book on Hoffman's lap. "Speaking of magic books, is that the ritual you mentioned earlier?"

"Yes," said Hoffman, stroking the page. "If I can get close enough to the golem and I'm able to recite this fully, the incantation should release it from Geller's control."

"And will you then be able to control it yourself?"

"As I created it, yes." Hoffman nodded. "From what I can understand of this text, I believe it will revert to obeying my commands. Then we'd have to extract the scroll from its mouth and it will transform back into clay. The incantation is lengthy, but I've been reading it over and over on the way here to ensure I remember everything."

"Allow me to assist." Reaching over, the detective ripped out the page and handed it to him. "Here, take it with you and read it when the time comes. You can't trust this to memory and you'll need to be word perfect."

"Have you..." Hoffman gaped at the torn page, horrified. "Have you *any* idea how valuable this book is?"

Quist nodded. "Ordinarily I'd cherish such historical works of the literary art, but our current enterprise is far more important." He pulled away and drove along the Esplanade. "The book itself is too large and unwieldly to carry and use, but now you have everything you need on that page."

Watson smiled uneasily at Hoffman's shocked expression and returned to peering out of the window.

Whitby had changed very little since Bram Stoker penned the

story of *Dracula* in 1897 and, if the author walked these streets today, he'd find the place virtually as he described it over a century ago. The Royal Hotel dominated the West Cliff promontory with the Captain Cook monument in a small area of parkland outside. The explorer's statue stood beside a tall arch, formed by the aged and bleached jawbones of a whale that commemorates the hunting fleets that once sailed from this port.

"Wow!" said Watson. "Look at these guys."

A popular tourist spot, the benches and lawns around the whalebones were usually crowded with visitors drinking in the stunning views of the town and harbour below. Tonight, the little park was filled with vampire wannabes, the men sporting black cloaks and the women wearing the creepy gossamer negligees seen in old Hammer horror films. Even Captain Cook's statue had been kitted out with a cape, glued-on fangs and rubber bats dangling from the hands.

"Goths," said Quist, smiling. "One has to admit, they can be darkly inventive."

The panoramic view from here was quite stunning and Watson gazed across at the opposite headland. He could see the distant flight of steps that wound up the precipitous hillside and the church and ruined abbey beyond, both dimly illuminated by golden floodlights.

"So Geller's over there, is he?" he said, frowning apprehensively. "According to your mate Psychic Sally, he's up there at the church with his pet golem?"

"Correct," said Quist, turning down the steep road into town. "That's where we're heading."

"Ah, no need to worry." Rex grinned at the anxious teenager. "This will be a piece of cake and your boss and I will protect you."

"You're far too complacent, Rex," warned Quist. "You're also excited and eager about this and that could be hazardous."

"Yeah, right." Rex winked at Watson.

Hoffman gave the three men a confused glance. He had no idea what Quist was planning to do when they met up with Geller, but he and his young friend in sunglasses couldn't protect *anyone* from the golem.

"Who's worried?" mumbled Watson. "Sara's granddad is going to read a magic spell to stop a monster from tearing us to bits. It's not like this is dangerous or anything."

They arrived on the busy Whitby seafront to find vampires everywhere, some in groups and some drifting eerily about on their own. A firm fan of horror movies, Watson saw that many impersonated Christopher Lee's *Dracula*, some had opted for the Bela Lugosi look, and others wore the top hat, sunglasses and sophisticated outfit of Gary Oldman's version of the Count. Attractive girls with fangs and pallid complexions floated around in white nighties with next to nothing underneath, and some had dressed as Morticia, Vampira and, for some obscure reason, the goddess Hela from the *Thor* movies. The younger crowd mimicked characters from the *Twilight* saga and all furtively inspected one another to determine who had the better costume.

"So why is everyone dressed as Frankenstein?" asked Rex, bemused.

"*Dracula*," corrected Watson, glancing at him disbelievingly. "They're all vampires."

"Same thing." Rex shrugged. "So why?"

"Halloween in Whitby is a really big celebration for the Goths," explained the teenager. "They come to the town from all over and do this every October the 31st. Certain other nights of the year too." He pointed to an approaching furry figure. "Hey, now this guy is definitely no vampire."

The werewolf ran into the road and pretended to attack the car, waving its paws and growling ferociously at them before its hairy trousers fell down. Watson had seen scarier characters on *the Muppets* and Quist and Rex exchanged deadpan glances.

"What's going on with this bunch up ahead," asked Rex.

Amateur Goth actors were performing horror street theatre in various locations and a small group were hammering a wooden stake through a vampire girl outside a fish and chip restaurant. A priest waved a crucifix and the spectators cheered as spurts of fake blood shot out, splattering Quist's car as it passed by.

"Yeah, whatever," drawled Rex. "I suppose it beats busking."

"Horrible," said Hoffman, watching uneasily as the gore ran down the window.

"Indeed." Quist glanced at the *Key of Honorius* page in the old man's trembling hand. "Although I suspect we may witness far worse horrors before this Halloween is over."

* * * *

Chapter 42

The twilight had darkened into night, the clouds had cleared and a bright half-moon sparkled silver on the ocean below Whitby's eastern headland. Churchill wore a dark blue coat over his suit and climbed the 199 worn stone steps that curled up the hillside to St. Mary's churchyard.

Black railings flanked the steep flight and ancient iron lamp posts stood on the turns, once lit by gas and now fitted with low wattage electricity. Constructed over two centuries ago, the Victorian builders had thoughtfully broken the climb every so often with rest areas and benches. These small landings were originally designed to allow coffin bearers to pause on their route to the church, but they now provided the less athletic tourists with a chance to catch their breath and take countless photographs of the view on their phones.

Churchill sneered at the groups of vampires smoking on the seats and the howling werewolf that ran down past him waving its furry arms. A girl with fangs glanced up over her phone and hissed theatrically, but he ignored her and continued his ascent. He definitely wasn't in the mood for such childish crap tonight.

The man shook his head angrily. *Who could have known his safe combination and planted those drugs in the office?* He'd find out somehow through his friends in the police and whoever it was would definitely pay with their life. But his fingerprints on the SS dagger and his childhood photograph were the problem. His true background as Kurt Schneider would soon be exposed and the White Rose Party was finished. Devastating as this was, it was merely a setback in the planned race war, however the man known as Dominic Churchill would now need to vanish from existence.

Nearing the top of the steps, he peered over the moonlit rooftops to his right and smiled to himself. All those years ago, when the Churchill personality had been expensively created, he'd had another fake identity and background carefully prepared for just such an emergency. There was plenty of cash in his secret offshore accounts and it was time to disappear, relocate under the new name of David Wellington and begin a fresh political movement after a little plastic surgery. Cornwall would be a good choice. Like Yorkshire, the Cornish people were proud of their county and it would be a hell of a lot warmer down south. This unexpected donation from Rupert Grant would help, if indeed it was authentic.

Why the hell would anyone propose a meeting in an isolated place like this?

Churchill reached the hilltop cemetery and narrowed his eyes. He'd been suspicious since the surprising phone call and the more he thought about it, the more he decided this could be a trap of some sort. But if that was the case, what kind of trap and who could be behind it? One thing was for sure, if this wasn't genuine, the perpetrator would really regret it.

The Victorian graveyard covered the headland, extending beyond St. Mary's church and across the grassy summit to the distant cliffs. Weathered by ocean salt and bowed by innumerable winter storms, ancient headstones sprouted everywhere like crooked grey teeth. Costumed goths in cloaks prowled the overgrown terrain around them and the ruins of the Benedictine abbey loomed behind the church, the tall arches gaunt and spectral in their amber glow of floodlights. Churchill had read the novel *Dracula* as a youth and this place featured memorably in the story. The famous bench was still here, the Victorian seat beside the church where the Count fed upon the Lucy character one moonlit night.

He frowned curiously as someone waved to him from it. The elderly man had a thick moustache and sat waiting beside a younger brown-skinned character who wore a raincoat. Walking closer along the church path through the tombs, Churchill noticed the shaven-headed man had bare feet and legs. Either he was wearing shorts in late October, or he was naked from the waist down beneath the coat.

"Good evening, Dominic," said the older man, as he approached. "It's a lovely night, isn't it? Just look at this incredible view – the old piers and the lighthouses."

"I assume you're Rupert Grant's employee?" Churchill paused some ten feet away, guarded on hearing the man's accent. "The one who called me at the pavilion? You didn't sound German on the phone."

"I made a point of disguising my voice." Daniel Geller climbed to his feet. "But yes, that was me. I've seen you at your party meetings, but it's so nice to meet you face to face."

"The feeling's mutual." Churchill smiled sarcastically. "I believe you have something for me? A holdall with a donation from Grant?"

"I'm afraid I haven't brought any money." Geller patted his pockets. "The offer was just a ruse to get you here, Dominic. Or should I call you Kurt Schneider?"

"Well, now this is interesting." Churchill quickly looked around, but apart from the drunken vampires in the graveyard a couple of hundred feet away, they were alone. He glanced at the man's young companion, but he sat with a blank expression and didn't appear to be listening. "Why would you call me that name?"

"Because you *are* Schneider, aren't you? I discovered your true identity yesterday." Geller smiled cruelly. "Shortly after killing your uncle Dieter and then your father Stefan."

"I see." Churchill stiffened, but managed to contain the rage building inside. "If that's true, whatever would possess you to do such a thing?"

"Oh, it's true. They killed my parents many years ago in Munich." Geller shrugged. "I could go into the details, but why bother? Suffice to say, I really enjoyed killing them and the four men in your Task Force too."

Churchill nodded. "As you can imagine, I've been very eager to meet the lunatic responsible and here you are."

"And here I am. Geller is the name, Daniel Geller."

"So *you're* Geller, the one who sent the letters to my father and the police? Presumably you lured me to this secluded spot at night with the insane notion of murdering me too?"

"That's the general idea." Grinning widely, Geller turned to the seated figure. "Tonga, stand up. This is Dominic Churchill."

"Tonga?" Trembling with anger, Churchill glared at him. Now that this young man was standing, he could see the coat was unbuttoned and, bizarrely, he appeared to be naked underneath. He showed no interest in the situation and stared blankly into the distance. "Yes, according to my police contact, that was the name of the fake carer who showed up at Wisteria Lodge. The description fits too, right down to the bare feet. He'll be your hired muscle, I take it?"

"That's one way of describing him." Geller laughed. "Tonga is the one who crushed Dieter's head and broke your father's back."

"Is that a fact?" Churchill reached into his coat, produced an automatic pistol with a silencer and fired without warning.

Geller grunted and staggered back, clutching his side.

"Oh, dear," said Churchill, looking around to ensure they were still alone and unseen. "I don't imagine you were expecting that, were you?"

The wounded man jumped for cover behind the motionless Tonga. He certainly *hadn't* expected it.

"You asked me to meet you in an isolated graveyard," snarled Churchill. "Did you honestly think I'd be stupid enough to come here without protection? So this is your bodyguard and hired assassin? Well, *my* bodyguard is this Luger from the war; I take it everywhere hidden in my car. It's a German SS gun that I'm sure killed Jews back in the day. It's time it killed another, along with this witness. This is for my father."

Churchill shot Tonga twice in the chest, but he didn't flinch. Frowning, he fired again. Holes appeared in the raincoat, but the young man continued to peer silently at the ocean with dead eyes.

"Tonga," snapped Geller, wincing at the intense pain pulsing in his side. "Dominic Churchill is your target. Kill him now."

The young man shrugged off the raincoat, his naked brown body swelling as he grew five inches in height.

"What in God's name is *this*?" stammered Churchill, freezing as the golem's eyes glowed red and it lumbered forward. "What *is* it?"

The silencer coughed again and again. Rooted to the spot petrified, he gaped in terror to see clay chippings fall from its torso around the gleaming red symbols which had appeared. He'd seen things like this in fantasy horror movies, but this was real. This thing was *real* and it was walking towards him.

His mind somehow forcing his body to move, Churchill backed away from the advancing creature, but his ankle caught one of the low tombs behind him and he stumbled, falling backwards onto the flat headstone.

"Careful, Dominic," hissed Geller, clutching his wound. "Watch you don't hurt yourself there."

Scrambling to get up and firing again, Churchill moaned to hear the click of an empty magazine, the moan rising to a squeal of agony as the golem grabbed his gun hand and effortlessly crushed it. The broken pistol fell from his pulverised fingers and the creature pressed a huge clay foot on his midriff, pinning him down on the horizontal granite slab. Churchill turned his head to stare pleadingly at Geller, but knew it was pointless.

"You were quite right," admitted Geller. "I didn't expect that gun, but I dare say you weren't expecting *this*."

"Dominic Churchill?" said Tonga.

"Yes," he croaked, assuming he was about to be asked a question by this thing.

The golem gripped an upright gravestone beside the tomb and brought it down hard onto Churchill's head. Crushed flat between the two slabs, the man's brains gushed out from the stone sandwich like bubbling raspberry porridge. Wisps of steam escaped and the half-moon glittered upon the splatter.

"Goodbye, Dominic," said Geller, grinning manically. "Give my regards to your father and his brother."

Nauseous from the pain in his side, he glanced around to ensure there were no witnesses. The Goths cavorted spookily in the cemetery some distance away, totally oblivious to the drama that had just taken place. Satisfied, he pressed a folded handkerchief over the bullet wound and grimaced.

"Tonga," said Geller. "Return to human form and put on your coat."

The golem obediently complied, transforming once again into the smaller shape of a young man and returning to the bench to pull on the raincoat.

"It's time to leave." Leaning on the silent creature for support, Geller looked back at the twitching corpse beneath the heavy slab and smirked. "I must say, Tonga, you're becoming remarkably inventive as you progress in our crusade."

* * * *

Chapter 43

Flowing down from the moorland, the River Esk runs into the North Sea through Whitby's harbour and a main road has traversed the water at this spot for over seven-hundred years. Quist drove across the current iron swing bridge and turned left into Church Street, entering the oldest part of the seaside town.

The cobbled thoroughfare was narrow, with winding alleyways leading off, and ancient inns and twee shops on either side. Costumed Goths filled the road ahead, wandering around in their cloaks and staggering from pub to pub, many intoxicated from copious amounts of *Dracula's Ale, Stoker's Stout, Bat's Blood Lager* and *Bram's Brew*. The detective braked and crawled along at a steady pace, careful not to collide with anyone.

"You say we're almost there?" Rex lowered his sunglasses and winked at a scantily clad vampire. This olde worlde place reminded him of the Shambles in York. "So where are these famous 199 steps up to the church?"

"Around the bend at the end of this street," said Hoffman.

"I honestly can't wait," muttered Watson, still tense and very nervous. He wondered how it was possible to tremble and perspire at the same time. "What's the plan, Guv?"

"We find Geller," said Quist. "If we can somehow distract him whilst Adam reads his occult incantation, the golem will be released from his control and hopefully it will obey Adam instead. Then we remove this scroll from its mouth to transform it back into clay."

"Oh, right." Watson nodded. "When you put it like that, it sounds easy."

Rex laughed. "Like I said earlier, a piece of cake."

The route became tighter still after the old Wesleyan chapel on their right and a dense crowd blocked the way.

"What's going on here?" asked Hoffman.

"I don't know," admitted Quist, "but I can't possibly get through them." He brought the car to a halt outside a jeweller's shop trading in Whitby jet. "No matter. The road is so narrow up ahead, I doubt I'll be able to park any closer to the steps. It would be more prudent to proceed on foot from this point."

The four men jumped out and soon realised the crowd were watching another group of actors performing horror street theatre. Quist led the way, pushing through the throng, and saw a priest and his helpers exorcising a young girl dressed as a nun who hissed and thrashed as they pinned her down on the pavement. Watson hurried past, aware that, at any moment, he could be on the receiving end of a projectile spurt of green vomit.

"You should see a doctor about that," advised Rex, wincing at the girl's cracked demonic face and bright red eyes.

The detective rushed by the Board Inn and around the corner onto Church Lane to reach the bottom of the precipitous 199 steps up the hillside. The winding stone flight above them looked to be empty, the Goths having come down to watch the exorcism show they'd just passed. They began to climb and then came to a halt three quarters of the way up as two descending figures appeared around the turn, the pair illuminated by the old iron lamp post beside them. Watson guessed the older one with the thick moustache must be Geller, his bald, brown-skinned companion with the raincoat being something of a giveaway.

"Shit," mumbled the youth, gulping and quickly moving behind Quist. They stood fifteen feet apart, but he'd seen how fast Tonga could run.

Rex peered at the golem, unable to see what all the fuss was about. "Is that *him*?" he whispered. "Is that Gollum?"

"Ah, Adam." Geller paused in his descent and grinned widely. "It's good to see you again."

"No thanks to you, is it?" snarled Hoffman, shaking with rage. "I can't believe you tried to murder us, you crazy bastard."

"All's fair in love and war," joked Geller. "I notice you've brought three friends." He narrowed his eyes curiously. "Including someone wearing sunglasses at night. Aren't you going to introduce us?"

"I'm Bernard Quist," said the detective, warily eyeing the silent creature by his side. "I presume Churchill is up there at the church and he's dead?"

"He is." Geller nodded sympathetically. "I don't know if you were thinking of sending flowers to the funeral, but he was quite fond of roses, especially white ones."

"There's a coincidence," said Rex, missing the sarcasm. "Because his political party was called…"

"You tried to kill Sara last night," snapped Watson, his frightened gaze still fixed on the motionless Tonga. "A totally innocent girl. Now that was a real twat's trick, mate."

"And who might you be?" enquired Geller. "Ah, presumably the private detective boyfriend that Adam told me about?"

"Just a friend," corrected Rex, quickly. "Sara doesn't have a boyfriend… yet."

"I know why you've been doing this," said Quist. "But it has to end tonight, Daniel. You can't continue killing…"

"Of course I can." Geller clutched the sodden handkerchief to the wound in his side and held onto the railings that ran alongside the steps. "There are plenty more out there just like Churchill. You must know what these people stand for and how evil they are."

"I can't help but notice you've been hurt." The detective gestured to his bloodied coat. "You're in obvious pain and I strongly suggest you accompany us to my car where we can talk about how to end…"

"That isn't going to happen," snapped Geller. "And *I* strongly suggest you all move out of our way."

"Listen to me," sighed Quist, "I know all about how your parents died and I understand this *crusade* of yours. To be truthful, I could almost sympathise with you, but then you sent your creature to kill Adam and his granddaughter. This is over."

Geller glanced at the young man in sunglasses and stiffened slightly. Hoffman had moved behind him, partly concealing himself from view, and he appeared to be reading aloud from a page of parchment.

"Kada nostra, kada estra," recited the elderly man. "Kada nostra, kada estra…"

"Adam, my old friend," growled Geller. "Whatever that mystical gibberish is, you'd better stop it right now."

Hoffman continued, raising his voice and speeding up the recital.

"As you wish." Geller turned to the silent figure behind him. "Tonga, Kill Adam Hoffman. Kill him now."

Tonga threw off his raincoat and instantly transformed, the fiery Kabbalistic symbols gleaming on the swelling body and the eyes in the flattened face burning red like rubies. Quist had witnessed a great many strange things in his time, but even *he* watched with utter amazement.

"Bloody hell," whispered Watson, gaping in terror at the full-sized creature, a creature which now looked to be as hard as rock. "Er, Guv, this isn't good."

"Whoo!" Rex peered over his sunglasses as the golem began to move forward, swaying slowly from side to side as it methodically descended one step at a time. "He's a big boy, isn't he?"

Quist glanced over his shoulder. From this position above the Whitby rooftops he could see the cobbled street and the buildings at the base of the winding flight and, for the moment at least, they were alone. Judging from the sound of the distant cheering and shouting, the crowds on Church Lane below were still preoccupied with the exorcism show around the corner.

The golem lumbered closer to Hoffman, reaching out its hands as the man reached the end of his incantation. "Uriel Seraphim Io Potesta Zati Zata Galatim Galata."

Geller frowned warily as the creature paused, its arms still outstretched. Clasping his wound, he followed it down the five steps. "Tonga, kill Adam Hoffman," he repeated. "Then kill these others. What are you waiting for?"

There was no response and Watson watched anxiously, his

257

heart pounding. Silver moonlight glinted on the golem's wide shoulders and head. Thanks to the blank clay features and tiny red eyes, he couldn't be certain, but the motionless creature gave the impression it was thinking things over.

"Do it." Geller slapped a hand on the golem's back and attempted to shove it forward. It was like pushing at a brick outhouse. "I said kill them all. Do it now."

"I'm afraid you're wasting your time," said Quist. "That murderous thing was under your exclusive command, but Adam's incantation just released it. The creature no longer obeys you and this is over."

Geller glared furiously at Hoffman, then glanced at Tonga's slit-like open mouth, an idea quickly forming. The golem had been rendered immobile, but perhaps there was a straightforward resolution to this. Tonga had obeyed him because he was the one who had placed the magical scroll in there. Maybe Hoffman's mystical mumbo-jumbo could be overcome by simply removing and then replacing it, much like switching a faulty electrical appliance off and on.

He reached for its blank face, only to grunt in pain as motion suddenly returned and one of the outstretched arms smacked his hand away. *Tonga had recognised what he was about to do and had prevented him. Surely not? Could he be somehow making his own decisions?*

"Now listen to me, Tonga," said Geller. His heart raced as the creature slowly lowered its head to gaze at him with eyes burning like hot coals. "You know me and we're partners in this crusade. Remember that we're *partners*. You will do as I command and you will…"

"No," said Tonga.

Geller whimpered as the golem's large hands clamped tightly onto his shoulders like bench vices, wrenching the right towards itself whilst forcing the left backwards. Steam billowed on the cold night air and he glanced down, realising it had escaped from his exposed internal organs. Just as one might tear a sheet of paper in half, Geller's body had been ripped apart from neck to waist.

Yes, he'd been correct back there in the graveyard. Tonga was definitely becoming more inventive with his killings.

"Oh my God," croaked Watson, his throat tight with fear. "Oh, God, no. I'm going to see that shit every time I close my fuckin' eyes."

Dropping the corpse, the golem began lumbering down the steps towards the four men.

"Halt," called out Hoffman. Backing away, he stared in horror at the entrails which had spilled from Geller's torn remains, realising his own body may soon resemble this ghastly mess. A torrent of blood from the dead man gushed down the stone flight, sparkling black in the cold moonlight. "You will now obey *me*. You will obey *only* me and you will stop right there."

It continued to descend, the red eyes gleaming brighter.

"Damn, it isn't working," snapped Quist. "It seems you were wrong, Adam. The control hasn't reverted to you, as you assumed. It no longer obeys *anyone*. This thing is now free to do whatever it wants and, thanks to Geller, it only knows how to kill."

"Well, that's just great," said Watson, trembling.

Racing down twenty-five steps to put some distance between himself and the ponderous creature, Quist quickly tugged off his shoes and stuffed them into his overcoat pockets. Knowing a transformation might be necessary, he'd left his watch and signet ring in the car earlier.

"I don't know how to stop it," moaned Hoffman, following with Watson and Rex. "God help me, I *can't* stop it."

"Don't worry." Rex slipped his sunglasses into his jacket and grinned. "Just leave this to the experts."

"Rex, listen to me," hissed the detective, angrily. "We have to extract that scroll and you need to restrain your excitement and exercise caution."

"Yeah, yeah," chuckled Rex, removing his Rolex and winking. "No problem."

"You can't go near it," stammered Hoffman. "It would be suicide."

Shrugging off the overcoat, Quist passed it to him. "I wonder if you could hold onto this for me, Adam? We may need your occult knowledge here so, whatever you do, please don't run away when you see what I'm about to do. If the concept of a supernatural golem didn't perturb you, then hopefully you should be able to cope with *this*."

"Yeah, hopefully." Watson moved back even further. "Good luck, mate."

"Cope with *what*? What are you talking..." Hoffman's words ended as Quist dropped into a squat, his bones crackling, his body growing and his features elongating into a lupine muzzle. "What in the name of... What in *God's* name?"

Too petrified to even notice the temperature plummet, the old man turned to see Rex transforming too. Shirts and trousers were ripped apart as the men swiftly shapeshifted, black furry torsos and limbs expanding until two enormous wolves stood upright in their place. Unable to move, he gazed at the huge teeth, the pointed ears and glowing amber eyes. The younger werewolf broke the spell by handing Hoffman his leather jacket.

"Careful with that," he growled, wagging his tail. "It's Gucci and really expensive."

"What in God's name?" repeated Hoffman, his voice a strangled croak.

"Are you ready, Rex?" asked Quist, staring at the golem. It had almost reached them and he debated how best to attack. Whatever he decided upon, he knew this would be like assailing a granite boulder. "We need to flank this thing and work together to get it onto its back. You go left and I'll go right."

"Er, my left or Gollum's left?" asked Rex.

"Just *go*," snarled Quist, darting forward. "Be very careful."

"Didn't I tell you this would be a piece of cake?" Rex grinned at Watson. "Just watch this."

Ignoring the instruction, Rex ran directly at the creature, then yelped as a powerful and unexpectedly fast arm shot out, effortlessly swatting him away. The wolf's flying body slammed hard into the staircase handrail, twisting the metal and snapping its spine.

Watson watched with bulging eyes as Rex fell in a furry broken heap.

"*Brilliant*," drawled Quist, shaking his head. "What a marvellous help *you* were."

Hoffman felt dizzy and realised that, for the past several seconds, he'd actually forgotten to breathe. He gazed in sheer disbelief as Quist ran by the golem on all fours, dodging the grasping hands, to wrap his arms around the creature's upper thighs from behind in a futile attempt to unbalance it. The bizarre spectacle seemed unreal − almost like a slow-motion cartoon − and Hoffman knew it had to be shock.

"Are you okay?" stuttered Watson, grabbing his hand and panting with fear.

"Okay?" murmured Hoffman, dreamily. "Er, yes, of course. Your boss is a werewolf and he's fighting Tonga. Yes, of course I'm okay."

"It's like you're in a trance." Watson turned from his blank face as Quist squealed in pain; the golem had gripped the wolf's shoulder and crushed the bone. "Listen, mate, you really have to snap out of this. We have to stop it. What the hell do we do?"

"Er, right…" mumbled Hoffman, mesmerised by the wrestling. "The, er, the scroll, it needs, er it…"

Taking a deep breath, Watson did something he never imagined he'd ever do to Sara's grandad and smacked him hard across the face.

Hoffman sucked in air and shook himself. "Yes, yes, we have to stop this," he spluttered, returning to something approaching normal, or at least what *passed* for normal right now. "This is all my fault. Yes, stopping this thing is my responsibility."

Rex's broken spine had healed and, climbing unsteadily to his feet, he ran again at the golem to help the wounded Quist, clamping his enormous wolf jaws onto its left leg. *Not the wisest of moves*, he decided, as three teeth painfully splintered and fell out.

"Hold the arms," yelled Hoffman, finally finding his voice and moving closer. "Try to prevent those arms from moving so I can get in there."

Quist grabbed the right arm, wrapping his large body tightly around it and grunting at the agony in his shoulder. Rex leapt up to snatch the left and swung on it with his full weight. Somehow managing to push aside his terror, Hoffman took the opportunity to rush forward. Quickly sticking his trembling fingers into the golem's open mouth, he fumbled around frantically and pulled out the small roll of parchment.

"I have it," he yelled, scuttling away. "It's out."

The creature instantly stiffened, its eyes losing the red gleam and the Kabbalistic body markings vanishing. It twisted its left arm and jerked it out straight, casting Rex off.

"Shit," he growled, flying through the air a second time.

Narrowly missing Watson, the flailing Rex rolled down twenty stone steps, snarling guttural profanities on every excruciating bounce. Not wishing to be knocked off his feet by airborne werewolves, the teenager darted up the flight and past the violent scuffle.

"The scroll is out," repeated Hoffman. "It's just dry clay now."

Quist felt the strength waning in the creature's arm and, releasing his grip, he pushed hard. The golem tottered, swaying back and forth, and summoning the tiny amount of courage he had left, Watson slammed himself into its back. The clay figure toppled forward and Hoffman jumped aside as it hit the steps face-first to noisily shatter in a cloud of brown dust. An avalanche of rubble cascaded down the flight and past the returning Rex.

"I can't believe I just did that," gasped the terrified teenager, shaking uncontrollably. "Did I just *do* that?"

"You did indeed," said Quist, breathing heavily and massaging his healing shoulder. Well done, Watson."

"Yeah," said Rex, dodging the tumbling clay fragments and smiling uncomfortably. "Er, didn't I tell you it would be a piece of cake?"

Quist looked down the steps and froze, alarmed to see that a small crowd of people had gathered on Church Lane at the bottom. He hadn't noticed them during the fight and the Goths stood silently watching with open mouths. Luckily, all seemed far too astounded to take out their phones and film anything. One suddenly began to slowly clap, followed by another and then the rest.

"Amazing," whispered Quist, as the spectators began to cheer. "Listen to me. Everyone just act natural. Watson, gather up our torn clothing and then the three of you follow me."

The teenager scurried around picking up the garment scraps as Quist retrieved his leather overcoat from the trembling Hoffman and slung it flamboyantly around his shoulders like a cloak. Rex did the same with his Gucci jacket and the wolves descended the steps on their hind legs to escalating applause, whooping and whistling. Watson and Hoffman followed through the dust cloud, the youth glancing down as he passed the lumps of shattered clay. All had crumbled to brown powder and there was nothing left to indicate that the murderous Tonga had ever existed.

"Absolutely brilliant, lads," enthused one of the crowd, clapping wildly as they approached. "That had to be the best horror street theatre ever."

"Why thank you," growled Quist. "Your praise is much appreciated."

"You're too kind," said Rex, nodding approvingly at the cheering. "There'll be a repeat performance at midnight."

"That was bloody amazing," agreed an applauding werewolf. "I thought *my* costume was good, but *those* are absolutely fantastic."

"Thanks," said Watson, taking the offered tips as he moved through the throng. "I made them myself. My mate here did the clockwork clay guy and the waxwork body up there on the steps."

Hoffman jerkily nodded and somehow managed a rigid smile. The incredible realisation of everything that had happened in the last couple of minutes was finally sinking in. The golem was no more and, inconceivable and insane as it might seem, he was strolling through Whitby with two real-life werewolves.

A drunken vampire girl darted between the wolves and took a phone picture of herself with them. She scribbled her number on a scrap of paper and, assuming it was part of a fake head mask, pushed it into

Rex's left ear for safekeeping.

"Ooh, you're fuckin' gorgeous," she slurred. "Ring me."

"Cheerio for now," said Quist, swiftly leading the way along Church Lane. "That was fun and hopefully we'll see you all again at midnight for the next show."

Reaching the corner of the street, he glanced back and saw that some of the crowd were now climbing the steps to where Geller's torn corpse lay bleeding. They would undoubtedly compliment the waxwork on how realistic it appeared, but only for a short time, before reality dawned, the screaming and puking began, and the police were inevitably contacted.

"We need to move fast," he said, quickening his pace. "Come on, before anyone gets a chance to take down my vehicle registration."

Hurrying along the street, Watson and Hoffman jumped into the detective's parked car, with the two wolves crushing their furry bulk into the rear seat. Rex slammed the door, grunted in pain, then pulled in his tail and closed it again. Despite his lack of driving license, Watson gunned the engine and accelerated away down the narrow cobbled thoroughfare.

The teenager let out a short staccato laugh, a nervous release of tension. *Right now, driving without a license would be the least of their worries if any cops stopped the car and saw Fido and Bonzo in the back.*

"I noticed there was no CCTV," growled Quist, glancing over his shoulder. "Watson, I need you to think carefully; did anyone photograph either you or Adam?"

"No, I was watching out for that," said the youth, turning onto the main road. "They were far too busy looking at your *costumes* and no one was bothered about us. Mind you, that pissed-up bird got a pretty good shot of you both."

Rex plucked the telephone number from his ear and read it. "Ooh, apparently she's called Donna." He smiled sexily, or as sexily as possible for a wolf. "Mmmh, this lucky girl will soon be getting a call from…"

Sighing and taking the paper, Quist screwed it up and tossed it out of the window. "That photograph doesn't matter," he said, relieved. "It's Halloween and, as you say, we were obviously wearing *costumes*. Speaking of which…"

Hoffman froze, his bowel lurching, as a large paw of talons clutched his shoulder and Quist leant forward from the rear seat. He whimpered slightly as the wolf's head appeared beside his face, the eyes glowing amber in the darkness. Attempting to calm him down, the wolf smiled warmly, but the wide mouth of gleaming fangs didn't help matters.

"We did it, Adam," said Quist. "The golem and Daniel Geller are no more and, thanks to your occult knowledge and that incantation, his homicidal crusade is finished. This terrible situation is finally over, however, I need to ask a large favour. Could I implore you *never* to mention anything about werewolves?"

"No, I won't say anything," said Hoffman, his voice a strangled whine. "Of course not. No, I didn't see *anything*."

"You can't even tell your granddaughter." The wolf shrugged. "It's a simple matter of trust. Don't mention our lycanthropy and Rex and I will never mention your involvement and how you created a creature that killed all those people."

"I won't say a word," stammered Hoffman. "I owe you so much for saving Sara in Leeds, for stopping Geller and for keeping me out of this. I promise you I won't mention anything about how you and Rex are… No, no, absolutely not. No."

"Thank you," said the wolf, eyeing his petrified expression. "Er, actually I need to ask a further favour. Could you please try your best to not soil my car seat?"

* * * *

Chapter 44

Rain clouds rolled over Scarborough Castle and the afternoon seafront was blustery, with a high tide and white waves smashing against the harbour walls. Yelping and chattering, the ever-present gulls and kittiwakes danced on the wind above Madame Selene's promenade cabin where Quist, Watson and Rex sat around the elderly clairvoyant's table. Candles flickered and a small brass incense burner filled the air with a rich jasmine aroma.

The detective opened the leather bag on his knee and smiled at Vera. "I have an exceptional memory…" he said.

"Yeah." Watson grinned. "And incredible modesty."

Quist gave him a sarcastic glance. "When we first met last Monday, I recall you telling me how you'd never tried caviar…"

"That's quite true," said Vera. "Or met a werewolf."

"Well, I decided it was time to remedy that." Quist produced a ceramic jar from his bag and a packet of cracker biscuits. "The finest Beluga caviar from a specialist outlet in York." He brought out a bottle encased in a cooling sleeve to maintain its icy temperature. "And a little something to wash it down – Pol Roger Champagne, the favourite drink of Churchill. My old acquaintance Winston Churchill, that is. Not the recently departed leader of White Rose."

"Oh, my," whispered Vera. "This is so kind."

"Paul *who*?" Rex inspected the bottle over his sunglasses. "Couldn't you get Bollinger? Most of the models I date seem to live on the stuff. Well, that and cocaine."

"Champagne," snorted Watson, shaking his head. "Basically fizzy white wine for dickheads with more money than sense."

"Which is why I brought you something more upmarket." Quist handed the youth a can of lager. "Enjoy."

"Oh, cheers, Guv." The teenager's face lit up. "Brilliant."

"Thank you so much," said Vera, watching misty-eyed as the detective placed three crystal flutes on her table. "This will be my last day working here. I don't have very long now and it's a really nice gesture. I never expected this."

"Really?" Watson opened his can and smirked at Rex. "I heard you were a clairvoyant."

"I thought it appropriate," said Quist. "Merely a small expression of appreciation for your assistance yesterday." Popping the cork and filling a glass, he passed it to her. "And also a thank you for saying nothing about me."

"Saying nothing about the *two* of you." Vera peered at Rex. "I can sense that you're the same as Bernard. And as for you, young man…" Turning to Watson, she touched his shoulder. "Oh, you're just normal, aren't you?"

"Er, yeah." He gave a dry laugh and raised his beer. "Thanks for that, luv."

Vera took Quist's hand and squeezed. "It's gone," she said, wistfully. "That large, dark figure I sensed when we first met was the golem. Its presence hung over you like an evil shadow, but it isn't there anymore."

The detective nodded. "That's correct and, as I said, it's partly due to you. Much as I truly loathe the destruction of books, the three of us were present this morning when the golem's creator burnt a certain dangerous volume on the occult, so any further appearances are highly unlikely." He gave her a lopsided smile. "I just wish we had the time to get to know one another better, Vera. I'm certain we could have become good friends and, with your exceptional gift, you could definitely have helped with my work."

"I'm sure you're right," said Vera, shrugging. "But I suppose that's life, or in my case, a rather definite lack of it."

"Mmmh, this Paul Rogers is pretty good." Rex knocked back his drink in one gulp and refilled the glass. "Being a connoisseur, I can always tell a decent bottle if the fizz makes my nose tickle."

Quist visibly shuddered. "Pol Roger should be savoured," he pointed out, testily. "Never guzzled."

"Hey, you're talking to an expert." Rex laughed. "I've drunk buckets of champagne and I know all about the stuff. Did you know it was accidentally invented by a blind monkey?"

"Er, yes." Quist wearily massaged the bridge of his large nose. "As a matter of fact I *have* heard something along those lines. I believe the animal's name was Dom Perignon."

"That's right," said Rex. "Come on, let's try the caviar."

"Absolutely." The detective rummaged in his bag. "And anticipating my assistant's views on such gourmet delicacies, I've brought him three packets of cheese and onion crisps,"

"Yes, the darkness has lifted." Vera studied Quist thoughtfully and sipped her drink. "The darkness and the danger have fortunately both vanished."

"Not to worry," said Watson, swigging his lager. "Knowing the Guv, I'm sure there'll be plenty more where that came from." He clanked his can against their champagne flutes. "Cheers, everyone and, as we're in a fortune-teller's parlour, here's to the future."

The End

About The Author

Ian was born in the north of England, where he worked for three hectic decades as an operational firefighter with West Yorkshire Fire and Rescue.

He's spent the past thirty-something years in a village near Selby, where he now writes humorous detective mysteries with a supernatural twist. The novels are set in York and feature the eccentric private investigator Bernie Quist and his assistant Watson.

Ian travels regularly, usually though Asia and the Americas, and his interests include walking the North York Moors and Yorkshire Dales, natural history, with an emphasis on birds, real ale, and ridding the world of all known evils.

He also feels decidedly peculiar speaking in the third person and may have to do this in the future using a sinister ventriloquist's doll.

www.ianjarviswriter.com

Also from Ian Jarvis

The Bernie Quist Series

Cat Flap
The Music Of Sound

Cat Flap: *"An excellent tale of a Sherlock Holmes type sleuth based in York - but with an unexpected twist. Humorous with historical observations, and not a little intrigue. As you would expect from a "Conan Doyle type" - an excursion into the supernatural. Highly recommended!"* AS

The Music of Sound: *"Ian Jarvis fans take note; he hasn't lost the sense of humour – every page drips with gags and one-liners ranging from the funny to the laugh-out-loud hilarious. As with Cat-Flap, this lifts the story and takes the edge off the tension and terror."* VC

Also from MX Publishing

The Missing Authors Series

Sherlock Holmes and The Adventure of The Grinning Cat
Sherlock Holmes and The Nautilus Adventure
Sherlock Holmes and The Round Table Adventure

"Joseph Svec, III is brilliant in entwining two endearing and enduring classics of literature, blending the factual with the fantastical; the playful with the pensive; and the mischievous with the mysterious. We shall, all of us young and old, benefit with a cup of tea, a tranquil afternoon, and a copy of Sherlock Holmes, The Adventure of the Grinning Cat."
Amador County Holmes Hounds Sherlockian Society

Also from MX Publishing

The Detective and The Woman Series

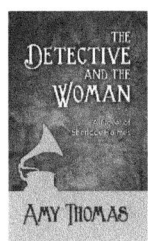

The Detective and The Woman
The Detective, The Woman and The Winking Tree
The Detective, The Woman and The Silent Hive
The Detective, The Woman and The Pirate's Bounty

"The book is entertaining, puzzling and a lot of fun. I believe the author has hit on the only type of long-term relationship possible for Sherlock Holmes and Irene Adler. The details of the narrative only add force to the romantic defects we expect in both of them and their growth and development are truly marvelous to watch. This is not a love story. Instead, it is a coming-of-age tale starring two of our favorite characters."
Philip K Jones

When the papal apartments are burgled in 1901, Sherlock Holmes is summoned to Rome by Pope Leo XII. After learning from the pontiff that several priceless cameos that could prove compromising to the church, and perhaps determine the future of the newly unified Italy, have been stolen, Holmes is asked to recover them. In a parallel story, Michelangelo, the toast of Rome in 1501 after the unveiling of his Pieta, is commissioned by Pope Alexander VI, the last of the Borgia pontiffs, with creating the cameos that will bedevil Holmes and the papacy four centuries later. For fans of Conan Doyle's immortal detective, the game is always afoot. However, the great detective has never encountered an adversary quite like the one with whom he crosses swords in "The Vatican Cameos.."

"An extravagantly imagined and beautifully written Holmes story" (**Lee Child**, NY Times Bestseller, Jack Reacher series)

Also from MX Publishing

Here is a collection of five previously unknown cases from the astonishing career of the consulting detective and his ever-loyal partner. An Affair of the Heart demonstrates the critical interplay between the two men which made their partnership so memorable and endearing. The Curious Matter of the Missing Pearmain is a classic locked-room mystery, while The Case of the Cuneiform Suicide Note sees Dr Watson using his expert knowledge in helping to solve the mystery surrounding the death of an academic. In A Study in Verse the pair assists the Birmingham City Police in a complicated case of robbery which leads them towards a new and dangerous adversary. And to complete the collection, we have The Trimingham Escapade, the very last case the pair enjoyed together, which neatly showcases the inestimable talents of Sherlock Holmes.